The Perfect Game

Books by Leslie Dana Kirby

The Perfect Game

The Perfect Game

Leslie Dana Kirby

Poisoned Pen Press

This book is dedicated to my father,
William H. Dana,
who played a truly perfect game in the game of life
and made me believe that any goal could be
accomplished through hard work.

Chapter One

(Saturday, July 23–Sunday, July 24)

The young man was dead, the unfortunate result of excessive speed combined with bald motorcycle tires and an unhealthy attraction to wind blowing through his hair.

Lauren discontinued chest compressions as her supervising resident, Dr. Stone, called it. "Time of death is 1452 hours." Like his name, Stone was solid in both physique and character.

Lauren glanced at the face of the dead man. Who had loved him? Who would grieve? She swallowed a lump in her throat.

The staff transitioned from rescue efforts to cleanup mode, removing the debris that accrues during emergency interventions, drifting out of the room to check on other patients, write notes, or gossip at the nurses' station. Soon, only Stone and Lauren were left in the room.

Stone ran his fingers through his dark crew cut and sighed. "Have you ever heard that Seinfeld bit where he says helmet laws are designed to protect brains that are too stupid to know to protect themselves?"

Lauren smiled grimly, recognizing the gallows humor that doctors used as their defense mechanism of choice. "Unfortunately for this guy's brain, Arizona doesn't have a helmet law."

Stone nodded in tacit agreement. "There's a rare lull in the action right now. You should grab a bite to eat while you can."

"Okay, thanks," Lauren murmured, but she loitered in the room as Stone headed out to check on the other interns.

The patient's head was no longer gushing blood. Lauren cleaned the gaping wound and carefully began stitching it up.

"There you are!"

Lauren started at the loud words in the quiet room.

"Gotcha," Ritesh said. Lauren had bonded with the five other emergency medicine interns at Phoenix Good Samaritan, but she was particularly fond of Ritesh, the handsome Indian with the mischievous sense of humor.

"No, you didn't." Lauren continued stitching up the gash. "Why did you practically jump out of your skin?"

"Autonomic startle response of the sympathetic nervous system. Do you remember that little lesson from medical school or do you need me to review it for you?"

Ritesh grinned, then surprise registered on his face. "Whoa. Are you sewing up a dead guy?"

"Keen observational skills. What was your first clue?"

"The fact that your stitches are so neat. They never look that good on real patients."

In between stitches, Lauren launched a swat at Ritesh. "Did you come looking for me for a reason or did you just want to torture me with your witty repartee?"

"Oh yeah. There's somebody here to see you."

"Me? Is he tall, dark, and handsome? 'Cause that's what I ordered."

"No, I wasn't referring to myself," Ritesh smirked. "She's petite, blond, and gorgeous."

"Liz? I wonder what she's doing here."

"I have no idea, seeing as I don't know who Liz is."

"My sister."

"Which explains the striking resemblance. Only she's much nicer than you."

"Only because she doesn't know you yet."

"So, are you going to go talk to her? Because if you'd rather stay in here treating the dead guy, I'd be happy to entertain her for you." He wiggled his eyebrows suggestively.

"Quit with the eyebrows. She's married."

"So? I don't discriminate against married women."

"Happily married."

"I thought happy marriages were mythological like flying pigs or smart blondes."

"Or funny Indians," she retorted before worrying this joke was too politically incorrect, but Ritesh just laughed. "Can you tell her I'll be out in a minute? I want to finish cleaning this guy up."

"Why? His dating days are over. Why don't you just pull up the sheet and call the morgue?"

"Because somebody who loved this donorcycle-riding idiot is going to have to identify his body. And I don't want their last image of him to be crushed skull fragments and exposed brain matter."

"You are such a marshmallow, Lauren. You should have been a social worker." As he sauntered out of the room, he quipped, "Better not leave me alone with your sister too long. I might ruin the last happy marriage in America."

Lauren took a few more minutes to adjust the patient's long-ish hair to hide the stitches as best she could. She took a deep breath as she pulled the sheet up over the patient's face.

The hospital cafeteria was crowded, nearly every table filled with hungry staff members or rundown-looking visitors. Lauren paused at the doorway to scan the room. Liz was always easy to spot in a crowd. Look for the table attracting the most surreptitious glances and . . . sure enough, there was Liz sitting in the far corner with Ritesh. Liz sparkled like a diamond in a box full of coal, somehow managing to look cool on this sweltering day, with her sleek hair, thin tanned arms, and crisply pressed white linen pants. Lauren wound between the small tables and cheap plastic chairs to make her way toward them.

"You know why they put nails in coffins?" Ritesh was saying.

"No, why?" Liz asked.

"To keep the oncologists out."

Liz's laugh filled the entire room, its uproarious noise surprising from such a delicate beauty. When she spotted Lauren, she jumped up to give her a tight squeeze. Ritesh excused himself back to the ER, but not before tousling Lauren's ponytail.

"Look at you dressed as a doctor," Liz exclaimed as Lauren attempted to tame her hair. "You look so…grown up."

Lauren glanced down at herself. Her scrubs were shapeless, making her feel like a green Pillsbury Doughboy. "Newsflash. I've been a registered voter for nearly eight years, in case you hadn't noticed."

"School is like a suspended state of adolescence. Now, you're all professional and important."

"Hardly. They say internship is the most humbling year of one's life. It's when you find out how little you really know."

"I wish Mom and Dad could see you now. They'd be proud of you."

"Yeah, yeah. They'd be proud of you, too." Lauren started to eat the nachos Ritesh had left behind on the table. "What brings you to this neck of the woods?"

"I thought I'd drop in and see if you could take a break for a few minutes. Now that we live in the same city, we can do this kind of stuff."

"True, true. I'm so happy to live close to you and Rose-ma again."

"The Rose sisters are reunited at long last. We can go shopping and hiking and play tennis. Do you have to work tomorrow?"

Lauren paused to think. She worked so many crazy hours that the days had begun to run together. "Nope. I have one whole day off."

"I was hoping we could get together. Maybe take Rose-ma to Mass and do brunch afterwards. I have something I need to tell you both."

"Is everything all right?"

"Yes, but I do have some news to share."

"Why don't you tell me now and put me out of my suspense?"

"Because I want to tell you and Rose-ma at the same time. Patience never was your strong suit," Liz said.

"Dear Pot, please stop calling me black. Love Kettle," Lauren said. Then they both laughed because if anybody had a problem with patience, it was Liz. Lauren resisted the urge to ask more questions.

"Your friend Ritesh told me you just lost a patient. Are you okay?"

Lauren let out a long sigh before answering. "It's always tough. I have to keep reminding myself that we can't save them all."

"The world would be terribly overpopulated if you could." Liz smiled before switching topics. "So, I got my official invitation for my ten-year reunion in the mail today."

"Let me guess. Cowboy-themed. Wear your best Levi's."

"Worse. A 'gala under the stars' coordinated by Lori Grimwood." Liz made a face.

"Lori? I wouldn't have thought she'd have the time. She's been awfully busy since high school. Isn't she on her third marriage?"

"Yep, she's been putting up some impressive numbers. Three marriages, five kids."

"I ran into her a couple of summers ago in Tehachapi. When I told her I was in medical school, she said, 'You're *still* in school?' I wanted to remind her that not everybody could be as productive as she is."

Liz giggled. "Let's hope most folks have matured after ten years. So will you come as my plus one?"

"You're not taking Jake?"

"He'll be working. I'll hire a car and driver. We'll arrive in style. It'll be fun."

"Remember all those times you didn't want your little sister tagging along?"

Liz grinned. "Maybe I've matured after ten years."

Lauren changed the topic. "Get this. I found out that Darcy already moved in with Michael."

"Good," Liz responded, surprising Lauren. "Those two deserve each other. And you deserve someone so much better than Michael. While you move on to something better, he's going to be stuck with that bimbo. At least until they start cheating on each other."

Lauren nodded, appreciating the logic of her sister's opinions even while she struggled with her own mixed emotions about her ex-boyfriend.

"Someday soon you are going to meet the perfect man for you. I promise," Liz offered with a smile.

Lauren's beeper went off. "Sorry. I have to get back to the ER. Stat," Lauren added, knowing the medical lingo would amuse her sister. "I'll meet you at Rose-ma's tomorrow morning at around eight."

"Okay, go save some lives," Liz ordered as Lauren rushed back toward the ER.

"Dust storm caused a multiple car pileup on the 101," Stone told Lauren as soon as she pushed through the heavy fire doors into the ER's staging area. "Several majors coming our way. ETA is five minutes. Stick with me. We'll take the first one."

Within moments, the ambulance entrance burst open with urgency as frenzied paramedics rushed in pushing a gurney. Lauren tried to keep up while they gave the patient report at a mile a minute, "Jamie Fuller…fifteen-year-old female passenger…probable fracture to left forearm…mother still being extracted from the vehicle."

As Lauren hurried alongside the gurney into a trauma bay, she knew she should be assessing injuries, triaging by order of urgency. But all she noticed was the look of terror in the young girl's eyes. "Hi, Jamie. I'm Dr. Rose. We're going to take good care of you."

"I want my mom," the girl moaned through obvious pain.

"She'll be here any minute. Can you tell me what hurts?"

Soon Lauren lost track of time in the intensity of the case, ordering X-rays, checking labs, setting a splint, and hooking up IVs. More than an hour passed before they had done all they could for Jamie, making her comfortable with a generous dose of morphine. Only then did Lauren find time to go look for information on the mother.

She checked several trauma bays before she found the one

with the same last name: Fuller, Sarah. Her heart sank when she noticed CPR being administered.

"No response," Stone was saying. "Time of death is…"

"No!" Lauren interrupted impulsively. "There must be something more we can do."

Most residents didn't appreciate second-guessing from interns, but Stone merely shrugged his shoulders. "What would you suggest?"

Kevin, another intern, continued CPR.

"Epinephrine."

"Tried it."

"AED."

"Three times already. No response."

"Internal heart massage."

"She's had catastrophic injuries. Who knows how long she was down in the field before the firefighters were able to extract her? You think cracking her chest is going to make a difference?"

"I don't know, but we have to try," Lauren pleaded.

"Okay, grab a Gigli saw and rib spreader. You're going to assist with this one."

Lauren hurried to gather up the necessary equipment. She returned to the bedside, nervously making eye contact with Kevin, whose case she had just hijacked. Unnaturally nice, Kevin smiled to communicate no hard feelings. Stone wasted no time in cutting an incision between two ribs on the left side and forcing the chest open violently.

"Okay, Dr. Rose, grab the heart and show it some love," Stone said. "See if you can sweet talk it into restarting."

This was Lauren's first time touching the heart of a living patient. Feeling uncertain, she reached into the woman's chest, located the heart, and began squeezing it rhythmically.

Nobody said a word, watching with anticipation. Nothing. Minutes passed, but Lauren refused to give up.

Stone said, "I admire your effort, but it's time to call it. We've done everything we can on this case. Other patients need our attention."

Ignoring him, Lauren pumped the heart several more times, willing it to start beating. It did not. Finally, she withdrew her hand.

"Time of death is 1723 hours," Stone said.

Her second dead patient today. Lauren fled the room, detouring into the supply closet as if she had an urgent need for gauze. Instead, tears came flooding out in long, silent sobs. She allowed herself the luxury of tears for only a few minutes before pulling herself together. She stopped in the restroom to splash water on her face, examining herself in the mirror. Her green eyes were still bloodshot, but she could credibly blame fatigue.

She dreaded returning to Jamie's trauma room, but did not dawdle. After delivering the terrible news, she pulled up a chair and sat with the young girl while she bawled. "I can't live without my mother. I can't. I can't."

"Yes, you can," Lauren reassured. "You don't want to, but you can. And you will."

Lauren took on several other cases that evening, but she returned to check on Jamie frequently. Shortly after midnight, Ritesh summoned Lauren out of Jamie's room. "Shift's over, Lauren. We're all going over to the Tilted Kilt for some drinks. You ready?"

"You guys go on without me. I don't want to leave until her dad gets here. We finally reached him and he's driving back from San Diego."

"How often do we get a chance to hit the town together? Besides, I heard you owe Kevin a drink."

"More like a six-pack. Next time. I swear."

"Maybe I should call your sister and see if she wants to fill your spot," he teased.

"Maybe you should settle down with that nice Indian dentist your parents picked out for you."

His eyes narrowed. "Wow. Now you have crossed the line."

Lauren's eyes widened. "I'm sorry, Ritesh. I didn't mean to hurt your—"

"Ha! Gotcha again. You're an easy mark today."

She laughed, grateful for Ritesh's ability to make her do so on a day like this.

"Good night, Marshmallow. See you tomorrow." He waved over his shoulder as he departed.

Lauren returned to Jamie, whose hand she would hold for several more hours. When the father finally arrived, Lauren was forced to deliver the same terrible news twice in the same evening.

Exhausted, physically and emotionally, Lauren was a few feet from the employee exit when she heard Dr. Stone call her name. She turned as he rushed to catch her.

"I know you're already way overtime, but there are a couple of detectives looking for you. They say it's urgent."

"Detectives? About which case?"

Stone shrugged his shoulders. "Shootings, stabbings, drunk driving accidents. The ER is a hotbed for crime victims. Take your pick."

She walked back with him to one of the consultation rooms, which were mostly used for death notifications.

The two men stood as she entered. They looked fatigued, but then again, it was already well past dawn.

The older man stepped forward. He was probably in his fifties, his face lined with deep creases, as if years of worry had aged him prematurely. He compensated for his receding hair with a bushy gray mustache. "Dr. Rose, I'm Detective Wallace with the Scottsdale P.D. And this is Detective Boyd." He indicated the younger man with a jerk of his head.

Detective Boyd was about six feet tall with broad shoulders and thick dark hair. Late twenties or early thirties. His startling aqua-colored eyes were many shades brighter than the navy suit he wore. He shook Lauren's hand.

She pulled back. "May I ask why you want to see me?"

"We should take a seat," Detective Wallace directed.

Lauren sat on the small love seat in the room. Detective Wallace took the chair opposite her while Boyd continued to stand.

"I'm afraid we have some bad news," Detective Wallace said. "Your sister, Elizabeth, was killed last night."

Chapter Two

(Sunday, July 24)

Lauren's heart hammered in her chest. This couldn't be happening. Not to her. And not to Liz. The two of them had suffered enough, hadn't they? She struggled to catch her breath, "There must be some mistake. I'm on my way to go meet her now."

Detective Wallace shook his head. "I know this is a shock, but there's no mistake. We've already reached Mr. Wakefield. He's catching the first flight back from D.C. He told us about your parents...and asked us to notify you in person."

◇◇◇

The moment Lauren stepped out of the employee exit, she was accosted by a mass of reporters, all shouting her name: "Lauren. Lauren, over here. LAUREN!"

Liz had learned to manage the media interest in her life, but Lauren was unprepared for this onslaught. She ignored the rapid-fire questions, hustling toward her aging white Honda Civic in the parking garage. Video cameras and microphones were shoved in her face.

Several reporters blocked her path. Lauren forced herself to speak, shouting over the noisy crowd, "I know this must be a great news story for you, but it's a tremendous tragedy for me." The din instantly quieted. Lauren could hear the sound of her own ragged breathing. "So, please let me grieve in peace."

◇◇◇

Lauren knocked on her grandmother's apartment door at the Desert Pointe Assisted Living Facility in Scottsdale. Rose-ma greeted her at the door. Lauren bent to hug her petite grandmother. Rose-ma smelled of powder; her L'Oreal #44 chestnut hair was pulled back into its usual meticulous bun.

"You look so tired, dear," Rose-ma observed. "They aren't working you too hard at that humdinger, are they?" Lauren knew her grandmother meant to say hospital. She was typically unaware of the word substitutions that had plagued her since the stroke. "How about some breakfast?" Rose-ma turned to her kitchen and began rummaging through her refrigerator.

"Thanks Rose-ma, but I'm not hungry. I need to tell you something."

"You're not obsessing about Michael again? He was a sweet boy, but there are so many other fish in the sea."

"No, it's not Michael. It's Liz."

The tears came now. Lauren took a deep breath and repeated the information the police had given her.

"That's fucked!" her grandmother said, dissolving into tears.

Lauren had never heard Rose-ma use such language before. She could only assume that this was another occasion on which her grandmother had unknowingly substituted one word for another.

But in this case, the new word was exactly the right word after all.

◇◇◇

Lauren agreed to attend church only for her grandmother's benefit. Her parents' deaths, and now Liz's fueled Lauren's certainty that God did not exist. She could not believe in a God so cruel. Still, Rose-ma's faith was stronger than Lauren's doubts.

The stained glass windows, the candles burning near the pulpit, and the hushed tones elicited memories of her parents' memorial service. Lauren imagined Liz's funeral, then forced herself to stop, refocusing on the hymnal in front of her.

Throughout the sermon, Lauren's cell phone had been vibrating repeatedly in her purse. As they walked back toward her car, Lauren checked her phone. Seventeen missed calls, including four from Jake. She called Jake back.

He answered on the first ring. "Lauren? I'm so glad to hear from you. Are you okay?"

"I'm in complete shock. How are you?"

"The same. Terrible, actually." There was a touch of strained humor in his voice. "Listen, I'm at my folks' house. Will you come over?"

"I need to drop Rose-ma off first and then I will."

"You remember how to get here?"

"I think so."

"Lauren, I need a favor. I wish there was somebody else I could ask, but it has to be an immediate family member."

"Of course. What can I do?"

"Somebody has to identify…" His voice cracked…"her. Her body."

Lauren had seen plenty of dead bodies, but she wasn't up for this impossible task. There had to be somebody else that could do it. But unless Lauren wanted to send her eighty-six-year-old grandmother into cardiac arrest, it came down to either Jake or herself. Liz wouldn't have wanted Jake to have to see her that way. So Lauren had to step up.

"Lauren? I'm sorry." Jake was crying on the other end of the line. "It's too much to ask of you. Forget it. I can do it. I just…"

Numb, Lauren said, "No, it's okay. I'll do it."

Chapter Three

(Sunday, July 24)

The coroner's assistant, dressed in maroon scrubs, led Lauren downstairs to a windowless room and showed her an image on a large monitor. The picture depicted a woman's head and shoulders, the face half-covered by a sheet. Even in death, the visible left side of the face was gorgeous. Flawless complexion, full lips, arched brow, thick blond hair.

The sheet shifted under its own weight and fell to the floor. The right side of the face was a mangled mass of blood, hair, and bone fragments. Lauren gasped. The technician apologized and the sheet was hastily pulled back up to conceal the ruined half again. The woman on the screen looked peaceful. Lauren nodded and they led her out of the room, up the stairs, back to the land of the living. Lauren signed a few documents and then escaped back to her car.

Her usual radio station was playing as she drove toward Paradise Valley. She was lost in thought when the rock music was interrupted by a news report.

"Elizabeth Wakefield, wife of Arizona Diamondbacks' pitcher Jake Wakefield, was found dead this morning in their Scottsdale home. A police spokesperson confirmed the death, which is believed to have been the result of a botched burglary. Several expensive jewelry items are reportedly missing from the home. Jake Wakefield, who was scheduled to pitch today against the Washington Nationals, has returned to the local area. Liz Wakefield was a well-known advocate for Mothers Against Drunk Driving."

Lauren approached the Wakefields' neighborhood. Journalists—video cameras and microphones at the ready—trampled the flower beds in front of the gate to the community. Security had been beefed up today as several private security guards were monitoring the gate. One of them corralled the reporters back as another checked Lauren's ID against an authorized guest list before allowing her to proceed through the gate.

Even in this upscale neighborhood of multimillion-dollar homes, the Wakefield home was impressive. Large pillars framed the front entry and supported the sweeping balcony. A large marble fountain in the front yard served as a centerpiece of the estate.

Lauren pulled into the circular drive and parked behind several luxury cars, including Jake's bright-red Porsche Spyder.

Lauren rang the doorbell and heard a sophisticated chime behind the leaded glass windows at either side of the front door, which was soon opened by Jake's mother. Buffy Wakefield was tall, thin, and tanned with silver hair styled in a perfect bob. She wore tailored black slacks and a black blouse with a plunging V-neckline. Her breasts were suspiciously high for a woman of her age. Lauren inhaled a combination of Chanel No. 5 and Scotch as Buffy pulled her into an embrace.

"Lauren, darling, such a dreadful thing. But we shall endure it. There is simply no choice. Can I get you something to drink?"

Lauren politely declined and followed Jake's mother through the vaulted entry, Buffy's Manolo stiletto heels clicking on the travertine tile. Buffy led the way up the winding staircase into the subdued lighting of the upstairs den. The walls were lined with cherry cabinetry holding classic leather-bound books, silver vases, and expensive crystal decanters of liquor. Several people were in the room watching a large television centered on the opposite wall. Jake was sitting on one of the leather couches, talking to several people in muted tones. When he spotted

Lauren, his face looked pained. He stood to greet her, pulling her into a firm hug.

"Did you find out anything more?" Lauren asked him.

"Not yet. I spoke to the detectives briefly when I got in. They said they'd call when they had more information. My phone has been ringing off the hook." As if to prove his point, his cell phone rang and he paused to answer it.

Jake was six foot three with broad shoulders and a slim waist. And, if you believed thousands of baseball fans, the "best butt in the major leagues." He had thick sandy hair that was always perfectly trimmed. Liz had used to joke that Jake had always either just gotten his hair cut or was just about to. His ocean-blue eyes were brighter than usual because he had been crying. He wore khakis and a button-down blue shirt.

Jake's voice cracked as he graciously accepted the condolences being offered on the other end of the line. He thanked the caller and hung up. He patted the seat next to him on the sofa. "Come sit down, Lauren."

She took a seat beside him, saying, "It's impossible to believe."

"I know. It's not sinking in for me either."

Something on the television caught Jake's eye. "Hey, Lauren, it's you." He gestured toward the TV.

Lauren turned to the screen and saw footage of her disheveled self taken at the hospital parking lot. That seemed so long ago already.

"Maybe we could call the detectives for an update," Lauren suggested.

"I'll give them a call in a minute. But first, we should discuss the memorial. I'd like to have it on Tuesday."

"So soon? Will they even release her by then?"

"Yeah, they should be done by then. Tuesday works best because I have to be in Houston on Wednesday."

"Houston?"

"We're playing the Astros. Houston's tough and we have a shot at the play-offs. I want to be there."

"You're going back to work this week?"

"Well, it will help take my mind off things. I'm sure you're going back, too, aren't you?"

Work had been the furthest thing from Lauren's mind. But, yes, she would have to go back. If she missed more than eighty hours of her internship year, she could be dismissed from the program with no guarantees of being accepted back into the prestigious Good Samaritan emergency medicine residency the following year. Lauren also needed her paycheck to pay her rent. "Yes, I have to. Everything is just happening so fast."

"I know. It's so hard. I'd like to have the service at Valley Presbyterian Church here in Paradise Valley."

"Valley Presbyterian? But we're Catholic."

"You and your grandmother are Catholic, but Liz and I attended Valley Presbyterian quite a bit. It's my parents' church and Liz loved it. It's gorgeous. And spacious. I expect a huge turnout. I'm sure this is what she would have wanted."

Lauren had assumed that Father Paul would conduct the service, but it sounded like Liz knew the pastor at Valley Presbyterian better. She nodded. "Okay. What about burying her in Tehachapi, near our parents?"

Jake looked distraught. "You think so? She told me she wanted to be cremated."

"Cremated?"

"That's what she said she wanted," Jake reiterated. "She said she didn't want to be put in the ground to be eaten by worms."

Jake knew Liz best. Liz hadn't told Lauren that she wanted to be cremated. The thought of a secret between them stung Lauren. What else hadn't she known about her own sister?

As Lauren reflected, Jake added, "I have to respect her wishes. It's all I can do for her now." Tears rolled down his cheeks.

Lauren gave him a hug and said, "Of course you're right. We should do exactly what she would have wanted."

He nodded and continued to cry.

Chapter Four

(Sunday, July 24)

Moments later, Jake's cell phone rang again. After hanging up, he announced he was going to the police station to give a statement.

Buffy fussed, asserting that Jake should be allowed time to grieve. Jacob Sr. insisted Jake needed a lawyer. As Jake interacted with his father, Lauren was struck by their physical similarities. Although he was in his sixties, Jacob Sr. looked much younger with his trim build and thick brown hair. He managed to look elegantly casual in an expensive sports jacket over khaki slacks. "They always want to pin things on the husband," he warned Jake.

"Dad, I was all the way across the country. They aren't looking at me. I need to do whatever I can to help the investigators."

"Let me give Bob a call and ask him to meet you there."

"Absolutely not. How is it going to look if I show up with the family lawyer? I've got nothing to hide and I don't want it to look like I do."

As Jake rose to go, Lauren followed suit. She did not want to be left behind in the Wakefields' museum-quality home, with their wealthy friends discussing Liz's death in hushed voices.

Buffy and Jacob Sr. hovered over her.

"Stay, dear, we insist. You shouldn't be alone at a time like this." Buffy said.

"I don't want to intrude."

Jacob Sr. waved his hand in the air in protest. "You're not intruding! You'll always be family to us, Lauren. You're welcome to stay. We'll have Yvonna make up the guest room for you."

"You're so kind, but I need to get home and make some phone calls."

The Wakefields relented and air-kissed Lauren good-bye before she left the house with Jake. He hugged her, promising to keep her posted. He donned his sunglasses, slid gracefully into his bright red convertible, and roared out of the driveway.

Lauren's one-bedroom apartment near the light rail line in Phoenix was exactly as she had left it. It seemed impossible that her world could be so different and yet look the same. She clicked on the television to see if she could glean any information. Liz's murder was breaking news on every local station. It was even featured on CNN and ESPN. Lauren viewed the same clips over and over: Liz's body being wheeled out to the coroner's van, detectives greeting Jake at the airport, herself begging reporters for privacy. There were no new developments.

Lauren's cell had been ringing all day. She let all the calls go to voice mail. But her heart leapt when she saw a familiar number on her caller ID.

She hurried to answer the phone, "Michael?"

"Oh, hey, Lauren, I wasn't sure you'd even pick up. I just heard about Liz. I am so sorry."

Lauren forced out a response through a throat tight with grief. "I can't even believe it's true."

"I know. It was so surreal when I heard her name on TV."

"I appreciate you calling."

"Of course. Liz was really special."

Lauren had no idea what to say and an awkward dead air lingered on the line.

Michael broke the silence. "If there is anything Darcy or I can do to help, call us, okay?"

"I think you and Darcy have done plenty already. I have to go." Lauren had barely finished saying the words before she hit the Call End button.

She watched her cell phone screen impassively as her phone vibrated several more times.

After a while, she took some time to listen to her voice mail messages. Friends, coworkers, Dr. Stone, all calling to express their condolences. And dozens of reporters calling to request interviews. They had already managed to find her phone number somehow. Then a message from somebody she did wish to speak with. Lauren called him back.

His telephone voice was professional. "Detective Boyd."

"Hello. This is Lauren Rose. Sorry I missed your call. I've been inundated."

"Yes, this case has stirred up quite a media storm. Ride it out, it should die down, I mean quiet down, in a few days. How are you holding up?"

"Um, okay. Has there been any progress in the investigation?"

"Nothing significant yet. It may take some time, but we'll sort it out. I was hoping I could come by and ask you a few more questions."

Lauren agreed, eager to have something to contribute. She settled back on the couch to await his arrival, continuing to watch the news. It was like a bad car accident. She did not want to see it, but couldn't resist looking. The ghastly news images were interrupted by a knock on the door. She checked the peephole, before opening the door to let Detective Boyd in.

"What can you tell me so far?" she asked.

"Not much. In an ongoing investigation; we aren't authorized to release much information."

"Not even to the family?"

"Not even to the family." He shifted uncomfortably. "We have to consider everybody a suspect until we can rule them out. That's partly why I'm here."

"I'm a suspect? I thought you said it was a burglary?"

"That's how it looks at this point, but most homicide victims are killed by somebody they know. The sooner we can rule out family and friends, the better. I was hoping I could see the clothes you were wearing last night."

Last night seemed an eternity ago. Lauren glanced down at the rumpled scrubs she was still wearing, "You're looking at them now."

"I need to take them into evidence if you don't object. You'll get them back as soon as forensics is done examining them."

"No problem. There's more where these came from. The hospital provides fresh scrubs by the cartful. Let me just change out of them."

Lauren stepped down the short hallway to her bedroom. She threw on the first clothes she could find, shorts and a T-shirt. She folded the scrubs and placed them in a plastic grocery sack before handing them to Detective Boyd. "It's possible that you might find body fluid splashes from different people on those."

Detective Boyd raised an eyebrow. "That should make the forensics team earn their paychecks. What time did you work last night?"

"My shift was scheduled from noon to midnight, but I didn't actually get off until this morning because of a tough case."

"Did you run out for Starbucks or anything?"

The very idea struck Lauren as funny, but she couldn't muster a laugh. "No. We don't usually have much time to eat. Sometimes, we don't even have time to use the bathroom. We joke about inserting catheters so we don't have to."

"Is there somebody at your work that could verify your shift?"

"The best one would be my resident. I doubt I could get out of his sights for more than thirty seconds without him noticing." Lauren provided contact information for Dr. Stone.

Boyd hesitated for a moment, "Miss Rose, did you know you were the sole beneficiary on your sister's life insurance policy?"

"Are you sure?"

"Yes. She changed it just recently from Jake to you. Any idea why?"

"None. I didn't even know she had life insurance."

"Was she having marital problems?"

"No, not that she mentioned."

"And would she have mentioned it to you if she was?"

"Yes," Lauren answered immediately, but then hesitated. She hadn't even known that Liz wanted to be cremated. "At least I think so."

Chapter Five

Unable to sleep, Lauren was relieved when her bedroom lightened at dawn, giving her an excuse to quit trying. She headed out for her morning run. She had been plagued by insomnia after her parents died and running had given her an excuse to start her day early.

Afterwards, she showered before perusing the Internet, hoping the web might provide details about the investigation. Typing Liz's name into the search engine resulted in dozens of hits. Most were about the murder the day before, but none yielded more than Lauren already knew; the Scottsdale police suspected Liz had been victimized by a burglar who expected the house to be unoccupied. Several older articles were written about Liz's charity work. Others were society pages, heralding Liz and Jake's attendance at various events.

Lauren couldn't believe how many hits Liz's name produced. Previous Google searches of Lauren's own name produced only one mention of herself, an article listing her as one of ninety-seven medical school graduates from UCLA earlier in the year. Idly, Lauren entered her own name in the search engine and was astonished when several links popped up, identifying her as a surviving sister in news articles about Liz's death.

Lauren watched the clock, wondering how soon she could call the detectives for an update. She gave herself permission to call at eight o'clock, but at 7:47, she broke down and dialed Detective Boyd's number. He answered on the third ring.

"I'm sorry to bother you so early, but I was wondering if you have any news about the investigation?"

"I was actually waiting for a decent hour so I could call you. Would you be able to come into the station to give a statement? The more we know about the victim, the better."

"Absolutely." Lauren jumped at the chance to help.

Though she hadn't lived in Phoenix long, she was adept at navigating the city streets, which ran along predictable grids. The Scottsdale Via Linda Police Station looked more like a small resort than a government building.

A stout receptionist took Lauren's name and Detective Boyd soon rounded a corner to greet her. It looked like he had not shaved since the previous day and his hair was untidy. His tie knot had been loosened around his neck. Dark circles ringed his eyes. Lauren hoped his disheveled appearance meant he had been making good headway on the investigation.

"Wow. You made good time. I hope you didn't pass any of our local traffic cops. They hand out speeding tickets like candy around here. It's a nice little source of revenue for the city. Funds lots of donuts." Lauren forced a polite smile and did not dispute his assumption that she had been speeding.

He shook her hand and offered a warm smile. "How are you holding up?"

Lauren's eyes filled with tears and she shrugged her shoulders in response.

"I know this must be a terribly difficult time for you," he said. "Can I get you coffee or anything?"

"No, thank you."

As Boyd led Lauren down the building hallways, he said, "We'd like to tape the interview if you don't mind. It allows us to review helpful information later if needed."

"Sure. No problem."

They entered a small room with a table, two chairs, and a two-way mirror on one wall. Lauren doubted anybody cared enough to observe this mundane family member interview from the other side. The room was freezing and Lauren, who was wearing shorts and a T-shirt appropriate for the 107-degree day, wished she had thought to bring a sweater.

Detective Boyd encouraged Lauren to take a seat. The metal chair was cold and uncomfortable. Boyd offered coffee again and Lauren, now shivering, asked for tea. He arranged for warm tea to be brought in and Lauren was grateful when he draped his own suit jacket around her shoulders.

Despite the formality of the interview room and the whirring video camera in the corner, the conversation was comfortable. Boyd started by asking lots of questions about Liz. How did Liz spend her time? Who were her closest friends? What were her hobbies? Lauren answered to the best of her ability, uneasily realizing she no longer knew all the details of Liz's personal life. Liz had often visited Lauren in California, but Lauren had not often had the time to make the trip to Arizona. And since starting her internship in Phoenix, Lauren had been too busy to spend much time in Liz's world.

"Was Liz cautious? Did she lock doors and set her security system?" Boyd asked.

"She wasn't easily spooked. We grew up in a small town where nobody locked their doors. Jake worried about security, so Liz locked up and used the alarm, but she wasn't obsessive about it."

"Would she have opened the door to a stranger?"

"I don't know. She might have."

"Tell me about Liz's relationship with Jake."

"They met at Arizona State. He was on the baseball team, of course. And Liz was a cheerleader. They started dating when she was a sophomore and he was a junior. They were crazy about each other. When he got drafted by the Diamondbacks at the end of his senior year, Liz quit school so she could travel with him. They got married that summer. It would have been seven years this August."

"And they got along well?"

"Incredibly. He was the Ken to her Barbie."

"Except Ken and Barbie ended up splitting up."

Lauren almost smiled. "Wow, you have an impressive command of Barbie's personal life. I just meant that they seemed perfect for one another."

"And what about the relationship between you and Liz?"

"We were exceptionally close. Losing our parents really bonded us. I wouldn't have survived that without Liz. She's always the first person I want to call when something significant happens in my life." Lauren realized she had lapsed into the present tense when referring to Liz.

"Have you had any arguments lately?"

"None."

Detective Boyd asked Lauren to specify her movements the previous evening. She reiterated what she had told him before. She had spent all night at the hospital, staying until morning because of a tough case.

"Thank you so much for coming in this morning. I appreciate it," Detective Boyd said, wrapping up the interview.

"Of course. Any time."

"Detective Wallace would like to ask you a few more questions before you leave." He glanced at the two-way mirror and Lauren realized for the first time that other people *had* been watching the interview. Now, her shivering was unrelated to the temperature.

Boyd exited as Detective Wallace entered the room. He was wearing the same suit he had been wearing the day before, which looked rumpled. His eyes were bloodshot and watery. But he entered the room with a commanding presence.

"I have a few matters that we need to clear up, Miss Rose," he said.

"Of course."

"Isn't it true that you were jealous of Liz?"

"What? No. We—"

But Wallace interrupted, "Isn't it true that you were jealous of her wealth while you took out loans to get through school?"

"No." Lauren furrowed her brows.

Detective Wallace leaned in now, getting uncomfortably close. "Didn't you convince your sister to change her life insurance policy shortly before she was killed?"

As Wallace neared her, Lauren shrank back in her seat. She responded with absolute clarity. "That's ridiculous. You worked all night and that's the best you've come up with?"

"I think we're done here," Wallace said, departing the room without another word. As if on cue, Boyd re-entered. He smiled at her, but said nothing as he busied himself with the video camera. Lauren fired upon him. "What the hell was that all about? You guys can't seriously think I did this!"

Detective Boyd finished clicking off the equipment. "Don't worry about him. He's under a lot of pressure to solve this case. To him, everybody is a suspect until proven otherwise."

"But I was at work all night."

"We know. We already confirmed your shift with Dr. Stone. You were at the hospital for your entire shift, right?"

"And then some," she said.

Chapter Six

(Tuesday, July 26)

Everybody in attendance at the memorial, which seemed like every well-connected person in the Phoenix metropolitan area, commented on how beautiful the service was. The church was gorgeous, the flower arrangements were plentiful, the minister's platitudes were polished. Jake was overwhelmed by grief so Buffy had planned the service. The entire event resembled Buffy's house: flawless, ostentatious, and impersonal. The minister referred to Liz as Elizabeth. Several of Liz's "friends," in their black Armani dresses and mile-high Prada heels, spoke about how close they had been to "Elizabeth." Lauren didn't recognize any of them.

Jake spoke eloquently about the amazing life they shared while noisy television helicopters hovered overhead, trying to get video footage of the mourners.

Lauren didn't speak. She had offered to help with the service, but Jake had assured her everything had already been arranged. She and Rose-ma sat together in the front pew alongside Jake and his parents. Lauren felt detached, as if attending the funeral of a stranger.

After the memorial, Jake ushered Lauren and Rose-ma into one of several black Lincoln town cars heading to a mausoleum in North Scottsdale. They rode in silence, alone with their grief.

Lauren hoped the Wakefields had limited the cemetery service to family members. They had not. Dozens of cars lined up behind Jake's car with illuminated headlights. Policemen on motorcycles solemnly escorted the long procession to the cemetery. Hundreds of Jake's fans lined the streets, hooting, hollering, and holding up homemade signs. At Paradise Memorial Gardens, cooling fans blew mist on the large crowd as the minister launched into yet another long-winded sermon about God's wisdom.

Lauren began to count the times the minister used the word "mysterious." By the time he wrapped up thirty-five minutes later, she was up to thirty-eight. More than one per minute. That must be some sort of weird world record. Jake kissed the ornate urn before it was placed into a small vault that resembled Lauren's locker at work.

Anger reared up like a beast within Lauren's chest. Anger at God for taking Liz. Anger at Buffy for planning the world's most impersonal service. Anger at the minister for not knowing when to shut up already. Anger at all these society crowd looky-loos who wanted to be able to brag about attending the hot ticket event. Anger at the police for not catching the killer yet. And anger at Liz for leaving her. If Liz was here, she would make Lauren laugh about this ridiculous circus. If only Liz were here...

Despite the elaborate misting system, Rose-ma was wilting and Lauren needed to get her out of the sun before she suffered heatstroke. It took her a moment to locate Jake in the crowd, where he was being consoled by several of his teammates. He excused himself to greet Lauren as she approached. "I need to get Rose-ma out of this heat."

"Why don't you two head to my parents' house?" he offered. "Mom hired a caterer. Rose-ma can rest in the guest quarters if she likes."

Lauren didn't relish the prospect of making small talk with a bunch of strangers.

"I don't know." Lauren said, trying to think of a reasonable excuse.

Jake seemed to read her mind. "No worries. You can come by later if you feel up to it. Take any of the town cars. Just tell the driver where you want to go." He hugged Rose-ma and whispered in Lauren's ear as he embraced her, "I'll call you soon. Thanks for your support. It means the world to me."

The rest of the guests continued to mingle as if at some macabre cocktail party. Lauren helped to steady Rose-ma in her sturdy heels as they headed back to the cars.

"Lauren?"

Detective Boyd was hurrying across the grass behind them. He greeted them both courteously. "Is everything all right?"

Lauren explained that Rose-ma was overheating.

Boyd nodded understandingly. "Before you go, can you tell me if there was anybody at the service that you didn't recognize?"

Lauren hesitated. How did she tell him that about the only person she did know was in the urn? She fumbled over her words, explaining how she had been busy with school in California. How she had only recently moved to Arizona. How she and Liz squeezed in time together around Lauren's crazy schedule. Even to her own ears, it sounded like a series of excuses to explain why she hadn't even known who her own sister's friends had been. He assured her that he understood.

The cool interior of the car was welcoming. As soon as the car pulled away, Rose-ma said, "That was a very strange service." She appeared flustered and stammered, "I didn't mean to say strange. What I meant to say was that was a very sweet service. I'm sorry. Sometimes my words come out wrong." Lauren smiled wearily at her grandmother and patted her hand.

"Don't worry, Rose-ma, I know exactly what you meant."

Chapter Seven

(Friday, July 29)

True to his word, Jake called Lauren a few days later. Lauren took a break from work to take his call, hoping his name on her caller ID meant there had been a break in the case.

"Hey, Lauren. I was calling to check on you and Rose-ma," he said.

"We're doing as well as can be expected. How about you?"

Jake sighed. His inability to speak spoke volumes.

Anxious to break the uncomfortable silence, Lauren said, "You pitched a great game yesterday. Roger Smithson looked shocked when that last pitch broke into the strike zone at the last moment."

Jake chuckled a bit and the awkward moment passed. "You saw the game? Did you see how much grief Smithie gave the umpire for calling it a strike?"

"Yeah, but he knew it was a strike. When the reporters asked him about it after the game, he could barely conceal a smile."

Jake laughed again. "Who knew baseball required so many acting skills? Did you see Molten pretend to get hit by a pitch?"

"No, I missed that part. What happened?"

"He put on a huge show. Shaking his hand and cursing up a blue streak. The ump gave him a base. But on the slow-motion playback, the ball clearly hit the bat, not his hand."

"When you're ready to retire from baseball, I guess you'll be ready for primetime."

"So, how about you, Lauren?" Jake asked. "Didn't you go back to work, too?"

"Yesterday. The chief of staff offered to let me defer my residency by a year."

"That sounds good. You should take them up on it. Take some time off to…" Jake paused to find the right word, "…unwind."

"No way," she said. "Sitting around waiting for the detectives to call would land me in the funny farm in no time. Work is a welcome relief. Sure, it is relentless and challenging, but it also keeps me so busy that I don't have time to dwell on Liz until my shift ends. And the other interns have been amazing to me. I've only known them for a month, but they already have my back."

"I know what you mean." Jake said. "Most of the time, I can't stop thinking about Liz, but when I'm on the mound, it's just me and the batter. And the other players are like my brothers. Something like this makes you appreciate your real friends, you know?"

"Absolutely. Have you heard anything from the detectives?"

"Nothing of interest," he lamented. "I call those guys at least once a day. They tell me they're making progress, but they don't provide any specifics."

"Same here," Lauren said. "They always take my call, but they never tell me anything. I know nothing more than I did on day one."

"Those yahoos don't know what they're doing. I've gone back in there to talk to them a couple more times and they keep repeating the same questions. They're wasting their time on me instead of following up other leads."

"Wasting their time on *us*," Lauren said. "They called me back in for a second interview, too."

"They did?"

"And asked all the same questions again. Does that mean they don't believe me?"

Lauren was interrupted by Dr. Stone. "Med flight is en route. Child submerged in a backyard pool for three minutes.

Sometimes young ones bounce back in surprising ways. Come up to the helipad with me?"

Lauren nodded, and wrapped up the phone conversation as she followed Stone up the back staircase. "Jake, duty calls. Can I call you back later? Are you still in Houston?"

"Yep, we play the Astros again tomorrow. We'll be flying home tomorrow night. I have Sunday off, so I was hoping we might be able to get together then."

"I already promised Rose-ma I'd go to mass with her."

"Perfect. Why don't we all go together and go eat afterwards? We have a great brunch at our country club."

Lauren was touched by Jake's effort to look after her, recognizing the void that Liz's death had created in her life. "Sounds like a deal, pickle."

"You Rose girls and your weird expressions," Jake laughed. "Liz used to say that, too."

Chapter Eight

(Sunday, July 31)

Approaching her grandmother's apartment on Sunday morning, Lauren could hear Jake's infectious chuckle and Rose-ma's giggle. When Rose-ma let her in, Jake was holding a delicate floral teacup in his huge hands. "Don't forget to curl your pinky finger," she teased. Jake curled his large pinky compliantly.

"I was just telling Jake about the time Liz got stuck in the mud," Rose-ma said.

Lauren smiled at the image that came to mind. "She screamed so loud we thought she was being attacked by wild animals. My dad grabbed her and she came right out of her bright red boots."

Jake smiled, "Liz had a flair for the dramatic."

"That's an understatement," Lauren said. "During a genealogy project in fourth grade, Liz told her teacher she was half-vampire on her mother's side."

Rose-ma hooted, "Well, that would explain why you girls never got enough sleep. Liz did have a tendency to embellish things."

"One of the things I loved most about Liz was her ability to tell a good story," Jake said. "She could turn a routine trip to the grocery store into an epic comic adventure."

"Everybody used to think I was so quiet," Lauren said. "What they didn't realize was growing up with Liz made it hard to get a word in edgewise." They all laughed.

"Sit down and have a bite of breakfast with us before mass, dear?" Rose-ma said.

"I thought we were going to brunch afterwards," Lauren said.

"Yes, but you shouldn't go to church on an empty stomach. You'll be so weary, you'll fall on your face," Rose-ma persisted. If Liz had been here, she and Lauren would have shared knowing glances. Her grandmother had a reputation for force-feeding people.

Jake caught Lauren's eye and flashed a perceptive grin. "Yeah, come have breakfast with us." Jake had a grapefruit on a dish in front of him.

"I'd love some toast," Lauren said.

"Are you sure you don't want the other half of my grapefruit?" Jake's smile was sly.

"I couldn't take food out of your mouth."

After placating Rose-ma by eating a few bites, they headed off to church. Jake's convertible was a two-seater, so he had brought Liz's sedan. Lauren's breath caught in her throat when she saw the champagne-colored Lexus. The car was so inexorably linked in her mind with Liz that Lauren half-expected to see Liz behind the wheel. As they climbed in, Lauren caught a fleeting whiff of Liz's favorite perfume. Grief smothered her like a heavy blanket.

Jake dropped Rose-ma and Lauren off near the church door so Rose-ma would not have to walk in the heat. Several of the other parishioners stopped to offer condolences, well-intentioned expressions of sympathy that served as painful reminders of their loss. Rose-ma and Lauren slipped into a pew and took their seats. Several minutes later, Jake entered, surrounded by a huddle of buzzing people. He signed autographs, took pictures with strangers, and even held somebody's baby for a photograph. The crowd finally diminished as the services started and Jake slid into the seat next to Lauren.

Their return to the car after the service was similarly impeded by a crush of people anxious to meet the famous baseball pitcher. It took almost thirty-five minutes to make the short trek to the car in the parking lot. Jake cheerfully accommodated every autograph request.

Brunch at Jake's upscale country club was subdued by comparison.

"People here don't pester you for autographs?" Lauren asked.

"Nah. This is my parents' club, so most these folks have known me since I was a snotty-nosed little boy. Besides, this crowd considers it beneath them to ask for a common autograph. They'd rather pay extravagant prices for an autographed ball from some charity auction so they can write it off on their taxes."

The brunch menu offered tempting choices such as crepes, Bourbon-dipped French toast, and truffled Kennebec potatoes.

"Order whatever your heart's desire," Jake offered. "My treat."

"I'm going to have eggs Benedict," Lauren decided. "I'm sure my heart doesn't desire that, but my stomach sure does."

Lauren and Jake exchanged knowing smiles when Rose-ma ordered an egg-white omelet with a side of grapefruit.

"I'm going to bust my training diet for this meal," Jake announced before ordering the breakfast sampler of pancakes, eggs, hash browns, and bacon. The waiter served complimentary mimosas.

"Have you seen all of the crazy tabloid stories about me and Liz?" Jake asked after the waiter was out of earshot.

Lauren rolled her eyes. "The stories get more far-fetched every day. Apparently Liz had a stalker, you're gay, Liz was really a man. Should I go on?"

"Don't forget that I supposedly have 'roid rage. And my personal favorite is that Liz and I were swingers," he laughed. "I don't seem to remember any of it."

"Your amnesia will probably be tomorrow's headline."

Jake looked around the room. "Shhhh," he said theatrically, "the walls have ears."

"I love how the articles always reference anonymous sources close to the Wakefields. Who are these sources with their outrageous theories?"

"A bunch of money-grubbing, attention-seeking crazies," Jake said.

"You think they get paid for those stories?" Lauren asked.

"I know they do. Most of those trashy rags will pay anything for some good dirt, even if it's not true. And you'd be surprised how many people feel like they know me because I took a quick photo with them. I love my fans, but they can get pretty scary."

"Speaking of fans, how about those Dodgers?" Lauren teased Jake.

The conversation turned to baseball. Lauren had been a die-hard fan of professional baseball since she was young, when her father used to take her to games at Dodger stadium. Ironically, Liz had never shown any interest in baseball.

"I think Mikelski's a better shortstop than Barlow was," Lauren commented on the Diamondbacks' recent mid-season change.

Jake paused to consider this, "Just between you and me, I agree. But if Barlow ever asked me, I'd deny it to my death."

Lauren was disappointed to see the bill arrive. She had never realized how much she enjoyed Jake's company.

Chapter Nine

(Friday, August 5)

Lauren was removing a piece of metal from a patient's eye. The sliver looked like a toothpick under the magnification of the scope she was using, but to the naked eye, it was the size of an eyelash.

"There's your suspect," Lauren told the relieved man after removing it.

"That's it? It felt like barbed wire,"

"Things in your eye always do," Lauren said. "Next time you decide to do home improvement with a power tool, I recommend…"

"That I keep my eyes closed?"

"That you wear safety goggles." The patient thanked her and she headed out, looking forward to getting some food. She ran into Stone in the hallway.

"Jake Wakefield is here to see you," Stone told her excitedly. Stone must follow baseball.

Lauren rushed out to the waiting area, which was nearly empty for once. "Jake, is there news about the investigation?"

"Unfortunately no. I was in the neighborhood and thought I'd check in on you. I haven't seen you in awhile. Do you have a minute?"

"Your timing is good. I was just going to grab some lunch. Are you hungry? The hospital cafeteria offers five-star fine dining."

He laughed. "I can't pass up an offer like that."

They made small talk as they proceeded down the cafeteria line and picked out their food: pizza and Diet Coke for her, grilled chicken and apple juice for him. They took seats at a small table in the back corner.

"Have you heard anything from the detectives?" she asked.

"Crickets."

"I should've guessed," she said. "I call every day. Whenever I get Wallace, he says, 'These things take time.' If it's Boyd, I get 'we're making excellent progress.' Are those guys even on the same team?"

"No kidding. Are they even in the same league?"

"Do they even play the same sport?" They both laughed, Jake attracting admiring glances from other diners.

"How's your job going?" Jake asked.

"Frustrating. Rewarding. Crazy. The usual. We had a guy come in yesterday complaining of breathing problems. We ran some scans and discovered a growth in his lung."

"Cancer?"

"That's what I thought, too, but get this…it was a strawberry plant."

Jake choked on his juice. "You're kidding, right?"

"Nope. He somehow had inhaled a strawberry seed. It got embedded in his lung lining, which was moist and warm enough for it to sprout."

"Did you have to operate with pruning shears?"

"Something like that."

"Excuse me, Mr. Wakefield." A young boy was approaching their table. "May I have your autograph?" He held out a paper napkin and a blue crayon.

"Of course you can, but not in Dodger colors," Jake smiled. He pulled out a wallet-sized photograph of himself in uniform and a red pen. "What's your name?"

Jake personalized the photo and chatted with the boy about his Little League team where young Mitchell played shortstop.

He sprinted back to a nearby table to show the signed photo to his beaming mother.

"Wow. You always travel with photos?"

"I've learned to. It saves me from having to sign disgusting napkins or, worse, body parts. Always be prepared. I was a Boy Scout, you know." He held up two fingers in the scout pledge.

"I'm sure you were." Sitting in the cafeteria, she was reminded of something. "Jake, I don't mean to pry, but was Liz pregnant?"

"What? No. Where'd you get that? *The National Enquirer?*"

She shook her head. "Just another rumor." As she polished off her pizza, she said, "I guess I should get back to work. And we better get you out of here so I don't have to spend the rest of the afternoon treating multiple victims trampled in a quest for your autograph."

The hospital corridors resembled a maze so she showed him back to the ER waiting room. "Thank you so much for checking on me."

He hugged her tight. "Liz worried about you being alone if anything ever happened to her and I swore I wouldn't let that happen. It was a promise that I hoped never to have to act on, but now I plan to keep it. Call me if you need anything. I'll see you soon."

Lauren did feel less alone in the world as she watched him walk away.

Chapter Ten

(Friday, August 12)

Nearly three weeks after Liz's murder, Lauren finally received a call from the police.

"Would you be willing to take a lie detector test?" Detective Wallace asked.

All of the frustration that had been simmering below the surface boiled over. "Why are you wasting your time investigating me? You have some crazed murderer running around the streets, waiting to strike again. And your grand plan after three weeks of 'tireless investigation' is to give me a lie detector test? Me, who was waist-deep in ER cases that night at a hospital fifteen miles away, with a dozen witnesses to account for my whereabouts? Me, whose only friend in this entire city was Liz? Me, who had no motive whatsoever to kill her? A polygraph test, which any Psych 101 student could tell you is not even admissible in court? If I'm your best suspect and a polygraph is your best investigative tool, you have a fucking problem!"

"Okay, I'll note that you refused the polygraph," Wallace said coldly.

"Wait a minute. I didn't say I wouldn't take…" but Lauren was talking to dead air. Wallace had already hung up.

Lauren was dialing Wallace back to inform him that she would take the lie detector test when she received an urgent page. *I'll let him cool down and call him back later,* she decided as she sprinted to trauma Bay Three.

Lauren spent the next hour pumping a fifth of vodka out of the stomach of a teenager. Afterward, Ritesh caught up with her in the hallway. "Your order has arrived."

"What order?"

"Tall, dark, and handsome."

"Ha ha. Very funny. I wouldn't get between me and the Diet Coke machine if I were you," she said.

"You must secretly find me attractive," Ritesh said, "because you immediately assume I am referring to myself, but there's a cop here to see you. He's down by the nurses' station."

Lauren recognized Detective Boyd from a distance. She invited him into the doctors' lounge, which was empty. Despite all the jokes about golfing, ER doctors didn't have much time to lounge.

"Lauren, did you really refuse to take the polygraph?"

Feeling defensive and guilty at the same time, Lauren responded, "No, that's not what I said. Or at least that's not what I meant. Of course I'll take the polygraph, even though I don't believe in them. They're based on physiological measurements that can be affected by so many extraneous variables, like anxiety or medications or feeling guilty about something else. But I'll happily take it if it will help get the investigation going."

Detective Boyd let out a long sigh. His aqua eyes focused on her green ones. "I know this must be frustrating for you, especially since we can't tell you much. But you have to believe me when I tell you that this investigation remains in full-gear. One great thing about all the media coverage is that the brass responds to that type of pressure. We *will* solve this case. It's only a matter of time. Don't overthink this polygraph request. It just allows us to check you off the suspect list."

"But why me? Any more time you spend looking at me is time wasted."

Detective Boyd paused for a moment. "So, did you really take Wallace to task about the reliability of polygraphs?"

"I didn't mean to. He caught me off guard and—"

Lauren was interrupted by Detective Boyd's laughter. He began shaking at the waist and his eyes teared up, accentuating their vivid color. He was laughing so hard that she was having trouble understanding what was saying. "What I wouldn't have given to see the expression on his face when you told him that even intro psych students know that lie detector tests aren't admissible. Classic!"

Lauren was sucked into the infectiousness of his laughter and they shared a good, long laugh. She felt both relieved and ashamed as she enjoyed the momentary respite from her grief.

Chapter Eleven

(Saturday, August 13)

Lauren drummed her fingers, waiting for her patient's lab results to come in. Mr. Hanson was either high on drugs or acutely psychotic. Only the toxicology findings would tell. While she waited, her cell phone vibrated in her pocket. She dug into her scrubs pocket to answer it.

"Hey, Jake. How's everything?"

"Painful. How are you?"

"Surviving."

"Listen, I'm sorry for the late notice, but I'm calling to invite you to a charity event tonight. Liz is going to be honored by MADD."

"Tonight?"

"I know. I'm sorry. This was scheduled before Liz died, but with everything going on, I let the whole thing slip my mind. It's bound to be rough. Please come with me."

"What time is it? I don't get off until six."

"That's perfect. It doesn't start until seven. And it's okay if you're not there right on the button. These things usually don't start on time anyway."

Lauren was exhausted and had been looking forward to crawling into bed, but she didn't hesitate. An early bedtime would do nothing for her persistent insomnia. "Sure. I'll go with you."

"Great. I appreciate it. I should be there when it starts, but you just come when you can. I'll save you a seat." He gave her the address to the downtown hotel and she jotted it down on the back of a prescription slip.

As they said their good-byes, the computer screen blinked in front of her and she entered her password to learn that Mr. Hanson had no drugs on board. *Shoot*, she thought, *meth would have been easier to treat.*

Hours later, intern LaRhonda Jackson strolled in to relieve Lauren at 6:10, casually eating a bean burrito from Taco Bell. LaRhonda referred to herself as a triple threat; big, black, and beautiful. She was also bold and didn't worry about being chastised for tardiness.

Lauren provided the patient report as concisely as she could. "Back spasms in Bay One, slip and fall in Two, high as a kite in Four, broken arm in Six, drunk and belligerent in Seven. Have fun."

"Why you in such a hurry tonight?"

"I have someplace I need to be by seven."

"Mmmm hmmmm," LaRhonda said knowingly.

Lauren didn't pause to elaborate. Her naturally leaden foot allowed her to reach her apartment by 6:25, where she hurriedly changed into a little black dress, applied eyeliner and lipstick in a matter of seconds, and tried unsuccessfully to smooth the ponytail bump from her hair. She tottered back out to her car in uncomfortably high heels moments later.

She was glad to be going against traffic on the city streets, driving back into the city as most others were headed for the suburbs. She made her final turn at 6:50, relieved that she would arrive in the nick of time. However, traffic slowed significantly as cars in front of her merged into a single lane to avoid an accident in the right lanes. Like everybody else, Lauren could not resist looking to see what had happened. Apparently, a green light anticipator had slammed into a yellow light accelerator, a Corolla T-boned by a Mercedes. The Mercedes driver paced around his car as he assessed the front-end damage, talking animatedly into his cell phone. The Corolla driver, a young woman, sat in her car, door open, crying. Emergency personnel had not yet arrived.

Lauren fought an internal battle; most of her wanting to arrive on time to the charity event, some small portion feeling obligated to render assistance. She stopped. The Mercedes driver appeared more angry than hurt. Lauren approached the crying woman, "Are you okay?"

"I think so," the woman wailed, "but I'm worried about the baby."

Lauren scanned the car, spotting no child safety seat. She imagined an unrestrained infant thrown from the car in a bloody heap. "The baby?"

"I'm five months pregnant."

"The human uterus is well-insulated. I'm sure your baby is fine," Lauren reassured.

"I haven't felt her move since the accident," the woman sobbed.

Lauren's pulse quickened. She hurried back to her own car, grabbing her spare stethoscope from the trunk. Returning to the woman's side, she knelt on the ground next to her, placing the stethoscope on the woman's lower abdomen. Fetal heartbeats were difficult enough to find in a quiet office with a sophisticated heart monitor. It was going to be damned near impossible on the side of a busy road with only a stethoscope. Still she tried, moving the scope here and there. Each time she moved the scope, the pregnant woman became more panicked. Lauren began to wish she hadn't attempted this in the first place. In fact, she was regretting stopping at all. But then she located the sound that always reminded her of a racing train.

"I hear the heartbeat," she said, looking at the second hand of her watch. "Strong and healthy at 150 beats per minute."

The woman threw her arms around Lauren. "Thank you!"

When the paramedics arrived, Lauren issued a brief verbal report before rushing back to her own car.

Lauren arrived at the award venue forty minutes late, with untamed hair and dirty knees. A tall woman in a red dress was speaking on the stage. Lauren ducked down as she wound her way through the round tables looking for Jake. Naturally, his table was front and center, maximizing Lauren's embarrassment as she slid into the empty seat next to him.

He leaned over and kissed her on the cheek, whispering, "You look fantastic." The woman seated next to him glared at Lauren. Jake made a face as soon as the woman turned back to the speaker. Lauren suppressed a giggle.

"Elizabeth Wakefield was an extraordinary humanitarian," the woman in red was saying, "but Liz was also my friend. She was approachable, down to earth, and funny as hell. In her fundraising role, she hobnobbed with high society, pulling in big donations. But behind the scenes, she offered real and meaningful comfort to victims of drunk driving."

In her haste, Lauren had forgotten to bring Kleenex. She discreetly used her linen napkin to dab her eyes.

"Those of us who had the privilege to know Liz will miss her dearly. She was taken from us too soon. In honor of her generous nature, sense of purpose, and fierce determination, we would like to award this year's Spirit of MADD award to Elizabeth Rose Wakefield."

The crowd erupted in applause and Jake ascended the stage to accept the award.

"Thank you so much for recognizing Liz for her contributions. I've been thinking a lot about what Liz would have said if she had been here to accept this award." He began to choke up, but regained his composure. "And she wouldn't have focused on herself. She would have used this opportunity to urge us all to do more. More activism, more awareness, and more fundraising. In her memory, I would like to jumpstart that effort with a twenty-five thousand-dollar pledge. Open your hearts and your checkbooks. Let's make Liz proud tonight."

The ballroom rustled as at least two hundred people dug into their wallets. Lauren pulled out her own checkbook and assessed her balance. She wrote a check for one thousand dollars, reminding herself to transfer some money from savings to cover it.

People swarmed Jake as he descended the stage. Lauren made awkward small talk with others as the guests milled about greeting one another.

"Lauren?"

She turned to see the woman in red. "I'm Kathryn Montgomery. I was a friend of Liz's."

"Yes, thank you so much for your kind words. You seemed to really know her."

"Yes," Kathryn said, "and I absolutely adored her. She talked about you often. She was looking forward to spending more time with you."

Lauren's eyes filled with tears and she could only nod. Kathryn continued, "I wanted to let you know that…"

"Take a look!" Jake burst through the crowd, holding the award aloft. It was a round crystalline circle etched with a martini glass and car key. A dramatic diagonal line crossed through the image. Liz's name was engraved in the base.

"Jake, do you know Kathryn?" Lauren asked.

Jake stuck out his hand. "Thanks for your warm sentiments about Liz."

Kathryn hesitated before she reached out to shake Jake's hand. "Yes, of course. It's nice to finally meet you."

To Lauren, Jake said, "We ought to get you home. Aren't you going to turn into a pumpkin soon?"

"Something like that."

They said good night to Kathryn and several others who mobbed Jake as they wove their way to the nearest exit.

"Sorry I was late." Lauren started to explain.

"Don't be sorry. Be grateful. You missed a lot of boring talk about fundraising goals and arrived just in time for the good part. You did, however, miss a mediocre meal. Are you hungry?" Lauren realized she was.

Jake drove her to a nearby coffeehouse, which was virtually empty at this hour. Lauren explained about the car accident that she had encountered earlier.

"How great that you know enough to be able to help," Jake said. "And what a pain that you feel like you have to."

"The detectives contacted me yesterday. They asked me to take a polygraph."

"Those dipshits. They asked me to take one last week."

"They did? What was it like?"

"I didn't take it. I told Boyd he could shove that machine up his ass since polygraphs measure bullshit anyways."

Lauren's lower jaw dropped. "You did not."

"Like hell I didn't. You should refuse too, Lauren. The sooner they stop focusing on us, the sooner they can start paying attention to who really did this."

They chatted more about the investigation, her work at the hospital, and his baseball season. The Diamondbacks had beaten the Phillies earlier that day and would be playing them again tomorrow. "You should come to the game," Jake said.

"I wish I could, but I have to work."

He looked disappointed.

"Another time."

"Any time you can make it, let me know."

Lauren's heart quickened as he leaned toward her and touched her face. He used one finger to wipe away a dab of cream cheese.

Internally, Lauren chastised herself. What had she thought he was going to do?

Chapter Twelve

(Monday, August 15)

The polygraph was administered in an austere office at the Scottsdale Police Station. Aside from a table, two chairs, and the polygraph equipment, the room was empty. It was lit by overhead fluorescent bulbs.

Before he hooked up the equipment, the polygraph examiner explained the procedure and asked if Lauren had any questions.

"No questions, just a concern. I studied the polygraph for a college paper. And based on what I remember, I don't have the utmost confidence in these things."

The examiner was bland-looking. Nondescript brown hair, brown eyes, horn-rimmed glasses. He responded, "Given that you're a physician, I would think you could appreciate this physiological approach to the detection of deception."

"I understand the polygraph measures objective measures like pulse rate, muscular tension, and skin conductivity," Lauren said. "And all of those things are reliable measures of anxiety which could result from lying. However, that anxiety could also result from being suspected of a crime."

"True, but our interview techniques are very effective at distinguishing the two," the examiner said. Lauren had already forgotten his name. *I'll think of him as Mr. Brown,* she told herself. He was even wearing a brown suit.

"Really? I think studies suggest the reliability is about seventy percent at best," Lauren said.

"Are you refusing to take the test?" Mr. Brown's tone developed an edge.

"Not at all. I'll do whatever it takes to help find my sister's killer. I just want some assurances that this entire investigation isn't relying upon an instrument that has questionable efficacy under the best of circumstances."

"Duly noted," Mr. Brown said before he began hooking up the equipment. He instructed Lauren to answer each question with a yes or no response.

He started by asking easy questions to establish a baseline of truthfulness.

"Is your name Lauren Nicole Rose?"

"Yes."

"Were you born on September twenty-eighth?"

"That's what I've been told."

Mr. Brown sighed, "Answer with yes or no only please."

"I'm trying, but I don't want to imply that I remember being born on that date when I don't."

Mr. Brown shook his head and moved on to another question, "Are you employed at Good Samaritan Hospital?"

"Yes."

"Are you the sister of Elizabeth Rose Wakefield?"

Lauren hesitated. "I used to be."

Mr. Brown glared, but continued the test without comment. "Were you at Good Samaritan Hospital on the evening of July twenty-third for the entire time between the hours of seven p.m. and eleven p.m.?

"Yes."

"Are you right-handed?"

"No."

"Are you left-handed?"

"No."

Mr. Brown furrowed his brow. "I need you to answer these questions fully and accurately."

"I'm ambidextrous. I favor each hand for different tasks."

"I see. But surely you use one more than the other?"

"I use my right hand for most things, including writing and eating, but I kick with my left foot and I throw balls with my left hand."

He paused and made some notations on a strip of paper being generated by the polygraph machine on which writing tools were jumping about, creating wiggly lines based upon Lauren's answers.

"Do you swing a golf club with your left hand?"

Lauren hesitated. She had to answer the question with complete honesty. "I'm sorry, but I use both hands when I swing a golf club. Did you mean do I swing it left-handed?"

Mr. Brown let out a long sigh of agitation. "I'll rephrase the question." He made another notation on the paper strip, which was now pooling on the floor next to the machine.

"Do you swing a golf club left-handed?"

"Yes."

"Were you aware you were the sole beneficiary on your sister's life insurance policy?"

"Not prior to her death."

"Yes or no only."

"I am aware of that now, but I wasn't aware of it at the time of her death."

He sighed again. "Were you aware you were the sole beneficiary on your sister's life insurance policy prior to July twenty-fourth?"

"No."

"Have you been having financial problems?"

"No, not really."

Mr. Brown eyeballed her unpleasantly. Lauren couldn't answer with a simple yes or no response. Lauren didn't have money problems per se, but she did sometimes worry about making sure her paycheck covered her expenses, like most people. After paying rent and student loans on her intern's salary, she didn't have a lot in savings. Did that constitute financial problems?

"Do you know the code to the alarm at your sister's home?"

"Yes." *At least I used to*, she thought. *Maybe Jake changed it.* Knowing she might have answered that question 'wrong' made her nervous.

"Do you have a key to your sister's home?"

"No."

"Is there any reason why the forensics team will find Liz's blood on the scrubs you turned over to Detective Boyd?"

"No." *Were they trying to fluster her? If so, it was working well.* Then came the question that she had been expecting, but wasn't prepared for.

"Did you kill your sister, Elizabeth Wakefield?"

"No."

"Did you kill her by stabbing her?"

"No."

"Did you kill her by shooting her?"

"No."

"Did you kill her with medications?"

"No."

"Did you kill her by hitting her in the head?"

"No." *But somebody had.* Lauren felt her pulse racing.

"Did you have anything to do with her death?"

I've been interviewed by homicide investigators. I had to tell my grandmother she died. I identified the body. I attended the funeral. I've had way too much to do with her death, Lauren thought. "No."

"Do you know who killed her?"

Lauren's mind raced. *I don't know. Do I? Once I find out who did it, I might know that person.* "No."

After waiting for the examiner to review the yards and yards of polygraph data, he told her the results were inconclusive. Lauren knew this stupid test wasn't valid. Mr. Brown asked her if she would submit to the test a second time.

The cold instruments were re-affixed to her body. Again, she was asked the intrusive, offensive, ambiguous questions.

After taking an eternity to review the results, he finally spoke. "I'll turn the findings over to the detectives. You may discuss it with them. But there is one more thing we'd like to ask of you before you leave the station today."

"Yes?"

"Would you be willing to leave hair and blood samples with us for DNA analysis?

"Sure. DNA analysis. That's a verifiable science."

"Yes, Dr. Rose, I believe you've made your opposition to the polygraph crystal clear." His tone was caustic.

As she left, Lauren said, "I'm sorry I frustrated you, Mr. Brown, I genuinely appreciate your efforts on this case."

He gave her a sour look, "My name is Baxter, not Brown."

Lauren had accidentally referred to him by the name she had secretly assigned him. Thank goodness it was not something worse like "Bully."

◇◇◇

"Those are some serious scratches you have on your arm," the phlebotomist commented as he drew Lauren's blood in the police station laboratory.

"Yeah," Lauren agreed, looking at the fading scratches she had all but forgotten about.

"Maybe we should take some pictures of those," he suggested.

"Yeah, you probably should."

Chapter Thirteen

(Tuesday, August 16)

The next day at the hospital, Dr. Stone tracked Lauren down accompanied by an unfamiliar man in civilian clothing.

"Don't freak out," Stone said, "but this gentleman is here to serve you with a subpoena. We get these often. It's usually some patient haggling with their insurance company over payment." Lauren accepted the white envelope handed to her and Stone directed her to the office of Mr. Lawrence, the hospital attorney. She handed the subpoena to Mr. Lawrence for routine legal review. There, she learned she was not being subpoenaed regarding a medical case, but with a court order to report to the Scottsdale Police Department within twenty-four hours.

"It requires you to submit to photography of your person," Mr. Lawrence advised after a quick review of the document. "Any idea why?"

"I got scratched a couple weeks ago by a patient. The police asked me about the scratches yesterday when I was having my blood drawn."

"Seems like they're looking at you pretty hard in your sister's murder. I can't represent you because this doesn't involve a hospital matter, but I can recommend a good criminal defense attorney. Sounds to me like you need one."

Lauren felt as if she had the wind knocked out of her. She had never had so much as a traffic ticket before. Now, she needed a defense attorney for the murder of her own sister.

Lauren had few people in whom she could confide. She did talk to Rose-ma on the phone every day. But as much as Lauren adored Rose-ma, she was tired of hearing Liz's murder attributed to God's will. Additionally, Lauren felt she had to protect Rose-ma from some of the things that were bothering her most, such as her own treatment as a possible suspect.

Her fellow interns had been amazing. In a field renowned for vicious competition, their intern class had managed to foster a spirit of cooperation. Lauren could share any work-related concern with the other interns and feel supported. Still, she didn't feel comfortable sharing details of the investigation with them. They had picked up on this and had respectfully stopped asking.

Lauren still had frequent phone calls from old friends, all calling to express concern about her in the wake of the tragedy. Most seemed sincere, others appeared to be fishing for gossip. Given the constant stories that showed up in the press, Lauren found it hard to trust anybody with her innermost fears.

She found herself leaning most heavily on Jake. She had never been particularly close to him before. He was a famous baseball player and she had been his wife's little sister. But now, they seemed to have everything in common. He understood her feelings of grief, anger, and loneliness because he was riding the same emotional roller coaster. They discussed the case nearly every day. He was as obsessed with the status of the investigation as she was. And he was equally frustrated by the detectives.

So, Lauren immediately called Jake about the police summons for photographs. "That's fucking ridiculous," he raged. "Enough's enough. I don't think you should do it. What the hell could they possibly want to take pictures of?"

"I was scratched by a patient at the ER."

"Don't you have witnesses? Somebody must have seen it happen."

"No one else was there at the time."

"Did this happen before or after Liz's…" his words petered out.

"A few days before."

"And you still have scratches?"

"They're healed now, but the scars are still visible. Jake, have the police said anything to you about me? Do they really think I might have done this?"

"Of course not. Those jerks don't know what they're doing. Pretty boy Boyd is a know-nothing and Wallace is a know-it-all." Lauren was touched by his anger on her behalf. "I think you should stop cooperating. Force them to stop focusing on you and turn their attention to real suspects. Why don't you talk to my family lawyer? I'm sure I can get you a free consultation."

Lauren let out a sigh of relief. Her parents' life insurance policy had covered college expenses for both Liz and Lauren, but Lauren had taken out student loans to finance medical school. Now, she was making substantial payments on her loans. She could ill-afford an expensive criminal defense attorney.

"Thank you, Jake. I don't know how I would survive this without you."

"That's what family's for."

"Jake, did you know Liz changed her life insurance policy?"

"Of course I knew. The policy was up for renewal and we agreed she should change her beneficiary to you. Have you gotten the payout yet?"

"No. They said they can't pay it until the investigation is complete. It doesn't matter. I don't care about the money. I was just wondering why she changed her beneficiary."

"I didn't need the money. So we agreed the money should go to you if, you know…Do you need money, Lauren?"

"No, thanks. I'm just worried about how much a lawyer is going to cost. I can't believe this is happening."

"I know." He sighed deeply. "Me neither. That's why you should talk to my lawyer. Let me call him and I'll call you right back."

Lauren paced until her phone rang again a few minutes later. "Sorry, Lauren," Jake said. "I talked to Bob, but he said he can't help. He said it represents a conflict of interest since I've already consulted him. I don't get that legalese stuff. Anyway, he says he thinks you should stop talking to the police. He says they'll only try to use what you say against you."

"But I haven't done anything wrong."

"You know that. And I know that. But those jackasses haven't figured that out yet."

Chapter Fourteen

(Wednesday, August 17)

In the end, Lauren decided to comply with the court order, confident in forensic science. The day after the summons, she reported to the Scottsdale Police Department. She was required to strip down to her undergarments so the police photographer could take photos of her entire body. They focused several frames on the scratches fading on her upper right arm. The experience was humiliating and by the time she left the small windowless room, she was in tears.

As she was approaching the station exit, she heard somebody calling her name. "Miss Rose."

Lauren had become accustomed to people calling out to her. Perfect strangers recognized her from the exhaustive coverage of the case. Many felt they knew her. It had been surreal at first. Now, it was annoying. Every trite condolence offered by a stranger was a stabbing reminder of her loss.

Lauren increased the length of her stride. The building was closing in on her. She was desperate to get outside.

The calls became more insistent, "Miss Rose!" The voice sounded familiar, but she did not pause long enough to try to identify the speaker.

Lauren was speed walking, practically running. She hit the door at a brisk pace and forced her way out to the front steps.

She could hear somebody pushing through the door behind her. She descended the steps two at a time. Her ten-year-old Civic had recently died a quiet death from a blown gasket. Lauren had long ago promised herself a new car when she finished her internship, but she had been forced to buy a new car eleven months shy of that goal. Her shiny new emerald Acura beckoned to her from across the parking lot.

Reaching the last step, she miscalculated her footing and went sprawling across the parking lot. The latch on her purse sprang open and her keys, a bottle of Tylenol, and two tubes of cherry chapstick scattered across the ground. Her right knee ripped open on the rough asphalt.

Before she could collect her thoughts, somebody pulled her to her feet and began gathering up the contents of her spilled purse. Detective Boyd.

"Are you okay?"

"Fine," she snapped. "Nothing bruised but my ego. Did you need something?"

He looked surprised at the sharpness of her tone, his blue-green eyes reflecting the bright sunlight. "I spotted you leaving the building. I wanted to see how you were doing."

"I'll tell you how I'm doing. I've lost my only sister and my best friend. I've been falsely accused of her murder. I've been served a subpoena and taken a polygraph. I've been poked and prodded and photographed in my underwear. And now you have chased me down the stairs and literally onto my knees. And you want to know how I'm doing? I'm doing crappy. That's how I'm doing."

Boyd took a step back. His face was somber, but the corners of his eyes turned up a bit at the corners. "I'm very sorry I chased you onto your knees. I just wanted you to know that we now have a very real suspect in this case." He turned on his heel and bounded up the steps.

Now it was her turn to call after him. "Detective Boyd? Wait." But he disappeared into the police station without a backward glance.

A very real suspect? Finally! Lauren's immediate euphoria was quickly followed by a foreboding feeling. She had just been photographed in her bra and panties. Perhaps she was the "very real suspect" that Detective Boyd was referring to.

Chapter Fifteen

Returning to the ER, Lauren still had blood oozing from one knee. She was yanked into an exam room by LaRhonda. Lauren and LaRhonda had very different upbringings, but had immediately bonded over the fact that they had both been orphaned at about the same age. LaRhonda had never known her biological father, and her mother had succumbed to knife injuries incurred during a drug deal gone wrong when LaRhonda was fourteen, cementing LaRhonda's determination to become an emergency room doctor.

"Honey, you are a hot mess." LaRhonda began to swab Lauren's knee with antiseptic, removing tiny pebbles that embedded in Lauren's flesh. "How can so much gravel find a home in these scrawny legs of yours? Look, I know you don't like to share your personal business. You pride yourself on being tough. Believe me, I know all 'bout that, but you best tell me what's going on."

All of Lauren's frustration came spilling out, concluding with her paranoia about being Boyd's very real suspect. "They keep telling me they need to rule me out so they can narrow their investigation. That makes sense, right?"

"Wrong! They shoulda been able to rule you out long 'go. For some reason, they think you did it. I know you grew up in some white-bread town where the biggest crime was stolen panties off some little ol' lady's clothesline, but honey, this ain't Mayberry. You need to get yourself a lawyer and fast. You need me to come with you? Cause I will. I will march into that lawyer's office with you and demand justice."

Lauren could easily imagine LaRhonda taking the entire judicial system by storm. "No, you don't need to march anywhere with me. Mr. Lawrence gave me the name of an attorney. I'll call him."

LaRhonda finished off Lauren's knee with a fancy bandage. Lauren began to get down from the exam table.

"Where do you think you'se going?" LaRhonda asked.

"I need to grab some scrubs. That police brutality set me back and I need to get to work."

LaRhonda forced her own cell phone into Lauren's hand. "You're not going anywhere until you call and get yourself an appointment with a lawyer. And that's final."

Chapter Sixteen

The law offices of Dennis Hopkins were located on the seven-teenth floor of a fancy high-rise in downtown Phoenix. The picture windows in the waiting room offered an expansive view. Lauren spotted Camelback Mountain in the distance, Good Samaritan Hospital where she worked, and Chase Field where the Diamondbacks played.

At her three o'clock appointment time, she was escorted back by the receptionist, who introduced her to the man behind the enormous desk before exiting. Dennis Hopkins rose from his chair to greet Lauren with a hearty handshake. He was a large man with a protruding belly underneath his western shirt, jeans, and a large silver belt buckle. He had salt and pepper hair, with extra salt.

Dennis instructed Lauren to sit in one of the bulky armchairs across from his desk. No sooner had her butt hit the chair than he drawled, "I understand you are a suspect in the death of your sister."

"Who told you that?" Lauren asked, shocked by his bluntness.

"You did. Isn't that why you scheduled this consultation?"

"I suppose so," Lauren conceded. "The detectives are trying to rule me out so they can narrow the focus of their investigation."

"Uh huh. And what have they done so far to rule you out?"

"They've questioned me a couple of times. They collected the clothes I was wearing on the evening of the crime. They talked to colleagues to confirm my whereabouts. I took a polygraph test, actually two polygraph tests. I provided DNA and hair samples and they took pictures of my body."

"Once you get to know me, you'll learn I'm a real straight shooter," Dennis said. "I don't need to sell my services to those who don't need 'em because I have plenty of potential clients who do. So please believe me when I say you need a defense attorney. Don't hire me if you don't feel comfortable with me, but you need to hire someone. No kidding, no sugarcoating, no fooling around."

Dennis explained the need to formalize the business contract before having any further discussion, explaining, "Signing the contract establishes attorney-client privilege." They reviewed it together and Lauren hired Dennis by signing on the dotted line.

"I can begin making some phone calls on your behalf now that I officially represent you. I've practiced in this city my entire career. I even used to be one of those SOB prosecutors once upon a time." Dennis chuckled. "I'm well-acquainted with most of the judges in this town and a great many of the prosecutors. I'll start making calls today and find out why the police find you so interesting. I don't think it's because you're easy on the eyes, though that will help if we have to go in front of a jury."

Lauren usually felt uncomfortable when a man complimented her, but she knew Dennis was not hitting on her. He was simply sizing up her potential strengths and weaknesses in front of a jury. She imagined this came naturally to him, just as she was inclined to notice any obvious signs of disease in people.

"Now, Lauren. I never ask my clients if they are guilty…"

"I'm not guil—" she started to say before he shushed her.

"As I was saying, I never ask my clients if they are guilty or not and there are some fine reasons for that. First of all, it's completely irrelevant. That might sound strange to you. Most people think criminal prosecutions are about determining whether the accused is guilty or not guilty, but that isn't true. Trials are about determining whether the prosecution can prove the defendant guilty beyond a reasonable doubt, and that's a different question altogether. Second, I'm in a better position to defend my clients when I operate on a presumption of innocence."

That's probably because most of your clients are guilty, Lauren thought.

"Finally, it is my legal obligation to ensure you do not perjure yourself. If you are charged with this crime, it is your constitutional right to refuse to testify. However, if you did choose to testify on your own behalf, I could not allow you to testify to anything I know to be untrue. You see what I mean?"

Lauren nodded. His rhetoric was stoking her fear as she imagined being charged with Liz's murder.

"For this reason, you and I will often speak in hypotheticals. When I start a question with the phrase 'hypothetically speaking,' I'm not asking you to tell me about something that happened in your own life, I'm just asking you to explore the facts of the case as you know them in a hypothetical manner. You see what I mean?"

"Yes." Lauren was familiar with this strategy. Doctors used similar tactics to discuss cases with the hospital legal office.

"I take my job very seriously. Every citizen in this country is entitled to a rigorous defense and that is what I pledge to provide for you. You won't find any other lawyer in this state who would defend you as relentlessly as I will. And…" he paused for emphasis, "…I never violate attorney-client privilege, not even to my own wife. I say that because it is imperative you feel comfortable confiding in me. Do you have any questions whatsoever about that?"

"Yes," Lauren responded, thinking about doctor patient confidentiality. Most of the things patients told Lauren were legally protected from disclosure, but there were some exceptions such as threats of self-harm or issues affecting public safety. "Are there any exceptions to attorney-client privilege?"

"None. Zilch, zero, nada. Not even your death would vacate the privilege. Not disclosures of past crimes. There are absolutely no exceptions whatsoever save the one I mentioned already. I cannot knowingly allow you to commit perjury or any other future crime. Anymore questions for me?"

Lauren took a deep breath. "What makes you so sure I need a lawyer?"

"A very good question. When you've been in this business as long as I have, you know what is routine for police investigations and what is not. Asking you questions, confirming your alibi, that's all standard stuff. But collecting DNA and hair samples, and subpoenaing bodily photographs?" He shook his head. "Those things aren't typical. Other questions?"

"No, I guess not." Lauren's mind was racing, but she couldn't pin down her fears. There were too many.

"Allow me to ask a few of my own. Hypothetically speaking, would you have any reason to kill your sister?"

"No. I had no reason to want Liz dead. Quite the opposite, in fact. She was my best friend. I miss her every single day."

"Of course you do. And is there any reason, hypothetically speaking, why somebody else might believe you wanted to kill your sister? Would there be any recent fights or nasty emails or evidence of bad blood between the two of you, even if you had since patched things up?"

Lauren and Liz had occasionally fought like crazed animals before their parents' deaths. Over clothes, games, or the television remote. After losing their parents, they both appreciated how trivial such things were and had scarcely spoken a harsh word to one another since. "Apparently, Liz recently changed her life insurance beneficiary to me, but I didn't know that and I wouldn't have cared if I had known."

"And how much is the life insurance worth?"

"A million dollars, or so I've been told."

Dennis let out a long, low whistle. "Hypothetically speaking, is there any chance they are going to find any incriminating evidence on the clothes you were wearing? Any of your sister's DNA on your clothing?"

"They shouldn't. I was wearing fresh scrubs that evening. I did see my sister that afternoon briefly, but we barely touched."

"And, hypothetically speaking, are the detectives likely to find your DNA or your hair at the scene of the crime?"

"Hmmm, good question. I've visited my sister's home, obviously, so it's possible they might find my hair there or something like that. I don't remember ever bleeding at her house, but it's possible I might have at some point."

"Good, I appreciate your objective approach to these questions. Now, hypothetically speaking, did you leave the hospital for any reason at all on the night of the crime?"

"No."

"Excellent, and is there any other evidence you can think of that the police might have collected that would suggest you as a suspect? Like a murder weapon or fingerprints or anything else you can imagine? Hypothetically, of course."

"It's certainly possible my fingerprints could be at my sister's house from previous visits, but otherwise, no, I can't think of anything else."

"Do you know the results of the polygraph examination?"

"They told me the first test was inconclusive and told me nothing about the second test. I was already nervous about taking it, but I want the detectives to know that I am fully cooperating."

"Not anymore. I am going to call the detectives and let them know I represent you. They should contact me, not you, if they need anything further from you. If they try to talk to you directly, you are to call me. Immediately. And I am going to do some digging around to see what I can find out. I want you to continue your usual routines. Okay?"

"Okay."

Dennis leaned back in his large leather chair and pressed his fingers together. "You're in good hands. I can assure you of that. Do you have anything else you want to ask before we end for today?"

Lauren looked Dennis directly in the eyes. "I know you intentionally didn't ask me, but I want you to know I'm innocent. I didn't kill my sister, hypothetically or otherwise."

Chapter Seventeen

(Thursday, August 18)

As soon as she returned to her car, Lauren called Jake.

"Hey you," he answered right away. "What's the latest? Have the Keystone Kops harassed you yet today? The day's just not complete until you've experienced some insufferable request from Detective Walrus or Detective Pretty Boy."

Lauren giggled at Jake's comparison of Detective Wallace to a walrus. His jowly cheeks and bushy mustache did bear a striking resemblance to the creature.

"Now Jake, that's not fair."

"Why do you always have to be so nice? You know those idiots couldn't find their way out of a bathroom even if they had a map, a flashlight, and a compass."

"I only meant that wasn't fair to walruses everywhere."

Jake rewarded her with a loud laugh.

"I just hired an attorney," she told him. "He scared the living daylights out of me. He thinks the direction of the police investigation suggests I am Suspecto Numero Uno."

"Only because he doesn't know how hard they have been looking at me. Those detectives are so far up my ass, you'd be able to see them if you looked down my throat with one of those scope thingies you doctors use."

Lauren smiled. "Maybe they think we conspired together to pull off the perfect crime. No means, no motive, and no opportunity. In any case, I hope this lawyer is worth it. He's costing me a small fortune."

"How much, if you don't mind me asking? Seeing as I might need to hire my own here any day now."

"Five thousand dollars and that's just to get things started. His regular hourly rate is four hundred dollars per hour, but he reduced it to two-fifty for me."

"Five G's? That's nothing. I've had baseball fines for more than that."

"Yeah, but I don't make the big bucks like you. I'm only a measly medical intern."

"Why'd he drop his rate for you? Because you're so hot?"

The compliment surprised Lauren. Petite, slender, with big green eyes, Lauren enjoyed girl-next-door good looks, but she had always paled in comparison to Liz's stunning beauty.

"Uh, no, I think it's because defending the criminal of the century is incredible advertising. The kind you can't buy in the yellow pages anymore."

Jake chuckled. "Hey, you have the day off? Why don't you come over? We can watch a movie or something. I'll get some ice cream."

Lauren hesitated. Did he really want her to come over or was he just being nice to his late wife's kid sister? "I have to work early tomorrow morning."

"Work schmurk. You only live once, Lauren. You and I both know..." he trailed off. Lauren thought she could detect the same despair and loneliness in his voice she herself had been experiencing.

"If you're sure I'm not bothering you, I'd love to come over and drown my sorrows in a tub of ice cream."

"Bothering me? What else am I going to be doing? Visiting the Scottsdale interrogation room again? Come on over."

Lauren had been driving north toward her own empty apartment, but now switched lanes in order to merge onto I-10 and headed east before exiting on Scottsdale Road and heading north toward the estate homes located north of Lincoln. As she neared her destination, she realized this was the first time she would be in Liz's house since her death. She considered canceling. But Jake had seemed so pleased she had agreed to come. She didn't want to let him down. If he could live in the house, she could visit it.

Several reporters were set up outside the community gate, but they didn't recognize Lauren in her new car with its darkly tinted windows. Lauren punched in the four-digit number and waited for the gate to swing open. It did not. She tried a second time. No luck. She dialed Jake.

He answered immediately, "Don't tell me you changed your mind."

"Maybe *you* changed *your* mind. I can't get in the gate."

"Oh, I forgot. They changed the code after…" He provided the new code and she was soon parking in the driveway at Liz's house. Jake's house now, Lauren reminded herself. She took a deep breath as she approached the elaborately carved front door.

Before she could knock, Jake greeted her with a warm bear hug. "You look amazing. I don't know how you pull it off in this heat. I'm nothing but a puddle of sweat after I've been outside for thirty seconds this time of year." Jake looked more like an Abercrombie & Fitch advertisement than he did a puddle. He was wearing khaki shorts with a blue dress shirt.

Lauren stepped into the house and glanced around. She was standing in the tasteful foyer, which overlooked a spacious sunken living room. Through the large picture windows and patio beyond, she could see the infinity edge swimming pool and golf greens. She could also see a corner of the batting cage and pitching target that had been added to the expansive backyard. The house looked exactly as it always had, nothing out of place. Lauren wasn't quite sure what she had been expecting, a huge blood stain on the white carpet perhaps. She let out a sigh of relief.

Jake peered into her eyes. "You okay?"

"Yes. This is the first time I've been here since…"

He let out a sigh of his own. "Hard, huh?" I'm probably going to sell after the baseball season. Too many memories, plus I'm getting a lot of pressure from…" he didn't complete the sentence.

"Pressure from whom?"

"Whom? When did you become an English professor?"

She respected his careful attempt to change the subject. His parents were probably pressuring him to sell the place. Liz had complained of their meddling on more than one occasion.

Lauren responded in her best British accent, "You Yanks are a disgrace to the English language. Using who instead of whom."

Jake got a twinkle in his eye and pulled out his cheesiest Southern drawl. "Sorry about that, ma'am. May I interest you in some ice cream?"

Lauren followed Jake to the gourmet kitchen lined with glass-fronted cherry cabinets, dark marble countertops, and stainless steel appliances. As they entered, Teresita was unloading several grocery bags, lining the counter with countless pints of Ben & Jerry's ice cream containers, one in every available flavor.

"*Muchas gracias*, Teresita," Jake said to his quiet Hispanic housekeeper. She placed the last carton on the counter, efficiently added two bowls and spoons, and discreetly left the room.

Lauren counted the cartons. "Fifteen pints, Jake? When you said you were sending her out for ice cream, I didn't know you meant the entire company." She resumed her British accent, "Have you gone bloody mad?"

He laughed. "I might be able to eat one pint. But my snooty sister-in law?" He whispered conspiratorially, "She can really pack away the food."

Lauren, who had been teased all her life for being scrawny, giggled. "Enough already. I'm going to get a complex and you'll be eating fifteen pints all by yourself."

They investigated the flavors together, laughing at the bad puns Ben & Jerry's use to name their flavors, such as Cherry Garcia and Jamaican MeCrazy.

Lauren began to push all of the cartons containing chocolate to one side. "These are all yours."

"What? How can you not like chocolate? That's like not liking sunshine or baby bunnies or breathing air or…"

"I get the picture. I'm a freak of nature. But at least you don't have to worry about me eating your chocolate."

"Here's one you can eat. Chunky Monkey."

"Ha ha. You're hysterical. That's got fudge chunks. It's all yours."

"Oooh. How about Karamel Sutra?"

"Nope. I'm sold on Mission to Marzipan. Sweet cream ice cream with almond cookies and marzipan swirl," Lauren read from the label.

"That was Liz's favorite," Jake said in a tight voice.

"We Rose girls have always loved anything almond-flavored. I'm sorry to upset you."

"You didn't upset me," he cleared his throat. "You just remind me a lot of her."

They loaded up their bowls with ice cream and headed to the home theater. The large room had an enormous viewing screen with red velvet chaise lounges stacked in tiered rows. An old-fashioned popcorn stand stood in one corner.

"What do you want to watch?" Jake asked. "Teresita picked up a bunch of new releases."

"Just nothing sad."

"Agreed. If Teresita did her job correctly, nothing remotely sad should even be among the choices. I told her nothing depressing, gruesome, or scary."

They browsed through the DVD selection and selected a recent romantic comedy. Jake began hitting buttons on a remote, opening the curtains covering the screen, dimming the lights, and starting the movie.

Lauren settled into one of the chaises. "I'll probably fall asleep."

"If you do, I'll write something embarrassing on your forehead with a Sharpie. Maybe 'Doctor in Training' to give your patients that extra dose of confidence."

"You better not. Most of them already ask me how old I am. Or my personal favorite, if my mommy knows I'm out playing doctor."

"Just don't fall asleep and you won't have anything to worry about."

The movie was predictable with the usual plot points typical of romantic comedies: boy meets girl, they get themselves into a ridiculous predicament, loathe each other for the majority of the film as they encounter one silly obstacle after another, and fall hopelessly in love by the closing credits. Given the mediocre acting and banal script, Lauren was surprised to find herself crying at the end of the movie.

"None of that," Jake chided. "Or you are going to get me started and I'm going to have to send Teresita out for Kleenex and more ice cream."

"Sorry. It's just...everything."

"You don't have to apologize to me, Lauren. I get it." He gently wiped the tears from her cheeks. "Why don't you stay here tonight?"

"I shouldn't." Lauren's mind began to race. "I have to be at work early."

"All the more reason why you should stay here."

"I want to go running before work."

"And your point is? We do have places to run here in Scottsdale. They're called running trails. I'm assuming you've heard of them."

"Ha ha. Very funny. My point is I don't have my running clothes with me, Genius. I guess maybe I could wear something of Liz's."

Jake's shook his head. "That's not necessary. Teresita can pick something up for you." He pushed a button on the wall.

"Yes, sir?" came Teresita's accented voice through the intercom speaker.

"Will you meet us in the theater, *por favor*?"

Teresita came in and wrote down Lauren's sizes; small shirt and extra small shorts. "Don't forget shoes," Jake reminded. "You're about a size eleven shoe, right?"

"What? I'm nothing less than a twelve." Lauren wrote down her actual size, six, on Teresita's notepad. "Let me get some money."

"No. I've got it," Jake insisted. He handed his credit card to Teresita, whispering something under his breath to her. Teresita nodded and headed out.

Jake began messing with the remote control, closing the curtains to conceal the screen and technological components. While he did this, Lauren gathered up the dirty dishes and took them into the kitchen. Jake came in while she was loading them in the dishwasher. The ice cream containers were nowhere in sight.

"Looks like the ice cream fairy came and stole your leftovers," Lauren observed.

"What? You wanted more?"

"No. I just think it's amazing your house cleans itself. My housekeeping elves must be on strike."

"I asked Teresita to take the rest down to the food bank donation center, but I can give her a call and ask her to pick up some more. Will another fifteen pints suffice?"

"Better make it sixteen."

"Shoot. I forgot to ask Teresita to pick up pajamas. Let me call her." He dialed over Lauren's protests that he had done plenty for her already. "She's not picking up," he said as he put the phone down. "You can wear something of mine. Ready for some dinner?"

They stepped into the nearby dining room. Wainscoting lined the baseboards and a crystal chandelier was centered over a round antique table, six feet across and cut from a single piece of polished wood. Delicate scroll details had been hand-carved along the edges. The matching chairs were upholstered in rich brocade.

Fresh-cut lilies were arranged in a vase in the center of the table and candles were burning in the candlesticks. Lauren wondered if the table had been set to impress her or if Teresita pulled out all the stops for Jake every night. The table sat eight, but there were only two place settings at adjacent chairs. "I hope you don't mind sitting next to me," Jake said. "I hate trying to conduct dinner conversation across flowers at a six-foot distance."

Lauren marveled at the desert sunset, brilliant in shades of orange with layers of pink, gold, and purple framing the horizon. Palm trees at the edge of the property were stark black in contrast to the fiery sunset. "Arizona has the most beautiful sunsets."

"Said the native Californian."

"There may be no ocean here, but there is plenty of beach." She alluded to the vast Arizona desert sands.

Jake enthused about his new food delivery service. The meal was fresh fish covered with lemon sauce, steamed asparagus, and seasonal summer fruit.

Lauren cleaned her plate. "That was delicious. I would eat healthy too if I could afford to have these meals delivered to my doorstep."

Conversation flowed easily as they discussed the movie and Jake's trip to Colorado the following day to play the Rockies. "You should come with me. The weather there is a welcome change from this heat."

"I wish I could, but I have to work. Besides, I'm not allowed to leave the state."

"What? You didn't tell me that."

"Just kidding. Detective Walrus and Detective Pretty Boy don't have me on full lockdown yet."

"So you're making up excuses to avoid coming to watch me play."

"The work excuse is real. At least until I win the lottery. Speaking of work, I should get to bed. I need to get going early in the morning."

Jake walked her upstairs to the guest suite comprised of an enormous bedroom, sitting area with television, and full bathroom. Jake excused himself and soon returned with a soft white men's button down shirt, apologizing that it was all he could find for her to sleep in. Lauren wondered why he hadn't brought her something of Liz's, but she didn't pry. The topic of Liz was likely to trigger more tears.

"Liz kept this place stocked for guests so you should find everything you need, including gently used toothbrushes." He gave her a quick squeeze good night.

Teresita soon tapped on the door and entered with two large Nordstrom shopping bags. "I hope this will work for you, Miss Lauren."

"All of this can't be for me. I only needed a couple of things."

"Mr. Jake tell me to bring you three of everything."

"What?"

"Three shirt, three short, three pair socks, two pair shoes," Teresita said in broken English. "That way, we make sure you have something you like."

"I'm going running, not to the Inaugural Ball." Teresita looked downcast. "Thank you, Teresita. Really. These are terrific."

"No, it not that, Miss Lauren. You look like Miss Liz. I miss her very much."

"Me too," Lauren said, tears stinging her eyes.

Wearing the shirt with the faint scent of cologne, she fell into a fitful sleep full of disjointed dreams involving Dennis, Liz, blood, Jake, and prison.

Chapter Eighteen

(Friday, August 19)

Lauren crept down the stairs at 4:30 the next morning. She entered in the code that Liz had given her months before to disengage the alarm. Just as she hit the enter button, she realized that the code had likely been changed. She was relieved when the alarm clicked into off mode. As she reached for the doorknob, she was startled by a "What do you think you're doing?" from behind her. She jumped.

She turned to find Jake doubled over in laughter. "I'm sorry, Lauren. I didn't mean to scare you, but you should've seen your face. Did you think I was going to let you show me up by going running without me?"

"You want to come running at this hour? Don't you get enough exercise at baseball practice?"

"Not really. Half those guys can't run from first to second in less than an hour. Baseball's where the lazy athletes hide out. If you want to be fit, you play basketball or tennis."

"All right. Let's go. But do try to keep up."

They ran about four miles along a running trail that meandered past multimillion-dollar homes. It was a lot more scenic than the downtown streets she usually ran. Lauren maintained a good pace, finishing in twenty-eight minutes. Jake had been content to run by her side for most of the trek, but occasionally he would circle around her, yelling "Am I keeping up okay?" Lauren only smiled because she was too winded to speak.

As they rounded the final corner of the curving driveway, Jake launched into a full sprint for the final fifty yards. Lauren lengthened her stride in an effort to keep up, but still reached the front door a full five seconds behind him. She grabbed her thighs as she struggled to catch her breath. Jake grinned. "That was fun. Let's go again."

It was still only five a.m., but Teresita had already arrived. She lived nearby in her own apartment, but came to the Wakefield house to clean five days a week. Several fragrant candles burned and Teresita was setting the dining table.

"Stay for breakfast?" Jake asked. "Waffles from the delivery service."

"Healthy waffles?"

"They take the calories out and leave the flavor in."

Lauren took a quick shower while Teresita prepared breakfast. She would have to leave for work soon, so she let her hair dry naturally. The result was soft damp waves instead of her usual smooth, straight hair. Jake complimented the look.

Breakfast conversation was entertaining and Lauren realized how lonely she had been. She savored her independence, but it was nice to have somebody to discuss the newspaper with over whole-wheat waffles, fresh berries, and turkey sausage.

"Coffee?" Jake offered as he picked up the pot of fresh brew.

"No thanks."

"I forgot Liz told me you don't drink coffee. We could never understand how you made it through medical school without it."

"Lots of Diet Coke."

"I could send Teresita out for some Diet Coke."

"No need. I'll muddle through somehow," Lauren said, pointing to her glass of freshly squeezed orange juice.

After breakfast, Jake walked Lauren to her car, opening the door for her. "I really wish you could come to Colorado."

"I wish I could too, but duty calls."

"You're working too hard. Especially with all the other stuff you're dealing with. Maybe you *should* take the year off."

"Work keeps me sane. Besides, I have bills to pay. Remember?"

Lauren detected a linger in Jake's hug. "Let's get together as soon as I get back from Colorado."

"Sure." Lauren slid into her driver's seat. "When do you get back?"

"We're back on Tuesday. Then we play at home against the Dodgers on Thursday, Friday, and Saturday. You have to come to one of those games."

Lauren took a moment to consider her schedule. "I should have Friday off."

"Should?"

"I'm scheduled to have Friday off, but sometimes things come up and we have to work."

"That's perfect; I'm scheduled to pitch Friday. We just won't let anything come up. I'll put a moratorium on sick and injured people that day."

"Then I'll be there."

"Great." He smiled at her as he closed her car door. She sneaked a peak in her rearview mirror as she drove away and found he was still watching her until she rounded a corner out of sight.

Even though there wasn't much traffic on Saturday mornings, the trip to the hospital took thirty minutes. Feeling overwhelmed by swarming thoughts, Lauren turned up the radio to eardrum-damaging decibels and focused on the lyrics as she sang along. She pulled into the hospital parking lot later than usual, rushing to get to the patient report on time.

"Boy, am I glad to see you." Ritesh said as Lauren hurried up. "It's been a crazy night. Bay One is a gang member who got shot, through and through the right shoulder. He'll be fine, but you might learn some new vocabulary words from him. Bay Two is a one-year-old kid who took a header into the coffee table while learning to walk. Scalp injury, so there's loads of blood. The kid's okay, but the mom needs to be sedated. Bay Three is a genius who decided to shake a vending machine, which fell on him, crushing his right leg. We're waiting on X-rays and a Mensa evaluation. Bay Four is a recovering myocardial infarct; he's already been admitted to the cardiac unit. We're waiting for them to take him up. And Bay Five, my personal favorite, is a guy who 'slipped and fell' (Ritesh used his fingers to create the quotation marks for Lauren, grinning mischievously) on a carrot while naked. I'm thrilled to pass him off to you. I fear he might have enjoyed my medical intervention a bit too much. I suspect you aren't his type. Though your hair does look quite sexy this morning. Almost like you ran out of time. Late night last night?"

Lauren blushed, feeling as if she had a scarlet letter branded on her forehead. She had to remind herself she had done nothing wrong. "Behave. You better get gone before Bay Five requests your services personally."

"Say no more." Ritesh made an exaggerated about-face movement and headed toward the locker room.

Lauren did a quick mental inventory of the cases she had assumed responsibility for. Determining that Bay Four was the most acute, she headed to check on Mr. Steven Gunther, who had been lucky to survive a heart attack earlier that morning.

Lauren remained lost in her work until she received a text message from Jake at about two that afternoon.

Getting ready to board the plane for Colorado. I'm confirmed as the starting pitcher on Friday. I'll send a car to pick you up at 4. Game starts at 6. See you then. Call me if you need anything.

Lauren's heart skipped a beat and she couldn't resist the urge to smile. She finally had something to smile about.

Chapter Nineteen

Dennis called Lauren a few days later. "Time for straight talk," he drawled. "I've made several calls to Scottsdale P.D. and the county attorney's office. I do believe they consider you a suspect in this case. I know Wallace from way back and he's usually willing to offer me a little something, but he was completely tight-lipped. He would only tell me they were still trying to rule you out. I don't mean to scare you, but that doesn't sound good."

"There have been no leaks on the case. None. I've had my legal assistants running down every related news story. There are hundreds, but none of them have contributed any information other than what was released on day one. That's very unusual in a case of this magnitude. Usually some of the folks involved in the investigation can't resist sharing the goods with a friend on a big case like this. But not this time."

This part, at least, was good news. Investigative leaks compromised the integrity of the case. Lauren was grateful that autopsy photos of her sister hadn't been leaked for publication in some cheesy tabloid magazine alongside such headlines as "Tom Cruise Gets Liposuction." However, she would have loved to have gained some insight into the direction of the police investigation.

Dennis continued. "In a case with this degree of public scrutiny, the police will be looking to make an arrest as quickly as possible. If they had enough evidence to arrest you, they would be eager to do so with full press coverage. No news is good news."

"But I want the police to make an arrest in this case. I want a conviction. I want justice for my sister."

"I understand that, Lauren. But we don't want it to be *your* arrest and *your* conviction."

Chapter Twenty

(Friday, August 19–Friday, August 26)

Lauren slept in until 8:17 on Friday morning. For the first time in weeks, she had not had nightmares. During her morning run, she thought about the baseball game that afternoon with anticipation.

She ran twice as far as usual because she was brimming with excitement, but it was still only 9:25 when she returned home. Too distracted to sit still, Lauren used her day off to respond to a large pile of sympathy cards. Finally, she took a shower, carefully styled her hair and makeup, and deliberated over what to wear before settling on denim shorts and a red Diamondbacks tank top.

The car arrived promptly at four o'clock. Lauren had only traveled in a limo once before, at Liz and Jake's wedding. On that occasion, the car had been filled with the excited chatter of Liz and the other bridesmaids. By comparison, this trip was tranquil.

"The bar is stocked with food and drinks. Please help yourself," the driver said over the intercom.

Lauren opened the miniature refrigerator, marveling at the selection of beer, wine, and snack foods. She wasn't a big drinker, but she decided to indulge in some chardonnay.

While other cars waited in long lines to get into Chase Field, the limo driver entered a VIP entrance and proceeded to the stadium gates. Lauren gave her ticket to a man at the gate, who escorted her to a skybox behind home plate. The box was immaculately furnished. Lauren was greeted coolly by several baseball wives. All of them were dressed to the nines with high heels showcasing long legs. Lauren felt conspicuously under-dressed. The other women warmed up considerably when she introduced herself, proceeding to tell her how much they had all adored Liz.

In general, the players' wives seemed more interested in the open bar than they did in the game. Lauren, however, watched every minute of play. During the seventh-inning stretch, she stood and sang "Take Me out to the Ball Game" in her off-key alto. Jake caught her eye from the field and rewarded her with a wave. Lauren beamed as she waved back.

Jake was pitching a perfect game thus far, but the score was still tied at zero. The Diamondbacks had gotten several hits, but had been unable to translate any of those into runs. The excite-ment was escalating about Jake's flawless pitching performance. Conventionally, the pitching coach would pull him after the seventh inning to protect his pitching arm, allowing a closer to finish off the game. As the Diamondbacks took the field in the eighth inning, the crowd went wild with applause when Jake returned to the mound. He would get his chance to complete his perfect game.

Tommy Moranda, a well-respected relief pitcher, was warm-ing up in the bullpen. Jake would be pulled from the game if he gave up a hit. Lauren sent up a silent prayer to a god she didn't really believe in.

The eighth man in the Dodger lineup was up to bat. Generally speaking, the bottom of the lineup represented weaker batters. Jake easily struck him out.

The next batter was the Dodger pitcher, Peter Davis. Davis had been pitching a strong game, having not given up any runs himself. However, the Dodger manager pulled Davis in favor of their strongest pinch hitter, Ray Robinson. Robinson had one of the highest batting averages in the league and was especially skilled at batting against southpaw pitchers.

Tall and muscle-bound, Robinson sauntered toward the plate. Lauren observed Jake for signs of stress, detecting none. He exuded confidence. Without hesitation, he fired two pitches straight down the strike zone, even though Robinson was crowding the plate. Robinson didn't swing at either of them. On the third pitch, Robinson stepped into an enormous swing. Strike three.

Returning to the top of their lineup, the Dodgers' first baseman came up to bat. On the second pitch, he tapped the ball to the shortstop, who caught it handily. Jake was one inning closer to the perfect game.

Batter number four for the Diamondbacks stepped up to the plate. Lauren hoped the home team would score some runs this inning, taking some of the pressure off Jake when he returned to the mound. But it wasn't meant to be. Three up and three down, leaving the game still tied zero to zero at the start of the ninth inning.

The crowd erupted as Jake resumed his position on the pitching mound. He quickly struck out the first batter, but the second batter was another southpaw by the name of Hudson. Jake had to adjust his windup due to Hudson's left-handed batting stance. Jake threw three balls and no strikes before delivering a fourth pitch directly into the strike zone. Hudson lined up on the ball, struck it with the sweet spot of the bat, and it sailed far into left field. Spectators leapt to their feet to watch the trajectory of the ball, which was heading over the fence. The Diamondbacks left fielder made a spectacular play, leaping to catch the ball at the fence and securing the second out.

Next up was the cleanup hitter for the Dodgers, their burly catcher named Garcia. Garcia was having an outstanding hitting season relative to previous years, prompting rumors that he was taking steroids. Normally, Jake might intentionally walk a player like Garcia to prevent him from winning the game with a homerun, but that would ruin Jake's shot at a perfect game. Instead, Jake fired pitch after pitch over home plate. Garcia got a bat on each one, tipping a total of seven foul balls. Jake glanced up at the skybox and grinned at Lauren. Before she could return his smile, he turned on the mound, slid a knuckle ball down the center of the plate, and Garcia went down swinging.

Music blared, fans whistled and cheered, and everybody jumped to their feet. But it wasn't over yet. Jake had pitched nine perfect innings. No hits, no runs, no errors. However, they were still tied at zeroes; the Diamondbacks could still lose this game. And the bottom of the Diamondbacks lineup were coming up to bat, making it less likely they would score this inning.

The Dodgers brought in outstanding relief pitcher Toby Bennett, who had a reputation for squeezing wins out of tightly contested games like this one. He decisively struck out Diamond-back batters number seven and eight. Jake was number nine. Most pitchers were not strong hitters and Jake was no exception.

Jake approached the batter's box. The cheering escalated to a roar so loud Lauren could no longer hear the commentary on the television a few feet away. Jake grinned contagiously and the crowd began chanting his name.

He allowed the first pitch, a strike, to pass. The umpire called the second pitch a strike even though it looked high. The crowd booed. On the third pitch, Jake swung with gusto. He had committed now; he would either hit the ball or strike out trying. The bat cracked against the ball, which sailed over the shortstop's head, a line drive low and hard into left field. Jake rounded first and slid safely into second base just before the ball arrived from the left fielder.

There were now two outs, Jake was on second base, and the leadoff batter, Antonio Santos, was coming up to bat. After several agonizing minutes and five pitches, it was a full count against Santos. Lauren watched, mesmerized. Santos whacked the next pitch forcefully, launching it into right field, the sound of bat against ball resonating around the stadium. The second baseman jumped, nearly catching the ball, but it hit his glove and veered off in another direction forcing the outfielders to change direction to pursue it.

Santos stopped at first. Jake rounded third and, totally ignoring the advice of the base coach, barreled for home. He slid in a storm of dust just as the catcher caught the ball. The crowd watched the umpire expectantly, who skipped a beat before throwing out his arms in the safe signal. The Diamondbacks had won. Loud cheers erupted from the crowd.

Pandemonium broke out on the field. Jake was nearly crushed by the enthusiastic congratulations of his teammates. He had pitched one of only a handful of perfect games in the entire history of baseball.

Santos' wife, Eva, touched Lauren gently on the arm. "Are you okay?"

"I'm just so happy for him," she said, realizing tears were streaming down her face. For all the tears she had shed since Liz's death, these were the first that were tears of joy rather than despair.

Chapter Twenty-one

(Friday, August 26)

Eva escorted Lauren to the press box, where they watched the players provide post-game interviews. Jake conveyed exactly the right combination of enthusiasm and humility. The questions continued for over an hour as the room crackled with the collective excitement of the perfect game along with the Diamondbacks' obvious trajectory toward the playoffs.

Players began drifting in from the locker room in twos and threes, collecting their wives or girlfriends as they headed home. Because he had to ice down his arm, Jake was the last player to emerge. Still more excited than a kid on Christmas, he grabbed Lauren and swung her around in a circle before they headed toward the parking lot.

The team lot was now empty except for the limousine. Jake explained he had caught a ride to the game with another player, so the two of them could ride together afterwards. He waved the chauffeur back, holding the door for Lauren before bounding in behind her. He grabbed a bottle of Dom Pérignon from the refrigerator, opened the moon roof, and popped the cork into the steamy night air. He poured two flutes and held his up in toast. Lauren clinked her glass to his. "To your perfect game."

"To the perfect evening," he smiled. The bubbles tickled Lauren's nose as she took a long indulgent drink.

They enjoyed a pleasant mixture of warm night breeze and pressurized air conditioning as they rehashed the game. Jake was impressed by Lauren's ability to discern between a knuckleball and a slider. They had been talking nonstop for about ten minutes before Lauren realized they were heading in the wrong direction.

She began pushing buttons to try to get the driver's attention. "I need him to take me back to my place."

"I use this car service quite a bit. They probably assumed I was headed home. You can stay over. I can give you a ride in the morning."

"Or the driver can just take me home after dropping you off."

"What? You can't stomach another night at my house?" he mock-pouted. "Are you afraid I'll try to force-feed you chocolate ice cream?"

Feeling the effects of the alcohol, Lauren giggled more loudly than the joke deserved. "I don't want to put you out. Why can't the driver just drop me off first?"

"Why can't you just crash at my place?"

"Because I have to work at six tomorrow morning."

Disappointment flashed across Jake's face before he made a valiant effort to disguise it with a smile. He pressed the intercom button, "George, we need to drop my friend at her place first."

"Of course, sir. The address?"

Lauren gave her apartment address and the limousine slowly rounded in a graceful U-turn.

Chapter Twenty-two

(Saturday, August 27)

The following morning, Lauren sprinted into the ER just as the current cases were being briefed by the outgoing interns. Stone stood nearby observing and asking pointed questions. Lauren attempted to apologize for her tardy arrival, but Stone simply stuck up his hand in a stop motion. Lauren redirected her attention to Emily, who was describing a severely obese patient who had presented to the ER with shortness of breath.

"Dr. Rose, why don't you have a listen to Ms. Dewell's lungs and tell us what you think?"

Putting Lauren on the spot was Stone's method of chastising her for being late. Using her stethoscope, Lauren listened to breath sounds in the enormous woman's chest.

"I hear a strange crinkling sound," she said tentatively.

"Crinkling?" Stone stepped forward with his own stethoscope to take a listen. He looked perplexed. "Wait a minute." He reached into the folds of the woman's abdominal fat, pulling out a Twinkie still wrapped in cellophane. "Here's the source of your crinkling sound."

"Hey, I've been wondering where that went," the patient said. The interns watched in disbelief as she tore open the wrapper and devoured the Twinkie.

Work occupied Lauren's full attention. At around three-fifteen her cell phone vibrated in her pocket, alerting her to an incoming text message. It was from Jake: **Important game tonight. Please come. You are my good luck charm.**

She was not on-call that evening but she was well aware that she should spend the evening at home to catch up on her sleep. She texted back: **I'll be there.**

He replied: **Terrific news. I will leave a suite ticket for you at Will Call.**

At Chase Field that evening, Lauren watched the game with single-minded enthusiasm. Having pitched the entire game the night before, Jake was not playing this evening, but there was still plenty of excited chatter about his momentous achievement the previous night.

The Diamondbacks beat the Dodgers three to two. Observing the postgame interviews with some of the other women, Lauren imagined the life of a baseball wife: traveling to all the games, staying in fancy hotels, and helping the hubby celebrate the wins.

Jake bounded out of the locker room, freshly showered and smelling of bubble gum. He greeted Lauren with a big smile. Lauren maintained an appropriate distance though she longed to throw her arms around him. The Diamondbacks were heading to the playoffs.

As they walked toward the parking lot, Jake said, "Look, I've been thinking about this a lot and wondering if it's wrong for us to spend time together. I miss Liz like crazy and there's nothing I wouldn't do to bring her back, but she's gone and…" he paused, "…I know she would want us to move on with our lives. As much as I loved her and you loved her, it makes sense for us to tackle this thing together, don't you think?"

Tears streamed down Lauren's cheeks as Jake said all of the same things she had been saying to herself. She nodded.

He continued, "I really care about you, but who knows how the media might spin this. The last thing we need is to give people more reasons to whisper about us. So, we should keep our friendship on the down-low for a little while."

Lauren nodded, relieved that he agreed with her.

He walked her to her car and gave her a long hug before holding the door open for her. "Drive carefully."

Chapter Twenty-three

(September 1–28)

The weather finally began to turn, offering relief from the unrelenting heat that had tortured Phoenix since May.

Outside of her long shifts at the hospital, frequent calls to the detectives for updates, and her regular visits to Rose-ma, Lauren spent time with Jake. She attended as many of his games as she could fit in around her crazy work schedule. He began purchasing general admission tickets for her, concerned about attracting unwanted media attention if she repeatedly showed up in the VIP suite. The seats were always top-dollar and Lauren felt more comfortable when she didn't have to make idle chitchat with the players' wives. Afterwards, they often met up at his house where they would rehash the game highlights. Jake gave Lauren a key to his house so she could come and visit discreetly.

On September twenty-eighth, Lauren's phone vibrated all day with birthday texts from friends and Rose-ma called to remind her of their plans for a birthday celebration lunch on her next day off. But Lauren did not hear from Jake. Liz had always commemorated Lauren's birthday with carefully selected gifts signed from both Liz and Jake. She was reminded now that Jake probably had little to nothing to do with those. He might not even remember Lauren's birth date. She decided to let it slide, not wanting to put undue pressure on him.

She did receive a brief text message from him toward the end of her shift that read, **Are you still coming over for dinner tonight?** Although there was no mention of her birthday, time spent with Jake was gift enough.

When she arrived at Jake's house, dinner was already on the table. Halfway through dinner, Jake reached over and pulled a piece of glittery confetti from Lauren's hair. He raised one eyebrow.

"The other interns trashed my locker today. I'm going to be finding that stuff for weeks."

Jake smiled and pulled a small black velvet box from his pocket. "Did you think I forgot your birthday?"

"Jake, you didn't have to…"

"That's what everybody says and nobody really means it. Now open it."

Lauren did as she was told. Nestled inside was a spectacular ring. The large diamond was set in a vintage platinum setting flanked by several smaller diamonds on both sides. A diamond ring? Lauren was speechless.

"Liz saw it in an antique store and had to have it. The problem was she thought it was too special to actually wear. So you have to promise me that you'll wear it more often than she did."

"It's gorgeous. Tears threatened to spill down her cheeks. "Thank you."

"I know she would have wanted you to have it, so that's a gift from both Liz and me."

Lauren took a deep breath and silently wished the investigators would soon solve her sister's murder. She wanted justice for Liz, but she also couldn't help wondering how her relationship with Jake would evolve when they were no longer living under the oppressive spotlight of suspicion. Then she blew out all twenty-six candles.

Chapter Twenty-four

On the evening after Lauren's birthday, LaRhonda relieved Lauren shortly before midnight.

"There you are. I've been worrying 'bout you. You okay?"

"I'm okay. It's been busy. There's a drug overdose in Bay One, a dog bite in Bay Two, and a guy with third-degree burns in Bay Four. He was trying to impress the ladies with his pain tolerance skills using a lit cigarette. The ladies didn't come in with him, so I'm guessing they weren't that impressed."

"I ain't asking 'bout work. I'm asking 'bout you. Are *you* okay?"

"Me? I'm fine. Running on fumes as usual. Why? Are my eyes bloodshot again? Maybe I could moonlight as a vampire."

"You haven't heard yet, have you?"

"Heard what?"

"Come with me." LaRhonda led Lauren to the doctor's lounge. Kevin and Emily were there, rummaging through their lockers. They eyeballed Lauren uncomfortably, indicating they also knew something Lauren did not yet know.

A thirty-inch television was mounted on the wall. Lauren had never seen anybody watching it, but LaRhonda turned it on now. A late-night talk show host was interviewing Madonna. LaRhonda changed the channel to CNN.

"What is it?" Lauren asked anxiously.

LaRhonda shook her head and muttered, "Wait for it."

They watched several news clips together, nobody saying a word. A picture of Liz appeared on the screen. The news anchor launched into the story in tones far too perky for the issue at hand. "Now an update about the homicide of Elizabeth Wakefield, the wife of Diamondbacks pitcher Jake Wakefield. Elizabeth was killed in her home on July twenty-third in what was initially a suspected burglary. Elizabeth's younger sister, Lauren Rose, has now been identified as a prime suspect." Lauren's yearbook photograph from her college days now materialized on the screen. "Sources tell us that money was the probable motive for the killing as Rose was recently named as the sole beneficiary of Elizabeth Wakefield's million-dollar life insurance policy. Rose has hired high-priced attorney, Dennis Hopkins, best known for defending death penalty cases. These recent developments lead many to speculate that Lauren Rose will soon be charged with the crime. And now, a more lighthearted story, a Japanese woman has eaten a record-breaking number of chicken wings…"

The others in the room looked at Lauren uncomfortably, clearly not knowing what to say. After a few beats, Kevin took an awkward stab at it. "You can't believe everything you hear on the news. I'm sure the police know what they're doing. Everything is going to be o—"

"Screw that!" LaRhonda interrupted. "You better call that high-priced lawyer of yours and make sure he is earning all that money you is payin' him."

It was now well after normal business operating hours. Lauren was wondering if this was ample justification to call Dennis on his personal cell, when her own phone vibrated in her scrubs pocket.

"Have you seen the news this evening?" Dennis asked her without any preliminary pleasantries.

"Yes. Just now. What does it mean?"

"It means…" he drawled, "…that our airtight case just sprang a major leak."

Chapter Twenty-five

(Friday, September 30)

For the first time since moving to Phoenix, Lauren detected a slight chill in the air during her morning run. She was not scheduled to work that day and had plans to go to Jake's first playoff game against the Braves later that afternoon.

Several reporters were camped outside of her apartment, bombarding her with questions when she emerged from her apartment. She offered a courtesy "No comment" and lost them as she sprinted toward the running path. She returned from a different direction, eluding detection until she was ascending her outdoor staircase. The reporters could not legally enter her stairwell without her permission.

Hoping to glean more information about the investigation, Lauren Googled her own name. She had many more hits than she had just a few weeks previously, the newest stories all identifying her as a suspect in Liz's murder. Lauren was reading through them when she was interrupted by a knock at her door.

She opened the door to Detective Wallace along with several other men she did not recognize.

"Lauren Rose," Wallace said without preamble. "We have a warrant to search these premises. Here's a copy of the warrant for your records."

Lauren quickly perused the document. It was written in legalese. "I'd like an opportunity to have my attorney review this."

Detective Wallace nodded. "You may contact your attorney, but the search will commence immediately. You may observe, but any interference with the searching officers will result in an arrest for violation of court order, is that understood?"

"Yes."

"I need my cell phone from my bedroom so I can call my lawyer," Lauren directed to Wallace, who was already issuing instructions to the officers queued up on her front stoop.

"Boyd will accompany you to make that one call. Then we'll be taking your cell phone into evidence."

As if on cue, Boyd stepped forward from the crowd of officers. He smiled warmly as if they were meeting at a cocktail party.

Lauren telephoned Dennis, who advised her to say nothing until he arrived. Lauren handed her phone to Boyd. They stood awkwardly together in the kitchen while the other officers donned latex gloves and began systematically uprooting her home.

Finally, Boyd said, "You know, we could clear up a lot of things if you'd just talk to us, but your lawyer keeps shutting us down."

Lauren knew she was not supposed to respond, but she snapped. "Really? I tried cooperating with you guys and you didn't believe me."

"I believed you. I still do."

"You really believe me? Or have you just been cast in the role of good cop today?"

He looked her directly in the eyes. "I really believe you."

Lauren caught herself and said nothing further, silently wondering if he were being truthful.

Dennis' offices were fifteen minutes away, but he arrived in less than ten. He quickly scanned Lauren's copy of the search warrant. Then he drawled casually to Boyd, "I'm afraid I'm gonna have to ask you boys to cease and desist this search."

"Why's that?"

"Because you've executed the warrant on the wrong location. Says here this search warrant is valid for Unit D and this here is Unit C."

"You're kidding." A look of immediate worry developed on Boyd's face.

"Oh, I don't kid when I have an innocent client being intimidated and harassed. So pack up your little fishing expedition and take it on back to the judge."

Boyd quickly peeked outside the front stoop to check Lauren's unit number and then hurried off to find Detective Wallace.

Dennis smiled broadly at Lauren. "Beautiful morning, isn't it?"

"What now?" Lauren asked.

"It won't take 'em long to get a new search warrant, but it will give us a little time to chat first."

From the recesses of her apartment, Lauren heard Detective Wallace explode. "Are you fucking kidding me? I'm going to have somebody's head on a platter by lunchtime." Wallace stormed around the corner into the small dining area where Lauren and Dennis were standing. The searching officers filed out the front door and stomped down the stairwell.

"Miss Rose." Detective Wallace addressed her as if Dennis was not there. His face was red and splotchy. "We need to correct a minor clerical error before we can continue our search. May I please have your copy of the warrant back so we can get this rectified?"

"I'm afraid this copy has already been issued to the resident," Dennis answered, deliberately folding the warrant and tucking it into his front suit pocket. "She's entitled to keep it for her records."

"As you've already pointed out, it hasn't been served to the resident of the proper apartment unit."

Dennis shook his head. "I can certainly understand why you'd want this here warrant back. It's quite an embarrassing error, isn't it? However, this copy was served in good faith to my client and I must advise her to exercise her legal right to keep it. You see, even though she is innocent of any involvement in her sister's murder, you appear intent upon implicating her. As the attorney who has pledged to defend her, I must begin collecting evidence for a vigorous defense."

"Dennis," Lauren said. "Can't we just let them finish it now so there won't be a need to go through this again later?"

Dennis chuckled heartily. "Isn't she sweet?" he said to Wallace. And to Lauren, he added, "I know you don't have anything to hide, but it would be unlawful for these officers to continue to search these premises without a valid warrant."

"Then let somebody stay until they can get the new warrant. I don't want them to think I'm hiding anything."

"Why don't you and I step into the other room for a mini-sidebar."

In the kitchen, Dennis whispered urgently, "Are you sure you don't need some time to tidy up before they return with a new warrant?"

"I'm not worried about anything they might find. I'm more concerned about what it would imply if I make them leave while we're waiting for the new warrant."

Dennis pulled a device from his pocket. "This here device will incapacitate your hard drive and I assure you it's perfectly legal. Your computer's listed on the warrant. Are you sure you don't want to scramble the hard drive before we turn it over?"

"There's no need to do that."

"Okay. We'll allow them to stay if you're sure you don't need a little time to clean up?"

"Not at all."

"You are a very unusual client."

"So you've said." She stepped back into the dining area. "Gentlemen, you're welcome to stay until you can correct the warrant. Can I offer either of you a Diet Coke? I'm afraid that's all I have." Both detectives politely declined. Wallace excused himself to go see the judge.

Lauren's cell phone had been placed in full view on the kitchen table. Under Boyd's watchful eye, Lauren began copying down her most important phone contacts to a piece of paper.

Once she was done, Dennis asked Lauren to step out to his car where they could talk in private. He asked Boyd to vacate the premises, allowing him to sit on the front stoop in front of the locked apartment.

Reporters swarmed the parking lot, shoving microphones at them and shouting questions. Dennis offered smooth assurances that Lauren would be vindicated as they walked to his luxury Mercedes. Dennis turned on the air conditioning full-blast, both to cool the car and to mask their conversation from anybody who might try to eavesdrop from nearby.

"Sorry, but I had to turn Boyd out of your apartment. Something stinks in this case and I don't trust those bastards not to plant evidence. There must be some reason they are so intent on pursuing you, but I sure as hell can't figure out what it is. They'll be back with a new warrant in two shakes of a lamb's tail and I want to review this search warrant with you, line by line before they return. The first thing on the list is all of your shoes."

"All my shoes? As in all of them?"

"You'll get 'em back eventually. I'm guessing they want to examine your shoes for blood evidence."

"Some of my tennis shoes might have some blood from the ER, but they shouldn't find Liz's blood."

"Next, they're looking for anything that might be the murder weapon in this crime, which they are estimating to be a blunt object long enough to swing with momentum, approximately four inches wide at one end. Do you have any bloody two by fours lying around the house?"

"No, I don't have anything long enough to swing except my golf clubs."

"I hope you don't have a lot of tee times lined up. They're probably going to confiscate your clubs. They also plan to seize your computer. That's standard. You'd be surprised how many people hang themselves with their Internet searches. A lot of folks don't realize deleted items can be recovered by forensic computer experts." He eyed her intently. "So, think hard before you answer this question. Have you done anything weird on your computer lately, any Internet searches, emails, funds transfers, that might incriminate you?"

"No."

"Have you ever done an Internet search on getting away with murder, the perfect crime, disposing of evidence, anything like that?"

Lauren laughed out loud before catching sight of Dennis' expression. "Oh, you're serious?"

He nodded soberly. "You'd be surprised what some people do."

"Not me."

"Okay. The next item, as you already know, calls for seizure of your cell phone. Cell phones are miniature computers these days so the same rules apply. Any incriminating web searches, phone calls, text messages, or the like, even if you deleted them?"

Lauren hesitated.

Dennis immediately picked up on it. "Look here, most people have some sort of secret. Unusual sexual practices, pornography habits, illicit drug use, adulterous affairs, and the like. You name it and I've had a client involved with it. I can assure you that I'm not here to judge you. But I am here to protect you from the people who will try to. Prosecutors have a field day with stuff like this. They'll try to convince a jury that if you have one secret, then you probably killed somebody. You and I both know that isn't true. Whatever it is that you're mulling over in your mind, it's in your best interest to share it with me."

"It's about my sister's husband."

"Uh huh. Do you have some sort of dirt on him?

"What? No. It's just that we've been spending a lot of time together since Liz died and…"

"I see. And is there evidence of your relationship with Mr. Wakefield on your cell phone?"

"Nothing explicit. Just phone calls back and forth and occasional text messages."

"Do the text messages imply the relationship has become more than friendly?"

"No. We've been spending some time together and he's gotten me tickets to several of his games, but we've been…" she struggled to find the right word, "…cautious."

"Thank you for sharing that. I don't think you've done anything wrong, but the cops might interpret your relationship with Mr. Wakefield as a motive to kill your sister."

"But there was nothing between us until after she died."

"I believe that's true, but a jury might not. I'm going to advise you to cool things off with Mr. Wakefield for the time being."

Tears welled in Lauren's eyes. Jake was her primary source of support.

Dennis patted her consolingly. "It's not forever. If he really cares about you, he'll be waiting for you on the other end of this. All righty now, the next thing on the list is your financial statements. Do you anticipate any surprises there?"

"I had to take out loans to pay for medical school."

"No other big debts or big purchases?"

"My old car crapped out a few weeks ago so I bought a new car." Dennis nodded again.

"And I wrote another huge check recently."

Dennis looked apprehensive. "What was that for?"

"Your retainer."

"Ah, yes. And that's it?"

"That's it."

"Okay, the final thing on the list says jewelry items. Anything to worry about there."

"Not really."

"Not really?"

"Jake did give me one of Liz's rings. He thought she would want me to have it."

Dennis pursed his lips. "And where is that ring now?"

"In my jewelry box."

"And Jake will confirm he gave the ring to you?"

"Of course."

"Okay. That's everything."

As if on cue, Detective Wallace drove back into the parking lot. Lauren and Dennis returned to watch as the police turned her apartment upside down.

Chapter Twenty-six

(Saturday, October 1)

The search officers filed out shortly after noon, lugging Lauren's computer, cell phone, all of her shoes and jewelry, and her golf clubs, providing Lauren with a few evidence receipts in exchange. Wallace even confiscated the flip-flops Lauren had been wearing, leaving her with no footwear other than a gaudy pair of fluffy white bunny slippers friends had once given her as a joke.

Lauren still hoped to make it to Chase Field before the 4:10 start time. Despite Dennis' admonitions, she longed to call Jake in the worst way.

It took her well over an hour to put things back where they belonged. Then she headed out in her Acura. Spotting a pay phone at a gas station, she fed it coins and dialed Jake's cell number. He would already be at the stadium, but she hoped to catch him before his warm up. Instead, she got his voice mail.

"Hey, it's me. Umm…" Lauren started before remembering that she didn't have a number to leave for him. "I don't have my phone right now. It's a long story. I'll tell you when I see you."

Lauren's shopping excursion to Kohl's in her white bunny slippers attracted quite a few bemused glances and at least one out-loud snicker, but she was able to purchase tennis shoes and a pair of flip-flops in less than fifteen minutes.

As soon as she entered the AT&T store, she was bum-rushed by an employee. "Hey, my name is Cody. How can I help you today?" His eyes widened in surprise. "The Wakefield case, right? I recognize you from the news." He was tall and gangly, about twenty years old. He might have been cute if not for the bizarre piercing protruding from his lower lip.

"Don't believe everything you hear on TV."

"No worries. I don't think you offed your own sister."

Lauren attempted a polite smile. "Ummm, so I need a new phone."

Cody seemed overly eager to help her out. She wasn't sure if it was because he felt sorry for her, was impressed by her infamy, or was on commission.

When the transaction was complete, Cody gave her the new phone, accessories, and his phone number. "Call me some time. We could grab a pizza and hook up."

Lauren's mouth fell open.

"What, you don't like pizza?" he grinned.

Lauren bolted from the store, interpreting the curious stares of all the other customers as accusations boring into her back as she fled.

She headed straight for the stadium. The four teams in the National League divisional playoffs from best to worst records were the Atlanta Braves, the Arizona Diamondbacks, and the Chicago Cubs, with the Cincinnati Reds as the wild card team. The Diamondbacks were hosting the Cubs at Chase Field. Jake was slated to pitch, so Lauren had arranged to swap this evening's shift with Ritesh.

As a matter of discretion, she no longer parked in the VIP lot. She impatiently waited in line for public parking, then hurried to Will Call to pick up her ticket. She was still in the long line when the game started.

"Lauren Rose," she told the Will Call clerk.

The older woman searched the R tickets twice. "Is Rose the last name or the first name?"

"Last, but people do reverse it sometimes. Maybe it's under the L's."

"Sorry, it's not there either. We can search for it using the credit card you bought it with."

"A friend bought it for me."

"It probably got filed under her name. What's that?"

Lauren hesitated. Discretion was paramount, but she was already missing the game. She could hear the crowd cheering periodically. "Wakefield."

"Like the pitcher?"

"Exactly like the pitcher," Lauren said with a straight face.

But the clerk still couldn't locate the ticket. Lauren gave up and approached the sales booth. "Sorry, but we're all sold out. Everybody wants to see Jake Wakefield pitch now that he's back on the market." The gum-chewing girl in the ticket booth giggled.

Of course it was now impossible to call Jake to ask about her ticket. Why did the cops choose today of all days? She might not get another chance to see Jake pitch again this season. If they lost this series to the Cubs, the Diamondbacks would be done for the year.

Disheartened, Lauren was trudging back to her car when a scalper offered her a ticket. The seat was terrible, especially compared to those she had become accustomed to, and he was asking three times face value for the ticket, but Lauren leapt at it. When she finally settled into her seat in the middle of the second inning, the Diamondbacks were winning one to zero.

She indulged in a bag of peanuts and the game allowed her to forget her worries of the day. The crowd was chanting Jake's name. More than one female fan held up "Marry Me, Jake!" signs. He pitched a great game before he was pulled in the eighth inning to allow a fresh-armed replacement to close the game. The jumbotron showed a close-up of Jake waving as he jogged off the field. Lauren felt uplifted when the Diamondbacks won the game, three to two.

After the game, Lauren headed to Jake's house where they had agreed to meet for a late meal and post-game discussion. She sat alone at the dining table where she had placed a Chick-Fil-A bag with a salad (his) and chicken nuggets (hers). A long hour passed and she began to worry that he had forgotten that they were meeting tonight. Her work schedule only allowed for erratic attendance at his games.

Suddenly, Jake was hugging her from behind, whispering in her hair, "I've been worried sick about you. When I got that voice mail from you, I thought you had been arrested. I tried to call back and there was no answer. I called the detectives, but those bastards wouldn't tell me anything. I almost pulled myself from the game. I've been so worried."

Lauren filled him in on the day's events. He laughed appreciatively when she told him about the mistake on the search warrant. "Those detectives are so dumb, blondes tell jokes about them."

"Dennis said you're going to need to confirm you gave me that ring."

"Happy to. I'll give Detective Walrus a call first thing in the morning and let them know it was a gift. I gave them an inventory of the missing jewelry so it shouldn't be a problem anyway. I keep telling those jerks they're barking up the wrong tree, but they seem to enjoy chasing their tails."

"Dennis asked me to stop spending time with you," Lauren said, her eyes filling with tears.

He nodded. "My lawyer called last night when all those news stories about you started going viral. He told me the same thing. It sucks, but we'll survive it."

"Your lawyer?"

"The family lawyer. The guy my dad keeps bugging me about. My parents are paranoid. They go on and on about how husbands always get accused. Of course, this might be a good thing. They won't find anything suspicious in your apartment. After they figure that out, maybe they'll finally change direction on this thing. Then we can get back to our usual lives. In the meantime, we just have to be careful."

Lauren swallowed a lump in her throat and nodded.

"On a happier note, did you enjoy the game?"

Lauren explained how she hadn't been able to retrieve her

ticket from Will Call and he swore under his breath. "Damn it. I bought an awesome seat for you. I can't believe they lost it."

Lauren joked about her nosebleed seat in the third tier. They analyzed the game in great detail as they always enjoyed doing. Jake was exalted about the win. This was the best year he had ever had.

That is, the best year in baseball.

Chapter Twenty-seven

(Sunday, October 2–Friday, October 7)

The other interns rallied around Lauren, recognizing her life had become a hurricane and she was in a sinking rowboat struggling to bail water. Practical jokes were rampant in an effort to lighten the mood. For one shift, Lauren had opened her locker to discover that Ritesh had adorned her stethoscope with Mickey Mouse stickers. More patients than ever before had questioned Lauren's age and credentials. In return, Lauren and LaRhonda stuffed Ritesh's locker full of free handouts from the public health department. When Ritesh opened the door, hundreds of condoms rained down on him.

New media stories about Lauren were released nearly every day. Dennis' team was reviewing each of them and he had promised to file legal action against any news outlet reporting slanderous information. However, most of the news stories skated on the edge of deception, combining factual information (such as the search of her apartment) with salacious "allegations" that Lauren had killed Liz.

Dennis capitalized on every opportunity to address the media on Lauren's behalf. "I implore the Scottsdale Police Department to stop these prejudicial leaks which falsely implicate Lauren Rose. Such breaches are unethical and unprofessional. Any member of the investigative team releasing information outside of their chain of command is acting in direct violation of procedure and undermining public confidence. It is unconscionable to try Dr. Rose in the press when she has never been charged with any crime."

The Scottsdale Police public affairs officer was also frequently featured, emphatically denying that leaks were emanating from the department.

Jake remained a beacon of hope in Lauren's stormy world. Despite the risks, they maintained telephone contact and he convincingly reassured her everything would turn out fine. However, she had not seen him for the entire week. Between her work hours, his trips to Chicago, and reporters following them both, it had been impossible to get together.

Jake contacted Lauren after each of his games so they could discuss the plays, coaching calls, and pitching decisions. Debating game strategy allowed them both to tune out the outside world for a short time. Jake called from Chicago shortly after the Diamondbacks won their third game against the Cubs. "Now if we can just get past the Braves, I'm going to the World Series. Can you believe it?"

"Of course I believe it. You deserve it. And you guys are definitely going to get past the Braves. Have you seen their batting averages? They couldn't hit a pitch thrown by a Little Leaguer."

"I've dreamed of a World Series ring since I was playing T-ball." He paused. "It's been a strange year. One of the worst and one of the best all at the same time."

Lauren briefly allowed herself to imagine a future with Jake. "I know what you mean."

Chapter Twenty-eight

(Saturday, October 8–Thursday, October 13)

The Diamondbacks did indeed get past the Braves over the course of the next week, taking four of six games. Lauren hadn't been able to attend any of them.

Jake called after the final win. "Next year, you'll be watching every single home game from the VIP suite." Lauren was heartened by his projections for a future together.

"I wish I could see you now. I've missed you." She allowed herself to say the words and then held her breath.

"I know. I miss you, too. Now that I have some time off before the Series starts, we'll find a way to get together when I get back from Atlanta. I promise."

But before he could keep that promise, the day Lauren had been dreading arrived.

She was at work, rushing to the supply room for a suture kit when she spotted Detective Wallace heading her direction. He was accompanied by the medical chief of staff and the hospital attorney. Their mood looked grim. Detective Wallace was walking with a sense of purpose. Lauren felt frozen to the spot, as she did in so many of her recent nightmares.

"Dr. Rose," Chief Cantor greeted Lauren. "This detective needs to have a word with you."

"Right now? I'm right in the middle of my shift."

"I'm afraid so. I'll make sure your patients are covered. We've arranged for you to use the first floor conference room. Our attorney, Mr. Lawrence, will accompany you."

Mr. Lawrence led the way. As she followed him, Lauren felt as if she was walking to her own execution. The four of them filed into a room with a large conference table surrounded by leather-bound chairs.

"Have a seat, Miss Rose," Wallace said.

Lauren broke into a cold sweat. She had a strong urge to bolt, vividly imagining her flight path out the ER doors. Instead, she sat down. Her hands started to shake and she attempted to control them by clasping them tightly together in her lap. Mr. Lawrence sat next to her. Detective Wallace and Chief Cantor took chairs on the opposite side of the table.

Wallace cleared his throat. "I'm here to advise you that we have issued an arrest warrant for the murder of your sister."

Lauren's mouth was painfully parched. *Was he going to hand-cuff her and parade her out in front of all her coworkers? Would he take her out the front door where news reporters nearly always loitered these days or would they be kind enough to use the employee exit in the back?* Lauren glanced at Chief Cantor. He was a giant in the field of trauma surgery and she has been so eager to impress him when she first started her internship. *I'm sure this is making quite an impression upon him all right.*

"Okay," she forced out.

"Detective Boyd has just taken Jake Wakefield into custody at Sky Harbor Airport upon his return from Atlanta."

"What?"

"Mr. Wakefield has been our primary suspect for quite some time, but we only recently compiled enough evidence to secure a warrant for his arrest."

The room began to spin around her. "Jake? Jake didn't kill Liz."

"You should wait until you hear the evidence before you make up your mind about that."

"I doubt you have any evidence that could make me believe he killed her."

"We'll see. Look, I understand that you have gotten…" he cleared his throat, "…close to Mr. Wakefield. We have taken a lot of negative press for leaks in this case so I'm not at liberty to discuss the evidence with you at this time." He looked at her meaningfully and Lauren knew he was referring to Dennis' press releases. "However, I have been authorized to advise you that the source of the leak has been identified."

"And?" she asked.

"The negative information released about you came directly from Jake Wakefield."

Chapter Twenty-nine

(April 27, the following year)

Lauren slid into the hard wooden bench seat in the courtroom gallery and settled in to wait for the hearing to start.

The brunette seated at the Prosecution table turned to greet her.

"Thanks for coming," the woman said in a strong Southern twang. Candace Keene was a seasoned prosecutor with a flawless conviction record. She had joined the Maricopa County Attorney's Office straight out of law school sixteen years earlier because she had a passion for "putting scumbags in the slammer." She was tall and slender, with chocolate-brown hair and caramel-colored eyes. Nicknamed Sugarless Candy for her sharp-tongued courtroom demeanor, she looked like a debutante and swore like a sailor.

"Of course," Lauren responded, meaning it this time.

When Lauren had attended Jake's arraignment in October, she had still been certain of his innocence. She had taken a seat behind the Defense table and anxiously awaited his arrival. Jake had been escorted into court at the last moment by a sheriff's deputy and managed to evade the media circus in the room by responding only to the judge. After entering a plea of "absolutely not guilty," his bond had been set at five million dollars. He had then been whisked away into the recesses of the court building while his parents made arrangements to post his bond.

As soon as Jake had been released on bail, Lauren had tried to reach him by phone. And learned his cell phone had been disconnected. She understood that he was taking appropriate measures to avoid the media onslaught and knew he would make contact with her as soon as he could.

Except he never did.

The second court appearance had been November fifteenth. On that date, Lauren had been sure that Jake would clear things up with her. Instead, he had deliberately avoided making eye contact with her, shielded on either side by his parents, both furiously protesting his innocence. Lauren's anticipation about court on that date lasted longer than the hearing itself, which was just long enough for the judge to grant the Defense's request for a continuance. Subsequent court appearances in January and March had been similarly uneventful. Lauren approached today's court date with low expectations.

The courtroom erupted in an excited murmur behind her and Lauren knew, without looking, that Jake had arrived. Her heart tugged heavily when she finally did look. His dark suit flattered his athletic build and he flashed his famous smile to the reporters seated in the gallery. He looked relaxed as he took his seat at the Defense table, his World Series ring prominent on his right hand.

The judge had refused to grant Jake's request to leave the state for away games, but he had been a full participant in home games. He even led his team to victory in game four of the World Series by pitching an impressive no-hitter. Despite the circumstances, Lauren had watched the Series games, habitually making mental notes of plays to discuss with Jake before remembering she would not be rehashing the game with him afterwards. The Diamondbacks had won a tightly contested seventh game to secure the championship. Shortly thereafter, Jake had signed a new contract with the Diamondbacks. The dollar amounts were substantial, but the new contract included a bailout clause, effectively firing Jake without severance in the event of a conviction.

Jake was joined at the Defense table by his lawyers. Following his arrest, Jake had hired John Fisher, a prominent defense attorney who had defended several celebrities and professional athletes over the years. This would, by all accounts, be the biggest case of Fisher's career.

When it had become evident that Jake would not be able to dodge the charges, he had also hired Richard Pratt. While Fisher was best known as a publicity spinmeister, Pratt was nationally respected for his litigation skills.

Pratt had a reputation as a bulldog in the courtroom and resembled one as well—short, balding, and heavyset, with a harsh New York accent. Fisher, on the other hand, looked distinguished with his thick wavy hair silvering at the temples and tall trim build. He wore exquisite Armani suits, Italian shoes, and ties that cost more than Lauren's monthly salary. Always camera-ready, Fisher served as the public face of the Defense's campaign.

While Jake was the one charged by the county, Lauren continued to be tried in the press. Candace opined that the Defense was responsible for the ongoing public assassinations on Lauren's character. "We've got so much evidence against that bastard, he's got no other choice but to point the finger elsewhere. But it doesn't matter, we've still got that little prick by the short hairs."

Inexplicably, Lauren still missed Jake. For several weeks following his arrest, she had stubbornly defended his innocence. The ongoing efforts of Wallace and Boyd to convince her of Jake's guilt proved ineffective for she had still been leery of the detectives themselves. In the end, the fact that Jake never attempted to contact Lauren after his release on bond forced her to reach the only logical explanation; he had never really cared about her. Even so, she still missed the person she had believed him to be.

Now, the bailiff called the courtroom to order. "Hear ye, hear ye, court is now in session. The honorable Judge Robles presiding."

Robles was a no-nonsense, experienced judge with a large build, balding pate, and sterling reputation. "Court is called to order in the case of People versus Wakefield."

Fisher stood up. "The Defense is prepared to proceed to trial."

Candace, who had been making careful notes on her yellow legal pad, looked up with surprise. Lauren glanced at Candace's notes: bananas, Lucky Charms, Jack Daniels. She had clearly been expecting the Defense to request another postponement.

Candace leapt to her feet. "Your Honor, the People request a continuance until July first in order to allow the victim's sister, Dr. Lauren Rose, to attend the trial. Dr. Rose is completing a demanding medical internship, which won't wrap up until June thirtieth.

Richard Pratt was quick to his feet. "The Defense objects. Mr. Wakefield's life has been completely uprooted by these unfounded charges and he is eager to exonerate himself. The People are attempting to deny our client his constitutional right to a speedy trial."

Candace snorted. "That's ludicrous. I'm sure it has not escaped Your Honor's notice that it is the Defense that has delayed this case over the past six months. The People are merely asking for another sixty-four days in order to allow the victim's sister to attend the trial."

Pratt responded. "Your Honor, our client wishes to exercise his right to a speedy trial. Additionally, we object to the attendance of Lauren Rose and ask to have her permanently excused from the courtroom."

"On what grounds?" Candace demanded.

"She is a witness in this case."

"We are prepared to call Dr. Rose as our first witness and would ask that she be allowed to attend the remainder of the trial following her sworn testimony."

Pratt strutted a few feet closer to the bench. "Your Honor, we are not referring to Miss Rose's testimony for the People. We intend to call her as a witness for the Defense. She is a material witness in support of our case."

Candace laughed out loud. "She's not even on your witness list."

"We've just added her today."

"This is a classic example of the Defense's shenanigans. This is simply manipulation of legal procedure for the sole purpose of denying Dr. Rose her opportunity to put a human face on this case. Surviving family members have a right to attend."

"The victim is also survived by her grandmother," Pratt interjected.

"Who is eighty-six years old with serious health issues," Candace snapped.

Judge Robles cleared his throat pointedly before rendering his ruling. "Dr. Rose shall be the first witness for the People, and the Defense will have ample opportunity to cross-examine her. She may then attend the trial as a representative of the family. The Defense may recall her as a Defense witness if they so choose. However, this trial shall not be delayed further to accommodate witness work schedules. I am prepared to set a trial date. Let me check my docket." The judge flipped several pages in a calendar book in front of him. "As it turns out, I cannot schedule a case of this magnitude until after the Fourth of July holiday. We shall return for jury selection on July fifth."

Candace smiled. She had lost the battle, but won the war.

Before adjourning, Judge Robles cautioned, "Counsel on both sides are reminded that the suppression order is still in place. Any public statements will result in immediate consequences for contempt."

As Jake filed out of the courtroom, he laughed loudly at something Fisher was saying.

Candace turned to whisper to Lauren. "He may be the best butt in baseball now, but pretty soon he's going to have the best butt in the state pen."

Chapter Thirty

(Wednesday, June 28)

Candace had asked the detectives to dig up information she could use to dispute Jake's public image as a golden boy with a fairy tale marriage. Fortunately, Jake made that fairly easy to do. Behind the scenes, Jake had been leading a playboy lifestyle with plenty of booze, women, and gambling. Unfortunately, all the detectives could produce were secondhand accounts of Jake's bad behavior; finding admissible evidence was proving much more difficult. Jake's teammates all stuck to the party line that Jake was a good friend and a hell of a ball player. Whether this was out of a sense of loyalty to Jake or to protect their own indiscretions was unclear, but the detectives had been unable to dislodge any dirty little secrets from the tight band of baseball brothers.

Jake's financial situation had been far more precarious than anybody had suspected. Eager to establish his reputation as a high roller, he had been living well beyond his means. He did command an impressive salary, but managed to spend significantly more than he made. Deeply in debt, Jake was upside down on his house and maxed-out on several high-limit credit cards. Financial gain was a reasonable motive for the murder, given that Liz's valuable jewelry collection had been stolen and Jake had believed he was the beneficiary of Liz's sizable life insurance policy. Yet again, these facts were difficult to substantiate with objective evidence. Following Jake's arrest, his debts disappeared, expediently erased by the old money coffers of Buffy and Jacob Wakefield, Sr.

As press coverage of the case escalated to a feverish pitch, the detectives caught a break. A stripper from San Francisco named Amber Sanders sold information to a tabloid about a supposed one-night tryst with Jake. Under normal circumstances, the story wouldn't even have warranted publication, but because of the public's rabid obsession with the Wakefield murder case, *Insider* magazine paid Sanders fifteen thousand dollars for her story. With little real optimism that it would be productive, the detectives flew to California to interview Sanders.

Lauren happened to be consulting with Candace at the Prosecutor's office when Wallace and Boyd returned from the trip, looking discouraged.

"Well…" Candace asked without preamble, "…did she really do the nasty with our guy?"

"Hard to say," Wallace hedged. "She did provide a detailed account of their encounter. Says Jake and some of the other players rolled into her club last year on the evening of May twenty-eighth. That is the correct date of the Diamondbacks' final game against the Giants in that match-up. They dropped a bunch of money on drinks and lap dances. She claims Jake took a special interest in her and, after shoving several hundred dollars down her G-string, invited her back to his hotel room."

"Was it the right hotel?"

"It was. But the thing is, we researched it, and we were easily able to find the dates and hotel information with an Internet search."

"And the Defense will be quick to point that out," Candace sighed. "So that's it? We can't prove that Jake slept with her."

"She did provide one detail that might be useful," Wallace added, shooting a surreptitious glance in Lauren's direction.

"Spit it out."

"We were wrapping up and it wasn't looking promising, but then Boyd asked her if there was anything else that she could add that might substantiate her story."

"And?"

Boyd responded, "She said she was stoked about landing Jake out of all the players, but she ended up being disappointed."

"Because?" Candace prodded.

Boyd's face flushed pink. "Because she claims, and I quote, that Jake's hung like a newborn baby."

Chapter Thirty-one

(July–August)

As it turned out, Candace needn't have worried about postponing the trial start date to allow Lauren to attend. Jury selection stretched on for nearly two months as both sides attempted to out-maneuver one another. The original jury pool consisted of over two hundred people, all of whom were given lengthy jury questionnaires compiled by jury consultants from both sides. Only forty-nine jurors were left after Judge Robles excused those who admitted to following the Wakefield case in the news.

In private, Candace fumed about the inadequacies of the remaining jurors. "They have to be lying about not being familiar with this case. You can't fall out of bed in the morning without hearing something about it. And if they are telling the truth, they must be complete idiots who never read, watch the news, or listen to the radio. I mean, who the hell are these imbeciles?" While questioning these same potential jurors, Candace was the epitome of Southern charm.

Lauren was not allowed to attend the voir dire process; the courtroom was closed to everybody but the defendant and the lawyers. However, she sometimes met with Candace and the prosecutorial jury consultant. Dr. Joseph Fritz was an older psychologist with coke-bottle glasses, a gray goatee, and an impressive résumé including multiple publications on the topic of jury interactions.

Because Lauren knew Jake well, Candace welcomed her input on jury selection. If she wasn't working, Lauren spent her evenings meeting with Candace and Dr. Fritz along with the second chair who had been assigned to the case, Kyle Simmons. Kyle had schoolboy appeal and considerable expertise in physical evidence.

"Kyle's a great match for me because he's everything I'm not," Candace confided. "Young, tactful, and patient as hell. I'm also hoping he might offset Jake's swoon effect on female jurors."

Kyle was good-looking, kind, and smart as a whip, but Lauren wasn't convinced he could hold a candle to Jake in the charm department.

Behind closed doors, Dr. Fritz advised on jury selection. "We need older, conservative, white males. We want blue-collar types that will be resentful of Jake's outrageous salary."

"And they can't be fucking baseball fans," Candace added.

Dr. Fritz continued. "The Defense will be looking for the opposite, of course. They're going to want young, liberal women who love baseball and those who have a general mistrust of the legal system."

By night, they debated which jurors to challenge and by day, Candace and Kyle went to battle with the Defense, each side working to dismiss jurors favored by the other.

Finally, the jury candidates were whittled down to twelve seated jurors and six alternates. They were sworn in and sequestered on Friday, August twenty-fifth. The trial would officially begin on Monday, August twenty-eighth, more than a year after Liz's murder.

Chapter Thirty-two

(Saturday, August 26)

Lauren spent the weekend preparing for her testimony.

Candace warned Lauren that the cross-examination would be vicious. "They'll ask you trick questions like 'Do you still beat your dog?' If you respond with an indignant 'no,' they'll make it look like you admitted that you once beat your dog."

Candace role-played the defense attorney and Kyle played the role of prosecutor. As she practiced her testimony, Lauren got tongue-tied several times. They coached her through it. On cross-examination, Lauren was instructed to pause to allow Candace time to object before she answered the question. Conversely on direct examination, she should answer quickly before the Defense had an opportunity to object. Even if her answer was subsequently stricken from the record, her words would still linger in the jurors' memories.

In her role as the defense attorney, Candace asked rapid-fire questions, knowing the real Defense would do the same in order to make Lauren look confused, short-tempered, or deceptive. Lauren gradually caught on, improving her response style significantly. Lauren had secured the whole weekend off from work and the sessions ran late on Saturday night. After midnight, they all began to feel a bit punchy.

"Isn't it true you envied your sister's lifestyle?" Candace threw at her.

"No, Liz..."

Candace interrupted with another question, "Isn't it true that you killed your sister for the life insurance?"

"No, I wouldn't..."

Candace interrupted again. "Isn't it true that Jake Wakefield has a tiny pecker?"

The three of them exploded into fits of laughter before Candace announced, "I think we can break for the night."

Chapter Thirty-three

Detective Boyd knocked on Lauren's front door promptly at seven on Monday morning.

The Wakefield case was the most covered court case since the O.J. Simpson trial of 1995. Traffic congestion would make it very difficult to get to the Maricopa County Superior Courthouse, where all high-profile cases were held. The detectives had been assigned to drive Lauren to court each morning. Lauren voiced concern that chauffeuring her to court was excessive, but Candace insisted that the public needed to see that the Scottsdale Police Department supported Lauren. Because of the enormity of the case, Detective Boyd had been assigned to attend the trial full-time so evidence could be researched on a same-day basis when necessary. Already assigned to the trial, he would double as Lauren's driver.

The usual gaggle of reporters was loitering in the parking lot of Lauren's apartment complex. Lauren ducked her head as countless photos captured her sliding into Boyd's government-issued vehicle, a dark blue sedan.

There was an iced chai tea sitting alongside Boyd's own Starbucks coffee cup.

"How did you know I drink chai tea?"

"Oh, I'm sorry. Didn't you hear? I'm an investigator. It's been all over the news."

Lauren laughed. They sat in awkward silence for a few beats before Boyd asked, "So, did you take some time off work in order to testify?"

"Nah, I'm scheduled to work an overnight shift tonight."

"I hope you're kidding."

"Actually…I am," she admitted. "I am off for the duration of my testimony. After that, I am going to work from six p.m. to midnight on weekdays and noon to midnight on weekends."

"Is that all?" Boyd joked. "I was worried that you might be planning to keep your usual hours."

"You're one to talk. You must be getting up at the crack of dawn in order to pick me up. And driving me around is extra duty on top of your regular work tasks."

"Ah, no worries. This court assignment is a great gig. How often do I get to focus on just one case instead of dividing my attention between several? Wallace is the one who drew the short straw."

"I don't mean to sound ungrateful, but driving me to and from court seems like overkill."

"Excellence. Initiative. Integrity." Boyd quoted. "It's what we do."

Her chai tea was refreshing as they debated where the court traffic would begin. They were both wrong by several miles. Traffic was backed up well over ten miles with journalists, entrepreneurs hawking Free Jake memorabilia, and spectators all trying to secure a golden ticket into the "Trial of the Century." Boyd had to turn on his police lights and drive down the breakdown lane to reach the courthouse on time.

"Okay, I concede. Maybe it really is necessary for you to drive me to court. I never would have made it on time," Lauren admitted.

The Maricopa Superior Court tower was a massive multi-story building with copper facades. THE FIRST DUTY OF SOCIETY IS JUSTICE was spelled out in bold letters across the building. Boyd held his badge out in his left hand to force his way through the crowds outside and he ushered Lauren in with his right arm.

The courtroom was already packed when Lauren and Boyd took their reserved seats in the front row behind the Prosecution table. Jake was already seated at the Defense table, looking sharp in a new suit. His parents, perfectly dressed and coiffed, sat in the front row behind him. Jake did not so much as glance in Lauren's direction, but Lauren did catch eyes with Buffy Wakefield. Lauren smiled out of habit. Buffy's eyes ran up and down in a disapproving assessment, glared icily, and turned away.

Candace and Kyle had their heads together, reviewing notes in front of them. Candace looked stunning in a black suit with a crisp white blouse. Kyle had gotten a fresh haircut and looked somehow more mature today.

At nine o'clock, the court clerk called the court to order. Judge Robles looked appropriately intimidating as he took his seat on the bench.

In her opening statement, Candace provided a meticulous preview of the evidence the State planned to introduce at trial. Lauren already knew the Prosecution's case, but it was compelling to hear all of the evidence woven together so concisely. Jake frequently shook his head as if to dismiss everything Candace was saying.

Candace's presentation had been polished and convincing. She had captured the full attention of the jurors. She wrapped up with a plea to the jury. "You may like the way he looks. You may admire the way he plays baseball. You may find it hard to believe he would throw it all away. But if you decide this case based solely on the evidence, as you have pledged to do, you will find Jake Wakefield guilty of first-degree murder."

Court recessed for lunch. Candace and Kyle remained in court to address yet another motion filed by the Defense. There was not enough time to leave the mayhem of the courthouse in the allotted time, so Boyd and Lauren dined on a lunch purchased from vending machines. As they ate, Lauren shared her fears about her upcoming testimony.

"You want to hear about the first time I testified?" Boyd asked.

"Of course."

"I was a brand new patrol officer and I had apprehended a guy driving a stolen car. I was all pumped up because this was my first collar. The prosecutor called me to the stand and asked me where I had pulled the guy over. Since this was my first case, I had prepped for it. I knew I sounded confident and professional. But as soon as I finished speaking, the defense lawyer moved to have the case dismissed for lack of jurisdiction and the judge affirmed it. The bad guy walked out a free man while my head was still spinning. I had forgotten to establish jurisdictional boundaries."

Lauren's face betrayed her confusion.

"A cop has to testify he had the proper jurisdiction to make an arrest. I had given the exact location where I pulled the guy over, but had forgotten to mention this was within my jurisdiction."

"And the guy got off because of that?" Lauren gasped.

Boyd nodded. "The legal system has all sorts of weird loopholes. But I never made that mistake again."

"If this is you trying to make me feel better about testifying, I think it's backfiring." They both laughed.

Lauren appreciated his efforts, but she was still overwhelmed with anxiety. Candace had warned her repeatedly that the Defense would try to make her slip up. Saying one wrong thing during her testimony might damage the entire case.

Candace was certain Pratt would take the Defense's opening statement. Kyle was betting on Fisher. It was apparent these two lawyers were battling to be top dog for the Defense team. "There's more adversarialism between Fisher and Pratt than between the Defense and us," Candace had joked.

When the trial resumed after lunch, Fisher rose to deliver the Defense's opening statement and Candace lost a twenty-dollar bet to Kyle. Fisher looked the part in his well-tailored suit and expensive shoes. The hair at his temples looked more silver than gray. Lauren wondered if he might even dye his hair to make him look more distinguished.

"Ladies and gentlemen of the jury, these false charges boil down to this one thing. A rush to judgment. The detectives in this case were so determined to make an arrest worthy of the front cover of every newspaper in this country that they charged an innocent man, even though the evidence points directly to another suspect. A suspect who had more means, motive, and opportunity. If you listen to all of the evidence in this case, not just the scraps of evidence the Prosecution has forced to fit their version of events, you will find a more obvious suspect. Now granted, if the detectives had arrested anyone other than Jake Wakefield, there wouldn't be as many news reporters covering this story. And that would surely be a disappointment to the Police Department and the County Attorney's office."

Candace leapt to her feet, "I object! To suggest we would charge somebody in order to garner publicity is outrageous."

"Overruled," Judge Robles said. "Ms. Keene, the Defense is permitted to summarize their theory about the facts in the opening statement. And their theory may differ from the Prosecution's." Many observers in the courtroom laughed. "You may continue, Mr. Fisher."

Fisher had memorized his opening statement, but the interruption had caused him to lose his place. He stood still for a moment, finally glancing down at the wrinkled note pages he held in his hand.

"If the detectives had arrested this other person, they wouldn't have gotten as much media attention and that would surely be a disappointment.

"Objection, redundant," Candace whispered to Kyle, who suppressed a laugh.

Fisher shot a dirty look at Candace, regaining his momentum now. "The Defense will show the evidence in this case suggests that Elizabeth Wakefield's own sister, Miss Lauren Rose..." Fisher pointed dramatically at Lauren, "...had more motive to commit this crime."

Candace was on her feet, screaming over Fisher's ongoing narrative, "Objection! There is no credible evidence to implicate Dr. Rose."

"Mr. Fisher, are you prepared to submit evidence to support these claims?" the judge asked.

"We are, Your Honor."

"Then I'll allow it."

Fisher continued. "The Defense will not only show reasonable doubt in this case, but the jurors will be left wondering why Mr. Wakefield was arrested instead of Liz's conniving sister."

The Defense's opening statement confirmed Lauren's worst fears. The pressing need for her to provide convincing testimony the following day settled over her like a wet blanket.

Chapter Thirty-four

(Tuesday, August 29)

Despite trouble sleeping, Lauren was up before her alarm, which was set for 5:30. As she picked up speed on her morning run, she managed to escape the swarm of reporters along with their rude questions and intrusive cameras. Upon her return home, she showered and slipped into a conservative black dress.

Boyd arrived promptly. The cold chai tea he had waiting for her was refreshing on this muggy August morning. Thunderclouds brewed threateningly in the distance, but rain never arrived.

Boyd offered words of encouragement, but Lauren remained distracted and he soon fell quiet, allowing her time to brood.

Candace and Kyle had deliberated long and hard about whether or not to introduce Lauren's flirtation with Jake. Prosecutors typically preferred to introduce potentially embarrassing testimony on direct examination rather than allowing the Defense to expose it on cross-exam. However, Candace feared the jury would condemn Lauren for getting friendly with Jake so quickly after Liz's death. The silver lining was that the relationship reflected equally poorly on Jake so the Defense would not be eager to raise the issue themselves. Furthermore, cross-examination was limited to issues introduced on direct examination. If the Prosecution did not ask Lauren about the relationship, the Defense probably could not do so either. In the end, Candace and Kyle had decided to avoid the topic altogether, gambling that the Defense would follow suit.

When Boyd and Lauren arrived, Candace whispered last minute reminders before court was called to order.

Lauren was called to testify. She approached the witness stand with a pounding heart and sweaty palms. As she took her seat on the stand, she noted she had a good view from this vantage point. She looked into Jake's eyes for the first time since his arrest. He stared back coldly. There was no recognition on his face, no warmth in his eyes.

Candace started the questioning. "Please state your name and spell your last name for the record."

"Lauren Nicole Rose, R-O-S-E."

"And what is your relationship to the victim in this case, Elizabeth Rose Wakefield?"

"She was my sister, only sibling, and best friend."

"How and when did you learn of your sister's murder?"

"I was notified by Detective Wallace and Detective Boyd of the Scottsdale Police Department. They came to my work on the morning of Sunday, July twenty-fourth, at about six-fifteen in the morning."

"What was your immediate reaction?"

"I was shocked."

"Did they tell you how she had been killed?"

"Yes, they said her death was caused by blunt force trauma."

"Are you aware that several news reports have insinuated you had some involvement in her murder?"

"Yes. I am hurt deeply by those lies. I never would have harmed Liz."

"Do you have any idea why those news agencies have falsely accused you?"

Pratt interjected, "Objection, Your Honor, speculative."

"Sustained."

Candace didn't break stride. "Did the detectives in this case tell you somebody had been leaking false information about you to the press?"

"Yes, they said Jake was responsible for the inaccurate information leaked to the newspapers."

"And by Jake, you mean the defendant?"

"Yes."

"Dr. Rose, when is your birthday?"

"September twenty-eighth."

"And for your birthday last year, did Jake Wakefield give you a gift?"

"Yes. A diamond ring."

Candace picked up an evidence bag and showed it to Lauren, "Is this the ring?"

The brilliant diamond sparkled beneath the dull plastic of the evidence bag, symbolizing so many lies and empty promises.

"Yes."

"And did Mr. Wakefield tell you why he was giving you the ring?"

"He told me it used to belong to Liz and she would have wanted me to have it."

"I have no more questions for this witness, Your Honor."

Candace deliberately kept the direct examination short with the intention of limiting cross-exam to key topics. Lauren turned expectantly toward the Defense table. She expected the cross-examination to be ruthless, but she didn't know which lawyer would conduct it. Finally, Fisher stood. "Good morning, Miss Rose."

"Good morning."

"You've testified that Elizabeth Wakefield was your best friend, is that correct?"

"Yes."

"How many times did you see Elizabeth over the year prior to her death?"

"I can't say for sure, but I would estimate..." Lauren paused to count. Thanksgiving, Christmas, Lauren's birthday, a long weekend or two, a few visits after moving to Phoenix. "About five or six times, but some of them were visits that lasted several days."

"You only saw your *best friend* five or six times over the course of an entire *year*?" Fisher asked as if this was one of the most absurd statements he had ever heard.

"I was living in California and Liz lived here. We both had busy schedules. We saw each other when we could for birthdays and other special occasions. And we talked on the phone frequently and emailed and texted."

"So, you saw Liz on her birthday?"

"Not her birthday, no. We got together for my birthday, but I couldn't get away from school for Liz's birthday."

"Do you know how she spent her birthday that year?"

Lauren paused. How had Liz spent her final birthday? Lauren couldn't distinguish one birthday from another after so much time had passed.

"Not exactly, but I think she did something with Jake and her friends to celebrate."

"Her real friends, you mean?"

Candace was on her feet. "Objection, argumentative."

"Sustained."

"I'll rephrase the question," Fisher said. "Isn't it true Liz spent more time with other friends than she did with you?"

"At that time? Certainly. I lived in California."

"Were you jealous of the time Liz spent with her other friends?"

Lauren paused. This was one of those crazy questions that was impossible to answer. Yes, she was envious of others who got to spend more time with Liz, but not in a pathologically jealous manner. "I wish I could have spent more time with Liz, but the distance made it difficult."

"Move to strike, nonresponsive." Fisher roared as if Lauren had rattled off a string of obscenities.

"Sustained."

"Weren't you jealous of the time Liz spent with her other friends?" Fisher repeated.

"No. I was glad Liz was enjoying her life. Her other friends didn't get in the way of our bond. We were unusually close to each other. We've been through a lot together."

"Meaning you've had a lot of conflict in your relationship with one another?"

"No. Meaning we lost our parents when I was thirteen and Liz was fifteen. That horrific experience brought us closer together."

"You have testified that Liz was your best friend, is that correct?"

"Yes."

"And were you Liz's best friend?"

Lauren hesitated. Hadn't she been Liz's best friend? Or would Liz have said Jake?

"Yes, I think so."

"You *think* so?"

"Yes. I can't speak for her and she isn't here to speak for herself, but I think I was her best friend." Lauren said to convince herself as much as to convince the court.

"Miss Rose, did you cry when the detectives notified you of your sister's death?"

"I have cried many times about the loss of my sister. I still cry sometimes."

"I asked if you cried *during* the notification?"

Lauren paused to reflect on that awful morning. "No, I didn't cry at that time. I was still in shock."

"So, detectives told you that your sister, your only sibling, and your *best friend* had been killed and you didn't cry?"

"Not at that time. As I have said, I cried many…"

Fisher interrupted. "Did you fall to your knees? Did you scream? Did you cry out in despair?"

"No, it hadn't sunk in yet."

"So the detectives gave you this devastating news and you failed to react appropriately?"

"I have done many death notifications and I would say shock and disbelief is the most common reaction."

"Your Honor," Fisher exclaimed. "This witness is not answering the questions being asked. Move to strike."

"Sustained."

"You testified media coverage suggesting your involvement in your sister's death is false, is that correct?"

"Yes, completely false."

"How many news stories would you say have suggested you were involved in some way?"

"Too many to count."

"Would you say it's more than one hundred news stories?"

"Yes."

"More than two hundred?"

"Yes."

"More than five hundred?"

"Probably. The same ridiculous accusations show up in multiple publications."

"Out of these hundreds of news stories that accused you of being involved, how many have you filed defamation lawsuits against?"

"My lawyer has filed a few lawsuits on my behalf. I don't know exactly how many."

"Is it more than five hundred?"

"No."

"More than one hundred?"

"No."

"More than ten?"

"No, I don't think so."

"So, hundreds of false stories have been written about you and you have filed suit against less than ten?"

Lauren took a deep breath. She had to remain calm, which was proving difficult. "News articles are strategically worded in order to avoid lawsuits. They reference unknown sources of information and use the word 'alleged' to prevent litigation. How many publications have reported Jennifer Aniston is pregnant when she's not? I don't see her suing all of them."

"But being accused of being pregnant is somewhat less deplorable than being accused of killing your own sister, don't you think?"

"Absolutely, but my point is that the tabloids know exactly how to avoid defamation lawsuits. I'm pretty sure Jennifer Aniston doesn't have a dozen babies."

Several jurors chuckled.

"Objection," Fisher roared. "Nonresponsive. Move to strike."

"Overruled."

Fisher moved on. "Isn't it true you were jealous of Liz's lifestyle?"

"No."

"No?" Fisher pronounced the two-letter word with three syllables. "You have testified that Jake gave you this ring..." he shoved the evidence bag in front of her, "...on September twenty-eighth of last year. Is that correct?"

"Yes."

"And did anybody else see him give you this ring?"

"No, we were alone at the time."

"Of course you were," he said sarcastically. "It is a gorgeous ring, is it not?"

"Yes."

"So, who did you show the ring to after he gave it to you?"

"Nobody."

"You got this beautiful ring for your birthday and you didn't show it to any of your friends or family?"

"I haven't much family left." Lauren realized she sounded bitter, but she was just speaking the truth. "And I didn't have much opportunity to show it to friends. I was working long hours and I can't really wear rings to work."

"You can't wear rings to work?" he asked with exaggerated incredulity.

"I take surgical gloves on and off all day long at work," she answered. "That's hard to do with rings, especially big rings, without ripping the latex."

"Isn't it true the reason you never showed the ring to any of your friends or family was because you stole that ring on July twenty-third after killing your sister?"

"No."

"Isn't it true you aggressively pursued a romance with Jake Wakefield shortly after your sister's death?"

"Objection," Candace shouted, jumping to her feet. "Beyond the scope."

"Sustained."

Fisher turned back to Lauren, "Isn't it true you killed your own sister because you were jealous of her and you wanted to inherit her money, marry her husband, and live her life?"

Lauren struggled to maintain her composure. "No, nothing could be further from the truth."

The judge was already sustaining Candace's objection before Lauren could finish speaking, but she was able to get all of the words out anyways.

"Mr. Fisher, you are reminded to limit your cross-examination to the scope of the direct examination," Judge Robles admonished.

"Your Honor, this witness has material information about this case," Fisher complained.

"Unless it was introduced in direct examination, you can't ask about it now," Robles said. "You may recall this witness as a Defense witness if you so choose."

"We intend to do that."

"Very well," said the judge.

Silence settled over the courtroom.

"Do you have any more questions for this witness at this time, counselor?" Judge Robles prodded.

Fisher pulled his shoulders back defiantly. "Not at *this* time."

"Re-direct, Ms. Keene?" the judge asked.

"Just a few," Candace replied. "Dr. Rose, did you know your sister listed you as the sole beneficiary on her life insurance policy?"

"No, apparently she changed the beneficiary from Jake to me shortly before her death, but I didn't learn about that until after she died."

"Do you know why she changed her beneficiary?"

"No, but I have an idea."

"Objection, calls for speculation," Fisher interjected.

"Sustained."

"Dr. Rose, did you collect your sister's life insurance policy?"

"Yes, but I didn't keep it."

"You didn't keep it?" Candace asked incredulously, although of course she already knew this.

Lauren had received the money back in March after Candace had reassured the life insurance company that Lauren had been cleared of any involvement in Liz's death. Candace had urged Lauren to use the money to take a leave of absence from work so she could attend the trial full-time.

"No, I donated it all to Mothers Against Drunk Driving, a cause that was important to both Liz and me because our parents were killed by a drunk driver."

"How much was the payout?"

"A million dollars."

"A million dollars? Surely you kept a little bit for yourself, to pay off your college loans or pay the legal fees necessary to defend yourself against the false accusations in this case or to take some time off of work so you could attend this trial?"

Fisher stood up. "Objection, counsel is leading the witness."

"Sustained."

Candace smiled. "I'll rephrase the question. Exactly how much of the million dollar payout did you donate to MADD?"

"Every penny of it."

"No more questions, Your Honor."

Fisher stood, "No more questions."

Lauren breathed a sigh of relief as she stepped down. Judge Robles called for a short recess. Lauren slipped back into her usual seat behind the Prosecution table.

Candace leaned over to whisper to Lauren. "I knew Fisher was in over his enormous head. He's been so busy preening for the cameras that he doesn't even know the facts of this case."

Lauren caught Boyd's eye and he nodded at her almost imperceptibly as if agreeing she had done well.

Chapter Thirty-five

(Wednesday, August 30–Thursday, August 31)

With her own testimony behind her, Lauren settled into her courtroom role representing the family. Candace wanted Lauren front and center to remind the jury of Liz. "Your striking resemblance will help humanize her for the jury."

"Striking resemblance?" Lauren laughed.

"If you don't think you look like your sister, you've been smoking your lunch."

"Thank you. That's a very flattering comparison, but Liz was larger than life. Gorgeous, funny, charming."

"Look in the mirror sometime," Candace said.

Lauren was determined to attend every minute of the trial, happy to finally be doing something. Detective Boyd drove her to court each day. Lauren had offered to get an apartment closer to the courthouse, but Candace had advised against it, not wanting to invite any speculation that Lauren was trying to advance her status. Boyd reassured Lauren it was not inconvenient to drive her to court as he was already attending to provide investigative support. He sat with Lauren in court each morning, but often left to track down information, always arriving back in time to drive Lauren home. On the way to court each day, they would anticipate the day's testimony and on the way home, they would analyze how the trial was unfolding.

The judicial gag order imposed on the lawyers did not extend to Lauren. At Candace's urging, she began to speak candidly to the press about her hopes for a conviction. When reporters attempted to ask Lauren about the false accusations that had been lobbied against her, she responded with a short "I won't dignify that with a response," turning immediately to the next reporter. Lauren had a very sharp memory and she shut out any reporter who had attempted to associate her with her sister's death. Most of the reporters learned not to cross that line. Of course, there were always a few tabloid reporters who persisted in asking insulting questions, but Lauren became adept at ignoring them. Lauren, who had always stayed comfortably in her sister's shadow, began to shine in front of the cameras, capitalizing on the media attention to demand justice for Liz.

The Prosecution's first objective was to dismantle Jake's public image as an all-American sports legend. Candace had decided against calling the stripper to the stand. Given that Sanders had sold her story for personal gain and was employed as an exotic dancer, the Defense would easily destroy her on cross-examination.

However, the Prosecutor's office was soon inundated with phone calls from women all over the country. Apparently, it was not unusual for the Diamondback players to celebrate their last night in a city by taking strippers back to their hotel rooms for a night of no-strings sex.

"It's weird they all came forward at the same time," Lauren commented to Boyd on the way to the courthouse that morning.

"I know," Boyd agreed. "It's like the floodgates have broken, but I have a theory about that. Once Sanders went public, these women were pissed to find out there were others. Jake made each woman feel like she was special to him and they remained loyal to him until they realized they weren't unique. He always said something along the lines of 'I've never done anything like this before, but you're so amazing.' And they all fell for his bullshit. Can you believe that?"

"Yeah…" Lauren said without hesitation, "…I can believe it."

"I wasn't talking about you," Boyd said. "Your situation was totally different."

Jake's womanizing habit turned out to be good fortune for the Prosecution's case because it provided the necessary ammunition to destroy his golden boy persona.

Candace refused to call several women who had sold their stories because of their tainted credibility. However, plenty of others abided by Candace's requirement that they not speak to the media. Perhaps they genuinely wanted to assist justice or maybe they just realized their stories would be worth even more after they testified. Candace didn't mind when she lost a few to tabloid payouts because Jake was also getting lambasted in the court of public opinion.

In the end, the Prosecution verified Jake's dalliances with fifteen women when each mentioned Jake was not well endowed. Candace continued her case by calling these witnesses, eliciting graphic testimony about their sexual encounters with Jake. The Defense asked a few derisive questions of each woman about her chosen occupation before summarily dismissing them. After the first four women testified, the Defense stipulated to Jake's extramarital affairs with eleven additional women. Candace was disappointed; she would have preferred to parade Jake's procession of women in front of the jury. Jake appeared determined to avoid having his small penis size introduced in open court.

"So his pride is more important than his Defense against murder charges?" Lauren asked.

"Apparently. Rumor has it he told his lawyers he won't be satisfied with an acquittal." Candace made a face. "He also expects his lawyers to rehabilitate his public image."

Chapter Thirty-six

(Friday, September 1)

Candace called Kathryn Montgomery, the executive advisor for the Arizona Chapter of MADD, the same woman who had presented Liz's award almost a year earlier. Tall with neatly styled short auburn hair, she wore a gray dress adorned with a small red MADD pin.

Under Candace's careful questioning, Kathryn described her friendship with Liz, which had blossomed over their collaboration on charity work. They shared the common bond of losing loved ones to drunk drivers, Kathryn having lost her twin sister. Over several years of working together on various fundraisers, Liz had gradually opened up to Kathryn.

According to Kathryn, Liz had become unhappy in her marriage. Having confronted Jake about his infidelities shortly before her death, Jake had become increasingly controlling, preventing Liz from talking to anybody outside of their close circle of baseball friends.

Lauren was pained by this testimony. She already felt remorseful about not spending more time with Liz. Lauren had simply believed their busy lifestyles were prohibitive. Had the infrequency of their interactions actually been the result of something uglier?

Kathryn testified, "Liz disclosed more and more disturbing information about Jake's behavior."

"And then what happened?" Candace asked.

"Finally I got up the nerve to ask Liz if Jake had ever hit her and…"

"Objection, hearsay."

"… she admitted he had." Kathryn forced out the rest before Judge Robles could rule on the objection.

Judge Robles called for a sidebar. The attorneys approached the judge's bench for a whispered conversation outside of earshot of the jury, the television cameras, and the courtroom spectators.

Candace looked grim as the sidebar broke up.

"Ladies and gentlemen of the jury," Judge Robles said. "Ms. Montgomery has been offering testimony about things Elizabeth Wakefield told her. This is called hearsay testimony, which is not admissible in court. I am going to strike all of Ms. Montgomery's testimony thus far from the record and you are reminded not to consider this testimony in your deliberations."

Candace composed herself. "Ms. Montgomery, when was the last time you spoke to Liz Wakefield?"

"She called me from her cell on the afternoon of Friday, July twenty-second. She was excited as she told me 'I finally did it.'"

"Objection, non-responsive," Pratt interjected.

"Sustained. The witness is directed to answer only the question posed."

"It was Friday, July twenty-second, at about 4:35 in the afternoon," Kathryn said.

"What was her demeanor on the phone?"

"Objection, speculation," Pratt interrupted.

"Overruled, the witness may answer."

"She was excited and happy and relieved," Kathryn responded.

Lauren knew what the jury did not. Liz had called Kathryn to tell her she had hired a divorce attorney. However, most of that conversation would not be admissible under the hearsay exclusion. Candace was trying to help the jury put the pieces together.

"Before you ended the conversation, did you make plans to speak to Liz again?"

"Yes, she said she would call me Saturday night as soon as her husband left the house."

"And, Ms. Montgomery, did Liz Wakefield call you as she had promised?"

"No." Kathryn Montgomery's composure crumbled as her voice quivered, "I never spoke to her again."

"No more questions for this witness," Candace said.

Pratt approached the witness stand. "Ms. Montgomery, did you ever observe Jake and Elizabeth Wakefield together?"

"No, but…"

"No more questions."

Kathryn Montgomery was excused from the stand without having shared the pertinent secrets she knew about the Wakefield marriage.

Court recessed for lunch. Lauren and Boyd traversed the pedestrian tunnel that connected the court building to the County Attorney's office. They joined the prosecutors in the war room, which allowed them a place to strategize in between court sessions.

Candace was pacing the room like a caged tiger. Kathryn Montgomery sat nearby, looking discouraged.

"Damn it," Candace said. "I needed your testimony to establish motive. This case is going to be a helluva lot harder to prove without it. Tell us again what Liz told you."

"After Liz confronted Jake about the infidelity, he clamped down on her. His precious image would be tarnished if she left him. He threatened to kill her if she ever left. To her credit, that didn't stop her from trying. She had it all planned out. She consulted with a divorce attorney on Friday, July twenty-second, and planned to move out on Saturday as soon as Jake left town. She also planned to file for a restraining order and have him served with it at the airport when he returned from D.C. I offered to let her stay with me, but she planned to get her own place and said she could crash with Lauren for a few days if necessary."

"But why didn't she ever tell me any of this?" Lauren asked, the hurt obvious in her tone.

"Things were unfolding pretty quickly. She had only just found out about the affairs. She didn't want to tell you on the phone because Jake was tracking her cell phone and computer usage."

"But she called you on the phone."

"Yes, but she kept it really brief. We were working on a fundraiser together so she didn't think that Jake would get worried about a quick phone call to me. But an extended phone call to you…"

Candace believed Jake had discovered Liz's plan to leave him and killed her in a fit of rage, clumsily attempting to cover up the crime as a burglary. Liz's disclosures to Kathryn provided the Prosecution's entire theory about Jake's motive. Candace had intentionally scheduled Kathryn's direct testimony for Friday, hoping her disclosures about Jake would marinate in the jurors' minds over the long Labor Day weekend. But the hearsay ruling had ruined that plan.

Candace was fit to be tied, "Damn it all to hell!"

"We knew it was a long shot, but it wasn't all for nothing," Kyle reassured. "The jury still heard Kathryn say Jake hit Liz. They won't forget that, even though the judge told them to."

Lauren was lost in her own thoughts.

"Are you all right?" Detective Boyd asked her.

"Why didn't I pick up on the fact that Liz was being abused? If I hadn't been so busy with work, would Liz have shared her troubles with me? Maybe things could have been different."

"You can't think like that," Boyd told her. "You'll drive yourself crazy. Don't let the what-ifs get the best of you. Liz's death is not your fault. It's Jake's fault."

Chapter Thirty-seven

(Friday afternoon, September 1)

Candace and Kyle launched into crisis mode. Which witness could they call on short notice to do serious damage before the long weekend?

They contacted the divorce attorney Liz had hired. He wasn't scheduled to testify until the following week.

Kyle hung up the phone. "It's a miracle. He's available and agreed to be here by one o'clock."

"That's great news, but it's no miracle," Candace remarked. "He probably just ordered his secretary to clear his schedule. This trial is the best publicity money can buy."

Ronald Bourk was a reasonably good prosecution witness. He refused to disclose details Liz had shared with him, citing attorney-client privilege. However, he confirmed Liz had hired him on the afternoon of Friday, July twenty-second, paying his retainer of twenty-five thousand dollars with a personal check.

"Mr. Bourk," I know you can't comment on Liz Wakefield's case specifically, but can you tell the court what kind of law you practice?" Candace asked.

"Family law."

"And what kinds of cases are included in family law?"

"Divorce and child custody cases, primarily."

"So you're a divorce lawyer?"

"Objection," Pratt said. "Ms. Keene is putting words in the witness' mouth."

"Sustained."

Candace switched gears. "Mr. Bourk, do you happen to have one of your business cards with you?"

"Yes." He reached into his pocket.

Pratt was on his feet. "Objection! Does the Prosecution plan to introduce this into evidence without prior notice?"

"Your Honor," Candace argued. "We are merely attempting to establish what kind of law Mr. Bourk practices. I thought his business card might shed some light on his specialty."

Judge Robles' eyes smiled, but his face remained impassive. "Ms. Keene, you haven't seen his business card before this moment?"

"No, Your Honor."

"I'll allow it."

Bourk handed his card to Candace, who glanced at it before returning it to him. "Mr. Bourk, can you read the top two lines aloud for the record, please?"

"Ronald M. Bourk, J.D., Divorce Attorney."

"You identify yourself as a divorce attorney?"

"That's correct."

"Mr. Bourk, you testified Elizabeth Wakefield paid you with a personal check on July twenty-second. Do you remember what date you deposited that check?"

"Yes, I deposited it that same afternoon."

Although Bourk was obscure about his conversation with Liz, the significance of his testimony was clear. Liz had hired a divorce attorney the day before she was bludgeoned to death.

"Mr. Bourk, have you ever met the defendant in this case?"

Bourk glanced uncomfortably in Jake's direction. "Yes."

"Under what circumstances?"

"He made an appointment with me on August fifth of last year."

"And what was the purpose of that appointment?"

Bourk looked uncomfortable, but he could not assert client-attorney privilege. Jake hadn't hired him.

"He asked me to refund the money his wife paid me."

"And how did you respond?"

"I refunded the money."

"Why?"

"Because I was no longer needed to represent Mrs. Wakefield."

"So Jake was spared expensive divorce proceedings by Liz Wakefield's untimely death?"

"Objection," Pratt bellowed. "The Prosecution is providing testimony in the form of her questions."

"Sustained," Judge Robles raised his eyebrows at Candace in silent warning.

"I'll rephrase the question. Mr. Bourk, how did you know you were no longer needed to represent Mrs. Wakefield?"

"Because she had been murdered."

Candace was satisfied. "No more questions, Your Honor."

At the Defense table, Pratt stood. Although he was short and stout, he managed to look imposing with his expensive suit and haughty demeanor. The dark bags underneath his hooded eyes suggested he had been putting in late hours. He cleared his throat phlegmatically. "Good afternoon, Mr. Bourk."

"Good afternoon, Counsel."

"Since your business card identifies you as a divorce attorney, does that mean you can only represent divorce cases?"

"No."

"You're free to take on other types of cases?"

"Yes."

"For example, if a client wanted to hire you to assist her in filing an order of protection against her own sister, you could take that case, couldn't you?"

"Yes, I could."

"No more questions, Your Honor," Pratt returned to his seat, smiling.

Candace stood up. "Mr. Bourk, over the past year, how many cases have you represented that were not divorce cases?" Candace was taking a gamble.

Bourk didn't even pause. "None."

"So you know a fair amount about divorce law in Arizona?"

"Yes."

"If a man is worth ten million dollars and he gets divorced in Arizona, how much can he expect to lose to his wife in the divorce?"

"Objection, irrelevant," Pratt was putting up a good fight.

"I'll allow it," Judge Robles ruled.

"Arizona is a community property state so he can expect to lose half of what he accrued during the marriage."

"And do divorcing men enjoy the idea of handing over half of their net worth to their soon to be ex-wives?"

Bourk chortled, "No ma'am, they do not."

"One more question, Mr. Bourk. What time did Liz Wakefield leave your office on July twenty-second?"

"Let's see. Her appointment started at three-thirty and lasted about an hour. She left my office about four-thirty."

"Just five minutes before 4:35?" Candace asked suggestively. She was stating the obvious, but Candace wanted to remind the jury that Liz had called Kathryn Montgomery in a jubilant mood shortly after leaving Bourk's office.

"Objection, irrelevant." Pratt's face was scarlet. "The State is trying to provide testimony in the form of a question."

"Sustained."

Candace grinned. "No more questions for this witness."

Pratt declined re-cross, Bourk was excused, and court adjourned for the week.

Chapter Thirty-eight

(Friday afternoon, September 1)

As Boyd drove Lauren back to her apartment, they discussed the day's testimony.

"At least Jake donated that twenty-five thousand dollar refund to MADD," Lauren mused.

"Didn't Candace tell you?" he asked.

"Tell me what?"

"I'm sorry. I thought you already knew. Jake never paid that donation to MADD."

"What do you mean? I was there when he pledged it."

"Oh, he pledged it alright. He just never paid it."

Lauren thought of her own thousand-dollar check that night. The one that had been inspired by Jake's incredible generosity. The one she could ill-afford. She shook her head.

"Do you think Pratt and Fisher believe Jake's innocent?" Lauren wondered aloud.

"There's no way defense attorneys can believe *all* of their clients are innocent. Prosecutors will only take on the surest cases so, realistically speaking, most defendants are guilty. To be fair, I guess defense attorneys must *occasionally* believe their client is innocent. Hell, those guys might actually believe Jake is innocent. He's a very convincing liar; I can attest to that. But the evidence against him is compelling. And Pratt and Fisher don't want to know if he's guilty. It's easier to defend him if they believe that he is not."

"But he was convincing when you guys talked to him?"

"Absolutely. That was before we had so much evidence against him, of course. But he agreed to talk to us without an attorney present. And he was incredibly relaxed. He certainly seemed adamant that you were guilty."

"Did you think I was guilty?"

"No, I never believed it, but Wallace entertained the idea for a while."

"Wallace thought I did it?"

"Not necessarily, but he wasn't willing to rule you out either. He's a very solid detective. He doesn't guess, doesn't operate on hunches, doesn't take into account his personal feelings. He's all about the cold hard facts and the facts ultimately pointed to Jake."

"When he came to the hospital last October, I thought for sure he was coming to arrest me."

"You? You never proved to be a viable suspect."

"Then why'd you search my apartment?"

"Sorry, I thought Candace already told you all this. During the investigation, we established an anonymous tip line. As soon as it launched, we started getting regular calls from some guy who insisted you did it. At first, he didn't have any specifics to back up his accusations, but he kept upping the ante. He said you had confessed your involvement to him. When that didn't work, he called to say you showed him a ring stolen from Liz. Acting on that tip, we got the warrant to search your apartment. You know who the anonymous male caller was?"

"Jake?"

"Yep. After his arrest, we were able to establish that he had been calling into the anonymous tip line from his cell phone after blocking the number. Pretty weird for a guy who claimed to be cooperating with us. Why not call us directly?"

"So they're going to admit those phone calls into evidence?"

"Unfortunately, no. Since the tip line was advertised as anonymous, we're obliged to protect the identity of the callers. But we have more than enough evidence to convict him." Boyd paused and shook his head in disbelief. "I can't believe you thought we were going to arrest you."

"I wasn't so sure you guys knew what you were doing."

Boyd laughed. "I wanted to come notify you myself, but Wallace let me serve the arrest warrant since this is my first homicide case. That was really generous. In a huge case like this, most lead detectives would hoard the glory for themselves. You know, Wallace wanted to become a police detective because his father was falsely convicted for murder."

"Really?"

"He doesn't talk about it much, but his father did two years of prison time before some cop uncovered the truth and got his dad released from prison."

"Wow."

"So, he's a real stickler for facts. He won't identify somebody as a suspect until he is positive about the evidence."

"What about you? Why'd you become an officer?"

Boyd sighed heavily and Lauren realized she had hit a nerve. "I'm sorry. I didn't mean to pry."

"No, it's okay. My grandfather was murdered and his killer was never caught."

"Wow," was all Lauren could manage for the second time in a matter of seconds.

"My grandpa had a huge heart and used to pick up hitch-hikers. Sometimes, he'd go well out of his way to get them to their destination. We think he gave a ride to the wrong person. Somebody shot him, dumped him in the desert, and stole his car and his wallet."

"And they never caught the guy?"

"Nope. They found Grandpa's car a few days later engulfed in flames down near Tucson. I was twelve years old and I resolved to become a cop and track down the killer. Sounds silly, huh?"

"Not at all."

"The case is still open. I pulled the file, but there's not much to go on. The fire destroyed any physical evidence that might have existed."

Lauren didn't know what to say so she patted his hand.

"What about the driver that killed your parents?" he asked. "What happened to him?"

"It was a her. Angela Martin. She was twenty-four years old and it was her third drunk driving arrest, though she liked to remind everybody that this was the first time anybody had ever been *hurt*. She pled guilty to two counts of vehicular manslaughter and got sentenced to two ten-year prison terms, but the judge let her serve them concurrently. She got out of prison after only seven years for good behavior." Lauren laughed bitterly. "Good behavior. Like a kindergartner who doesn't eat paste."

She paused for a moment before continuing. "My dad was declared dead at the scene. My mom was still alive when she got to the hospital, but the doctors weren't able to control the bleeding in time. I guess that's why I ended up in emergency medicine."

"Weird, huh?" Boyd asked softly.

Lauren nodded. "You, me, and Wallace. All chasing the ghosts of our pasts."

Chapter Thirty-nine

(Tuesday, September 5)

As a matter of routine, the bank records were already on the Prosecution's list of discovery. However, they took on new significance when they learned Bourk had deposited Liz's check on the day before her murder. Boyd spent part of his weekend re-interviewing Cheryl Davis, the bank manager who would be testifying about the Wakefields' bank records.

"Boyd's my secret weapon with female witnesses," Candace confided to Lauren as they convened back in court on Tuesday morning. "He charms them into a cooperative state of mind."

Ms. Davis testified that Liz's check to Bourk had cleared the Wakefields' joint checking account on Friday, July twenty-second. Coincidentally, Mr. Bourk used the same bank as the Wakefields. Liz couldn't have known the check would post so quickly.

Candace asked a follow-up question, "Ms. Davis, can you tell us if and when the account was checked online between the dates of July twenty-second and July twenty-third?

"Yes, it was checked one time on those dates. Somebody pulled the account balance on July twenty-third at 6:33 pm and then they clicked on check #1273 to view the details."

"So, the person who accessed the online system on July twenty-third would have seen check #1273 was a twenty-five thousand-dollar check payable to Ronald Bourk."

"Yes."

Pratt did a solid job of muddying the water. "It could have been Mrs. Elizabeth Wakefield who opened the online system of July twenty-third, couldn't it?"

"Yes, it could have been anybody who had the account number and password," Ms. Davis agreed.

Ms. Davis was the last of the motive witnesses, those called to demonstrate for the jury that the Wakefield marriage was far from the perfect union.

Having established motive, Candace moved on to her time line witnesses. William Dallas was tall and thin with graying hair. Despite the one-hundred-plus degree temperatures outside, he wore a tennis sweater and slacks to court. A neighbor of Jake's, Mr. Dallas testified he saw Jake's red convertible hurriedly exiting the community gates at about seven-fifteen on the evening of July twenty-third. This was important because Jake had told police he left for the airport at six-thirty and the time of death was estimated between seven and eleven p.m.

Under Pratt's careful cross-examination, Mr. Dallas was forced to admit he couldn't be one hundred percent certain the car he had seen was Jake's car. On re-direct, Candace elicited confirmation that the car was the same make, model, and color.

"You'd have to be an idiot to believe another convertible red Porsche Spyder just happened to be in the neighborhood that night," Candace muttered as they were leaving court that evening.

Boyd was driving Lauren home when she received a phone call from an unfamiliar number.

"I'll come right away," she said in a trembling voice.

Boyd expressed concern the moment she hung up. "Everything okay?"

"No. That was the nurse at Desert Pointe. My grandmother is being sent to the hospital for chest pain." Her eyes welled up.

"Which hospital?"

"Scottsdale Shea."

"I can take you there now."

"No, that's too much to ask. Just take me home, I can drive myself out there."

"That makes no sense. Taking you home first is going to cost you too much time in this traffic."

Lauren reassured herself that Boyd lived in Scottsdale himself. He could drop her off at the hospital on his way home, reducing his own commute time. Having eased her own mind about Boyd, she resumed worrying about Rose-ma.

Boyd navigated quiet side streets in order to make better time. "Is she in the emergency room?"

"She must be. They were transporting her by ambulance."

He pulled into the circular drive of the ER. Lauren flung the car door open before the car had even reached a complete stop.

Lauren paused outside the open car door. "Thanks for the ride. I'll see you in the morning." She shut the door and rushed into the ER lobby. She identified herself to the receptionist, who led her back to one of the trauma bays.

Her grandmother looked tiny, wrapped up in soft white blankets on the hospital bed. She was hooked up to a pulse oximeter, cardiac monitor, and automated blood pressure cuff. She smiled weakly when Lauren entered. "Here's my favorite doctor. How are you, dear?"

"I'm fine, Rose-ma. More importantly, how are you?"

"Oh, nothing worth reporting. Just a little discomfort in my chest and the Desert Pointe staff insisted upon sending me here. By ambulance no less! I'm feeling much better now. It was probably just heartburn."

"Better safe than sorry, Rose-ma. I'm so glad you're okay."

"Enough about me. How are you? I hope you haven't been working too hard. I always worried about the way you girls went without sleep, so distracted by homework and sports and boys. Do you remember the time Liz dreamed her alarm went off in the middle of the night and she got up, showered, and got herself ready for school? I found her eating breakfast at two o'clock in the morning!"

Lauren remembered. "Her dream was so convincing she argued with you about the right time for fifteen minutes before she noticed it was still dark outside. The hubbub woke me up and we all had some o.j. before going back to bed."

They were laughing at the memory when the receptionist returned. "Excuse me for interrupting, but there's a gentleman asking for you." Boyd was lurking in the hallway beyond the curtain.

"Detective Boyd, come on in. Do you remember my grandmother?"

"Of course I do," Boyd said as he stepped into the room. He briefly took Rose-ma's small hand in his large one. "It's nice to see you again, Mrs. Rose. It's good to see you looking so well. You gave Lauren quite a scare."

"Well, Lauren scares easily."

Blood warmed Lauren's cheeks as Rose-ma and Boyd shared a laugh at her expense.

Boyd turned to Lauren. "I don't mean to intrude. I just wanted to let you know I was here. I'll wait in the waiting room until you're ready to go and then give you a ride back to your place."

"Thank you, but that's unnecessary. You should head home. I can catch a cab…" Lauren was interrupted by the clanging alarms of her grandmother's cardiac monitor.

Instinctively, Lauren flew into action. She hit the code button located on a nearby wall and started CPR. "Tell a staff member I need a crash cart stat," Lauren directed to Boyd. She continued chest compressions as the room quickly became a flurry of activity around her. An ER doctor began calling out orders. He was preparing to shock her grandmother's chest with the defibrillator. Lauren stopped chest compressions as he shouted, "Clear!"

The physician was still tending to Rose-ma. "Get the family members out of here." Lauren and Boyd were hustled unceremoniously back to the lobby, Lauren listening intently for the distinctive monitor sounds that would indicate Rose-ma's heart had resumed beating. She didn't hear them.

Her muscles were trembling from the rush of adrenaline and she paced the waiting room. Boyd stood nearby, respectfully allowing her time to herself.

Moments felt like hours, but finally a nurse emerged from the treatment area. She invited Lauren into a private triage room. Boyd came along without waiting for an invitation and squeezed Lauren's hand supportively as they took seats.

"The doctors were able to restart your grandmother's heart. They've taken her into emergency surgery where they'll work to insert a stent to restore the flow of blood to her heart. The doctors are doing all they can, but the cardiac enzymes were extremely elevated, indicating a significant cardiac event. At her age, the anesthesia alone can be a considerable risk. You should prepare for the possibility she may not survive the surgery. I recommend you ask the rest of the family to meet you here. The surgery will take at least an hour. The surgeon will come out to talk to you when it's over."

Lauren felt numb as she and Boyd returned to the waiting room. She pulled out her cell phone, but was harshly reminded she had no family left to call. Instead, she called Stone at work to let him know she wouldn't be in for her shift that evening. "You should get going, Detective Boyd. This is going to take awhile. I'm sure you have better things to do than babysit me." She found herself wondering about his home life, a topic she knew very little about.

"You can stop trying to get rid of me. I'm not going anywhere until we know your grandmother is all right. But you can do something for me."

"Of course. What is it?"

"Will you please stop calling me Detective Boyd? I feel as old as Wallace when you do that. You can call me Ryan."

"I'll try."

"Do you want to get some dinner?"

Lauren shook her head. "There's no way I could eat right now."

"Why don't we go down to the hospital chapel?"

Lauren exhaled audibly. "I don't really trust God anymore. He's let me down so many times already."

Lauren saw no judgment on Ryan's face, only compassion. "Then come with me and I'll pray enough for both of us." He led her down a series of hallways until they reached the chapel, which was devoid of other visitors. It was a small room with wooden pews filling the majority of the space. The faux stained glass windows were illuminated by backlit light bulbs, no matter the time of day.

Boyd crossed himself as they entered and Lauren followed suit, realizing he was Catholic himself. Somehow, this revelation comforted her. He steered her to the front pew, both of them kneeling in the aisle before taking their seats. Ryan bowed his head and shut his eyes. Was Lauren willing to confide in God? She decided to try.

Heavenly Father, I beg you, please don't take Rose-ma from me right now. I know I'll have to let her go at some point, but not yet, not right now. Without her, I will have nothing. I would be lost. I know I haven't been the most faithful of servants. I'm trying to renew my trust in you. I know I can't make my faith contingent upon you answering this prayer, but please don't take her from me. I may not deserve your grace, but Rose-ma does. She's the most faithful person I know.

Tears flowed freely down Lauren's face as she imagined a world without Rose-ma. Ryan wrapped his arms around her and let her cry until she could cry no more. Afterwards, they returned to the waiting room to await news from the surgeon. Ryan's cell phone rang several times. Most times, he hit the ignore button and returned the phone to his pocket. But on one occasion, he murmured to Lauren, "Sorry, I have to take this." He retreated to the corner of the room to take the call in relative privacy. Lauren could not resist the urge to eavesdrop, but he spoke in subdued tones and she couldn't make out much from his end of the conversation.

Soon he returned to the seat next to her. "Sorry about that. It was work."

"If they need you, you should go."

"I'm not leaving here until the doctor comes out to talk to you. Anyway, it was nothing urgent. They always call me when they have trouble with the computer system. We have a whole IT team, but I'm the only one that seems to know how our system actually operates."

"You are truly a jack of all trades—investigator, chauffeur, spiritual advisor, computer technician."

He smiled. "Master of none."

They sat in impatient silence. The cardiac surgeon finally emerged and greeted both of them as if he already knew them. This happened to Lauren frequently these days and probably to Ryan as well. He introduced himself as Dr. Randall and invited them back to a private consultation room. Lauren feared the worst.

"The good news is your grandmother survived the surgery. We were able to insert the stent and re-establish blood flow to the posterior descending artery. The bad news is it took us quite some time to revive her. We aren't certain of the extent of oxygen deprivation to her brain. We won't know about the impact upon her cognitive functioning until she wakes up."

"Can I see her?"

"Yes, but remember she's still recovering. We won't know for sure what we're dealing with until the anesthesia has fully dissipated."

Lauren turned to Ryan. "Will you come with me?"

"Of course."

Rose-ma was sleeping peacefully. Lauren squeezed her hand. "Rose-ma? Can you hear me?"

"Yes, dear, of course I can. I had trouble with my heart, not my ears," Rose-ma said as she slowly opened her eyes. "I've just seen Liz."

"No, Rose-ma," Lauren said, somewhat embarrassed by Rose-ma's confusion. "Liz isn't here anymore, remember? You've had surgery, but everything went well. You need to focus on getting better now, okay? I love you."

"*Oui, oui.* Don't worry about me, dear. I'll be fine. Liz sent a message for you. She asked me to tell you that you have always been her favoritest sister. I scolded her poor grammar, but she insisted I had to say it just like that. She said you would understand."

The hairs on Lauren's arms stood up. After their parents had died, Liz had taken to cheering Lauren by saying, "Always remember, you're my favoritest sister!" Initially, Lauren would protest, "That's because I'm your only sister," but eventually they reached an unspoken understanding about the true meaning behind the silly phrase. Underneath it all, they would always have each other.

Lauren was left to wonder if her grandmother's recovery was the result of medicine. Or something more.

Chapter Forty

Lauren felt badly when she spotted Ryan yawning in court the following morning. They had been at the hospital until well past eleven the previous night. Then Ryan had insisted upon driving her home. He must not have gotten home himself until nearly midnight. Lauren was long accustomed to keeping crazy hours, but felt guilty for dragging Ryan into her chaotic life. Rose-ma was recovering well, with no signs of additional memory loss. She would soon be discharged from the hospital to return to her apartment at Sierra Pointe.

The next Prosecution witness, Jonathan Schope, looked like an Iowa farm boy with his freckled face and strawberry blonde buzz cut. He was a regional manager for Sprint telecommunications and Candace had called him to help establish the Prosecution's time line.

Liz's phone records confirmed she was on her cell frequently, typically starting around eight in the morning and continuing until about ten most nights. But her cell phone usage came to an abrupt stop at 6:39 p.m. on the evening of Saturday, July twenty-third when Liz had sent her final text. She had been in the middle of exchanging text messages with a friend. The friend sent a text at 6:46 p.m. asking Liz if she was attending an upcoming charity event, but Liz never responded. Additionally, Liz hadn't answered her phone after 6:39 p.m. despite several missed calls reflected on her cell phone records that evening, including one from Lauren's cell phone at 8:23 p.m.

Lauren reflected. She remembered leaving a hurried message that night. As she listened to the testimony, she realized Liz had likely already been killed, lying dead and bloodied as the incoming call from Lauren rang and rang.

The medical examiner had estimated the time of death somewhere between 7 and 11 based upon stomach contents and body temperatures. But the cell phone records told a more compelling story; Liz had become lost to the rest of the world somewhere around 6:39 p.m.

Mr. Schope testified that Jake was also a "high cell phone utilizer." He had used his phone regularly on July twenty-third with the exception of one time frame. Between the hours of 6:28 and 7:18 p.m., he had initiated no calls or texts and had failed to answer two incoming phone calls.

Pratt attempted to mitigate Schope's testimony by getting him to admit all cell phone users miss calls on occasion. However, the implications were still quite damaging. Liz had been too busy dying and Jake had been too busy killing her between the hours of 6:39 p.m. and 7:18 p.m. for each to answer their phones.

Todd White was the next Prosecution witness. He was an attractive, broad-shouldered black man who worked as a skycap at a private hangar for U.S. Airways. When Candace called for him, he sauntered to the stand, clearly enjoying his moment in the spotlight. After taking his oath, he testified about checking in Jake's bags on the evening of July twenty-third. As a big Diamondbacks fan, White had recognized Jake immediately. White consulted automated records and confirmed Jake had checked in at 7:44 for his 8:15 flight that evening. Jake had autographed a photo for White before hurrying to catch his plane.

White's testimony supported the Prosecution's time line. The detectives had timed the drive from the Wakefield home to the airport several times. Even when traffic was heavy, the trip took no longer than thirty-five minutes. If Jake had left home at

6:30 as he said he did, he should have checked in at the airport by 7:15 at the latest. The fact that he didn't check in until 7:44 suggested he left at least thirty minutes later than he said he did.

Pratt gently chipped away at White's testimony, asking if it was uncommon for people to check in thirty minutes prior to their flight time.

"Not at all. We tell people to check in at least an hour before their departure time, but many folks don't check in as early as they should. Lots of folks show up late, running up to us all crazy like, worrying about missing their flights. And when folks are private passengers, like Mr. Wakefield, they can check in a little later because they get preferential security, so they aren't so pressed for time as regular Joes."

Pratt smiled. Although White had been called by the Prosecution, he seemed eager to help the Defense make their points. "Mr. Wakefield signed an autograph for you?"

"Yes, sir. We aren't supposed to ask our customers for stuff like that, but he just gave it to me 'cause he could tell I was a fan, and I was real glad to get it. It's worth about fifteen hundred dollars on eBay now."

A Jake Wakefield autograph wouldn't have been worth more than fifty dollars a year ago. Wakefield memorabilia was now selling for extravagant prices. Jake's supporters would argue it was because of his perfect game and World Series win, but in reality, the media exposure of the trial had strangely enhanced Jake's celebrity status. Before the trial, Jake was famous among those that followed sports, but Jake Wakefield was now a household name.

"What was Mr. Wakefield's demeanor that evening?" Pratt asked White.

"He was real pleasant. He was just like a regular ol' customer that night even though he's a real big star."

"Thank you." Pratt concluded. As Todd White exited the courtroom, he leaned over to shake Jake's hand. Candace objected and Judge Robles directed White to exit the courtroom, but the damage had been done. Courtroom decorum was out the window and Prosecution witnesses were fawning over Jake's autographs. This wasn't a trial, it was a three-ring circus.

Candace had been on the fence about calling the Wakefields' housekeeper to testify. On the one hand, Teresita had discovered the body. Candace also suspected Teresita had witnessed Jake abuse Liz, verbally and physically. And Teresita has been close to Liz. On the other hand, Jake paid Teresita a generous salary, which she stood to lose if Jake went to prison. Candace elected to roll the dice and call her.

Teresita cried throughout the entire direct examination. It was difficult enough to understand Teresita's accented English under normal circumstances, but when she was crying, it was practically impossible. Teresita appeared to be exaggerating her accent to avoid answering Candace's questions. If so, it was effective. Her testimony was painfully slow to elicit. Still, she described entering the Wakefield home very early on Sunday, July twenty-fourth. She had been going about her cleaning when she discovered Liz lying dead on the master bedroom floor in a pool of blood. She had dialed 911 and awaited the arrival of the responding officers.

"Did you ever hear the Wakefields argue?"

"No."

Candace rolled her eyes. "You worked full-time for the Wakefields for three years?"

"Yes, ma'am."

"You spent a lot of time in the Wakefields' house?"

"Yes, ma'am."

"And you never saw or heard the Wakefields argue with each other?"

"No. Never."

Candace nodded incredulously. "Did you ever see Jake Wakefield physically abuse Elizabeth Wakefield in any way to include hitting, punching, grabbing, biting, kicking, or restraining her?"

"Never, never! Mr. Jake is a very good man. He is very good to me."

Teresita composed herself for cross-examination, appearing anxious to do a good job for the Defense. She glanced at Jake frequently and he nodded at her in encouragement. She proceeded to answer all of Pratt's questions with what a 'good man' Jake was.

"Ms. Gomez," Pratt asked gently, "you had a lot of opportunity to observe Mr. and Mrs. Wakefield interact with one another, isn't that correct?"

"Yes, sir."

"And would you say Jake Wakefield was a good husband to his wife?"

"Oh, yes sir. Mr. Jake is a very good provider."

That much was true, Lauren thought ruefully. Teresita had been raised in a shack in Central Mexico with dirt floors and no indoor plumbing. Maybe she couldn't distinguish between a good provider and a good husband.

When Pratt had no more questions, Judge Robles recessed court for the day.

"That filthy little liar," Candace fumed as the courtroom emptied. "Jake and Liz never had so much as an argument? I never should have called her to the stand."

Lauren countered, "That's the very beauty of her testimony. Any juror on the panel who has ever been in a relationship, let alone married, isn't going to believe her. They are going to know she lied about that, so they will assume she also lied about the domestic violence."

"Don't be so sure. The jury themselves are a bunch of liars, remember?"

"Yes," Lauren agreed, "and liars recognize other liars."

Chapter Forty-one

(Friday, September 8–Monday, September 11)

Washington D.C. detective, Vincent Castiglione, was next to testify. At Wallace's request, Castiglione had provided a courtesy death notification to Jake at the St. Regis Hotel in D.C. According to Castiglione, Jake had not seemed surprised at the news of his wife's death, his tears had appeared feigned, and he had forgotten to ask how his wife had died until several minutes had passed. When Castiglione had offered to drive Jake to the airport, Jake required no time to pack up. Castiglione said it was as if Jake had been awaiting his arrival. The Defense objected to this as speculative and had it stricken from the record. Still, the image of Jake, bags packed, just sitting and awaiting notification made an impression. Maybe he had even rehearsed his tearful response.

Next, the Wakefield life insurance agent testified that Liz had come in alone to change her beneficiary from Jake to Lauren a few days before her death. Liz had offered no explanation for the beneficiary change and the agent had not asked for one.

The next witness, Sonia Jamison, worked for the twenty-four-hour insurance claim line. She testified a male had called to inquire about a life insurance payout at about six-thirty a.m. Phoenix time on July twenty-fourth. The caller had identified himself as Jacob Wakefield and indicated his wife had died. Ms. Jamison had advised the caller that information about the life insurance benefit could only be released to the designated beneficiary, who was not listed as him. The caller had become angry and belligerent, demanding to know when the beneficiary had been changed. The call had ended with the caller threatening, "You can expect to hear from my attorney."

During cross-examination, Jamison admitted that she couldn't be sure the caller had really been Jake Wakefield. Candace whispered something to Ryan who quietly exited the courtroom.

"In fact, the caller could have been any number of people, right?" Pratt asked.

"Whoever called knew Elizabeth Wakefield's social security number," Jamison hedged.

"The caller could have been a news reporter trying to get information about this case, isn't that right?"

"I suppose so."

Ryan returned to court just as Pratt was wrapping up his cross-examination, slipping some documents to Candace before resuming his front-row seat next to Lauren. Candace reviewed the document and turned around to reward Ryan with one of her hundred-kilowatt smiles.

When Jamison had been excused, Candace jumped up and asked to be heard on a motion.

Judge Robles recessed for lunch, but asked the attorneys to stay back so he could hear the motion. "What's that all about?" Lauren asked Ryan as they headed to the war room for lunch.

He grinned. "I tracked down the phone records for the insurance company on the morning of July twenty-fourth."

"And?"

"There was only one incoming call to the claims office between the hours of six and seven that morning. It came in at 6:27 a.m. Want to guess where the call came from?"

"Jake's cell phone?"

"Not quite, but almost as good."

Lauren shook her head. "I give up."

"A pay phone at Washington National airport in D.C. The

first thing the grieving widower did was call about the insurance payout."

"Why would he use a pay phone, but identify himself by name to the insurance clerk?"

"Why does anybody ever use a pay phone? Because they don't want the call traced back to them."

Lauren thought about the recent occasions on which she had used a pay phone and nodded in agreement.

Ryan continued. "He wanted to conceal the fact that he called the insurance company right away so he took the extra precaution of using a pay phone. That would give him plausible deniability later if he needed it. The phone company employee I spoke to this morning is on standby. Candace is probably petitioning for permission to call her this afternoon."

Lauren heard a commotion in the hallway outside. Candace and Kyle arrived like the victors of war.

"Pratt is fit to be tied," Candace crowed. "He's been whining to the judge about not having enough time to prepare on such short notice, but Robles ruled in our favor anyways. We get to call the phone company rep this afternoon. Robles allowed an extra hour for lunch so the Defense can prepare their big cross. What a joke. There's nothing to cross."

This reality didn't prevent Pratt from trying. After the heavyset woman from the phone company testified the only incoming phone call that morning had been initiated from a pay phone at Washington National airport, Pratt jumped up to vigorously cross-examine the poor woman, who had awakened that morning with no clue she would be at the center of a public spectacle this afternoon.

"Ms. Hanford, does Qwest have any way of determining which individual might have initiated a particular phone call?"

"I'm sorry. I don't understand the question."

"Allow me to simplify it. You can tell what phone line a call came from, but you can't tell who dialed that phone, isn't that correct?"

"Yes."

"The phone call in question came from a pay phone at Washington National Airport, right?"

"Yes."

"Do you have any way of knowing who initiated that phone call?"

"No, I couldn't know that."

"It could have been any one of thousands of people at that airport that morning, could it not?"

"Yes."

"And if we called that number right now, would you have any way of knowing who would pick up the phone?"

"Of course not."

"Indeed, why don't we find out? Permission to have the witness call the phone number, Your Honor?"

"Objection, Defense counsel is grandstanding for the jury," Candace charged.

"Overruled. I've allowed you some leniency today, Ms. Keene, and I will allow this."

The rattled witness was handed a speakerphone. "Ms. Hanford, please dial the number for the pay phone we have been discussing," Pratt directed.

Court spectators could hear the phone ringing through the microphone on the witness stand. One ring, three rings, five rings.

Somebody answered after nine rings. "Hello?"

"Hello, this is Richard Pratt calling from the Arizona Superior Court."

"Right, and I'm Judge Robles," said the voice. Then the line went dead.

The court exploded in laughter. But Pratt had managed to make his point. Anybody could have initiated the call from that phone.

Several people went to the press the following day claiming to be the "mystery phone witness" in the Wakefield murder trial.

Chapter Forty-two

(Tuesday, September 12–Friday, September 15)

The following morning, Candace called the medical examiner to the stand. Dr. Brian Gunther had thick gray hair, wire-framed glasses, and a meek demeanor. He spoke in medical jargon such that Candace had to ask him to explain his testimony in layman's terms on several occasions. His testimony was explicit. Candace had given Lauren permission to excuse herself if necessary, but Lauren felt compelled to hear the details as if it would somehow force the truth to sink in. However, she could not bear to view the photos as they were projected onto a large screen each time one was introduced into evidence. Although she didn't look, Lauren could hear Dr. Gunther discussing the extent of the injuries in minute detail. It was not unlike many of the graphic lectures Lauren had endured in medical school, but something altogether different when depicting the anatomical damages to somebody you loved.

Jake stared dispassionately as Dr. Gunther described Liz's horrifying injuries. Thirteen of the twenty-two bones in Liz's skull had been broken, with three of her teeth dislodged. She also had fractures in both arms, defensive wounds acquired as Liz had used her arms to shield her head. Dr. Gunther estimated Liz was hit with a solid object similar in size and shape to a two-by-four plank of wood at least twice. Lauren's stomach churned. Jake now buried his face in his hands as if he was crying, but no tears fell.

Given the trajectory path of the blows, Dr. Gunther opined that the assailant was likely left-handed. This revelation caused a stir in the courtroom as people stared at the famous southpaw pitcher at the Defense table.

Dr. Gunther asserted the injuries were consistent with an assailant taller than the victim because the blows were executed in a downward fashion. He guessed the assailant to be male based upon the force of delivery.

As expected, Dr. Gunther estimated time of death to be between the hours of seven p.m. and eleven p.m. on the evening of July twenty-third.

The Defense didn't spend much time on cross-examination. Medical examination was a relatively straightforward science. The cause of death was not under dispute. Pratt did manage to get Gunther to admit it was possible that the blows had been delivered by a physically fit female. Gunther also conceded the assailant may not have been taller than Liz, especially if Liz had been hunkered down to protect herself.

The next Prosecution witness was the state criminalist. Dr. Lantu Wong, an Asian American woman with a Ph.D. in microbiology, was employed as a senior supervisor at the Scottsdale Police Department crime lab. A seasoned expert witness, Dr. Wong clearly summarized the findings in the Wakefield case. The only fingerprints found at the scene belonged to Liz, Jake, and Teresita. The only hairs recovered at the scene were consistent with those of Jake and Liz Wakefield. Blood spatter patterns confirmed the killer was left-handed. There was less than a one in 21,257,984,722 chance that the DNA found under Liz's fingernails belonged to anyone other than Jake. No other DNA was found at the scene. The presence of significant blood in the master bedroom shower drain suggested the killer had cleaned up in there, which would be strange behavior for a burglar.

"Dr. Wong, did you find any evidence suggesting Lauren Rose was involved in this crime?"

"None whatsoever."

Pratt was unable to do much to mitigate the power of Dr. Wong's scientific testimony on cross-examination. The jury would have the whole weekend to contemplate the CSI findings. Candace was in a celebratory mood and invited the others out for an early dinner.

"Oh, I don't know," Lauren hesitated, glancing sidelong at Ryan, who was her ride home.

"Come on," he urged. "What else are you going to do? Start work early?"

"No," she said with mock indignation. "I was planning to do a little leisure reading and finish *Gray's Anatomy*. The textbook, not the show."

They were the last people left in the otherwise empty courtroom. Candace and Kyle took a side exit to drop paperwork at their offices before heading to the restaurant. Lauren and Ryan moved toward the courtroom doors. They were chatting as Ryan pushed the heavy door open and Lauren rounded the corner. Slamming into somebody standing in the hallway, she lost her balance. Ryan grasped her left elbow to prevent her from tumbling to the floor. Reflexively, Lauren reached out and grabbed hold of somebody with her right hand before regaining her footing. "Oops, sorry," she apologized to the person she had nearly tackled.

It was Jake. He stared at Lauren coldly as he wrenched his arm free from her hand, thrusting her backward roughly. If not for Ryan's grip on her other elbow, he would have sent her sprawling on the floor.

His ocean-blue eyes were stormy. Lauren knew it was childish, but she did not want to look away first. He held her gaze for a few long moments before turning on his heel and catching up with his legal team who were already outside on the front steps. The television cameras rushed Jake. He was one of the most newsworthy faces on the planet these days.

Ryan continued to hold Lauren's arm gingerly as he led her out the side door of the lobby. The courthouse reporters were so preoccupied with Jake that Lauren and Ryan slipped away unnoticed.

"What a jerk," Ryan seethed.

Lauren nodded, dark ideas invading her thoughts. As Liz took her last breaths, had she known she was about to die at the hands of the man who had promised to love, cherish, and honor her?

Majerle's was a nearby sports bar where prosecutors often convened after work. Candace was entertaining a small crowd of admirers with ribald jokes when Lauren and Ryan arrived.

Kyle casually touched Candace's back as he steered her into the dark leather booth and Lauren wondered if the two were more than colleagues. Kyle was more than ten years younger than Candace, but they were both single and consenting. Lauren found herself hoping they were blowing off a little steam together on the side. It must be hard for them to make any time for themselves in the midst of this madness.

Lauren found herself musing again about Ryan's personal life. Despite the time they spent together, she knew little about his time away from work. Like the others at the table, this trial had been consuming his life. She stole a glance at him. His thick dark lashes framed his aqua eyes, which crinkled as he laughed at one of Candace's inappropriate jokes. He was a good-looking decent man; of course he probably had a woman in his life.

Kyle gestured at the television. Coverage of the trial was the top story on the news nearly every night. The restaurant crowd hushed as the television anchor began discussing the case. There was grainy coverage of Lauren stumbling into Jake in the courthouse lobby and Jake shoving her roughly away. A news photographer had captured the incident through a dirty window.

Candace grinned. "This is priceless. Jake's true colors shining through. I'm sure every juror has already heard about it, even though they're 'sequestered.'" She used her fingers to put air quotes around the word. Candace remained skeptical about the objectivity of the jury members. Rumor had it that Juror Number Six was already writing a book.

Candace raised her glass to Lauren. "To your killer heels. That little stumble of yours may have just won us this entire case."

Chapter Forty-three

(Friday, September 15–Thursday, September 21)

"What time do you get off?" Ryan asked as they pulled into the hospital parking lot.

Is he asking me out? Lauren wondered, noticing a warm tingling sensation at the prospect.

"My shift ends at midnight, but I often work later depending on how busy it is. And weekend nights usually get pretty crazy."

"I can be here by midnight to give you a ride. Or I can stay later if you have to work longer."

"I can catch a ride from one of the other interns," Lauren insisted. "I'm pretty sure your professional escort assignment doesn't extend to weekend duty."

"This time, I was offering as a friend." He smiled.

"That's thoughtful of you, but I can catch a ride with Ritesh. He lives near me."

"Okay, if you're sure…" he let his words trail.

"I'm sure," she said, suddenly not feeling sure at all. Had she just declined a date or a polite offer made out of a sense of obligation? Was he disappointed or relieved?

"Okay, have a good weekend."

And that was the last she heard from Ryan until he arrived to drive her to court on Monday morning.

Candace had saved Wallace for last, calling him to wrap up the entire police case with a pretty bow for the jury. Wallace was an experienced witness, not easily rattled on the stand.

Wallace's immediate impression upon arriving on the scene was this was a homicide staged to look like a burglary. The jewelry chest in the master bedroom was left with drawers hanging open, but nothing else in the house had been disturbed. A Rolex watch was still visible on a dresser in the same bedroom. There was no evidence of forced entry into the home.

Wallace testified Jake Wakefield had demonstrated considerable self-confidence during his initial police interview along with an unusual display of emotion. While Jake had made sobbing noises throughout the interview, Wallace testified he had seen no tears. The rapidity with which Jake alternated between weeping and coherence made Wallace suspect Jake wasn't really crying at all.

Jake had been wearing a long-sleeved shirt despite the 114-degree temperature that day. On a hunch, Wallace had asked Jake to roll up his sleeves. Jake had hesitated before agreeing. Detectives had observed fresh scratches on Jake's right forearm. Candace introduced several police photographs of the scratches. The injuries were consistent with those that might result from someone engaged in a violent struggle.

Jake had refused to take a polygraph test on July twenty-fifth and had "lawyered up" at that time, making it impossible for the detectives to question him further. But that hadn't stopped Jake from calling the detectives to place the blame elsewhere.

Jake told detectives almost immediately that Lauren was the beneficiary of Liz's life insurance, insistent that Lauren might have killed Liz for the payout. A few days later, Jake had called the detectives to report Lauren was spending money lavishly and had purchased an expensive new car. And the day after Jake had given Lauren the diamond ring, he had called the police to report he had spotted her wearing one of Liz's stolen rings.

This accusation prompted the search of Lauren's apartment. They had tested every pair of her shoes for Liz's blood and found none, did a forensic examination of her computer which revealed nothing suspicious, and looked for a possible murder weapon, finding nothing. Detective Wallace emphasized they had absolutely no reason to suspect Lauren other than allegations instigated by Jake.

On cross-examination, Pratt forced Wallace to acknowledge that the expensive antique diamond ring had been found in Lauren's apartment. Pratt also accused Wallace of a rush to judgment regarding Jake's guilt, therefore failing to investigate other leads. But ironically, Jake's accusations had forced the police to investigate Lauren with comparable intensity, which Wallace pointed out. Pratt then delighted in belaboring the investigative efforts that had focused on Lauren.

"Isn't it possible that the real killer had been after Elizabeth Wakefield's jewelry specifically?" Pratt demanded.

Wallace offered a measured response. "I suppose that's a possibility, but I don't know of any burglars that would overlook an expensive Rolex watch sitting out in the open."

"Unless the female perpetrator wanted only women's jewelry she could later wear?" Pratt sneered.

"Was there a question for me in there or were you just planning to testify for me?" Wallace asked. Scattered laughter followed.

"Isn't it true that deep scratches were also found on the upper arm of Lauren Rose shortly after the crime?" Pratt asked.

"Yes, but those were unrelated to the crime."

"How can you be so certain?"

"None of Lauren Rose's DNA was found underneath Liz Wakefield's fingernails. The blood and skin tissue found there belonged solely to Jake Wakefield. Additionally, Dr. Rose was able to provide a credible explanation for the scratches on her arm."

"And what was that explanation?"

"She had been scratched by a combative patient."

"And you have a witness to this?"

"No, there were no witnesses."

"You must have spoken to the patient?"

"Yes, we did."

"And the patient admitted to scratching her?"

"He said he might have."

"He said he *might* have?" Pratt asked sarcastically.

"He had been driving under the influence and he resisted Dr. Rose's medical blood draw because he feared she was taking a legal sample. He admits he may have scratched her, but he can't remember because his blood alcohol level was 0.232. He has no memory for most of that evening."

"How convenient for Miss Rose," Pratt said.

"It would have been much more convenient if he remembered scratching her."

Wallace was forced to admit they never found bloody shoes or clothes belonging to Jake, but Wallace postulated Jake disposed of both the clothing and murder weapon on the way to the airport. "There are at least nine dozen dumpsters between the Wakefield home and the airport."

"And did you search those dumpsters?"

"With countless potential dumping places? No, we didn't attempt to search every dumpster in the Phoenix metropolitan area."

Pratt pushed on. "Are you aware Lauren Rose has access to fresh scrubs at her hospital?"

"Naturally. She's a doctor."

"Isn't it possible Miss Rose wore hospital scrubs, cap, and booties to commit the crime and returned those items to the hospital laundry where blood-stained scrubs wouldn't attract any attention?"

"Almost anything is *possible*. It's possible I'll win the lottery tomorrow, but I haven't quit my day job."

More laughter in the gallery.

A vein on Pratt's forehead began to visibly pulse. "Objection. Nonresponsive."

Judge Robles looked over his glasses at Wallace. Wallace had testified in Robles' courtroom on several previous occasions and the two men were friendly with one another, but neither man showed signs of familiarity now. "Sustained. The witness is reminded to limit his responses to the questions posed by counsel."

"Detective Wallace, isn't it possible Miss Rose wore hospital scrubs and booties to commit the crime and returned those soiled items discreetly to the hospital laundry room?" Pratt asked again.

"I can't answer that. I have no idea."

Pratt continued with a different line of questioning, "What evidence do you have that Jake Wakefield gave this ring to Lauren Rose?" He thrust the bagged ring under Wallace's nose.

"Dr. Rose told us that is how she came in possession of it."

"And you took her at her word?"

"We have no evidence that Dr. Rose was deceptive with us."

"Didn't she fail a polygraph in this case?"

"Objection, inadmissible," Candace raged.

"Sustained." But the jurors had already heard the damaging question.

Pratt grinned like the Cheshire cat. "Isn't it possible Lauren Rose came in possession of the ring when she murdered her sister and stole her jewelry?"

"That's not what the evidence shows."

"So you have proof that Lauren Rose did not kill her sister, Elizabeth?"

"We have alibi witnesses confirming Dr. Rose was at work for the entire evening on July twenty-third. We have absolutely nothing to implicate her."

Pratt grinned broadly. "Nothing except for an extravagant ring that Miss Rose coveted since the day it was given to her sister by Jake Wakefield?"

"Only if the ring was really stolen at the time of the crime and I only have Jake Wakefield's word about that, which doesn't mean much because he has lied and stonewalled so many times."

"Detective Wallace, did you personally witness Miss Rose take possession of the ring?" Pratt asked.

"No."

"So it's possible that Miss Rose stole the ring from Elizabeth Wakefield's jewelry box?"

"Anything is possible, but using that logic, there are a lot of pawn shop owners that should be considered suspects in robberies because they come in possession of stolen property all of the time."

Pratt attempted to discredit Wallace one final time, "Detective Wallace, isn't it true you focused so exclusively on Jake Wakefield that you ignored credible evidence that might exonerate him, including evidence implicating Lauren Rose?"

Detective Wallace responded decisively. "That is patently untrue. This investigation took seventy-five days, two full-time detectives, several criminalists, countless other police officers, and more than twenty-four hundred man hours to complete. This was an exhaustive, careful, and cautious investigation and all of the resulting evidence points squarely at Mr. Wakefield."

"I guess, you have to believe your own theory," Pratt said.

"Because it's based on the facts," Wallace retorted, but Judge Robles was already admonishing Pratt for making speeches in the courtroom.

Chapter Forty-four

(Thursday, September 21)

Detective Wallace agreed to join the others for happy hour to celebrate his performance on the stand. Wallace had recently been featured on the cover of *People* magazine. Ryan teased him mercilessly about his celebrity status. Wallace accepted the ribbing good-naturedly, but he clearly despised the attention being showered upon him. He steered the prosecutors onto the topic of the Defense team, which was relatively easy to do because skewering the Defense was one of their favorite pastimes.

Kyle did an excellent impression of Fisher, pretending to buff his fingernails while holding a press conference. Candace joined in with an impression of Pratt sputtering indignant diatribes to the judge. Lauren produced a spot-on impression of Jake, admiring his World Series ring and bemoaning the fact that this "pesky little murder trial is interfering with my pursuit of scandalous women." With a general consensus that they had gained a significant advantage in the case, the mood was light.

Afterwards, Ryan drove Lauren to Good Samaritan for her six o'clock start time. She asked him to pick her up at the hospital the next morning because she was pulling call that evening.

"Are those on-call rooms how they show them on television?" Ryan teased.

"Hardly. Ever notice how all of the doctors on television programs are young, hot, and have time for their personal lives?"

"You're young and hot and would have time for a personal life if you weren't attending this bleeping trial."

Heat flushed her cheeks. "I can assure you those shows are unrealistic. They depict a lot of sex in on-call rooms, but if you offered a real resident a choice between sex and sleep, I'm pretty sure they'd choose sleep every time." As soon as the words escaped her lips, she wished she could rescind them.

Ryan smiled. "I guess it's a lot like police work. Too much work, not enough time. Why do people take these jobs?"

"The fame and fortune?"

They shared a laugh.

"Speaking of fame and fortune, they aren't going to call you to testify at all?" she asked.

"Nah. Wallace has a lot more experience on the stand. Besides, Candace is worried the Defense would try to discredit me because I've spent so much time with you."

"I feel terrible. I didn't know it was going to mean you wouldn't be able to testify."

"Because testifying is such a treat? I should be thanking you. You've saved me from one of Pratt's scathing cross-examinations. Besides, I enjoy being your designated driver. It's the most pleasant part of my day."

"Mine too," Lauren responded instantly. Both the trial and her work were stressful. The times she spent in Ryan's car were the most relaxing waking moments she had.

"The Defense would have been right anyway."

"Right about what?" Lauren asked, confused.

"I'm not impartial about you anymore. I haven't been for a long time."

Lauren considered the magnitude of his words. It had been more than a year since she been abruptly dumped by Michael and her fledgling relationship with Jake had never even taken off. She had declined several efforts by LaRhonda to set her up. Even hearing that Michael had recently married Darcy had not upset her much. She had been too busy to miss dating.

Lost in thought, Lauren wasn't sure how to respond.

Ryan pulled into the side entrance of the hospital and broke the silence. "See you in the morning…" he said, exactly as he always did.

She smiled cheerfully. "Great. See you then." As she opened the employee door, she turned to wave, but Ryan's sedan was already disappearing around the corner.

Chapter Forty-five

(Friday, September 22)

Lauren had tossed and turned all night thinking about what Ryan had said and kicking herself for the way she had handled it. Why hadn't she told him how grateful she had been for his support or how much she enjoyed his company? She ruminated about how her silence must have sounded like a deafening rejection to him. How he must have been eager to escape when he pulled away so quickly.

As she waited outside on a hospital bench for him to pick her up the following morning, she agonized about what she could say to fix the situation. She had stopped by the hospital cafeteria to purchase some pastries and clutched the white bakery bag in her sweaty palm. Ryan pulled up punctually. He would try to get out of the car to open her door for her if she didn't beat him to it so she jogged toward the sedan in her pencil skirt and high heels. As she did so, she stepped on an out of place landscaping rock. She lost her balance and threw out her arms in a desperate attempt to prevent a fall, wobbling back and forth before regaining her balance. Ryan watched from the car with alarm. To mask her embarrassment, she dipped into an elaborate bow with a flourish of her arms. She could hear the welcome sound of Ryan's laughter when she opened the car door.

"That was quite the performance."

"Thanks, I've been practicing in all of my spare time."

Lauren saw he had a Starbucks drink waiting for her, flooding with relief that he didn't appear to be upset with her.

"Thanks for the chai tea. That is exactly what the doctor ordered, both literally and figuratively. Bear claw?" she offered. He raised one eyebrow suspiciously and accepted the pastry.

Lauren's mind was racing about what she should say, but Ryan spoke first. "Candace plans to rest the Prosecution's case soon. Who do you think the Defense will call as their first witness?" They slipped easily into their usual dialogue about trial proceedings and Lauren lost her resolve to finish the conversation they had started yesterday. Maybe she had been reading too much into things. The tension she had feared did not exist and not wishing to stir any up, she decided to let the matter drop.

At the courthouse, there was more media pandemonium than usual. Television reporters were preparing sound bites, breathlessly speculating that the Prosecution would rest their case that day.

Candace called Wallace back for re-direct, hoping to keep him on the stand long enough to prevent the Defense from starting the presentation of their case that day. She wanted the jury to have time to contemplate the full magnitude of the Prosecution's case over the weekend.

"Detective Wallace, do you remember Mr. Pratt asking if you were able to prove that Dr. Rose was not involved in her sister's murder?"

"Yes, I remember."

"Can you tell us if that is how police investigations proceed?"

"I can tell you that is *not* how police investigations proceed. If police were required to prove everybody who did not commit the crime, we would be investigating the entire human population. However, we do try to eliminate all possible suspects until we narrow it down to the person responsible."

"And were you able to eliminate Dr. Rose as a possible suspect?"

"Yes. Dr. Rose has a reliable alibi. Several of her coworkers confirmed she was at work that evening. Additionally, Dr. Rose was fully cooperative with the investigation and provided consistent statements throughout."

Candace kept Wallace on the stand for as long as she could, wrapping up shortly before noon. Judge Robles recessed court for lunch.

The Prosecution team celebrated over Chinese take-out. They had presented a very strong case to the jury. They had not seen any Defense witnesses waiting in the courtroom lobby, suggesting the Defense would wait until Monday to call their first witness.

The conversation turned to the question of whether or not Jake would take the stand.

"Jake will insist on testifying," Lauren predicted. "He won't want to miss his moment in the spotlight."

"There isn't a snowball's chance in hell that Pratt will let Jake take the stand," Candace disagreed. "It's Defense 101. Never put the defendant on the stand."

The team made friendly bets on the issue. Ryan and Lauren betting against Candace and Kyle. Wallace, who had joined them today, abstained, commenting he had been surprised by trial outcomes so often that he no longer cared to guess what might happen. Lauren wondered if the wrongful conviction of his father was one of the "surprising court outcomes" Wallace alluded to.

"Is Pratt ballsy enough to call Lauren to the stand?" Kyle wondered aloud.

"Nope," Candace said. "Pratt is many things, least of which is an arrogant asshole, but he isn't stupid. Lauren's a terrible risk for them. They couldn't break her on cross-exam last time and she would be unpredictable as hell. They won't call her."

Lauren let out an audible sigh of relief.

"Of course, we're still going to have to prep you this weekend, just in case," Candace cautioned. "It wouldn't be the first time I was surprised by this fucking trial. Maybe Pratt and Fisher forgot to take Defense 101."

"Fisher took Publicity 201 instead," Kyle said.

"And Pratt was probably in Smoke and Mirrors 302; the advanced course," Ryan commented.

"So, what's your best guess?" Wallace asked. "Do you think they'll call me back for more cross this afternoon?"

Candace pondered. "That's a tough one. On one hand, I know Pratt would be loath to allow us the last word before recessing for the weekend. On the other hand, you've already embarrassed him a few times. I can't imagine he cares to square off against you again."

But when court resumed that afternoon, Pratt did approach Wallace on the stand once more.

"Detective Wallace," Pratt said in a voice smooth as silk, "you testified this morning you could not absolutely prove that Miss Rose was not responsible for the murder of her sister, did you not?"

"That's not what I said. I can't prove that you didn't kill Liz Wakefield either. All I do is testify about the evidence and let the jury interpret the facts."

Despite the fact that Wallace had scored yet another embarrassing point against him, Pratt grinned. "You also testified you were able to verify Lauren Rose's alibi. Can you tell us how you did that?"

"Yes, we spoke to Dr. Rose's immediate supervisor, a man by the name of Dr. Matthew Stone. He was able to confirm that Dr. Rose had been at work that evening for her entire shift of noon to midnight and that she had stayed until about six-thirty a.m. because she was busy saving the life of a child."

Pratt glared at Wallace for plugging Lauren with his response, but did not object. "And Dr. Stone had visual contact on Miss Rose for the entire evening?"

"Not the entire time, but they interacted frequently throughout the night."

"Detective Wallace, have you spent much time in hospital emergency rooms?"

"Yes, I'm afraid I have spent far too much time in emergency rooms."

"Is it fair to say ERs tend to be busy places?"

"Yes."

"And the people that work there tend to be busy people?"

"Yes."

"So, isn't it fair to believe that Miss Rose could have departed the hospital for a short period of time undetected by her supervisor?"

"Long enough to use the restroom or make a quick personal call? I would imagine so, but I doubt very much she had time to leave the ER, drive across town, commit a vicious murder, and return to the hospital without her absence being detected by somebody."

"You doubt it, but you don't know for sure because you weren't there, Detective Wallace."

"No, I wasn't and neither were you, Mr. Pratt. We have no eye witnesses to the crime, so we have to rely on the evidence, which implicates Jake Wakefield, not Dr. Rose."

"That's how you chose to interpret the evidence, but other possible interpretations do exist."

"Any logical person would draw the same conclusion. I believe these jurors are logical people, who will interpret the evidence accurately."

"Have you ever misinterpreted evidence, Detective Wallace?"

"Not that I'm aware of."

"Really?" Pratt asked incredulously. "I find it hard to believe that in all of your years of service, thirty-five years all together as you told us in your earlier testimony, that you've never made a mistake."

"I didn't say I've never made a mistake. We all make mistakes. But, to the best of my knowledge, I've never arrested the wrong person."

Pratt smirked, "Until now."

"Objection." Candace was on her feet. "Defense counsel is attempting to provide his own testimony in this courtroom."

"Sustained."

"I will withdraw the remark," Pratt offered. "No more questions for this witness."

"The witness is excused." Candace beamed at Wallace as he descended the stand and departed the courtroom. "On behalf of the people of the State of Arizona, the Prosecution rests, Your Honor."

The reporters in the courtroom began feverishly typing into their portable telecommunications devices. This was breaking news. After nearly a month of testimony, the State's case against superstar Jake Wakefield rested.

Pratt said, "Your Honor, at this time, the Defense would like to call Lauren Rose as a witness."

Candace was outraged. "The Defense did not advise Dr. Rose they intended to call her today."

"Your Honor, we did not anticipate the Prosecution would rest their case today," Pratt said. "We don't wish to delay the court proceedings. We are very mindful of the sacrifices this jury is making during their sequestration and we wish to get these jurors home as soon as possible. We would be pleased to open the Defense case today if you will allow us to call Miss Rose."

One couldn't help but admire the extent of Pratt's wily ways. Candace was now in a bind. If she protested, it would appear as if she had no regard for the jurors and as if Lauren needed protection. If she did not, she would be sending Lauren into the lions' den without any preparation. She asked for, and was granted, permission to consult the witness. Candace beckoned for Lauren to approach the Prosecution table and then whispered. "Are you ready for this?"

Lauren felt sick to her stomach. Candace and Kyle had been planning to prepare her over the weekend for the possibility the Defense might call her as a witness, which everybody thought unlikely. Now it was a grim reality. The Defense had an urgent need to make Lauren look guilty. They were clearly prepared to pull out all the stops to make that happen. Lauren's mind raced. What could she possibly say that wouldn't make her look suspicious to the jury? "I'm ready as I'll ever be."

Chapter Forty-six

(Friday, September 22)

After Lauren was sworn in, Pratt approached like a cat about to pounce. Lauren's heart was thumping so loudly, she worried the jurors might hear it.

"Good afternoon, Miss Rose," Pratt said chummily. The Defense team never addressed Lauren by her medical title.

"Good afternoon."

"You are the younger sister of Elizabeth Wakefield, correct?"

Lauren would soon be older than Liz had ever been. Because of the murder, she would reach ages Liz had never reached. "Yes."

"Liz enjoyed more financial success than you did?"

"Liz had more money than most people, including me."

"Do you think it's fair to say Liz was prettier than you?"

Candace objected, but Judge Robles overruled it, forcing Lauren to answer the offensive question. "Absolutely. Liz was very beautiful."

"And Liz enjoyed more romantic success than you, didn't she?" Pratt was warming up now.

"Everybody used to think that before they found out what a monster Jake is," Lauren responded.

"Did you think Jake Wakefield was a monster when you began spending time with him last September, two months after your sister's death?"

Candace had believed the Defense would not want to introduce this evidence. Candace had been wrong.

Lauren resisted the urge to squirm in her seat. "No. I believed we were both grieving for Liz. That was before I knew he killed my sister and then tried to frame me for her murder." She looked directly at Jake, who refused to meet her gaze. She hoped the jury noticed.

"You admit you became friendly with your sister's husband very shortly after her death? It sounds to me like you were hoping to step into your sister's expensive shoes."

"I was grieving and Jake made me feel like he genuinely cared about me. He created that illusion for many people, including my sister."

"Isn't it true you entered the words 'deaths from traumatic injuries' into the search engine of your home computer on the twenty-second of July?"

"I don't remember the exact date, but I did enter those search terms. I'm an emergency medicine resident and I was conducting research for..."

Pratt interrupted. "And you did another Google search on July twenty-second with the search term 'causes of death'?"

"I needed the information for my job because..."

Pratt interrupted again. "Miss Rose, isn't it true you were having some financial strain at the time of your sister's death?"

"No. That is not true."

Pratt moved to enter documents into evidence. After doing so, he handed one to Lauren. "Can you identify this for the jury?"

"That's my student loan statement."

"And how much money does it say you owe?"

"This one is a few months old so I owe less now, but this statement reflects a balance of one hundred sixteen thousand, eight hundred twelve dollars."

"One hundred sixteen thousand, eight hundred twelve dollars?" Pratt asked with exaggerated shock. "Isn't that a small fortune in student loan debt?"

194 Leslie Dana Kirby

"It's not uncommon for medical students to owe such amounts."

"So you don't feel like this is a large debt?"

"It is a large debt, but not one I can't reasonably pay off over time."

There was a commotion at the Defense table. A heavyset man in khaki pants and a polo shirt was whispering animatedly to Fisher. Pratt became aware of the disruption and returned to the Defense table where both Fisher and the stranger murmured to him excitedly, Jake listening in with a smile.

Pratt turned back to Lauren with a gleam in his eye.

"Miss Rose, will you please tell the court where you were between the hours of seven and eleven p.m. on the evening of July twenty-third last year?"

"I was at work at Good Samaritan Hospital."

"For that entire period of time?"

"Yes."

"What hours were you there that evening?"

"My shift started at noon so I got there around 11:45 in the morning. And my shift ended at midnight, but I was busy with an important case so I didn't leave until about six-thirty in the morning."

"Don't you get a dinner break?"

"We eat if and when we can find the time in between patients. There's a cafeteria in the hospital and vending machines. The nurses almost always have baked goods lying around. We don't practice the healthiest eating habits."

Several people in the courtroom chuckled.

"Do you remember if you ate on the evening of July twenty-third?"

"I snacked here and there, but I never sat down and ate a real meal. We were too busy that night."

"So you didn't leave the hospital at all that night, is that correct?"

"That's correct."

"The Defense would like to introduce into evidence a video-tape from the hospital filmed that evening."

Candace shot to her feet. "Your Honor, may we approach the bench?"

The judge called a sidebar. Lauren could hear only bits and pieces of the conversation. She heard Candace fume, "This is an outrage!" Pratt was clearly impassioned as he gesticulated wildly with his hands.

While the minutes stretched long, Lauren wondered what could possibly be on the hospital videotape that would be of interest to the Defense. She was aware of only one video camera at the hospital. It had been placed in the waiting area to allow the triage nurses to keep an eye on waiting patients. Hospital security also monitored it as many ER patients were drunk, high, belligerent, or some combination of the three. Secretly, the interns also surveyed the video footage to divvy up patients, Ritesh angling to be the treating provider for any and all attractive female patients. For a fleeting moment, she wondered if the Defense might have video of the interns dishing about patients or otherwise acting unprofessionally, but that was unlikely because the only camera was in the waiting room. The remainder of the ER was not taped in order to protect patient privacy.

Growing bored while the lawyers bickered, Lauren attempted to make eye contact with the jurors. The Defense was desperately trying to convince the jury that Lauren was capable of murder and she wanted them to see this wasn't true. She wanted them to know she wasn't afraid to look them in the eye. But most of the jurors were either staring at the spectacle at the sidebar or doodling in their notepads. One appeared to be asleep.

She scanned the courtroom for a comfortable place to rest her eyes. Jake was leaning back in his chair, laughing and joking with the front row of spectators behind him, which included his parents and several reporters. Most people in the gallery were browsing their cell phones. Even Ryan had been using the downtime to check his phone, but he suddenly seemed to sense Lauren's discomfort. He glanced up at her, feeling alone and small on the witness stand, and he smiled reassuringly.

After more than twenty minutes, the huddle at the judge's bench broke up. Candace looked grim and even irrepressible Kyle looked deflated. Meanwhile, Pratt and Fisher exuded victory.

"Ladies and gentlemen of the jury," Judge Robles instructed, "the Defense has filed a motion to introduce newly discovered evidence, which they have only uncovered today. We will recess early today to allow the Prosecution time to review the evidence. We will make some approved movies available for you to watch at the hotel over the weekend. See you back on Monday morning."

Chapter Forty-seven

(Friday, September 22)

"Not here," Candace snapped when Lauren returned to the Prosecution table. Candace was slamming documents into boxes, stacking the boxes roughly on a rolling rack.

They walked in silence through the long tunnel to the county attorney's office. Several passing people greeted Candace, but she barely acknowledged them. Lauren raised her eyebrows at Ryan in a questioning manner. He shrugged his shoulders in response.

No sooner had they entered the war room than Candace slammed the door shut, rounded on Lauren, and shouted "Did you forget to tell us something about the night of your sister's murder?"

"What? No. I've told you everything. Why? What did they say?"

"It's not what they said, it's what they found. They say they have video footage of you leaving the hospital at 6:42 p.m. on July twenty-third. Please tell me that isn't true."

"It isn't true."

"We're about to find out." Candace pulled a labeled DVD out of one of the evidence boxes. "Fucking Pratt. I wonder how long he's been sitting on this little nugget. He claims their investigator only discovered it today. I told Robles the timing was suspiciously convenient. They just happened to find this footage right when they get you on the stand. I'll bet. Pratt's been hinting at a problem with your alibi throughout the entire trial. I thought he was just grandstanding for the jury. Until now." Like a freight engine that had picked up steam, Candace continued her diatribe as she slammed the disc into a media system set up in one corner of the room. When it failed to load, she gave the unit a sharp kick. The familiar DVD logo popped onscreen and Candace hit play.

The video display was grainy. The image depicted the waiting room at Good Samaritan. The time and date stamp were on the bottom left of the image; 23 July, 18:40. There was no sound. The silence was deafening as they watched for the next ninety seconds. At 18:42, Lauren entered the waiting room and departed through the automatic front doors at the entrance to the ER. Candace eyeballed Lauren. "That's you, right?"

"Yeah, that's me. Are we sure this thing is date-stamped correctly?" Lauren felt a pit in her stomach.

"They swear up and down the tape has been authenticated by the hospital security staff."

"That's weird because I don't even use that door. We have a staff entrance that leads out to the parking garage. Does it show me coming back in?"

They watched in stony silence for several more minutes, but the video Lauren did not return.

"I can't believe we didn't catch this ourselves," Candace was saying now in an accusatory tone directed at Ryan.

"Hold up, Candace," he responded calmly. "Lauren's telling us this is inaccurate and I believe her. We can call Dr. Stone to the stand to verify she was at the hospital all night if we have to. We have his statement to that effect on file."

"Yeah, but he wasn't with her every second of the night. The Defense is claiming that Lauren snuck out to kill Liz, and the ER is such a busy place nobody missed her."

"Anybody that's ever worked in an ER is going to know that's ludicrous," Lauren protested. "You can't go missing from your shift undetected. I have a pager. I have patients asking for me."

"Anybody that has any sort of job knows that," Ryan agreed.

"People are going to notice you're missing and come looking for you. And with technology today, you can always be found."

Candace was still seething. "It doesn't matter. The Defense just created reasonable doubt. Lauren already testified under oath that she didn't leave the hospital at all that night so they're going to make her out to be a liar."

"Wait," Lauren exclaimed, pointing to the video screen. "There I am again." Kyle had been fast-forwarding slowly through the tape. At 19:47, Lauren reappeared on the screen. She could be seen talking to a patient in the waiting room and handing her some forms on a clipboard.

Candace looked relieved. "What time does it show her coming back in the hospital?" But it didn't. Both times that Lauren appeared on screen, she entered the waiting room from the treatment area. She exited the hospital at 18:42 and was not seen again until 19:47 when she re-emerged from the treatment area. They forwarded through the rest of the footage, but saw no more images of Lauren for the remainder of the video, which ran through 09:00 on the morning of July twenty-fourth.

"Why doesn't it show you leaving after your shift?" Candace asked warily. "You got off at 6:30 that morning, correct?"

"Yes, but I left through the employee entrance. You can see reporters flooded the waiting room at around 6:15 that morning."

Ryan nodded in support. He well-knew that Lauren used the side entrance to come and go.

"Do you ever use the front entrance?" Candace asked.

"Not really. The side entrance is close to the doctors' lounge where we change into our scrubs, put our stuff in our lockers."

"But that's you on the tape, right?"

"Right."

"Is there any chance that's somebody that just looks like you?" Candace asked.

Lauren watched the footage again. "No, that's definitely me."

"Why did you leave the hospital through the front door that night still wearing your scrubs?" Candace demanded.

But Lauren only shook her head. "I don't think I did, but I can't remember that night clearly anymore. It was more than a year ago."

"But you told the police you didn't leave the hospital that night for any reason." ·

Ryan nodded again. "That's right, Candace. I remember asking her about it on July twenty-fourth. Do you remember what you said to me, Lauren?"

"I told you I didn't leave," Lauren said defensively.

"Easy. I was agreeing with you. You said that with utter conviction. You laughed when I suggested you might have ducked out for some reason. Remember?"

Lauren thought back to the first day she had met Ryan, who had still been Detective Boyd to her back then. She nodded.

"There must be something fishy with this video." Ryan said. "Let me get the forensics guys to look at it and see if it's been tampered with."

Lauren breathed a huge sigh of relief. Of course, Ryan must be right. Something must be wrong with the video.

Chapter Forty-eight

(Saturday, September 23–Monday, September 25)

But the forensics team found nothing wrong with the tape. The hospital camera was consistently taping with the correct date stamp and there was no indication the tapes had been tampered with.

Lauren spent many hours over the weekend preparing for her ongoing testimony. Candace played the role of Pratt and Kyle acted as Candace. After several grueling hours, Kyle gave a spot-on send-up of Candace when he lodged an objection to the imaginary judge in a Southern accent. Candace was not amused. "Straighten up. This isn't high school lunch hour. This fucking tape could unravel our entire case." She was barely speaking to Lauren except to try to cut her to pieces in her role as Pratt. It wasn't method acting.

Lauren held up well under Candace's relentless questioning. She plausibly denied being jealous of Liz. She responded to questions about her relationship with Jake in a calm and reasonable matter. She was tempted to try to lighten Candace's mood with a joke about Jake's penis size, but she didn't dare.

The only area in which Lauren's testimony fell apart was when it came to questions about the tape. In her role as Pratt, Candace asked repeatedly where Lauren was going when she left the front entrance of the ER. Lauren could only answer, "I honestly don't remember leaving that night at that time."

Candace exploded. "That isn't going to fly, Lauren. Do you want to hand them this case on a silver platter? Answer the goddamned question!"

"But that's the truth, Candace. Do you want me to lie? Do you want me to make something up? I can say I was going out to look at the stars. I can say that I stepped outside for a nip of vodka. I can even say I was leaving to go kill my sister if you want me to. Anything I say other than I can't remember is going to be a lie. It was more than a year ago. Do you remember what you were doing a year ago?"

After this outburst, Candace relented a bit. They agreed Lauren would respond she didn't remember leaving, but must have quickly returned through the staff entrance. Candace was still displeased, but conceded it would have to do.

Even though she was exhausted, Lauren did not sleep well on Sunday night. She should have collapsed into a dreamless sleep. Instead she had fitful nightmares about going to prison.

After running and showering, Lauren selected her outfit carefully in anticipation of being grilled on the stand. She dressed in a black skirt suit and simple black heels. She wore an emerald green blouse, which was Liz's favorite color. She pulled her hair back in a French twist. Now she looked more like a doctor than she did at work where she wore scrubs and a ponytail.

Ryan arrived promptly to pick her up. Ever the gentleman, he always insisted on parking the car and coming to her apartment door. Lauren made a point of always being ready to go as soon as he arrived. When she opened the door, he took one look at her and issued a low long whistle. "You look amazing."

"I figured I could at least try to look good."

"You're going to do fine."

"Candace doesn't seem to think so."

"Candace?" he said. "What does she know about testifying? She's never even done it herself."

He was trying to make Lauren laugh, but she could only manage a grimace. When she slipped into his dark car, she found a bear claw and an iced chai tea waiting for her.

"Thank you," she said, trying to smile to show her apprecia-
tion.

"I thought bear claws were the accepted currency of consola-
tion." So he had understood her earlier clumsy attempt with the
bear claws all along.

"There are some things even a bear claw can't fix."

"All you can do today is tell the truth as you know it. You
may even gain some credibility in the jury's eyes if you admit
you can't remember why you stepped out that door. It was over a
year ago now. They're going to understand that. The video shows
you were already back to work when you reappear an hour later."

"Maybe or maybe they're going to conclude I used that hour
to speed to Liz's house, off her in a fit of jealousy, and rush back
to the hospital to resume healing perfect strangers."

"If you did that, then why wouldn't you make up something
better about why you were exiting the hospital? Something better
than you don't remember? All you can do is tell the truth."

Lauren nodded feebly, saying nothing. They made the rest of
the trip in suspended silence, Lauren steeling herself for what
was about to come.

Court convened at nine o'clock.

"Ms. Keene, I assume the State had ample time to review the
proposed evidence?" the judge asked.

"Yes, Your Honor, but I still object to the introduction of this
video into evidence. I have reason to believe the Defense knew
about these videotapes long before they turned them over to us."

Judge Robles excused the jury from the courtroom so he
could hear arguments about the Defense's motion to introduce
the video recordings into evidence.

Pratt acknowledged they had been in possession of the tape
for several weeks. "However, my team has been so inundated
with tips that it has taken us an inordinate amount of time to
sort through all of the evidence we have collected. We were
unaware of the significance of these tapes until moments before
we moved to introduce them into evidence."

"And I call bullshit," Candace retorted. "Isn't it convenient you just happened to discover these tapes right after Dr. Rose testified she hadn't left the hospital, with your investigator rushing in to do his Oscar-worthy acting job? You've been hinting for weeks that you planned to refute Dr. Rose's alibi. You knew about these tapes and you intentionally concealed them from the Prosecution. It's professional misconduct. You could be disbarred for such offenses."

"I could, if your baseless accusations were true. I was as surprised as you were when my investigator told me what he found on those tapes on Friday afternoon."

The battle raged for ten minutes before Judge Robles ruled the recordings would be introduced into evidence, reminding Candace she could appeal his ruling to a higher court for immediate review if she chose to do so. While the Prosecution might win the appeal, it would come at the cost of pissing off Robles for the remainder of the trial.

Candace stood up perfectly straight. "I elect not to appeal Your Honor's ruling, but I do intend to file a complaint of misconduct against Mr. Pratt with the Arizona Bar Association."

"So noted for the record," Robles answered.

The jury filed back into the courtroom and Lauren was recalled to the stand.

"Dr. Rose, you are still under oath," Robles reminded her. Lauren's cheeks grew hot. He said this to all witnesses when they resumed the stand, but Lauren could not help but feel Judge Robles knew she had been contemplating lying during her testimony today.

"Good morning, Miss Rose," Pratt said with unforced cheerfulness.

"Good morning."

"Do you remember testifying under oath that you were at work during the hours of 11:45 a.m. on July twenty-third to 6:30 a.m. on July twenty-fourth?"

"Yes."

"And do you remember testifying under oath that you did not leave the hospital during those hours for any reason?"

"Yes."

"Your Honor, at this time, the Defense requests permission to play a portion of a video recording from Exhibit Seventy-Four A."

"Permission granted."

Pratt made an elaborate show of taking the disc from its evidence sleeve and putting it into the courtroom DVD player. It was cued to right where it had been yesterday.

"Miss Rose, can you tell the members of this court where this room is located, please?"

"That is the waiting room for the ER at Good Samaritan Hospital, where I work."

"And will you read the date and time stamp for the record please?"

"It says twenty-three July, 18:40."

Using a remote control, Pratt pushed the play button. Lauren watched over a minute of footage before she saw the image of herself enter the waiting room on the screen.

Pratt paused the tape.

"Miss Rose, do you recognize this person?" Pratt flourished a red laser pointer at the screen, landing squarely on her own head in the image.

"Yes, that's me."

Pratt pushed play again and Lauren saw her video self exit through the electronic ER doors.

"And what do you see yourself doing here?" Pratt asked as the video showed Lauren leaving the hospital building. A buzz of excited whispering filled the courtroom.

"I'm going through a set of doors."

"And can you tell this court where those doors lead?" he asked with evident delight.

"To the ER entrance of the hospital," Lauren responded.

"Outside, you mean?"

"Yes."

"And for the record, can you read the date and time stamp aloud, please?"

"It says twenty-three July, 18:42."

"So this video shows you leaving the hospital at 6:42 p.m. on July twenty-third, isn't that right?"

"No, it shows me leaving the ER, not the hospital grounds," Lauren responded with an internal surge of defiance. "I stepped out to get my coat out of my car because I was cold."

Pratt, who had been pacing as he questioned Lauren, stopped in his tracks and did an abrupt about-face to square off against Lauren.

"Because you were cold?" he asked, his voice dripping with sarcasm. "On July twenty-third in Phoenix?"

"Yes. They keep the thermostat quite low in the ER because low environmental temperatures are beneficial for many traumatic injuries including crush injuries, near-drowning, and fevers. The temperature is…"

Pratt interrupted. "And you just happened to have a coat in your car?"

"I had left my lab coat in the car so I stepped out for a moment to retrieve it."

"And you chose to leave through the main entrance?"

"It was the closest door and it was an outdoor route that would allow me to defrost a little bit."

"And you just happened to have your car keys handy?"

"No. I didn't lock my car."

"You didn't lock your car? In downtown Phoenix?"

"I never used to lock my car. I grew up in a small town where we never locked our cars or house."

"Phoenix is hardly a small town, is it?"

"No, it's not."

"And before you moved to Phoenix, I believe you lived in Los Angeles?"

"Yes, in Westwood."

"And I suppose you didn't feel the need to lock your doors in Los Angeles either?"

"Not unless I left something valuable in my car."

"Something like your lab coat, you mean?"

"My lab coat? No. Nobody other than a doctor would want a lab coat and most doctors already have one of their own."

"So, if we were to go out to your brand new Acura in the courthouse parking lot, we would find your car doors unlocked?"

"My car isn't brand new anymore and it's not in the parking lot, but I do lock my doors now."

"So last year, you were a trusting naïve small-town girl, but now at the ripe old age of twenty-six, you started locking your doors?"

Candace jumped to her feet to object, but Lauren was burning to respond so she blurted out her answer, "Yeah, I stopped trusting people when I found out my sister was murdered by her own husband."

Candace grinned as she resumed her seat without voicing her objection.

As Pratt's direct examination continued throughout the morning, he challenged Lauren about the scratches to her arm to which she explained that she had been injured by a drunken patient. He pointed out that the videotape could not account for her whereabouts for more than an hour. Lauren responded she had been treating patients in the treatment area where cameras were prohibited. He questioned her about her purchase of an expensive new car shortly after Liz's death. Lauren responded her decade-old car had suffered a catastrophic engine failure. She testified to making the payments on her own, demonstrating she had not needed Liz's insurance money to afford the new car.

Pratt asked, "Why did you insist on identifying Elizabeth's body yourself?"

"What? I didn't insist on that. Jake asked me to do it. He said he couldn't handle it himself. Seeing my sister like that still haunts me. If I knew then what I know now, I never would have done it. Jake could have gone and identified her savaged body himself."

Pratt did ask Lauren to do one thing that puzzled her. He handed her a hammer and a pillow and ask her to hit the pillow with the hammer several times. Candace objected, but was overruled.

Lauren tapped the hammer lightly against the pillow several times and stopped. Pratt seemed disappointed, but he simply took the props away and proceeded with a different line of questioning.

When court finally recessed for lunch, Pratt was red in the face. *He looks discouraged*, Lauren realized, feeling satisfied. With Jake's assistance, Pratt had attacked her with vicious allegations. But Lauren had held her own. Today's testimony had bolstered, rather than diminished, Lauren's sense of self-confidence. She had entered the coliseum as the bull and had, against all odds, defeated the matador.

Chapter Forty-nine

(Monday, September 25)

Candace said nothing as she packed up her documents. The walk back to the war room was long and solemn.

As soon as they entered the war room and secured the door behind them, Candace let out a whoop. Kyle clapped Lauren on the back, and Ryan gave her a one-armed squeeze. Lauren caught a whiff of his cologne, an intoxicating combination reminiscent of pine trees and ocean breezes.

"Lauren, you let me worry all weekend, but you really pulled it out of your ass," Candace said. "That bit about going outside to warm up and fetch your coat from your car was sheer brilliance. Very believable."

"It was the truth," Lauren answered.

Candace's face betrayed her doubts.

"That's exactly why I went out those doors." Lauren persisted with a fierce determination to convince them all she was telling the truth. "When Pratt showed me the tape today, my memory finally clicked in. I suddenly got painfully cold that night so I ducked out of the ER through the closest door, knowing I would defrost outside. I'm pretty sure if you look at the image of me when I reappear on the screen an hour later, you'll find I'm wearing my lab coat."

Candace pulled out their copy of the video. "Isn't it interesting they had the time to dub us a copy and label it for us even though they supposedly discovered this footage moments before they brought it into court?" Candace commented while she fast-forwarded to the designated time on the time stamp.

They watched intently. At 6:42 p.m., Lauren departed the ER in her scrubs. When she re-emerged from the treatment area for the second time at 7:47 p.m., she was wearing her white lab coat.

"It was right there in front of us this whole time," Candace said. "Listen, Lauren, I'm sorry I gave you so much grief over this. I've never had my work so scrutinized. Idiots on the national news picking apart my performance and relishing in finding fault with me. And not just the way I'm prosecuting the case, but my hair, my suits, my shoes. It's driving me crazy. Can I plead temporary insanity?"

All was forgiven. Candace had given up so much of her personal life in her impassioned quest to secure justice for Liz.

Local restaurants donated lunches to the Prosecution team every day. "Apparently, there are some folks out there who support us," Candace observed.

"Either that or they're hoping we will plug their restaurant when we win this case," Kyle offered.

Today, they found several platters of Japanese food awaiting them. Lauren's favorite. As they enjoyed their meal of miso soup, salad, and several artfully prepared sushi rolls, they rehashed the battle of wits between Pratt and Lauren. The others unanimously declared Lauren the victor.

"What was the deal with that strange pillow exhibit?" Lauren asked. "Did Pratt think I would beat the living daylights out of the pillow until feathers flew everywhere and he could jump up and shout 'Aha' like Perry Mason?"

Candace laughed. "I think he was hoping you would use your left hand to hold the hammer so he could shout 'Aha' like Perry Mason. Shouldn't Jake have been able to tell him whether you were right-handed or left-handed?"

"Jake was too busy trying to frame me for his own crime to notice which hand I was using. Funny thing though, if Pratt had given me a golf club, I would have swung left-handed. I'm ambidextrous."

"Your golf clubs were on the search inventory list." Candace said as she rifled through her courtroom file box, pulling out a list of all of the things that had been confiscated from Lauren's apartment during the search. "One set of left-handed women's golf clubs. That must have made Pratt think you were left-handed. He must have been surprised and disappointed when you picked up that heavy hammer with your right hand."

It reminds me of an old joke." Although Lauren did not often tell jokes, she geared up to share this one. "After attending her first bullfight, a woman ate dinner at a nearby restaurant. She noticed the man at the next table was enjoying a delicious-looking dish topped with two big juicy meatballs. She asked the waiter for the dish, but he said it was a bullfight special called Espagueti Testiculos and only one could be served each evening because it was made with the testicles of the defeated bull. So she skipped the bullfight the following evening in order to be the first to order the Espagueti Testiculos. Her mouth watered in anticipation, but when her order came out, she was disappointed to find a plate of spaghetti topped with two shrunken meatballs. 'Waiter,' she complained, 'this isn't what I ordered. I wanted the same dish you served that gentleman last night.'"

"'But madam,' the waiter responded, 'the bull does not always lose.'"

Already in a punch-drunk mood resulting from weeks of intense stress, cumulative sleep deprivation, and the elation of the morning's victory, the others roared with laughter.

Chapter Fifty

(Monday, September 25)

Perhaps Pratt had gotten some sort of pep talk over lunch or maybe Jake had pumped him up with a fresh set of false accusations against Lauren. Whatever the case, Pratt looked rejuvenated. He dispensed with any niceties and launched immediately into quick-fire questions intended to rattle Lauren.

"I am going to ask you a series of yes-no questions and I would like you to respond with a simple yes or no answer. Is that clear?"

"No," Lauren responded.

"No? No? You don't understand?"

"No."

"Let me get this straight. You are a medical doctor with an advanced degree, but you are unable to comprehend the basic principle of answering questions with a simple yes or no?"

"Yes."

"Yes what?"

"Yes, I am unable to comprehend your request."

The vein in Pratt's forehead throbbed. He clearly wanted to explode on Lauren. She wished he would. Lawyers love to try to make witnesses lose their temper because it undermines their credibility. Wouldn't it be great if she could turn the tables on Pratt?

"Your Honor," Pratt whined. "Will you please counsel the witness?"

"Dr. Rose," Judge Robles said sternly, but Lauren detected a twinkle in his eyes. "Please do your best to answer Mr. Pratt's questions with a simple yes or no response."

"I would be happy to if Mr. Pratt asks simple yes or no questions," Lauren answered sweetly.

"Thank you, Your Honor," Pratt said as if the judge had just solved the problem of world hunger.

Pratt resumed glaring at Lauren. "Wasn't your sister, Elizabeth, more successful than you?"

"No."

"Wasn't she wealthier than you?"

"Yes."

"Didn't you feel like your sister was prettier than you?"

"Yes."

"Wasn't your sister more famous than you? Uh, at the time of her death, I mean."

"Yes."

"Isn't it true you were jealous of your sister?"

"About some things, yes."

"Were you the sole beneficiary of Elizabeth's life insurance?"

"Yes."

"Did you receive the million dollar payout, yes or no?"

"Yes."

"Isn't it true that within two months of your sister's death, you bought yourself a brand new Acura?"

"Yes."

"And shortly after your sister's death, you began to spend personal time with your sister's husband?"

"Yes."

"And, after your sister's death, you slept over at her house?"

"Once."

"Isn't it true you asked Mr. Wakefield if you could wear some of your sister's clothes?"

"Once, so I could go running because I didn't have any exercise clothes with me."

"Isn't it true you attended several of Mr. Wakefield's baseball games?"

"At his invitation."

"Isn't it true you called Jake Wakefield frequently in the weeks following your sister's death?"

"Yes."

"Would it surprise you to learn you called him at least fifty-four times between July twenty-third and October fourteenth?"

"How many times did he call me during the same time frame?"

Pratt exploded in a narcissistic fit of fury. "I ask the questions and you answer them, is that clear?"

Judge Robles was not amused. "Mr. Pratt, it is not your job to correct the witness. You may take the issue up with me and I will counsel the witness, is that clear?"

"Yes, Your Honor."

"Dr. Rose," the judge said. "I understand that answering complex questions with a simple answer can be challenging for all of us at times, but I do ask you to limit your responses."

"Yes, Your Honor."

"You may continue, Mr. Pratt," Robles instructed.

Pratt stood staring at Lauren momentarily, trying to remember where he was. Several journalists would later report that Pratt had attempted to stare down his first witness.

"Would it surprise you to learn you texted Jake Wakefield ninety-eight times between the dates of July twenty-third and October fourteenth?"

"No."

Pratt made a show of introducing Lauren's cell phone records into evidence and having Lauren confirm all of the times that Jake's phone number appeared. Lauren knew the following page of the same cell phone bill would show how many times Jake had called her, but Pratt didn't seem interested in asking about that.

"Isn't it fair to say you were obsessed with Jake Wakefield during that time period?"

How do I answer that question? At the time, she had been falling for Jake. But everything had changed so much since then. *The medical definition for 'obsession' was a persistent unwanted thought. Back then, my thoughts about Jake weren't unwanted.*

"Do you need me to repeat the question?" Pratt demanded.

"No. The answer to that question is no."

"No?" he asked again as he did when he did not like her response.

"No, not during that time period."

Pratt's eyes lit up. "Were you obsessed with him during a different time period?"

"I'm quite preoccupied these days with the idea of him being justly convicted for killing my sister, if that counts."

"Objection. Non-responsive. Move to strike," Pratt directed at the judge.

"Overruled."

"Isn't it true you attempted to conceal your relationship with Jake Wakefield?"

"We thought…"

But Pratt interrupted, "Yes or no, Miss Rose?"

"No."

"Didn't you choose not to sit in Jake's VIP seats at the ball games because others would know you were there to watch Jake?"

"Yes."

"And didn't you begin calling Jake from pay phones and other land lines after the police searched your apartment?"

"Yes, because…" but Pratt would not allow Lauren to finish her answer.

"When we saw that video tape taken at the hospital earlier today, you were wearing scrubs, weren't you?"

"In the first image, I was wearing scrubs. In the second image, I was wearing scrubs and my lab coat." There was whispering among the observers.

"There was no second image, Miss Rose," Pratt snapped.

"Oh, there is, the court just hasn't seen it yet."

Pratt's objection was sustained.

"And your scrubs are issued by the hospital, is that correct?"

"Yes."

"Miss Rose, would you be surprised to see one of your colleagues walking around the hospital with blood on their scrubs?"

"Not particularly. We change our scrubs when they get soiled, but we can't always do so right away."

"If your scrubs get dirty, you just change into new ones?"

"Yes."

"And where would you place your bloody scrubs after you were done changing?"

"In the hospital laundry."

"So, the hospital must wash a lot of bloody scrubs?"

"Yes."

"And you also use latex gloves at work?"

"Yes."

"So those gloves are readily available to you?"

"Yes."

Pratt continued his offensive. "Miss Rose, didn't you decline to attend the wake for your sister?"

"I attended the memorial service, but I didn't go to the Wakefields' home afterward. My grandmother was…"

Pratt interrupted. "Isn't it true you were offered a year off from work so you could grieve the death of your sister, but you declined?"

"Yes. I couldn't afford to take a year off from work."

"Even though you collected a million dollar life insurance payout?"

"I was never expecting that money, nor did I keep it when it was offered to me."

"Isn't it true you disparaged the detectives in this case by referring to them as Walrus and Pretty Boy?"

"Jake coined those nicknames."

"So you never referred to the Detectives as Walrus and Pretty Boy?

"I might have, but I was only repeating what Jake called them."

"So, you were eager to have Jake like you?"

"Yes, at that time, I wanted him to like me."

"You very much wanted him to like you?"

"I guess you could say that."

"Isn't it true you told Jake you have always loved baseball?"

"Yes, because I *have* always loved baseball."

"Isn't it true you asked Jake about Elizabeth's life insurance policy?"

"Yes, because…"

"And isn't it true you began talking like your sister when you spoke to Jake, using the same verbal expressions she used to use?"

"We used the same expressions because we were sis—"

"And isn't it true you told Jake you wished you could eat delivery meal services like he received all the time?"

"Yes, because…"

"And isn't it true you enjoyed the things Jake's money and fame could get you like limousine rides, VIP parking, and good baseball tickets?"

"Yes, but that doesn't mean…"

"And didn't you call your sister's cell phone at 8:23 p.m. on the night she was killed?"

"Yes. I wanted to…"

"And didn't you leave a message on her voice mail, saying "Hey, call me back as soon as you can?"

"Yes."

"And didn't you leave that message to try to disguise the fact you had just killed your own sister."

"No!"

"You were jealous of your sister and wanted what she had, so you snuck out of the hospital, drove to her house, let yourself in using her alarm code, bludgeoned her to death, returned to the hospital, changed out of your bloody scrubs leaving them in the hospital laundry, collected her insurance payout, and promptly pursued her husband?"

Candace's objection was overruled.

"No, none of that ever happened."

"None of that ever happened?"

"Correct, none of that happened."

"We know the jealousy part did happen because you have already admitted to that."

"I was jealous of her at times, but the rest of it didn't happen."

"You didn't collect the insurance?"

"Yes, but…"

"And shortly after her death, you slept in her home, and spent personal time with her husband, yes or no?"

Lauren made a concerted effort to maintain her composure. "Yes."

"No more questions for this witness," Pratt said victoriously. As Pratt had no doubt been counting on, Judge Robles recessed court for the day, which would allow the jury time to contemplate all of the dirty little secrets they had learned that day about the victim's sister. Things that were not nearly as dirty nor as secret as they appeared.

Chapter Fifty-one

Lauren felt like a punching bag as she descended from the witness stand.

Candace whispered to her as the courthouse noisily emptied. "The jury isn't going to like the fact that you got involved with your sister's husband. And there isn't too much I can do to pretty that up. However, I can clean up most of Pratt's ridiculous innuendos."

Tuesday morning, Lauren resumed the stand so Candace could 'rehabilitate' her. Doctors used the same terminology to indicate a patient's condition that improved with treatment, but lawyers used the term to refer to restoring a witness' credibility. And, admittedly, Lauren's credibility had taken a fairly big hit under the heat of Pratt's persistent accusations the day before.

"Good morning, Dr. Rose," Candace opened.

"Good morning."

"Dr. Rose, you struggled to answer most of Mr. Pratt's questions yesterday with a simple yes or no, didn't you?"

"Yes. Most questions can't be answered with a simple yes or no response because life isn't black and white. There are many shades of gray. Mr. Pratt's questions, in particular, were difficult to answer yes or no because they implied things that weren't accurate."

Candace waved her yellow legal pad, "I jotted down Mr. Pratt's questions yesterday and I thought I would ask those same questions of you today, allowing you more opportunity to explain your answers, okay?"

"Yes, great," Lauren responded.

"In what ways might you have been jealous of Liz?" Candace asked.

"Liz lived a glamorous life and I was happy for her, but I didn't want to be her. I was enjoying my own life and she was happy for me too. But have I *ever* been jealous of Liz? Of course I have. She was my older sister. I was jealous when she played Dorothy in *The Wizard of Oz* play in elementary school and I had to be a munchkin. She got to wear those fabulous ruby red slippers."

Laughter filled the courtroom.

"Pride might be the more accurate word. I was proud I had an older sister that was so beautiful and cheerful and generous. I suppose there were some things I envied like her shoe collection, but she'd let me borrow them any time. It would be nice to be as financially independent as she appeared to be, but not many people are. I was pursuing a career that would allow me to be financially secure. There was a time when I thought she was really happy in her marriage and I wanted to have a happy relationship myself some day, but now I know better. That was a happy face that she painted on the marriage, which is nothing to be jealous of."

"Do you think there were any ways in which Liz was jealous of you?"

"Again, I'm not sure jealous is the right word, but she was proud of me too. She was so excited when I got into medical school. She told anybody that would listen that her little sister was going to be a doctor. She dropped out of college after her junior year to marry Jake so she was proud of me for finishing school."

"Did you ever contemplate a relationship with Jake while your sister was alive?

"Never."

"You never even fantasized about it?"

"No. Honestly, I didn't know Jake all that well. I'd see him occasionally when I was visiting my sister, but we didn't really interact much. Plus, for a long time, I was involved in a serious relationship of my own."

"You testified earlier that you did a Google search for deaths from traumatic injuries, is that correct?"

"Yes, my supervisor at work asked me that day what percentage of deaths result from traumatic injuries. I didn't know the answer so I wanted to look it up and let him know I had found it."

"And did you report your findings back to your medical supervisor?"

"Yes. Unintentional injuries are the fifth leading cause of death in the United States and the number one cause of death for people under the age of thirty-four."

"Was he satisfied with those findings?"

"Yes, though he would have preferred I had known them without having to consult Google."

More laughter in the gallery.

Candace allowed Lauren to clarify several more issues before wrapping up and court recessed for lunch. Over a quick meal in the war room, Candace prepared Lauren for the upcoming re-direct. "Answer honestly, completely, and calmly. Don't let Pratt cage you in. And, remember he's only allowed to return to subjects broached by me so if he tries to open up something new, wait for me to object."

Although Lauren was the witness on the stand, the afternoon court session turned into the Candace vs. Pratt comedy sketch. Pratt attempted to rehash issues exhausted on direct examination. Candace objected on the basis that the question had already been asked and answered.

Reviewing his notes, Pratt fixed his gaze upon Lauren. "Do you remember testifying you did not fantasize about a relationship with Jake Wakefield because you were in a serious relationship yourself?"

"Yes."

"Can you tell us when that serious relationship ended?" Pratt asked.

"Objection, outside the scope," Candace said. But this time, the judge ruled against her, Pratt finally hit upon a topic he had not already exhausted.

"In May of last year," Lauren answered.

"And how long had that relationship lasted?"

Despite Candace's objection, the judge allowed Pratt to continue. As Pratt's face twisted into a self-satisfied smirk, Lauren got the distinct feeling he already knew the answer to these questions. Had somebody from the Defense team talked to Michael? Wouldn't Michael have had the courtesy to contact Lauren and let her know?

"It lasted about three and a half years."

"Three and half years? That sounds very serious. Had the two of you discussed marriage?"

"Yes."

"And what was the outcome of those discussions? Had you agreed to get married?"

"Not exactly. We were never officially engaged."

"But you were planning marriage in your future, weren't you?"

"Yes, we both thought that would happen after we graduated from medical school."

"But it didn't?"

"No."

"Why did the relationship end?" Pratt asked with a malicious grin.

"He got involved with somebody else," Lauren said, trying very hard not to allow the pain to show on her face.

"After three and a half years and plans for eventual marriage, he got involved with somebody else?"

She felt embarrassed and exposed. Details about her private personal life splashed around for public display as if she was a circus sideshow. "Yes."

"Did you know the other woman?"

"Yes."

"So your boyfriend of three and a half years got involved with a woman you knew?"

"Yes."

"And whatever happened between your ex-boyfriend and the woman he cheated on you with?"

"They got married."

"They got married," Pratt repeated. "That must have really hurt you, didn't it?"

"I was hurt at the time of the breakup, but now I feel relieved."

"Relieved?" Pratt asked as if he had not heard her correctly.

"Yes, my ex-boyfriend wasn't the man I thought he was. I'm so glad I discovered that before we married."

Several women in the courtroom nodded their heads.

"But you admit you were really hurt at the time of the breakup, correct?"

"Yes."

"And he broke up with you, hurting you, just a few months before your sister was killed, correct?"

Candace was on her feet. "Your Honor, I object to this entire line of questioning. Mr. Pratt is attempting to establish a link between two events when there is no evidence they are related."

"Ms. Keene," Judge Robles responded, "you have already been overruled on this matter. I will hear your motion to appeal my decision now if you so choose."

Candace paused as if she were deliberating the issue, "No, Your Honor."

"Very well, let's proceed."

Pratt didn't miss a beat. "And your hurt reaction to your relationship breakup occurred only a few months before your sister was killed, isn't that correct?"

Any idiot with a calendar could answer that question, Lauren thought. "Yes."

"So, last May you got dumped by your longtime boyfriend, in June you moved to the Phoenix area and started spending more time with Jake and Elizabeth, in July your sister was killed, and in August you started spending a lot of time with Jake. Is that accurate?"

"Not exactly."

"Not exactly?" Pratt mocked.

"I started spending more time with Liz after I moved here, but not really Jake."

"No, you didn't start spending time with him until after your sister was conveniently dead, did you?"

"I resent the representation that my sister's death was convenient. It has never been anything other than tragic to me."

"Allow me to rephrase the question. "You didn't start spending a lot of time with your sister's husband until after your sister's death, isn't that right?"

"We were supporting one another through the grieving process…"

"Yes or no, Miss Rose. Yes or no?"

"Yes."

He grinned and turned to the judge, "No more questions for this witness."

Court was adjourned for the day.

Lauren dreaded the questions Ryan might ask during the afternoon drive, but he did not pry. However, he did say with a small grin, "Detective Pretty Boy thinks you did a fantastic job on the stand."

Although Lauren felt beat down, she couldn't resist smiling. "He does? When did Wallace tell you that?"

It took a fraction of a second for Ryan to comprehend her response and then they both laughed.

Very little surprised Lauren anymore. Wedding pictures of Michael and his bride showed up on the covers of several tabloid magazines over the next few days underneath captions such as "Lauren Rose's Ex-Boyfriend Speaks Out at Last." Michael had capitalized on the trial publicity by selling his story to the tabloids. *He probably needs the money to support his gold-digging wife,* Lauren thought. He had staggering student loans and his new bride had quit her nursing job as soon as they had married. Lauren reminded herself once more of how lucky she was that she hadn't ended up married to that scruple-less scumbag.

Chapter Fifty-two

(Wednesday, September 27)

The following morning, Lauren returned to the stand for more cross-examination under Candace's careful guidance.

"Have you ever killed anybody, Dr. Rose?"

"No."

"In fact, you have taken a solemn oath to help people heal, have you not?"

"The Hippocratic Oath, yes."

"Under what circumstances might you intentionally kill someone?"

"Only if it were necessary to defend my own life or the life of somebody else."

"What if it would bring you fortune?"

"No."

"What if it would bring you fame?"

"No."

"What if it would bring you romance?"

"No."

"So, you didn't play any role in the death of your sister?"

"None whatsoever. I had nothing to do with my sister's death."

Candace left it at that.

Over lunch, the prosecutors reviewed the Defense witness list, debating who might be called next. Most of the people on the list were character witnesses for Jake, mostly fellow baseball players. Candace said, "I would love to cross-examine some of these guys, but I doubt the Defense will call them now that the lid has blown wide open on their out-of-town escapades. What are they going to say? That Jake adored Liz when he wasn't sleeping with other women? Besides, none of those guys is going to be willing to expose their own bad behaviors."

Candace bet Jake's parents would testify next. Kyle's money was on the hired gun the Defense had hired as an expert forensic witness. When court reconvened, Pratt called Mrs. Buffy Wakefield to the stand and Kyle owed Candace twenty bucks.

Buffy was dressed in an expensive platinum-colored dress. Her hair was perfectly coiffed, her eyebrows dramatic arches over her icy blue eyes. Too-tan skin and too-white teeth made her look like a caricature. The personification of wealth.

Buffy spoke with affected speech, which sounded like aristocratic British although she had been born and raised in Massachusetts. Perhaps she had once had a British nanny or had spent too much time watching *Mary Poppins*. In her polished manner, Buffy described Jake as the perfect son, a generous philanthropist, and the ideal husband.

Candace kept it brief on cross-examination. "Mrs. Wakefield, Jake is your only child?"

"Yes, we struggled to conceive and Jake was our miracle."

"And you love him very much, don't you?"

"More than anything else in the world."

"And you would be devastated if he were convicted of this crime, wouldn't you?"

"Very much so."

"No more questions for this witness." Candace had made her point; mothers don't make good witnesses.

And fathers aren't much better. Pratt called Jake's father next. Jacob Sr. looked impressive with his square shoulders, strong jaw, and expensive suit. He, too, testified Jake had been a joy to raise, demonstrating a special talent for throwing a ball from a very young age.

Ryan, who had been running an errand for several hours, slipped back into court and passed some documents to Candace before resuming his seat next to Lauren. Candace skimmed over the documents and rewarded Ryan with a smile.

Candace started her cross-exam with a line of questions similar to those she had asked Buffy. Jacob Sr. testified he and his wife had been thrilled to conceive after many fruitless years of trying and Jake had immediately become the center of their universe.

"And it would be impossible for you to believe Jake guilty of this crime, wouldn't it, Mr. Wakefield?"

"Yes. He could not have done this."

"And what makes you so certain?"

"He's simply not capable of it."

"Mr. Wakefield, isn't it true Jake got into some legal trouble when he was still in high school?"

Pratt leapt to his feet, "Objection, irrelevant."

Candace was ready for this. "Your Honor, this information directly relates to the impeachment of Mr. Wakefield's earlier testimony."

"Overruled."

Mr. Wakefield looked rattled. "He was never convicted of anything."

"But he was arrested for a crime and you had to pick him up from the police station, isn't that right?"

"That was many, many years ago," Mr. Wakefield waved his arm as if dismissing the matter.

"What was he arrested for?"

"He and his girlfriend had been in a…a bit of a minor scuffle at school."

"A minor scuffle?" Candace referred to the documents in her hands. "Wasn't he arrested for aggravated assault?"

Mr. Wakefield brushed his fingers through his silvering mane. "Yes, but he was never formally charged."

"And why wasn't he charged?"

"Objection, calls for speculation," Pratt shouted.

"Allow me to rephrase the question. Mr. Wakefield, do you know why your son, Jake, was not formally charged with that crime?"

Mr. Wakefield hesitated.

"I'll remind you that you're under oath," Candace prodded.

"Yes, I believe I do," Mr. Wakefield responded tentatively.

"And why was that?"

"The Paradise Valley Police chief felt the matter should be dismissed."

"Mr. Wakefield, aren't you friendly with the man who was the Paradise Valley Police chief at that time?"

"Well, I don't know about the word friendly, but we do belong to the same country club."

"And did you make an appeal to him about your son's arrest back then?"

"Not an appeal, but we did speak about the issue."

"So, you helped your son avoid punishment for a crime he committed?"

"A minor scuffle he was *accused* of committing," Jacob Wakefield, Sr. retorted.

"And wouldn't you like to help him avoid punishment for the crime he is now *accused* of committing?"

Wakefield looked at Pratt as if hoping for an objection, but none came. "Because he didn't commit this crime," he finally answered.

"And how do you know he didn't commit this crime?"

"Because he's my son and I just know, for crying out loud."

"Because you don't want to believe your son is capable of any wrongdoing, do you Mr. Wakefield?"

"Of course I don't."

"No, of course you don't," Candace agreed.

And the words hung in the courtroom air as court adjourned for the day.

Ryan filled Lauren in on the ride home. Candace had sent him out on a fishing expedition for anything that might be helpful in impeaching the rosy picture Mr. and Mrs. Wakefield intended to paint of their son.

"I didn't think it would amount to much, but I thought I might as well stop in at Jake's high school and ask around. The young receptionist at the front desk was sweet as punch with the same IQ. I asked her if there was any record of problems with Jake when he had been a student there. She gave me a glassy-eyed look and said she wouldn't even know how to find such information. It was a crapshoot in the first place so I was walking out the door just as an older woman entered. She must have recognized me from the trial. She addressed me as Detective Boyd before I could introduce myself."

"She probably liked the looks of you," Lauren remarked. Candace had not been joking when she said Ryan had the best success with female witnesses of any detective she knew.

"Please. She was old enough to be my mother."

"A cougar," Lauren made a purring noise. She got the result she was angling for when Ryan laughed.

"You're distracting me from this story, which is about to get good."

"Because it shows what a crackerjack detective you are?"

"Exactly. She tells me they only maintain school disciplinary records as long as a student is enrolled so Jake's should have been destroyed long ago. But then she confessed they don't always get shredded in a timely manner. I'm still thinking nothing is going to come of it when the cougar hit print on her computer and handed me a copy of the disciplinary report. Jake decked his high school girlfriend in the face when he found her talking to another boy at school. She was transported to the hospital with a broken jaw and Jake was arrested for assault."

"Then Daddy got him out of his *little scrape* with the law?"

"It pays to have money and connections."

"I wonder if they can track down the old girlfriend?"

"They can't introduce old crimes in court. Candace can only use it to impeach Mr. Wakefield's testimony that his son was the perfect angel."

"Geez, our legal system is biased in favor of the defendant," Lauren observed, thinking of other things the jury would never hear, like Kathryn Montgomery's knowledge of Jake's physical abuse and the phone calls Jake had made to the anonymous tip line.

"Ain't that the truth?"

"The truth, the whole truth, and nothing but the truth," Lauren agreed, reciting the oath she had already taken twice in this trial.

Chapter Fifty-three

The Defense called Dr. Scott Rankin as their next witness. Rankin had been a very well respected forensic pathologist working for the medical examiner's office in Chicago. He had since retired from that position and now consulted on high profile criminal cases.

Pratt spent the entire morning asking Dr. Rankin about the forensic testimony introduced by the Prosecution. No matter Pratt's question, Rankin offered a polished explanation replete with multisyllabic scientific terms that refuted the Prosecution's interpretation of the scientific evidence. He testified that Jake's DNA and blood could have gotten under Liz's fingernails during impassioned sex, the true killer might have worn gloves and a hat to avoid leaving behind evidence, somebody trained in medicine would be knowledgeable about how to avoid leaving DNA evidence behind at the scene, and so forth. Basically, Rankin provided several hours worth of testimony explaining why all of the evidence collected in this case could implicate Lauren.

When Pratt could think of no other questions that would enable Dr. Rankin to incriminate Lauren, he turned the witness over to the Prosecution.

Candace approached Rankin. "When was the last time you worked as a medical examiner?"

"I have consulted on dozens of cases over the past..."

"I'm so sorry," Candace interrupted with a smile that appeared genuinely apologetic. "I think you must have misunderstood my question. The question is, when was the last time you were employed as a medical examiner?"

"I haven't worked as a medical examiner for twelve years, but I have..."

Candace interrupted so seamlessly that it hardly seemed rude. "Twelve years. And since that time, you've served as an expert witness in ninety-six legal cases, is that accurate?"

Dr. Rankin's chest puffed out a bit, "Yes, quite right."

"And how many of those ninety-six times have you testified on behalf of the Prosecution?"

"The Prosecution uses government employees as their witnesses so I'm typically needed to testify for the Defense."

"So out of ninety-six cases, how many of those did you testify for the Defense?"

"Again, the Prosecution usually..."

"I'm looking for a number here, Dr. Rankin. Half would be forty-eight? Was it forty-nine? Sixty? Eighty? How many?"

"I'm always called by the Defense."

"Always? So in all ninety-six cases, you've testified for the Defense?"

"Yes."

"Have you ever turned down a case because you felt that the evidence implicated the accused?"

"That wouldn't be the only reason to turn down a case."

"Yes or no, Dr. Rankin, have you ever turned down a case?"

"No, because I believe that every individual is entitled to defend themselves."

"And to have you assist them in doing so?"

"No."

"Right, they only get you if they can afford your extravagant fee, right?"

Judge Robles sustained Pratt's objection.

"Dr. Rankin, how much are you being paid to provide your opinion in this case?

"Thirty thousand dollars."

"Thirty thousand dollars. And you have testified in ninety-six cases over the past twelve years. That sounds like a very nice income."

"I don't make thirty thousand dollars for every case."

"Oh, I know. Sometimes you make much more than that. I have no more questions for this *Defense* witness."

Court adjourned for lunch.

Lauren was the first to arrive at the war room. As she flipped the light switch, several staffers from the prosecutor's office jumped up in the dark room, yelling "Surprise!" A big banner on one wall read "Happy Birthday." Lauren's favorite sushi rolls lined platters on the big table along with a large birthday cake.

Tears welled uninvited in Lauren's eyes.

"Did you think we forgot?" Ryan asked her.

"I didn't expect you to know it was my birthday in the first place."

"Don't you know who you're dealing with here?" Ryan joked. "I am one of the most widely recognized investigators in this entire country." Due to his work on this trial, that statement was completely true. Lauren laughed at his expression of mock indignation.

The staffers, most of whom Lauren recognized from their work around the prosecutor's office, helped themselves to food and cake, wished Lauren a happy birthday, and gradually excused themselves. Soon, only Kyle, Candace, Ryan, and Lauren remained in the room.

The conversation soon returned to the trial. They enjoyed poking fun at Dr. Rankin, who was clearly more interested in lining his wallet than he was in the truth.

"Hey," Ryan said. "We should all go out tonight to celebrate Lauren's birthday."

"Absolutely." Kyle agreed. "Unless Lauren already has plans for her birthday."

"Huge plans." Lauren said. "I have to work tonight."

Lauren wished there was some way she could take them up on the offer. Between the trial and work, she had not gone out in ages. What had happened to that youthful girl who went out dancing with her friends? Ryan stepped out to return a phone call while Candace and Kyle continued to roast Pratt and Rankin. Lauren wondered if the Defense similarly enjoyed skewering the Prosecution team and could only assume they did. What did Jake have to say about her? Did the entire Defense team make fun of how easily she had fallen victim to his manipulation?

Lauren's cell phone vibrated inside her purse. Everybody that knew her, and even most people that did not, knew she spent her days attending the trial. She rarely received missed calls when court was in session, though LaRhonda did occasionally text her in the middle of the trial to comment on the "crap" the Defense was trying to pull.

This text message was from Dr. Stone: **Happy Birthday. Take the night off and go have some fun. And that's an order.**

Lauren smiled. Stone had a heart of gold, but she really doubted whether he remembered her first name, much less her birthday. Ryan tried to slip back into the room inconspicuously.

"Urgent phone call to Good Samaritan hospital?" Lauren asked him.

"I don't have any idea what you are talking about," Ryan replied with a straight face.

"Stone just gave me the evening off out of the clear blue sky."

"That's excellent news. And such good timing, too, on account of us all wanting to go out tonight to celebrate your birthday."

"Well, I guess if I can't go to work and be surrounded by sucking chest wounds and disembowelments, hanging out with you guys will have to do."

Lauren spent the rest of the afternoon sitting in court, but thinking about her first real evening out in months. She felt grateful to Ryan for recognizing her need to take an evening off. Despite the many hours they had spent together, they maintained a professional distance between them, like one of those invisible barriers that would deliver an electrical shock if you crossed it. Still, he probably wouldn't want to spend the evening out with Lauren, Candace, and Kyle if he had a girlfriend waiting for him at home, would he? Or had he invited her out for the evening out of a sense of obligation? Or worse, pity?

As Pratt spent the afternoon attempting to rehabilitate the credibility of Dr. Rankin, Lauren resolved to stop worrying about the reasons behind Ryan's actions and allow herself to enjoy the upcoming evening.

Chapter Fifty-four

(Thursday, September 28)

Kyle had proposed dancing at Myst, one of Scottsdale's trendiest nightclubs.

"Absolutely not," Candace vetoed. "I'm all for celebrating Lauren's birthday, but we have to keep it under the radar. We do not need to be calling attention to ourselves right now."

They settled on dinner at The Old Spaghetti Factory in downtown Phoenix. Candace and Kyle were returning to the war room to prep for court the next day, but would meet Ryan and Lauren at the restaurant at seven. After court, Ryan dropped Lauren at her apartment, promising to return to pick her up again at six-thirty.

"You don't have to drive all the way back here to get me. I *can* drive, you know."

"This is your first day off in weeks. Who knows, maybe you'll want to cut loose and have a drink or something."

As she walked to her apartment, she stopped to talk with the reporters loitering in her apartment parking lot. Keeping her promise to Candace that she would represent the family, Lauren offered her opinion about the day's proceedings, accusing Dr. Rankin of interpreting the data in a manner intended to favor the Defense.

The reporters thanked her for taking the time to comment. Several wished her a happy birthday as they packed up for the day and headed off to escape the excessive heat. Phoenix was experiencing an Indian summer and the high temperatures were still reaching the triple digits.

For the first time in ages, Lauren did not feel rushed. She stood under the shower nozzle enjoying the unfamiliar sensation of relaxation.

She took the time to flat-iron her long blond hair, which had a tendency to become unruly in the hot weather. Tonight it hung down her back in a sleek sheet. She applied makeup and picked out her favorite pair of jeans, a stylish T-shirt, and killer platform sandals. When she looked in the mirror, she recognized her old self.

The doorbell rang exactly at six-thirty. Did Ryan perfectly time his arrival or did he loiter outside waiting to ring her doorbell at the designated time? There was so much she hadn't figured out about him. When she opened the door, something about him was different. Had he gotten his hair cut? It took her a moment to realize this was the first time she had seen him in casual clothes. He wore trendy jeans and a closely fitting blue-green T-shirt, which matched the unusual color of his eyes and showcased his pecs and arms.

As they made their way to the car, Lauren was relieved to see the reporters were gone. "I gave them their sound bites on my way in."

"Thank God. Candace is so paranoid that I figured I might need to meet you at the grocery store down the street to dodge the media. I'm glad the vultures have fled the scene, to use official police lingo."

Surprise registered on Lauren's face when Ryan stopped beside a black Mazda RX-8 and unlocked the passenger door for her. "Yeah, this is my own car. I'm not driving the government-issued beast tonight." The car was sleek and low to the ground; the interior smelled like new leather, pine trees, and the beach.

As Ryan drove down the freeway, they had a great view of the sunset. Huge thunderstorms in the distance glowed in Crayola shades of burnt sienna, razzle dazzle rose, and vivid violet over the White Tank Mountains.

"Another beautiful day in paradise," Lauren said.

"True, but I wish it would rain already."

"No kidding, it's time to put the soon into monsoon," Lauren said, referring to the Valley's disappointing summer storm season, which had produced very little rain this year.

"Yeah, so far it's been a non-soon."

"I must admit Arizona does have the most beautiful sunsets," Lauren observed, and was reminded unpleasantly of a similar conversation she had with Jake the previous year.

"And the most amazing emergency room doctors."

"Not to mention their world-famous police investigators."

"I got a little something for you," he said, handing her a small gift bag, which he pulled from the backseat area. The bag itself was gorgeously arranged. Silver gift bag with purple and green paisleys, matching tissue paper peeking out the top.

"Wow, check out this wrapping job. Did you do this yourself?"

"Of course I didn't. The woman at the shop put it together, but I did pick out the colors."

"Thank you, it's exquisite."

"It's more than a bag. You're supposed to open it."

"You didn't have to do this," she said, secretly pleased he had. This was the first, and perhaps the only, birthday gift she would receive this year. Liz had always spoiled Lauren on her birthdays, overcompensating for the absence of their parents.

"I know I didn't have to, but I wanted to. It's not the Hope Diamond like you got from you-know-who last year, but it reminded me of you."

Lauren pulled the tissue out of the bag cautiously, reluctant to dismantle the lovely packaging. She pulled out a small heavy item, wrapped in more brightly colored tissue. She unwrapped it to reveal a small figurine of a bull carved out of dark stone. The bull was pawing one foot menacingly.

Lauren was touched by the meaningful memento. "Thank you very much. I love it."

"You are welcome very much…" he hesitated as if to say something more, but no other words came out.

The restaurant wasn't much from the outside, but inside, it had high wooden ceilings, hardwood floors, and antique furniture. They joined Kyle and Candace, who were already at the bar drinking dirty martinis.

Surreptitious glances from other customers were followed by furious whispering. The bartender approached with four shot glasses. "The finest Patrón from an admirer of your work," he said as he passed out the drinks. They each licked salt off the back of their hands, slammed the shots, and chased them with lemon wedges. The tequila burned down Lauren's throat.

She was relieved when they were called for seating so they could escape the curious stares from strangers. The hostess led them to a cozy table in the back corner of the restaurant. Several of the tables had been constructed from old antique bed frames, the headboard having been turned into bench seating on one side of the table and the footboard making a complimentary bench on the opposite side. This particular table was framed by an ornate wooden bed frame, with both ends being high enough to afford them considerable privacy. The men stood chivalrously while the ladies scooted in on either side, Kyle sitting beside Candace and Ryan beside Lauren.

"No shop talk," Candace warned even though the restaurant was noisy with clanking silverware and the constant chatter of other diners.

"Of course not," Ryan said. "This is a birthday celebration after all."

"We should all share stories about our most memorable birthdays," Kyle suggested.

"Excellent idea," Lauren agreed. "You go first."

"Okay," Kyle said. "On my twenty-first birthday, I went to Las Vegas for a weekend of debauchery with several of my fraternity brothers. It was one long binge of drinking, gambling, and strip clubs."

Candace rolled her eyes. "Vegas for your twenty-first birthday. How cliché."

"I suppose you have something better," he pressed. "What was your most memorable birthday?"

"Believe it or not, my mother was a very proper Southern belle and she was determined that I would be a debutante. She planned an elaborate sweet sixteen birthday party for me and invited all of my father's clients to our home for a formal banquet. She made me wear the most god-awful pink fluffy dress you can imagine and dragged me off to her beauty parlor, where they yanked my hair into some elaborate updo with a tiara. A goddamned tiara. The party was going exactly according to my mother's plan until it was time to serve the cake, a three-tiered pink frosted monstrosity. My mother was furious when they couldn't find me to blow out the candles."

Candace was interrupted by the waitress who arrived to take their order. Lauren was looking forward to the spaghetti with mizithra cheese sauce. Kyle ordered the chicken parmigiana and they all groaned when Candace ordered a salad.

"I have to watch my girlish figure. I'm drinking my calories tonight." She ordered a full bottle of cabernet.

When the waitress got to Ryan, he said, "I'd like the *espagueti testiculos*, please."

"I'm sorry," the bubbly young waitress said. "I don't actually speak Italian."

"I'll take the spaghetti and meatballs," he said as the others tried to suppress giggles.

"So finish your story, Candace," Kyle reminded her as the waitress cantered off. "Where were you when you were supposed to be blowing out sixteen candles?"

"Outside playing paintball with a bunch of the boys."

"In your pink party dress?" Lauren gasped.

"Hell no. I ditched that thing as soon as my mom got distracted by the cocktails. There was a great stretch of woods out back of our house so some of the boys snuck over their paintball gear. At first, they refused to let me play, but I threatened to snitch to their parents until they relented. I overheard them talking about how they would take me out first and then continue without me."

"Somehow, I'm guessing that didn't happen," Kyle said.

"You know me well. I had seven confirmed kills before I captured the other team's flag. Of course, knowing the lay of the land was to my advantage, but I was also very wily. Even back then."

The wine arrived and Candace poured full glasses for everybody, except for Ryan who declined because he was driving.

"Okay, who's up next?" Kyle asked.

"Of course, my fondest birthday memories are from my childhood when my parents were still alive," Lauren said. A familiar, uncomfortable hush fell over the table and Lauren hurried on, "but my most memorable birthday was my twenty-first birthday. Liz flew us out to New Orleans to celebrate. We went sightseeing by day and down to Bourbon Street at night. We drank the famous hurricanes at Pat O'Brien's, which were too strong for me. So I figured I'd order something tastier for my next drink. Have you heard of a mint julep?"

"You did not," Candace gasped.

"Yep, I'm afraid I did. I imagined it would be green and frothy and mint-flavored."

"I bet that was an unpleasant surprise," Candace said.

"Why? What's a mint julep?" Kyle asked.

"As best as I could figure, it consisted of about eight ounces of whiskey with a mint leaf on the top." Lauren responded with a shudder.

"Lauren, you exaggerate," Candace teased. "It's only seven ounces of whiskey mixed with an ounce of sugar water with a mint leaf on top."

"Needless to say, I have never been so drunk in my whole life!"

"You must've been miserable the next day," Ryan said.

"Not exactly," Lauren said. "I got a brilliant idea."

"As so many drunken ideas are," Kyle quipped.

"I figured if I didn't go to sleep that night, I couldn't wake up with a hangover in the morning."

"And that worked?" Candace asked skeptically.

"Sort of. I stayed up all night and the next morning, we took a streetcar down to the zoo and a paddleboat back."

"So, you didn't get sick?" Kyle asked.

"I think I was actually still drunk. I found the animals at the zoo very amusing. The following morning, we got up early to catch our flight home and, believe it or not, I was hung-over that morning."

"Two days later?" Ryan asked.

"Yep. When we got on the plane, the first thing I did was pull out the airsickness bag and clutch it pathetically. The man sitting on my other side took one look at me and said, 'Oh great.' But Liz piped up and said, 'Give her a break. She has a serious case of the weekend flu.'"

They all laughed.

"Okay, your turn," Lauren said to Ryan in order to break the quiet that had settled over the table as the others reflected on the witty sister Lauren had lost.

"Okay. I do have a good birthday story, but it wasn't my birthday," Ryan started. "I was six at the time, but I still remember this like it was yesterday. It was my brother's first birthday so my mom had him strapped into his high chair. She put the cake on the table in front of him and she was scrounging through the kitchen looking for a birthday candle.

"'Let's use this,' my dad suggested as he discovered a leftover Fourth of July firecracker in one of the kitchen drawers.

"Of course he was kidding, but my mom went right along with him. She said, 'Great idea, stick it in.'

"My dad didn't want to be the one to cave so he plopped the firecracker into the cake and told my mom, 'Okay, bring the matches.'

"Not one to be outdone, my mother calmly fetched the matches and handed them to my father. He struck a match and lit the firecracker, eyeballing my mother the whole time. My parents continued to watch each other, waiting to see who would blow it out first, when we all realized it was going to go off.

"We all ducked under the table, but of course Jason wasn't going anywhere because he was still strapped in his highchair. Kaboom! There was cake everywhere, including all over Jason, who proceeded to happily lick it off his face and arms. He didn't even cry."

The others just sat there disbelieving. "You're pulling our legs, right?" Lauren finally asked.

"No, I'm dead serious. We were still finding bits of cake in odd places weeks later." He grinned. "Now that was a memorable birthday."

The wine flowed. For the first time, they were not discussing the details of the trial. There was no shortage of funny stories as Candace shared stories from trials, Ryan from police investigations, Lauren from hospital patients, and Kyle from law school. Several inappropriate jokes were made about the size of Ryan's meatballs.

The waitress came back to check on them so frequently they concluded she was interested in either Ryan or Kyle. "Could be both, you never know with these sweet young things anymore," Candace remarked.

"Could be you or Lauren, too, because you *really* never know with these sweet young things anymore," Kyle added.

"I'm not sure which of us deserves the credit, but at least we are getting very attentive service," Lauren said.

Lauren's spumoni ice cream came out with a flaming candle in it. Lauren took a moment to reflect on what she wanted most out of life before she blew it out.

Candace and Kyle excused themselves immediately after the meal, complaining they had to return to the office for more trial prep before they could call it a night.

As they disappeared out of the restaurant together, Lauren asked, "Do you think they're more than friends?"

"They kind of make you wonder, don't they? I heard they sleep together sometimes, but Candace isn't interested in anything serious and that only makes Kyle pursue her more. I don't know if it's true," Ryan answered.

The two of them continued to sit side by side even though the other half of the table was now empty. Lauren nursed the rest of her wine, not wanting the evening to end. To his credit, Ryan did not rush her.

Eventually, Lauren drained the last drops of her wine and they slid out of the booth.

Chapter Fifty-five

(Thursday, September 28)

Lauren smelled it as soon as she walked outside. Ozone. It was raining at last. She stepped out from underneath the overhang of the restaurant and lifted her face to the gently falling raindrops, breathing in the sweet smell of clean air. Ryan smiled at her childlike enjoyment of the simple pleasure.

As soon as they were in the car, he held up a folded cocktail napkin. "Look what I got," he said dangling the napkin in front of Lauren. She took the napkin from him and unfolded it. She saw The Old Spaghetti Factory logo in one corner and scrawled across it in bright purple ink was written, Brittany 623-760-6955. Cute little heart to dot the i.

"The waitress' phone number?" she laughed. "I didn't even see her give it to you."

"She was very stealthy. She waited until you had your back turned."

"Did she ask you to pass it along to Kyle for her?"

Ryan laughed. Lauren handed him back the napkin, which he promptly crumpled up and chucked over his shoulder into the backseat.

As they neared Lauren's apartment, her heart began to race. *Should she invite him up? Would he say yes if she did?* Geez, it was her twenty-seventh birthday, but she was feeling like an adolescent girl.

"What? No fan club to greet your arrival?" Ryan said as they pulled into the parking lot, noting there were no reporters waiting for her.

"They all think I'm at work. The true diehards are probably standing outside in the rain at Good Sam right now waiting for me to get off shift in an hour."

"I thought they weren't allowed on the premises?"

"They're not, but that doesn't usually stop one or two from trying."

Ryan parked the car, pulled the keys from the ignition, and opened his door. It was still sprinkling as they headed toward her apartment. About halfway there, thunder crashed and the sky unleashed a torrent of gigantic raindrops. They dashed up her steps, and huddled under Lauren's small front stoop while she struggled to unlock the door, bursting through at last into the dry interior, slamming the door behind them.

They were both soaking wet. A lock of Lauren's hair had plastered itself to her cheek. Ryan used his thumb to brush it back behind her ear.

In her platform sandals, she would just be able to reach her lips to his if she dared. She reached up on tiptoes, but settled for wiping a raindrop from his cheek, allowing her hand to linger.

She saw conflicting emotions flit across his eyes and braced herself for him to make an excuse to leave. She desperately wanted him to stay. She did not want to spend yet another night alone. Not on her birthday.

She stepped closer and brushed her lips to his. The kiss was tentative. Lauren could sense hesitation in Ryan's stiff posture. She pressed her body against his, pleased to feel his body now responding to hers.

"We should get you out of those wet clothes," she said in a manner that was uncharacteristically forward for her. "You're in danger of catching a cold. I'm a doctor, you know."

She pulled his wet T-shirt up over his head, exposing his flat stomach, solid chest, muscular shoulders and arms.

"Are you sure you wouldn't rather go to bed and get some sleep? You are a medical resident after all."

Lauren felt stung before she remembered having told him that residents preferred sleep to sex. "Not this time. You know what they say about all work and no play."

"Then it's time to take a taste of your own medicine," he whispered in her ear. His hands pulled her wet shirt off easily as he kissed her more forcefully, exploring her mouth with his tongue.

As he kissed her, he unclasped her bra, releasing her modest but firm breasts. The bra, the best one she owned, dropped unceremoniously to the floor as he knelt now before her kissing her stomach and breasts. He worked at the button on her jeans, which he soon mastered, allowing them to slip off her ankles. He picked her up and carried her down the narrow hallway toward her bedroom.

The dainty lace panties she had picked out so carefully just a few hours earlier offered no resistance now.

Although she was no longer thinking clearly, Lauren realized Ryan was still wearing his jeans. For a moment, she worried the inappropriate jokes she and Candace had been making about Jake's manhood made Ryan feel insecure about removing his own pants in front of her.

Lauren sat up on the edge of the bed and began to unbutton his jeans with an urgency that sent his button flying across the room. "I must insist that you disrobe," she said in a voice that was unintentionally breathy. "Doctor's orders." He obliged, the rest of his clothes joining hers on the floor. Lauren could now see that she needn't have worried about him feeling insecure.

Afterwards, Lauren slept in Ryan's arms more soundly than she had in well over a year.

Chapter Fifty-six

(Friday, September 29)

When she woke up, he was gone.

She found her clothes, dry now, folded neatly on her dining room table, topped by a note written in tidy block letters.

SLEEPING BEAUTY,
I'LL PICK YOU UP AT THE USUAL TIME.
SLEEP TIGHT!
~R

Lauren had no idea what time Ryan snuck out. It was nearly six now. As she left the apartment for her morning run, she discovered he had considerately locked her knob lock on his way out.

True to his word, Ryan arrived promptly at seven to drive her to court. He was dressed in a suit and tie, driving the sedate government sedan once more. With reporters already camped outside, he greeted her professionally, and did not touch her as they walked side by side to his car.

"How did you sleep?" he asked courteously.

"Better than I have in ages. And you?"

"Like a baby."

They sat in silence in the car for a moment before he continued, "Listen, Lauren, about last night…"

Lauren's stomach clenched in anticipation of what he was about to say.

"I let myself get carried away. You looked so good, the meal was so fun, and the rain was so unexpected, but…"

"But?" she asked, steeling herself for his response.

"It was a mistake. I'm sorry. I exercised poor judgment and I can't let it happen again."

"So you do have a girlfriend?" she accused.

"A girlfriend? What? No. It's nothing like that."

"Then what is it?"

"I'm one of the lead investigators on this case and you're a material witness. I could lose my job. I thought you knew that."

"I guess I should've known that."

"Why did you think I never pursued you before?"

"The same reason lots of guys don't pursue girls. Because they aren't interested."

He laughed. "Hardly. Everybody has noticed my attraction to you. Except, apparently, you. Candace, Kyle, Wallace. I had to solemnly promise to stay professional when I volunteered for the driving gig and they keep reminding me I can't get involved with you so long as this case is unresolved. It could jeopardize the whole case."

"It could?"

"Unfortunately, yes. The Defense could accuse me of hiding evidence to protect you or manufacturing evidence to incriminate Jake. If the jury has any reason to question the objectivity of our investigation, it could screw up everything. Candace would have my head on a platter. So we can't right now, okay?"

"Okay," she answered. *Why do I keep falling for the one man that I can't have? Who was it that said, 'Man wants most what he cannot have?'* she wondered as she remembered the quote, but not where it came from.

Chapter Fifty-seven

(Friday, September 29)

There was an accident on the I-10 freeway and traffic was backed up for miles. Ryan turned on his flashing red light and drove down the breakdown lane in order to make it to the courthouse on time. He and Lauren had barely taken their seats when court was called to order.

Friday morning, the Defense called three witnesses who had interacted with Jake at the airport on the evening of July twenty-third as he departed for Washington D.C. All of them testified he had been friendly and relaxed. He hadn't been acting like a man who had just killed his wife.

Candace fired the same series of questions at all of them.

"Do you believe most criminals make an effort to avoid getting caught?"

"Yes," all of these so-called demeanor witnesses testified.

"And do you believe criminals accused of committing a terrible crime might try to act normal?"

They all agreed.

"And do you think some of those criminals who are guilty, but are putting on an act in order to appear innocent, some of them might be very convincing?

Again, all of the witnesses agreed.

Next, she asked, "Have you spent a lot of time with murderers?"

They all insisted they did not.

"Then you don't know with any certainty how someone who has killed his own wife, but is desperately trying to get away with it might act, do you?"

They all conceded they did not.

Those acknowledgements were enough to satisfy Candace.

Court recessed for lunch. Conversation was minimal until they reached the war room. Leaks in this case had been so numerous that Candace no longer trusted anybody.

"Have you seen this morning's newspaper?" Candace asked Ryan with pursed lips as soon as the door swung shut behind them.

"Not yet, why?"

She reached into her briefcase and pulled out that day's copy of the *Arizona Republic*, tossing it on the table for Ryan and Lauren to see. "Wakefield Trial Investigator and Witness Spotted in Bed Together" read the front-page headline. Lauren gasped audibly and Ryan paled.

Ryan opened the paper at the fold to reveal the rest of the article. A picture accompanied the story. Had a photographer managed to shoot a photo through Lauren's bedroom window?

Looking closer, Lauren could now see the photo had been taken at the restaurant after Candace and Kyle had left. Lauren and Ryan were sitting together at the table framed by the old bedposts, looking at each other and smiling. The photo was somewhat grainy, probably taken with another customer's cell phone camera and sold to the newspaper. The article itself was relatively benign, simply reporting the two of them had been observed dining together the previous evening.

"You can't seriously be mad about this?" Ryan said. "You were there with us."

"I let you talk me into that," Candace snapped. "How many times do I have to remind everybody that we're in a fishbowl? We can't afford for these things to get misconstrued by the press."

"Candace, we're allowed to eat," Kyle reminded her.

Candace softened visibly. Lauren didn't believe Candace didn't care about Kyle; she could see it on both their faces now.

"We're allowed to eat, but we're not supposed to be out having fun. Sorry guys, but none of us is to be photographed together outside of our activities for the trial. Is that clear? It could cost us this entire case."

The others nodded. Lauren wondered how furious Candace would be if she knew what had really happened the previous night, hoping she would never find out.

The mood was dampened as they ate their lunch in stony silence. Lauren's phone vibrated in her purse. She didn't recognize the phone number, but it could be work-related. As a second-year resident, she was now supervising first-year interns who occasionally contacted her with a question, though they usually texted her.

"Hello?" she answered.

"So you're fucking Detective Pretty Boy now?" asked the chilling voice on the other end of the line.

"And loving it. And now I have a question for you, why did you kill my sister?"

The line went dead. As she hung up the phone, she realized that Candace, Ryan, and Kyle had all stopped eating and were staring at her with looks of shock.

As she repeated the phone conversation for their benefit, she realized with panic that she had just impulsively disclosed the truth about her tryst with Ryan.

But Candace didn't address that part of the conversation at all, simply saying to Ryan, "Let's see if we can trace that phone call," before resuming eating her Caesar salad.

Ryan excused himself as the rest of them made their way back to the courtroom for the Friday afternoon session.

"How many more of these fucking airport witnesses do we have to put up with?" Candace asked Kyle.

"They have four more on the witness list."

"Great, an afternoon spent with four Jake Wakefield groupies eager to do their share to help a murderer go free."

Chapter Fifty-eight

(Friday afternoon, September 29)

As anticipated, the next witness was yet another airport demeanor witness, a young woman who had asked for Jake's autograph at the airport as he was rushing to his plane. "He was so gracious and kind," she gushed.

Lauren suppressed an urge to roll her eyes. She was having trouble paying attention to the court proceedings, distracted by her worries about Ryan. Wouldn't he be angry that she had accidentally disclosed their sexual encounter to Candace and Kyle?

When she could stand it no longer, she discreetly tapped a silent text message to Ryan, wherever he was. **I am so sorry. I didn't mean to say that. It just slipped out.**

Her phone vibrated in her hand a few moments later with his response. **No apology necessary.**

Immediately, another text came in from Ryan. **Wait! What do you mean that you "didn't mean to say those things"?**

Lauren grinned. She felt guilty about texting in court, which she had never done before, but was relieved that Ryan was not upset with her. **Oh, I meant what I said :) I just didn't mean to say it in front of Candace. Hope I didn't get you into trouble.**

Her phone soon buzzed with his reply. **No worries. Candace will be happy when I get the results of this phone search back to her.**

Phew! Lauren could now pay attention to the trial again. Candace was cross-examining the witness. The attractive young woman fell easily into the trap set by Candace, admitting she didn't actually know how a wife-killer would act. And, as Lauren knew, Jake was a gifted actor.

Ryan returned to the courtroom, silently handing Kyle some documents before slipping back into his seat beside Lauren. She smiled at him and he raised one eyebrow at her.

As Candace was finishing up with the witness, Lauren's phone vibrated again.

That red wine sure was delicious last night read the text message from Ryan. She glanced at him out of the corner of her eye, but he was looking straight ahead as if he were paying close attention to Candace's skillful cross-examination.

What? You didn't have any. She texted back, confused.

Lauren's phone vibrated. She glanced discreetly down at the message in front of her. **I know, but it tasted delicious on your tongue.**

Lauren couldn't suppress her smile while Ryan maintained a perfect poker face beside her.

After the demeanor witness was excused, Pratt leapt to his feet, "If it pleases the court, the Defense would like to call the defendant, Mr. Jacob Wakefield, Jr., to the stand at this time."

Chapter Fifty-nine

(Friday Afternoon, September 29)

The courthouse buzzed with excitement. The most anticipated question of this entire trial aside from the verdict had finally been answered. Jake Wakefield would take the stand in his own Defense.

It was late in the afternoon. The Defense clearly hoped to adjourn for the weekend with Jake Wakefield's convincing denials swimming in the jurors' heads.

Jake looked handsome as he strode toward the stand. Lauren had recently read he used tanning beds to even out his baseball tan.

He was wearing his wedding ring. He had rarely worn it when Liz had been alive. He claimed it interfered with his grip on the baseball.

He had a fresh haircut and looked sharp in a dark blue suit and complementary tie, which showcased his eyes. He flashed a grin at the jury. Lauren remembered how intoxicating a smile from him could be and worried about his potential impact upon the jury.

Pratt greeted him like an old school chum, "Good afternoon."

"Good afternoon," Jake smiled again.

"Mr. Wakefield, the Prosecution has painted an ugly picture of you thus far, haven't they?"

Candace sprang to her feet. "Objection, the State has been presenting evidence, not painting pictures."

"Sustained. Please rephrase the question, Mr. Pratt."

"Jake,…" Pratt slipped with the familiar use of the first name or perhaps he had done it intentionally, "…do you remember telling me a couple of weeks ago it was hard for you to believe the Prosecution was talking about you?"

"Yes."

"Can you explain why that was so hard for you to believe?"

"The Prosecutor keeps accusing me of being a bad person, a horrible husband, a monster, and none of those things are true. It is shocking to me how many inaccuracies have been introduced into this trial as evidence. I know the jury doesn't know exactly what the truth is, but I do. And I am *not* that person they have been making me out to be."

"But it is true you've had some…" Pratt cleared his throat, "…marital indiscretions."

"Yes, and I'm not proud of that fact, but at the risk of sounding like a jerk, that behavior is the norm among professional athletes. Most pro athletes, and I mean almost all of them, have extramarital sex. In fact, most of the wives accept that as one of the conditions of being married to an athlete. It's not a good excuse. I broke a marital vow to my wife, but I was never involved emotionally with those women. I didn't maintain contact with any of them."

That was probably true. Of the women who told credible stories about sleeping with Jake while he was married, all of them described one-night flings. However, Lauren did not believe that Liz had been accepting of Jake's infidelities.

"Would you consider yourself a good husband?"

"Again, I know this may sound strange…" Jake leaned forward in a gesture of sincerity, "…but yes. Aside from occasional indiscretions on the road, I was a very good husband to Liz. We attended church together and we socialized with friends a lot. We had a nice home to live in and money in the bank. We were active in the community. We had a happy marriage."

"Did you have an argument with your wife on the evening of July twenty-third?"

"Not at all. I was packing to get ready for my trip and she was helping me find stuff around the house. She went off to the hospital to visit her sister. She knew that Lauren had been feeling jealous and Liz was trying to make things right."

Candace jumped to her feet, "Objection, hearsay"

"Sustained. That last sentence will be stricken from the record."

"And what happened when she returned from the hospital?" Pratt asked.

"We made love that afternoon. I kissed her good-bye before I left for my trip. I tried to call her when I got in that night, but she didn't pick up. It was late, so I figured she was sleeping and I would catch up with her the next day..." Jake choked up, but no tears formed in his eyes.

"When you made love that afternoon, did your wife scratch you?"

"Yes, she did. You know, we weren't going to see each other for a few days and..." he paused and smiled shyly, looking up at the jury from underneath his long eyelashes. "She scratched me in a moment of passion."

"And you were notified the next day that she had been killed?"

"I couldn't believe it. We had a great security system and the detectives told me there was no sign of forced entry. I knew it had to be somebody Liz knew."

"And did you figure out who that somebody was?"

Candace was on her feet, "Objection, calls for speculation."

"Your Honor," Pratt protested. "The defendant has a right to assert his own theory of the crime."

"Overruled," came the ruling from the bench. Pratt nodded at Jake to continue.

"Not right away, but over time, Liz's sister started acting weirder and weirder. At first, we were getting close with each other because we were both grieving for Liz. I was so lost and confused and Lauren kept coming over to the house. She reminded me so much of Liz. They look alike and their voices sound identical. Lauren even started using a lot of the same phrases as Liz.

"But later it seemed like Lauren wanted to become Liz. She asked if she could borrow Liz's clothes. And she started wanting to come to all of my games and sit with the other wives. I didn't see it at the time because I was grieving, but eventually I realized she was trying to replace Liz.

"That's when I started to wonder if she might have killed Liz. I mean, it would explain so much, like why there was no sign of forced entry. Lauren has a key to our place and she knew our security alarm code. Or Liz would have let her in. When I saw Lauren wearing a ring that had been very special to Liz, a ring that had been stolen the night of the crime, that's when I knew for sure she did it. I called the police right away. I told them all of my suspicions. Lauren kept calling me obsessively. I continued to take her calls because I wanted to keep her talking. I wanted to see what I could find out to help the police solve the case."

Heat of fury and embarrassment flooded Lauren's face. Her blood pressure spiked. She was very aware that several jurors were looking at her. She did her level best to appear calm. Despite what the detectives had been telling her about Jake, it had been difficult to accept. Now she could hear it with her own ears, his blatant lies told with the full intention of accusing her of the murder of her own sister. She fought to control her breathing.

Lauren looked directly at Jake. Throughout this entire trial, he had refused to make eye contact. But now, as he accused Lauren of unthinkable things, he looked directly at her and they locked eyes. Lauren felt as if they were engaged in a battle of wills, one she refused to lose. Eventually, Jake shifted his gaze back to Pratt.

"Mr. Wakefield, did you check your online bank account on the evening of July twenty-third?"

"No, I never looked at that stuff. Liz managed the finances. I didn't even know our online passwords back then."

"Were you aware your wife had consulted with a family law attorney?"

"Absolutely. Liz and I figured we had a lot of blessings so we were considering adopting a special needs child. We hadn't told anybody yet because we were worried people would offer unsolicited advice. Liz was especially worried that her sister would disapprove. But last July, we decided to do it. We wanted to provide a loving home to a child who needed one. Liz went in to consult Mr. Bourk about legal assistance for the adoption."

Lauren was quite certain there was no truth to this, but Jake must have been desperate to explain why Liz would hire a family law attorney. Liz had wanted children, but Jake had not been ready; he kept telling Liz he wanted to enjoy his youth first. Now, Jake was laying it on thick.

Pratt glanced at his watch and strode across the courtroom floor to stand right in front of Jake and the jury box.

"Jake, did you ever strike your wife?"

"No, the notion that I ever would have hit Liz is repugnant to me. That is a pack of lies manufactured by people determined to frame me for this crime. I never hit my wife. Ever."

"And did you have anything to do with her death?"

"Absolutely not. I kissed her good-bye on the evening of July twenty-third, fully expecting to see her again a few days later when I returned from D.C." He started to choke up. Or at least he pretended to. "But I never saw her again. I still miss her every single day. I wish I could have been there to protect her."

"Your Honor, I have no more questions for this witness."

Pratt's timing was perfect. It was 4:56 p.m. Predictably, Robles recessed for the weekend.

Lauren spoke briefly to the press, "I am disgusted by the vicious untruths Jake Wakefield has lobbed at me in his blatant attempt to get away with the murder he himself has committed. However, I have absolute faith and trust that this jury will see his statements for what they are; disgusting lies told by a despicable man."

"Are you okay?" Ryan asked once they had navigated through the hoards of press to the relative quiet of Ryan's vehicle.

Lauren sighed. "No, but I will be."

Ryan said nothing more as he eased the car out of the parking spot and put the car into drive.

"Are we okay?" Lauren asked, wondering if Ryan might believe what Jake had said.

"No, but we will be."

What the heck did that mean?

After taking a deep breath, Ryan continued, "I care about you a lot and I hate to see your name get dragged through the mud. As much as I wish I could just whisk you away to Jamaica, we have to get through this. I know we will. But you heard Candace today; we can't see each other outside of professional capacity until this thing is over."

"I hope it's over soon."

"It should be. When the defendant testifies, they are usually the last witness. It looks like this crazy mess is almost over."

Lauren nodded again. Ryan added, "Candace was wrong about Jake not testifying."

"Yeah, Candace owes me a Diet Coke. I always knew he would testify. He thinks he can charm anybody into believing anything. I hope he's wrong this time."

Chapter Sixty

(Monday, October 2)

On their way to court on Monday morning, Ryan said, "Hey, I forgot to tell you I was able to track down that incoming call on your cell phone on Friday at lunch. It traced back to a pay phone at the court house."

"I didn't even have to ask. I know it was Jake. He didn't even attempt to disguise his voice."

"He probably told his lawyers he was going to the restroom and called you instead. You know what I think?"

"What's that?"

"I think it makes him crazy to see you and me together."

"No, he never cared about me. He just needed to pump me for information."

"Think about what he said on the phone. It kills him to see you with me. He's hated me since day one. Even when he was trying to be cool with us at the beginning of the investigation."

"He hates you because you're better looking than he is."

Ryan laughed as if Lauren were joking.

"I'm not kidding. The fact that he nicknamed you Pretty Boy says it all."

"Candace got some satisfaction out of knowing he was the one that made that phone call, but she can't introduce it in court. She can't prove anything with it."

Lauren nodded. "I guess not. Pratt would just make another show of calling a pay phone from the witness stand. I wish I had thought to turn the speaker phone on so you could have heard how cold and calculating he can be."

"You don't have to convince me, Lauren. I already know."

They arrived early enough to chat with the prosecutors before court convened.

"Are you ready?" Ryan asked Candace.

"Are you kidding me? I have been fantasizing about this day. Pratt will regret his decision to let Jake testify."

Jake looked more like a model than a defendant as he resumed the witness stand.

Candace launched a well-executed assault on Jake, but she wasn't able to rattle him. Despite her relentless questions, he maintained his composure.

"Isn't it true you gave that diamond ring to Lauren as a birthday gift?"

"No. That ring was stolen from my wife's jewelry box on the night of her murder. The next time I saw it, Lauren was wearing it on her left ring finger. I believe she wanted to pretend it was a birthday gift from me. I think she was hoping she and I might even get married one day, but I did not give her that ring."

"Isn't it true you discovered on the evening of July twenty-third that your wife was planning on divorcing you?"

"I discovered no such thing. My wife consulted Mr. Bourk about an adoption, not a divorce. That's one of many things that you misinterpreted."

"You realized your wife planned to leave you and you snapped?"

"No, that never happened. Liz was never considering leaving."

"Because nobody could ever leave *you*. After all, you're the great Jake Wakefield?"

"No, that's just another myth you have manufactured to try to make me look bad."

Candace proceeded with carefully constructed questions, and Jake responded with reasonably worded retorts. He had been very well prepared for his testimony and showed no signs of caving.

Lauren got goose bumps. For the first time in this entire trial, she worried Jake could be acquitted. Perhaps Candace was beginning to have the same concerns. She was irritable over lunch in the war room. She and Kyle spoke in hurried conversations about how they might be able to get Jake to crack. They occasionally asked Lauren to chime in about how Jake thought or behaved. But they could not identify the chink in Jake's armor.

Cross-examination continued for the rest of the afternoon. Candace was determined to keep him on the stand long enough to give the jurors something to think about that evening. She was hoping Jake would get testy or confused over time, but he didn't. Jake looked comfortable throughout cross-examination. He even unbuttoned his suit jacket and relaxed his posture. If Lauren had not known with certainty he was lying, she herself might have believed him. Lauren realized that in the entire courtroom, indeed in the entire world, only one person other than her knew the truth. And, right now, that one person was convincingly accusing her of lying.

Chapter Sixty-one

(Monday evening, October 2)

That evening at work, Lauren was rummaging through the supply closet, looking for the four by four gauze bandages she needed to treat her patient. The thirty-four-year-old married father of three had attempted to impress his friends that night by juggling full bottles of liquor. The three-inch gash on his forehead revealed how that had turned out.

While she was squatting down to check the lower shelves, Ritesh came in and began searching the higher shelving units for a nine-gauge needle. Shortly thereafter, one of the female interns opened the door, took one look at the two of them, murmured "Oops, sorry," and slammed the door. When Lauren emerged a moment later with Ritesh steps behind her, the female intern was whispering to several other interns who were all looking at Lauren and Ritesh and giggling.

"What are you guys going on about?" Lauren said to them. "Don't you have something to do? Because if you don't, I have a stool sample that needs to be collected from the guy in Bay One."

They tittered again and began to scatter, but one of the guys by the name of Cooper said, "Don't worry about it, Dr. Rose. We think you and Dr. Patel make a lovely couple."

"And I think you guys have been watching too much bad television. Sometimes, people go into the supply closet for actual supplies. Congratulations, Dr. Cooper, you just earned yourself the privilege of collecting that stool sample. Hope it comes out all right for you."

Lauren could hear Ritesh guffawing behind her. "You know, Lauren, that gives me an idea, I haven't been able to use all those condoms you guys gave me last year and..."

"Don't even bother finishing that sentence," Lauren retorted as she returned to her patient with the gaping head wound. She took extra care with the stitches since this guy was going to be sporting a visible scar. As she was finishing up, her cell phone vibrated in her pocket.

She checked her phone after wrapping up with the patient, including a notation to 'Quit Juggling' on his discharge instructions. Her heart skipped a beat when she saw she had a missed call from Ryan. He usually just texted if he needed to confirm a pick-up time or location.

She pushed the Call Back button. Her pulse quickened as the phone started to ring.

"Lauren?"

"Hey Ryan. I saw you tried to call, but I was with a patient. Is everything all right?"

"Everything's great. I just wanted to let you know that Candace said the verdict from the mock jury is in."

"Already?" The State's jury consultant had convened a mock jury to watch the videotaped testimony from the case and provide feedback. They had been using this data throughout the trial to determine what components of their case they needed to reinforce.

"Candace figures the Defense is probably going to rest their case tomorrow after they ask Jake a few more questions, so she requested a verdict from the mock jury tonight."

"And?"

"And they voted unanimously to convict."

"That's terrific news. Thanks for calling to let me know."

"No problem. I..." he paused awkwardly. "I'll see you in the morning."

"See you in the morning." Lauren was disappointed by the artificial distance between them, but was elated by the mock jury results. They were going to win this case after all.

Chapter Sixty-two

(Tuesday, October 3)

Pratt re-called Jake to the stand for redirect, but he asked only one question.

"Including jury selection, we have been in trial for nearly three months today. All of this time and all of this evidence is being used to answer one simple question. Mr. Wakefield, did you kill your wife?"

"No, I loved my wife and she loved me. I had no reason to want her dead. I could never have hurt her and I did not kill her."

When Candace declined additional cross-examination, Lauren waited for the Defense to rest their case.

"Your Honor, at this time, the Defense would like to call Detective Ryan Boyd to the stand."

Ryan stiffened in the seat next to Lauren. Candace was already on her feet, "Your Honor, may we approach the bench?" The judge assented and the lawyers huddled up with the judge for a private sidebar.

Lauren dared a glimpse at Ryan. He was staring at the sidebar with his jaw clenched. Whatever the Defense's intentions were, it couldn't be good.

The sidebar broke up and the lawyers returned to their tables. Candace looked tense, but the Defense lawyers didn't look all that happy either.

Judge Robles spoke to Ryan. "Detective Boyd, you may take the stand now."

Lauren knew the Prosecution had never prepped Ryan to testify. The State didn't need to call him as there was nothing he could offer that Wallace hadn't already covered. And nobody had ever guessed the Defense might choose to call him.

"Detective Boyd, you were one of the lead detectives in this case, were you not?"

"Yes."

"In fact, you are still assigned to this case, correct?"

"Yes, I am."

"You continue to track down leads on the case?"

"When the need arises."

"And you also escort Miss Rose to court every day?"

"Yes."

"Is that routine police protocol for criminal trials?"

"Not exactly, but this is hardly a routine trial."

"Why is it necessary for taxpayer money to be spent to escort Miss Rose to and from court?"

"I'm acting on orders from my police chief. I guess you'd have to ask him."

"He didn't tell you why he wanted you to escort Miss Rose to court?"

"He told me he wanted to make sure she arrived to court safely. As I'm sure you know, the traffic at the courthouse can make that very difficult most days."

"And yet the rest of us all manage to get here fine. Miss Rose is a licensed driver. I'm guessing she's capable of driving herself to and from court?"

"Yes, I imagine she could, but there have been threats made against her because of the unsubstantiated accusations that Jake Wakefield levied against her in the press."

Pratt looked pleased. "Some people are so convinced Miss Rose is guilty of this crime that threats have been made against her life?"

"Some naïve people that know more about unfounded

accusations than they do about the evidence," Ryan responded with some ferocity in his voice.

Lauren wasn't aware of any death threats, but it didn't surprise her. The press had initially crucified her. This explained why the Scottsdale Police Chief had been so insistent that she be escorted to court.

"So it's fair to say you have spent quite a bit of time with Miss Rose during all of your commutes to and from the courthouse?"

"Yes, that would be fair to say."

"I believe the two of you have dined together on several occasions?"

Candace objected but was overruled.

"We have lunch together almost every court day along with the Prosecution team and all of us have had dinner together a few times."

"But you have also dined with Miss Rose alone, have you not?"

"No."

"No?" Pratt asked in his exaggerated tone of incredulity.

"I haven't eaten alone with La—" Ryan caught himself, "… Miss Rose unless you count snacks in the car or lunches at the courthouse."

Pratt moved to enter something into evidence. It was the photo from the *Arizona Republic* article showing Lauren and Ryan at The Old Spaghetti Factory.

"Detective Boyd, doesn't this photo show you and Miss Rose eating dinner alone?"

"No."

"No?" Pratt's voice went up an octave.

"I can see why you might think that, but we dined with the prosecutors that night. They left a bit earlier than we did because they had to get back to work. We stayed another five minutes at the most, finishing our meal."

"Detective Boyd, have you become romantically involved with Miss Rose?"

Candace objected, "Your Honor, there is no evidence to support that question. This is nothing more than a fishing expedition intended to unfairly malign the reputation of my investigator."

Robles sustained the objection and shot a warning look at Pratt. "Mr. Pratt, we discussed this in sidebar. You are only permitted to ask questions that are predicated on established evidence."

Pratt looked back at the photograph of Ryan and Lauren in his hand, clearly looking for a way around the judge's limitations. "Detective Boyd, when you look at this picture, wouldn't you agree these two people appear to be in love?"

Candace objected again. Robles paused before issuing a ruling. "I will allow questions based upon the content of the photograph."

Ryan answered. "Why? Because we're smiling and laughing? I smile and laugh with a lot of people I'm not in love with. I think you're making assumptions without evidence and I wouldn't do that. So, no, I wouldn't make that assessment based solely upon that photograph."

"Detective Boyd, I would like to ask you a few questions about standard police procedure."

"Okay."

"Aren't police officers supposed to maintain objective relationships with their witnesses?"

"Yes."

"Wouldn't it be considered inappropriate for a police detective to get intimately involved with a witness in one of his cases?"

Outraged, Candace objected, but was overruled. However, Robles did caution Pratt, "Tread lightly, Counsel."

"Yes," Ryan agreed.

"And aren't you intimately involved with a witness in this case?"

Candace exploded and the judge was not far behind her. He sustained Candace's objection and called for another sidebar. Lauren was afraid to look directly at Ryan for fear the jury would see. She looked instead at the sidebar, trying to catch a glimpse of Ryan in her peripheral vision. He looked anxious, which made her feel nervous for him.

Judge Robles addressed the room. "Ladies and gentlemen of the jury, Mr. Pratt has been trying to ask this witness some questions for which there is no basis in fact. That is not permitted in a court of law. I strongly urge you not to consider these questions suggesting an intimate relationship between this investigator and one of the witnesses in this case." Several jurors looked at Lauren when he said that. "There is no basis in fact to suggest any such relationship exists. Because Mr. Pratt has overstepped his bounds on more than one occasion, he is not permitted to ask this witness anymore questions at this time." He turned to Candace. "Your witness, Ms. Keene."

"Detective Boyd, you have been involved in this case from the very beginning, haven't you?"

"Yes. The case was assigned to Detective Wallace and me as soon as it was called in as a homicide."

"It was assigned to you before you knew the identity of the victim?"

"Yes."

"Or the victim's husband?"

"Yes."

"Or the victim's sister?"

"Yes."

"So you knew nothing about Elizabeth Wakefield when this case was assigned to you?"

"Other than that she was married to the baseball pitcher, no I didn't."

"Detective Boyd, did you and Detective Wallace conduct a comprehensive and impartial investigation in this case?"

"Yes, we did. We took our time and investigated all credible leads."

"And can you tell the members of this courtroom why Jake Wakefield was ultimately arrested for this crime?"

"Yes, we arrested him on the basis of the evidence. The time line, the DNA match, the blood spatter evidence, the inconsistencies in his statement. Jake Wakefield is the only person who had the means, the motive, and the opportunity to commit this crime. All of the evidence in this case points to Jake Wakefield."

"Detective Boyd, did you maintain your objectivity in this case as you were investigating it?"

"Absolutely."

"No more questions for this witness."

Pratt requested another sidebar. Robles dismissed the rest of the courtroom for lunch while he met with the lawyers privately. Ryan looked solemn as he and Lauren walked back to the war room together in silence.

Once they were in the privacy of the war room, Lauren offered reassurances, "You did a solid job up there. Very composed."

But Ryan shook his head. "They didn't even ask me any questions about the evidence. They only wanted to know about my relationship with you. This is my first homicide case and I've botched it up for the prosecutors. The Defense knows about us somehow."

Lauren shook her head. "No, if they had any real evidence, they would have introduced it. Candace is right. They're just fishing. It's that stupid article in the *Arizona Republic*. I thought it was funny at first, but not anymore. I'm going to call that reporter and demand a retraction."

She called on her cell phone. As soon as she identified herself by name, the receptionist seemed more than eager to put Lauren in contact with the reporter who had written the story. "Yes, Dr. Rose, why don't I take your phone number and I'll have him call you?"

"I bet he'll call me. And call me and call me and call me. Why don't you give me his number and I'll call him?"

"I'll have to check with him to see if I can give you his number."

"Yes, you do that."

The receptionist called back in a matter of seconds, offering all of the reporter's contact information to Lauren. "He said you could call him any time."

Lauren blocked her phone number before making the call. The reporter, Doug Collier, picked up the call on the first ring.

Lauren didn't waste any time, "Your juvenile sexual innuendoes are putting this entire case in jeopardy. I want you to issue a retraction in tomorrow's paper or I am going to sue you for libel. Is that understood?"

The reporter was extremely conciliatory. "I'm so sorry. I didn't mean to cause any trouble. I'll ask the editor about printing a retraction."

"I want it on the front page, front and center, just like the article was. Tomorrow!"

"I'll see what I can do."

"Just make it happen."

Lauren hung up, still feeling dissatisfied. Ryan looked miserable. Candace stormed into the room with Kyle trying to keep pace behind her, slamming the door before confronting Ryan, "Pratt asked Robles for permission to subpoena your cell phone records. For the love of God, please tell me there's nothing incriminating on your cell phone." Ryan looked uncomfortably at Lauren. Candace immediately interpreted that look correctly, exploding at Ryan, "Were you born yesterday? You better hope and pray Robles doesn't grant that subpoena. He's researching the matter over lunch."

Candace shoved her salad aside and ate Ryan's Philly cheese steak sandwich instead. Ryan ate Candace's salad without complaint and nobody said another word over lunch.

Chapter Sixty-three

(Tuesday Afternoon, October 3)

They filed back into the crowded courthouse for afternoon session. The clerk announced the judge was still reviewing the motion before him and court would be delayed. Reporters tapped into their electronic devices, Jake laughed with his lawyers, Candace was writing furiously at the Prosecution table. Lauren and Ryan sat silently side by side, Lauren fervently hoping for a favorable decision from the judge.

Finally, the court clerk returned. "Hear ye, hear ye, court is now in session. The Honorable Judge Robles presiding. All rise." Everybody stood up as Robles ascended the bench.

"We are back on the record in the Wakefield matter. After considerable research into the issue before me, the Defense's motion to subpoena Detective Boyd's telephone records is denied for lack of probative evidence."

Pratt jumped to his feet to object, but Robles seemed to have anticipated this. "Defense counsel may appeal my decision upon verdict if so desired. You may bring in the jury."

Ryan relaxed on the bench seat beside Lauren. She let out a deep sigh, realizing she had been holding her breath since court was called to order.

Pratt indicated he had more questions for Ryan, who resumed the stand.

"Defense counsel is strongly cautioned that all questions must be limited to the content of Ms. Keene's cross-examination," Robles reminded Pratt.

"Detective Boyd, do you recall testifying that you conducted this investigation with objectivity?"

"Of course."

"And that wasn't the truth, was it?"

Ryan looked taken aback. "That was the absolute truth. Detective Wallace and I both took considerable care in conducting a sound investigation."

"But you are no longer objective about this case, are you?"

"I remain objective about this case. I continue to track down leads and let those leads take me where they will. I don't assume they are going to take a particular direction and yet they always do. They always lead me back to Jake Wakefield. For that reason, I guess you could say I am somewhat less objective today than I was when the case started because I am now convinced of Jake Wakefield's guilt."

"And nothing could persuade you that Mr. Wakefield was not guilty?"

Ryan paused to consider how to answer this trick question. "No, I think I could be persuaded otherwise if some compelling evidence to the contrary was presented, but thus far, I have only seen evidence that implicates him."

"Or maybe that's how you choose to see it, Detective Boyd?"

"No. I had no preconceived notions about a suspect in this case when we first started, but the investigation always led us back to Jake Wakefield."

"Isn't it true you are having a sexual relationship with Lauren Rose…" Pratt pointed an accusing finger at Lauren, "…and that has caused you to sacrifice your objectivity in this case?"

Robles was pounding his gavel before Candace could even jump to her feet. "The witness will not answer that question. Mr. Pratt, you have been warned several times that accusing this witness of an inappropriate relationship would not be permitted and you have defied my orders. I hereby find you in contempt.

Matters to follow immediately. You are done questioning this witness, Mr. Pratt. Ms. Keene, do you have additional questions for this witness?"

"No, Your Honor," Candace said, the corner of her lips quivering as she struggled to suppress a smile.

"Court is dismissed for the day. Mr. Pratt will remain behind." Robles said gravely.

Lauren and Ryan maintained a professional distance as they exited the courthouse. Lauren paused to speak to reporters, expressing her disappointment that the Defense would stoop to accusing the investigators of improprieties without any substantive evidence.

As soon as they were in the car, Ryan said, "It must've been Jake."

"What?"

"Jake told his lawyers about his phone conversation with you and they acted on it. That's why they pursued it so aggressively."

"You think Jake had the audacity to admit he called me?"

"It's the only thing that makes sense. Why else would Pratt be so determined?"

"The newspaper article?"

"I don't think so. The headline was suggestive, but the article itself was harmless. This is Jake's handiwork again."

"Well, Jake's nothing if not persistent."

"Persistently evil." Ryan let out an enormous sigh, "I feel like I dodged a bullet. I wasn't going to lie under oath."

"I know. I wouldn't have expected you to. You wouldn't be the person I like and admire so much if you were willing to lie on the stand."

"It is incredibly lucky the judge ruled I didn't have to answer that last question of Pratt's."

"Speaking of Pratt, I wonder how he's faring right about now. Robles looked none too happy with him."

"I don't envy that poor bastard right now, but he must've thought it was worth it. He knew that question would infuriate Robles and he asked it anyway. He really wanted the jury to think you and I were sleeping together. I hope it doesn't ruin the whole case."

Chapter Sixty-four

(Tuesday night, October 3–Wednesday, October 4)

Candace called Lauren that night to let her know the mock jury had not been influenced by Pratt's efforts to discredit Ryan. They still voted unanimously for conviction.

"Does Ryan know?"

"Yes, I just talked to him. He's doing much better now." Candace didn't apologize, but Lauren detected a tone of contrition in her voice.

Lauren was relieved not only because this meant they could still expect a guilty verdict from the real jury, but also because Ryan could stop kicking himself for a single night of indiscretion.

Lauren laughed when she found an entire box of bear claws waiting on the passenger seat, along with the morning edition of the *Arizona Republic*, when she climbed into Ryan's car the next morning. "Oh my. What are you guilty of?"

"I'm afraid I was testy with you yesterday. I was mad at myself, convinced I had screwed up this entire case, and I took it out on you. I'm sorry."

"That's how you act when you're angry? If so, I'll take it. You have nothing to apologize for. This stinking trial has been hard on all of us."

"Thank God it's almost over. The Defense should rest today and closing arguments should wrap by the end of this week."

"And the jury should vote to convict shortly after that."

"And we can all get our lives back."

"Except for Jake."

"Yeah, except for that rat bastard."

"I was worried that Candace would pull you off the trial."

"She definitely considered it, but she concluded that would make it look like I have something to hide. However, she did threaten to remove precious body parts if I so much as look at you sideways from here on out."

Lauren nodded and began to peruse the newspaper.

"Check out the story by your friend, Doug Collier," Ryan said.

"Wakefield Defense Attorney Found in Contempt" read the bold headline on the front page. The accompanying article described how Pratt had openly defied Judge Robles' established limitations when questioning Detective Boyd. It was followed by a formal retraction from the editor. Lauren read it aloud. "Correction. The September 29th edition carried a headline that inadvertently suggested that Detective Ryan Boyd and Dr. Lauren Rose, both of whom are key players in the Wakefield murder trial, were involved in an inappropriate relationship. The *Arizona Republic* has no facts to support any such suggestion and we sincerely regret any damage it may have caused."

"Nice work. You know how to take care of business," Ryan remarked.

"I do now."

As they settled into their front row courtroom seats, Candace turned around to greet them. "Can you believe this circus is finally about to pack up and leave town?"

Judge Robles opened the day's session with directions to the jury. "Yesterday, Mr. Pratt asked inappropriate questions of Detective Boyd in direct violation of this court. As such, Mr. Pratt had been charged with contempt of court, pled guilty, and been fined. You are strongly admonished to disregard any of Mr. Pratt's questions about a relationship between Detective Boyd and Dr. Lauren Rose, questions for which no factual basis had been established."

Judge Robles turned to the Defense table expectantly. Pratt got to his feet. "If it pleases the court, the Defense would like to file a motion to call a witness not previously identified on the witness list."

"Your Honor," Candace protested, "the State objects to the Defense's attempt to drum up new witnesses at the eleventh hour, witnesses that the State has had no opportunity to depose. This is another unconscionable effort by Mr. Pratt to distract this jury from the facts of this case."

The judge called for a sidebar. After the hushed debate among the lawyers raged for twenty-five minutes, Robles announced, "Court will be recessed for the remainder of the morning to allow attorneys on both sides to prepare oral arguments for the motion before this court. Those arguments will be heard in a closed courthouse this afternoon. For the rest of you, court will resume tomorrow morning at nine."

Candace beckoned Ryan over and the two of them consulted briefly before Ryan returned to talk to Lauren. "I have to try to chase down another of the Defense's red herrings. I'll give you a ride home first and explain on the way."

The courthouse was already clearing of its usual contents of journalists, Jake's groupies, and courthouse junkies. As Lauren exited down the center aisle, Buffy Wakefield smacked into her with her enormous Gucci bag. Upon impact, Buffy glared coldly at Lauren, but said nothing.

Ryan stayed quiet until they had retreated to the safe confines of his car. "The Defense is claiming to have an alibi witness for Jake. A young woman from Scottsdale. Candace is pissed as hell, to put it mildly. She asked me to dig around to see what I can find out about this woman in case Judge Robles allows her to testify."

"An alibi witness? I thought his alibi was he was on his way to D.C. at the time of the murder."

"Now they claim he stopped off to see this woman on his way to the airport."

"Who is she?"

"Her name is Madison Hart. Does that name mean anything to you?"

Lauren shook her head. "Never heard of her before in my life. If Jake was really with her the night of the murder, why are we just now finding out about her?"

"That's what I have to try to find out," Ryan replied determinedly.

Chapter Sixty-five

(Thursday, October 5)

Lauren was surprised when she opened her door to Detective Wallace the following morning. "Boyd got busy with some stuff," was all he offered by way of explanation.

The car ride to court was not as pleasant as usual. Lauren had mistrusted Wallace during the early phases of the investigation. She no longer felt that way, but it was hard to dismantle the wall that had been built between them. After making small talk about the weather and traffic, they made most of the trip in silence.

"Look," Wallace finally said. "I know how hard it can be when you've been falsely accused. You've taken a lot of heat throughout this whole crazy incident. How are you holding up?"

I'm fine, Lauren almost said. But she resisted the urge to answer with the socially acceptable response. Instead, she assessed how she was really doing. She had been operating on autopilot for so long, she didn't even know anymore.

"I'm beyond ready for this whole thing to be over," she finally said.

He nodded. "I'm sure you are. Look, Lauren, I want to apologize for whatever role I might have played in contributing to your stress. I was pretty hard on you. I never really believed you did it, but I was hearing a lot of accusations against you and I was just trying to do my job thoroughly. I hope you can forgive me."

"I already have."

The courthouse was more chaotic than usual. Even more satellite press trucks than usual lined the streets and it took Wallace, who was unfamiliar with this madhouse, quite some time to navigate the traffic and locate a parking spot.

Excitement vibrated in the air. The courtroom was abuzz with unrelenting speculation about the Defense's mystery witness.

Court was called to order and Judge Robles took his seat.

"I have considered the matter before me with the utmost gravity," Robles opened. "On one hand is the defendant's right to introduce witnesses on his own behalf and on the other is the State's right to discovery which allows them the opportunity to review the statements of Defense witnesses and conduct a deposition of their own. I am not pleased with the Defense's delay in adding this individual to the witness list. However, I do believe they did not previously intend to call this witness. I have weighed the rights of the defendant against the rights of the people and all things being equal, feel I must err on the side of the defendant who is presumed innocent until proven guilty. As a result, I will allow the Defense to call the witness, but they must first make her available to the Prosecution for deposition. Ms. Keene, how long will you need to prepare?"

"The better part of a week, Your Honor," Candace answered. Candace's body language betrayed her emotions. She was seething just beneath the surface.

"Very well," the judge continued. "I will allow you an entire week to prepare. Court shall reconvene next Thursday at nine a.m. sharp." He banged his gavel and court was dismissed.

Chapter Sixty-six

(Thursday, October 5–Thursday, October 12)

After months of attending the trial day in and day out, the following week was a strange liberation for Lauren. She wasn't quite sure what to do with herself. She scrubbed her entire apartment, caught up on all of her laundry, watched several DVDs, and even spent one entire day reading by the pool at her apartment complex, feeling oddly guilty.

LaRhonda and Ritesh insisted on taking Lauren out on Saturday night, jumping through several hoops to swap out schedules to make it happen. They went to Suede, a swanky Scottsdale nightclub where LaRhonda and Ritesh hit the dance floor with abandon. Lauren attracted a frenzy of attention there based upon her pseudo-celebrity status. Fearing photographers would show up and she would piss off Candace yet again, she begged off early, catching a taxi home.

Strangely, Lauren realized she missed the trial, that very beast from which she had been fantasizing about emancipation. Her household chores seemed insignificant compared to the mission of the Prosecution. Her days of leisure were boring relative to the endless twists and turns of the trial. Her brain didn't feel as challenged, not even when she was at work. She missed Candace and Kyle and most of all Ryan, all of whom Lauren now realized had become her closest friends over these past few months.

Lauren knew little more than the general public as she watched the news for updates about the case. While the trial continued to lead the news most nights, very little useful information was forthcoming. The press had not yet uncovered the identity of the "alibi witness" so they were left to speculate endlessly. The trial and all of its breathless spectators were on pause.

Lauren was relieved when the week had passed and her doorbell rang at seven on Thursday morning. However, she was disappointed to find it was Wallace again.

Wallace struggled to maintain a cheerful discussion on the trip to the courthouse. Lauren managed to keep up her end of the conversation, but was weighed down by her feelings of disappointment and rejection. Perhaps Wallace picked up on this. "Boyd has been busy running down leads for Candace." Lauren merely nodded.

Wallace dropped her off at the courthouse, citing cases he needed to return to. As Lauren entered the courtroom, her pulse quickened when she saw Ryan was already there, engaged in a hushed conversation with Candace and Kyle. She had neither seen nor spoken to him for more than a week. As Lauren took her seat behind the Prosecution table, nobody even turned to acknowledge her. Feeling conspicuously alone, she glanced around the room and noticed Jake somehow managing to look like the most relaxed person in the room. Lauren was struck by the incongruence between his demeanor and the gravity of the situation. If you photographed him, removed the background and showed the photo to a group of test subjects, they might guess he was about to be honored at an awards banquet.

When the clerk called the court to order, Ryan wrapped up his conversation with the prosecutors and took his seat next to Lauren. Lauren felt strangely uncertain. Should she look at him or not? When she caught his eyes, she saw an unfamiliar emotion there. Guilt? Anger? It didn't look promising.

After the normal courtroom preliminaries, Judge Robles nodded to Pratt, who rose to his feet. "The Defense would like to call Miss Madison Hart to the stand."

Everybody turned toward the back courtroom doors expectantly, eager to lay eyes on the mystery witness.

Madison Hart was not what Lauren had expected. She was very young and relatively unattractive, but meticulously groomed. Gleaming streaks of blonde and auburn were expertly woven into her own muddy brown hair, which was swept up in an elegant chignon. Her eyebrows had been plucked into flawless arches over her dark brown eyes. Her makeup was artfully applied with a heavy hand. She had slightly crooked teeth showcased by lipstick that was too red for daytime wear. Her acrylic nails were garishly long. Her suit had been professionally tailored, but still could not disguise the fact that she was carrying about fifteen extra pounds on her short frame. Lauren recognized the shoes as Christian Louboutins by their distinctive red soles as Madison clip-clopped her way toward the witness stand. Lauren was reminded of a young girl trying to look older by wearing her mother's clothes and makeup.

She was clearly nervous. Judge Robles had to remind her to speak up as she stated her name for the record.

Pratt got right to business. "Miss Hart, are you acquainted with the defendant, Mr. Jake Wakefield?"

"Yes," Madison said timidly.

"And can you tell us how you met Mr. Wakefield?"

"I was working at McDonald's and Mr. Wake—, I mean Jake was one of my regular customers."

"And when he would come in, did you know who he was?"

"Oh yes, of course," Madison responded with more animation. "We would all talk about how he was a Diamondbacks pitcher."

"And you saw him regularly at McDonald's?"

"Yeah, he came through the drive-through a lot and I'm the one that would give him his order most of the time."

"So, at first you just knew him as a customer?"

"Yes," her voice cracked.

"But your relationship changed over time, didn't it?"

"Yes. We started talking more and more when he would come through the drive-through and one day, he asked if I would meet him after work."

"And did you agree?"

"Yes, and we've been friends ever since."

"What kind of friendship do you have with Mr. Wakefield?"

"Oh, eventually we became like best friends," she responded with a juvenile level of earnestness.

"Where would you meet?"

"Well…we would meet in parks or stuff like that because I still lived with my parents and Jake, uh, lived with his wife."

"So you didn't tell your parents about the relationship?"

"No."

"Why not?"

"They've always been overprotective and, uh, Jake was still married."

"Miss Hart, did your relationship with Jake evolve into a sexual relationship?" Pratt asked gently.

Madison blushed. "Yes."

"When?"

"Jake and I first started hanging out in May of last year, but we didn't, uh, we didn't have sex until June."

"June of last year?"

"Yes."

"And, Miss Hart, did you see Jake Wakefield on the evening of July twenty-third last year?"

"Yes. He was on his way to Washington D.C. and he wanted to see me before he left town."

"Where did you meet him?"

"In a parking lot at Kiva Elementary School near his house. We met there and I got into his car, and we talked for a little while before he had to leave for the airport."

"What time did you meet that night?"

"At six p.m."

"And when did you leave?"

"It was seven when we left that night. I remember because he wanted to stay longer, but he couldn't or he was going to miss his flight."

"What were you doing together that evening from six to seven?"

"We were talking and stuff."

"What kind of stuff?"

"Oh, you know, we were just kissing and stuff."

"Did you have sex with Jake Wakefield that evening?"

Madison blushed again. "Uh, yeah."

"Miss Hart, you have known that Mr. Wakefield was on trial for murdering his wife that evening, correct?"

"Yes, of course."

"Didn't you think it was important you come forward with this information to help him defend himself against these allegations?"

"Definitely. I've been wanting to tell the police that Jake was with me, but he didn't want me to. He wanted to protect me from the reporters and stuff."

"So why did you come forward now?"

"I finally told Jake I couldn't let him go to jail for something I know he didn't do. He still didn't want me to testify because he doesn't want to see me get hurt by any of this, but I couldn't sit by anymore."

"And you are certain you were with him on the evening of July twenty third between the hours of six and seven in the evening."

"Yes, I'm positive. That's the reason why he was sorta late to the airport that night."

Pratt turned over the witness to Candace.

"Good morning," Candace said coolly.

Madison licked her lips. "Good morning."

"Miss Hart, can you tell us about the nature of your relationship with Mr. Wakefield now?"

Madison smiled nervously. "We're boyfriend and girlfriend."

"And you've been boyfriend and girlfriend for how long?"

"Since last May. I know it's wrong to date a married man, but I couldn't help falling in love with him."

"And what did he tell you about the status of his marriage?"

"Uh, he said he still loved her, but she didn't appreciate him the way I did."

"And were you aware he was having sex with other women while he was out of town?"

Madison practically whispered, "That was a long time ago."

"Miss Hart, you testified your relationship with Mr. Wakefield became sexual last June, correct?"

"Yes."

"Where did you and Mr. Wakefield have sex?"

Pratt bellowed, "Objection, irrelevant."

"Your Honor," Candace stated, "we are attempting to establish the veracity of this relationship."

"I'll allow it," Robles said.

"Where did you have sex with Mr. Wakefield?" Candace repeated.

Madison looked at Jake who nodded at her, "Uh, in his car."

"In his tiny convertible car in the heat of the Phoenix sun?" Candace asked with upraised eyebrows.

"Yes."

"How romantic," Candace quipped. Pratt roared another objection and Candace's comment was stricken from the record.

"How did you make arrangements for when and where you would meet the defendant?" Candace asked.

"He would come by my work and give me a note through the drive-through."

"You never called each other on the telephone?" Candace asked.

"No, we had to be careful."

"How did you feel about having to keep the relationship a secret?"

"Oh, I didn't care so long as I got to be with Jake, but the good news about me testifying is it doesn't have to be a secret anymore." She beamed at Jake.

"And did Jake Wakefield or anybody else offer you anything in return for your testimony today?"

Madison Hart squirmed in her seat. "No."

Judge Robles recessed court for lunch. As soon as the war room door closed behind them, Candace let out a derisive laugh. "God, those idiots must be desperate. Where did they find this dolt?"

Silence.

"Doesn't anybody have anything to say? Boyd, you couldn't dig up any fucking dirt on this girl?"

"Sorry, Candace. I told you I couldn't find anything. She's only nineteen years old. How much dirt can a nineteen-year-old have? She's been working at McDonald's for a couple of years. She graduated from high school last May. I talked to a bunch of her classmates and coworkers, but didn't come up with anything. She's a nobody."

"You know Jake best." Candace directed at Lauren. "Do you think there's any truth to any of this?"

Lauren shrugged her shoulders. "I don't know. At first, I thought there wasn't a chance in hell. I mean, she's not his type. The one thing you could say about all those other girls he bedded is that they were all gorgeous, right? But there must be some truth to it. The way she looks at him. She clearly adores him. Either she's completely delusional or there's some truth to it."

"If she is telling the truth, she was his girlfriend for two months before Liz was killed and all throughout his relationship with you. No offense intended."

"None taken," Lauren said.

"But why? What does he get from her that he wasn't getting from his other hook-ups? I mean, even if we suppose he was only cozying up to you to get information about the investigation, why would he continue to take the risk of seeing her?"

"Maybe he was worried she would turn information over to the police if he dumped her," Ryan speculated.

"Yeah, maybe she knows something," Kyle agreed.

"Or maybe he revels in her adulation," Lauren speculated. "I can see him getting off on the way she idolizes him. I hate to admit it, but I think I might have been the same way a little bit, at least about his baseball. Jake and I used to discuss the highlights after all of his games. He loved that I paid so much attention to his performance. It was the only part of our relationship that I think was real for him." It was uncomfortable for Lauren to discuss this at all, but especially in front of Ryan.

"Do you think Madison even knows anything about baseball?" Candace asked.

"You should ask her," Kyle suggested. "Ask her some questions about baseball and see if she can answer them."

"You interviewed all of her friends and coworkers?" Lauren asked Ryan.

"Yeah, none of them knew anything about her relationship with Jake. She did tell a friend about it a few weeks ago, but her friend didn't believe her."

"Does she have any old boyfriends?"

"No. This is her first relationship."

Candace snorted. "Relationship? It's casual sex in a hot car."

Lauren shook her head. Ryan was watching her, "What are you thinking?"

"I'm thinking there's no way an adolescent girl falls in love for the very first time with *the* Jake Wakefield and doesn't tell anybody about it."

"Jake asked her to keep things quiet because he was married and then because of the investigation," Ryan reasoned.

Lauren continued to shake her head. "She would still be bursting to tell somebody."

"She did eventually crack and tell one of her friends."

"After more than a year of dating him? I don't buy it," Lauren asserted.

Candace nodded in agreement, "Me neither."

Chapter Sixty-seven

(Afternoon, Thursday October 12)

Madison Hart returned to the witness stand after lunch. Her lipstick had been carefully re-applied.

Candace resumed cross-examination. "From your testimony, it sounds like it was sort of a big deal when Jake would come through the drive-through at your work. Is that right?"

"Because he's famous and everything."

"So you must have been pretty excited when he first asked to meet up with you, right?"

"Yeah, I was real excited about that."

"So, you probably told all of your coworkers that he asked you out, right?"

Madison paused. "No. I didn't tell anybody because I knew he was married."

"But you were so excited. You must have told somebody?"

"No, I didn't tell anybody."

"You're close to your older sister, right?"

"Yes. She's two years older than me."

"Did you tell her about your relationship with Mr. Wakefield?"

"No, I didn't tell anybody."

Lauren reflected. She had always told Liz everything. But sisters could keep secrets from each other. Liz had proven that.

"Even after you became romantically involved with Mr. Wakefield, you still didn't tell anybody?"

"No, because we didn't want his wife or my parents to find out."

Lauren watched the female jurors. Did they get it? How unlikely it was that a young inexperienced girl falls in love for the first time without confiding in anybody? Or were they too busy fantasizing about their own sexual trysts with Jake?

"And didn't your parents wonder where you were all those times that you were meeting the defendant secretively?"

"I told them I was going to a friend's house or to the library."

Candace saw her opportunity, "So you lied."

Madison hesitated. "Yes, about that."

Candace changed gears.

"So, according to your earlier testimony, Jake has been your boyfriend for about seventeen months now, is that correct?"

Madison beamed. "Yes."

"How many of his baseball games has he taken you to?"

"Well, I haven't been able to go to any of his games because we were keeping things secret, but I watch them on television."

"And you and Jake have probably talked a lot about baseball over the past seventeen months together, right?"

"Yes."

"Can tell me what ERA stands for?"

Madison looked alarmed and Pratt jumped to his feet to protect his witness, "Objection, Your Honor, irrelevant."

"I'll allow it," the judge ruled, looking interested in the response himself.

But Madison was shaking her head, "No, I don't know that one."

"How about RBI?"

Madison's eyes widened. "No, I don't know that one either."

"Okay, do you know what K stands for in baseball?"

Madison shook her head again. She was looking desperately at Jake. His demeanor remained calm, but Lauren could tell by the tension in his temporomandibular joint that he was clenching his teeth.

"I'm sorry, Miss Hart, but you need to speak your answers into the microphone. The court reporter can't capture you shaking your head. Was that a no?"

"No, I don't know that one. I don't know that much about baseball. All I know is I love to watch Jake play."

"According to your testimony, Mr. Wakefield was your boyfriend in September of last year, is that correct?"

"Yes," Madison said more confidently, clearly relieved to be off the hook from baseball terms.

"Something quite significant happened in Mr. Wakefield's baseball career that month. Surely you can tell the court what that was?"

But Madison shook her head again as her eyes filled with tears. Somehow, Lauren couldn't help but feel sorry for her. Just another hapless female victim of Jake's.

Looking satisfied, Candace asked no more questions.

Pratt did what he could to rehabilitate his witness.

"Miss Hart, tell us again why you didn't tell anybody about your relationship with Mr. Wakefield."

"It was private and personal. We agreed to keep it a secret between the two of us. Jake said that way nobody could hurt our relationship."

Pratt exaggerated his head nod as if her answer explained everything.

"Miss Hart, you didn't watch much baseball before you met Jake Wakefield, did you?"

"No. I never liked it before, but I love it now because I love Jake."

"And does not knowing baseball terminology make you love Jake any less?"

"Oh no. Jake doesn't know McDonald's terminology either, but I still love him like crazy." Several spectators chuckled.

Pratt turned over the witness. Candace approached Madison again.

"You still work at McDonald's, Miss Hart?" Candace asked.

"Yes."

"Those are lovely shoes you're wearing. Are those Louboutins?"

Madison looked flattered. "Yes, these are my first pair. Jake bought them..." but Pratt was on his feet, objecting to the irrelevance of the question. The objection was sustained.

"Are you sure you didn't get anything in exchange for your testimony today?" Candace asked again.

Pratt objected, but was overruled. Madison appeared to be uneasy with this line of questioning.

"No, I'm testifying about the truth. About what really happened because I don't want Jake to be convicted of something I know he didn't do."

"Who paid for your outfit and shoes today?"

"They're gifts from my boyfriend."

"And did Jake also pay for your haircut and nails?"

"Yes." She seemed proud of this fact, failing to recognize Candace's innuendo that Jake had been prepping her for her testimony today.

Candace dismissed the witness. Madison Hart shot Jake a loving smile as she departed the courtroom.

"The Defense rests," Pratt finally said.

Chapter Sixty-eight

(Thursday afternoon, October 12)

Lauren was pleased to see that Ryan would be driving her home. Mindful of the television cameras capturing everything on film, they walked more than an arms-length apart from each other. Lauren stopped to address the reporters, opining that Madison Hart's eleventh hour testimony was suspiciously convenient.

As well as she knew Ryan by now, Lauren was surprised to find herself nervous to be alone with him. But they quickly lapsed into comfortable conversation as soon as they returned to the familiar environment of the car, the place they had spent so much time together.

Ryan shared the busy rush of his week as he had attempted to track down information to impeach Madison's claims. However, more than a year had passed and proving her story to be untrue now had been impossible. People's memories faded with time and nobody in Madison's life could remember anything that contradicted her version of events.

They giggled at the fact that she seemed to know nothing about baseball. "I wish Candace had asked her even more rudimentary questions about the game," Lauren commented.

"It would have been hilarious if she didn't know how many innings are in a game or the meaning of full count," Ryan agreed.

"She doesn't love the game, she loves the player," Lauren said in a pretty good imitation of Madison's mousy voice.

"There's no way in hell that Jake wouldn't have rolled over on her immediately if she was with him that night. He had no trouble selling you out. Hell, I think he would throw his own mother under the bus if it would save his ass."

"He wouldn't have to. Buffy would jump under a bus for him."

Ryan nodded in agreement. Jake's parents were always on television complaining about how unfairly their precious son had been treated by the Scottsdale Police Department. They were practically comical in their unwavering support.

"Besides…" Ryan continued, "…what was he trying to protect Madison from at that point? Liz was already dead so they didn't need to worry about her finding out. Jake was willing to go to jail to prevent her parents from finding out about the relationship? I seriously doubt that."

"Maybe he wanted to protect his precious public image. At least it's almost over." Lauren said, realizing she had mixed feelings about the impending end of the trial.

"You can say that again," Ryan agreed. "This thing has gone on long enough. I'm ready to get my life back."

Although she understood his sentiment, Lauren could not help but feel hurt by his words.

Chapter Sixty-nine

(Friday, October 13)

"Friday the fucking thirteenth," Candace muttered when Lauren and Ryan arrived at court the next morning.

Lauren was surprised to hear levelheaded Candace making reference to this. "Surely, you don't believe in superstitions?"

"Like hell I don't. One time, a black cat crossed in front of my car and I rear-ended the guy in front of me immediately afterwards."

Probably because you were distracted by your unreasonable fear of black cats, Lauren thought. But she didn't say that. Instead, she offered, "It's Friday the thirteenth for the Defense, too. Maybe today is going to bring bad luck to them instead of us."

Candace delivered a flawlessly prepared summation. She reviewed the time line, the physical evidence, and the motive. She depicted Jake as a controlling husband who became infuriated at the prospect of his wife leaving him. He lost his temper and battered Liz to death. Attempting to defend herself, Liz scratched him in the process. Then the cover-up began. He had showered in his own shower, grabbed some of Liz's jewelry to make it look like a burglary, and dumped the bloody clothing and murder weapon somewhere on his hurried trip to the airport. Despite the Phoenix heat, he wore long-sleeved shirts to cover-up the scratch injuries. He pursued a relationship with Lauren to get information about the investigation and had given her the diamond ring in an effort to frame her for the crime. In the face of overwhelming evidence against Jake, the Defense had resorted to falsely accusing Lauren, discrediting the investigators, and calling an eleventh hour alibi witness telling a farfetched tale for the very first time.

The mood was celebratory in the war room over lunch. Nearly everybody in the office, including the County Attorney himself, came by to congratulate the Prosecution team on a job well done. There was an air of confidence in the building, but nobody explicitly predicted victory. Lauren imagined this was a superstition of another variety. Prosecutors won't predict a win for the same reason trauma doctors never comment on a quiet night in the ER.

After his disastrous first outing in the courtroom, Fisher had taken a marginal role on the Defense team, sitting day after day at the Defense table without uttering an additional word in open court. So Lauren was surprised to see him stand to deliver the Defense's closing statement. He looked striking with his silver hair and fit build.

Fisher delivered the Defense closing statement with style and gusto as if he was auditioning for an Oscar-worthy role. He blamed the Scottsdale Police for a rush to judgment, accusing them of focusing so closely on Jake Wakefield that they had overlooked evidence that pointed to Lauren's obvious guilt. He suggested Lauren had used her good looks and womanly ways to pull the wool over the eyes of the inept detectives, particularly Detective Boyd. Fisher argued that the evidence was both sparse and circumstantial, implicating Lauren more than Jake. He emphasized that Madison Hart's testimony was irrefutable proof that Jake could not have killed his wife, for she had been with him while Liz was still alive according to phone records. Fisher's summary was a bunch of baloney, but the delivery was eloquent. It was like baloney that had been diced into bits, covered with Hollandaise sauce, and wrapped in a delicate crepe. Disguised by its pretty packaging.

Because the Prosecution had the burden of proof, Candace had one last audience with the jury. "Ladies and Gentlemen of the jury, I know this has been a long, hard trial for you. I appreciate your sacrifices, but please make sure that we have used your time wisely. Once you have dismissed the theatrics of the Defense, you will be left with only cold, hard facts. And those facts will tell you what you have to do. You may find Jake Wakefield good-looking because he is. You may find him a good baseball player because he is. And you must find him guilty because he is."

As the judge issued the jury instructions, Lauren sized up the jury. Their faces were blank slates, impossible to read.

"It's all over but the waiting," Candace said as they exited the courtroom that evening. In accordance with trial superstition, there would be no celebration that night, not even to acknowledge their freedom from the time constraints of the trial. Any celebration would have to wait until the jury came back with a guilty verdict.

Lauren stopped to talk to the press and voiced her confidence that the jury would reach the appropriate decision to convict. Out of the corner of one eye, she could see Jake speaking to other reporters with equal confidence that the jury would be wise enough to acquit an innocent man. Lauren spoke louder as if drowning out Jake's words would rob them of their ability to come to fruition.

Ryan was quiet and contemplative on the car ride home. He engaged with Lauren briefly about the powerful closing statements, but refused to speculate about the possible outcome of the trial. Lauren wondered if police detectives submitted to the same trial superstitions that prosecutors did.

They rode most of the trip in silence. As they neared Lauren's apartment complex, Ryan finally spoke. "You know, I can't call you until the jury comes back with a verdict."

"I know. Let's just hope they come back quickly."

Chapter Seventy

(October 14–November 3)

But the jury did not come back quickly. Hours of waiting stretched into days, which then stretched into weeks. Speculation among the television pundits reached a feverish pitch. But for every on-air legal scholar who predicted the long deliberation meant certain victory for the Prosecution, another was equally certain that it favored the Defense.

Lauren was at a loss for what to do with her time. She asked to return to a regular shift at the hospital, but her supervision encouraged her to wait until the case concluded so she could attend future court dates including the reading of the verdict and the sentencing. So she continued to work her modified shifts. Compared to the hectic pace she had maintained while the trial had been in session, Lauren now had too much time to think. About Michael, about Jake, about Ryan, but mostly about Liz. The pain had not subsided and Lauren realized that even a guilty verdict would not diminish her sense of loss.

Lauren cleaned her apartment to spotlessness, though she had spent so little time there over the past few months that it had never had a chance to get messy in the first place. She finally took the time to respond to countless telephone messages and letters she had received from perfect strangers as well as old friends. The letters had been sorted for her by an intern at the prosecutor's office, who weeded out negative letters and turned threatening messages over to the police for investigation. It was astonishing how much "fan mail" Lauren had received, including requests for autographs and marriage proposals. Several female fans begged Lauren to introduce them to either Ryan or Kyle. She answered most of the letters with a standard form letter thanking the writers for their support, but she refused to autograph anything. She had already been appalled to learn that her "autographs" on such things as prescription slips were being sold on eBay and would sometimes fetch as much as one hundred dollars. She had asked Dennis to intervene and he filed an injunction to prohibit such sales.

The case took an unexpected twist on Saturday, October twenty-first, when the news media announced the marriage of Jake Wakefield to Madison Hart. Television coverage was provided by media helicopters, which hovered over the outdoor ceremony at the Phoenician Resort. Madison looked radiant in an extravagant designer dress with a nine-foot train. Jake smiled ostentatiously for the cameras. The newlyweds sold exclusive access to their wedding photographs to *Us Weekly* magazine, which covered all of the details of the exorbitant affair in a seven-page spread, including a separate box which discussed how Madison could not be subpoenaed to testify against Jake in any further legal proceedings given that spouses could not be compelled to testify against one another.

Several people had suggested a wrongful death suit to Lauren, but she had not given it any real consideration. She would be content to see Jake go to prison.

Halloween came and went without a verdict. The most popular selling costume was the Jake Wakefield costume. It was comprised of a baseball uniform with WAKEFIELD on the back. The team name was the Don'tcomebacks. Fake blood and brain tissue clung to the accompanying baseball bat made out of hard Styrofoam so you could pretend to beat up your friends with it. For an additional twenty dollars, you could buy a blow-up Madison bride doll carrying a Get-Out-of-Jail free card in her hand. The second most popular costume was Sugarless Candy, with a wig resembling Candace's hair, killer heels, and a button that read NO MERCY. Costumes for Lauren and Ryan were also on the market. They sold less often, but were frequently purchased together suggesting couples all over the nation were attending costume parties dressed as the pair.

Finally, on Friday, November third, shortly after noon, Lauren got the call she had been anxiously anticipating. It was Kyle. "The jury's back. Can you get to the courthouse by three?"

Lauren drove herself to court for the first time since the trial started. She left her apartment immediately, knowing court would be a madhouse. Traffic got increasingly outrageous as she got closer to the court building and ground to a halt about two miles away. She missed Ryan, who could turn on his police lights to circumvent traffic when necessary.

Frustrated with the snail's pace, Lauren parked her car at a metered space in downtown Phoenix electing to walk the remaining distance, figuring she would make better time on foot. As she fed the meter, nearby spectators spotted her and began to trail her to the courthouse. Some shouted support; others screamed obscenities. The hordes of people and reporters closed in and she was jostled about on the sidewalk as she tried to reach the courthouse on time.

She was very relieved when Ryan forced his way into the melee to come to her rescue. He used his size and his authority to clear a path as she followed right behind him. Once inside, they were given priority clearance through the metal detectors and into the relative peace of the courtroom, which was humming with excitement.

"Why didn't you call me for a ride?" Ryan whispered as they took their usual seats. "From now on, I escort you to the courthouse. Period."

Lauren nodded in mute agreement. That scene outside had gotten pretty hairy and she suddenly wondered what some of the threatening letters that had been written to her said, the ones that had been turned over to the police instead of to her.

Lauren imagined the next time Ryan would drive her to court. Victims were allowed to make statements at the time of sentencing. Lauren relished the idea of confronting Jake in a situation where he would be forced to listen.

Lauren looked at Jake. He was dressed in a midnight blue suit that set off his striking features. On the bench behind him, Lauren could see Madison Hart Wakefield had joined Jake's parents. She was wearing an expensive floral dress that did nothing for her dumpy figure. She was smiling brightly, completely inappropriate to the situation.

The crowd simmered down when the clerk called the court to order. Judge Robles took the bench and addressed the jury foreperson. "Have you reached a verdict?"

Lauren held her breath. A lot of the media pundits on the radio had been predicting a hung jury.

"We have, Your Honor."

Judge Robles addressed the room. "The jury has arrived at a verdict. I caution everyone here that there is to be no excessive reaction to the verdict when it is read. Any person violating this order will be removed from my courtroom immediately."

This threat was a fate worse than death. Most seats were reserved for family members of the defendant, of the victim, and for media members. The few remaining seats had been distributed each day on a lottery basis. This trial had been the hottest ticket in town.

Judge Robles continued, "Madam Foreperson, please pass the verdict form to the clerk who will pass it to me."

Time seemed to move in slow motion as the form passed from one to the next. The judge reviewed the verdict silently before speaking in a solemn voice. "Will the defendant please rise to hear the verdict."

Jake stood.

Judge Robles read, "We, the jury, upon our oaths unanimously for the count of murder in the first degree of Elizabeth Rose Wakefield, find the defendant, Jacob Charles Wakefield the Second, not guilty."

Despite the judge's earlier admonitions, the courtroom exploded. Celebration from the crowd surrounding the Defense table, expressions of shock and disbelief from the rest of the room.

Robles banged his gavel, demanding the room return to order. Two of Jake's baseball buddies continued to celebrate and were swiftly escorted out of the courtroom by sheriff's deputies. Judge Robles thanked the jurors for their service. Finally, he turned to the Defense table and spoke to Jake, telling him he was free to go. Jake hugged both of his parents, first his mother and then his father. He gave Madison an awkward squeeze before whooping in jubilation.

Lauren was overwhelmed by sadness for the Prosecution team, who had given their all for this case, and had gotten nothing but grief in return. She glanced around at them, all with expressions of grim defeat.

How could this have happened? She turned to look at the jurors. None of them would meet her gaze, but several were smiling at Jake as if he had just pitched another perfect game. Hadn't those people heard the evidence?

Candace hugged Lauren and murmured in her ear, "I am so, so sorry. I let you down."

Lauren whispered back, "You did your very best for me and Liz. You didn't let me down. Jake did, and then the jury."

After Candace let her go, Ryan bent over to look Lauren in the eye. "Do you want to talk to the press?"

"No, I just want to get out of here." Lauren fought an uncontrollable urge to run. She desperately wanted to escape before she burst into tears. She forced her way through the throngs of people, paying little attention to what she was doing, knowing only that she needed to get out of that room before she suffocated. As she pushed her way through, she came face to face with Jake, who narrowed his eyes before breaking into an enormous smile. Lauren did not stop, continuing to push and shove until she broke through the crowds near the back entrance to the courtroom, where she shoved her way through the heavy doors, out into the courthouse foyer, and finally into the warmth of the rays of daylight outside on the courthouse steps. Ryan was right behind her, steering her down the steps in the direction of his car. People were yelling her name, seeking her attention, but she paid them no mind. She sought sweet escape.

Which she finally found in the dark recesses of Ryan's car. No sooner had she settled into the passenger seat than the tears exploded down her cheeks. The trial was over, but the dreadful reality never would be. Liz was still dead and Jake was free to go about his new life with his new wife. He would even continue to play professional baseball.

Lauren decided to retrieve her car later since Ryan agreed to drive Lauren to Desert Pointe, where she would once again shoulder the burden of delivering bad news to Rose-ma.

Chapter Seventy-one

(Tuesday, February 4, three years later)

It was a cool morning in February. Lauren had already been out for her morning run and was reading the newspaper over a cup of warm chai tea when her cell phone rang. She glanced at her phone display and smiled at the caller identification, which read Darling Husband.

"Good morning, Honey," she answered.

"Hey, I have big news. Are you sitting down?"

She smiled at this expression and assured him she was.

"Madison Wakefield was found dead at her home this morning and Jake has just been arrested for her murder."

"What?"

"An anonymous caller called 911 in the middle of the night to report screaming from the Wakefield residence. When the responding officers arrived, it took Jake forever to answer the door. When he finally did, the police saw a body lying on the floor behind him with blood spatter on the walls. They took Jake into the station to interview him and they are booking him now as I speak."

"They're already arresting him? It took months last time."

"Yep. I'm sure his past arrest record isn't helping his credibility any. I haven't heard all the details, but he's saying he was at home all night and has no idea what happened to Madison."

"That's going to be a hard story to sell to a jury."

"That's his story and he's sticking to it. Look, I better get back to work. I just wanted to give you a heads-up. The media's already crawling all over this one. Things are going to heat up for Jake again. I don't know if you and I will get dragged into the coverage or not."

"Nah, we're old news now. I imagine they'll start hounding Madison's family this time. Not us."

"It wouldn't surprise me if they try to contact you to get your reaction, so be prepared."

"I'm an old pro at handling the media, remember?"

She could practically hear him smiling on the other end, "Yes, I remember well. I better run. I'll call you if I hear anything else. I love you. Enjoy your day off."

"I love you, too. See you tonight."

After she hung up the phone, she glanced at the television, playing quietly across the room. Sure enough, the story about Jake Wakefield's arrest, having been charged with the murder of his wife for the second time, was breaking now on the local station. Lauren watched, with significant levels of satisfaction, the news footage of Jake being escorted out of his own home in handcuffs and being pushed into the back seat of a police cruiser.

Hoping that, this time, his arrest would result in a conviction.

Chapter Seventy-two

(Tuesday, February 4–Wednesday, February 12)

The wheels of justice turn slowly. No longer privy to insider updates, Lauren and Ryan watched the case unfold along with the rest of the world. Ryan was careful not to press the Scottsdale detectives assigned to the case for information for fear his interest would give the Defense something to complain about when the case finally went to trial.

Jake had hired both Pratt and Fisher again. Clearly, he did not want to mess with the dream team that had secured his acquittal before. At his arraignment, he pled not guilty and was released on bail, which his parents promptly posted. Through a publicist, he proclaimed his absolute innocence, claiming, in a familiar refrain, that he was being framed for a crime he did not commit. He even agreed to do a television interview on a national news show. Lauren and Ryan watched with interest as he claimed to have no idea how Madison had been battered to her death in their living room while he lay sleeping in a nearby bedroom.

Lauren quipped, "Maybe he'll try to blame it on me again. It worked so well for him last time."

"Or maybe some random nineteen-year-old will step forward to provide an alibi so he will marry her. She can become his next dead wife," Ryan said.

Many of Madison's friends seemed eager to talk to television reporters, expressing their opinions that the marriage between Jake and Madison had been a sham. Jake pursued baseball and other women unabashedly while Madison tolerated it all for the privilege of calling Jake her husband. She lived a life of luxury in the home Jake had once shared with Liz and had all of the things money could buy. Still, friends described her as lonely and unhappy. Many reported she had turned to alcohol as a way to manage her emotional pain and isolation. Madison's fairy tale marriage had turned out to be a Grimm version with evil lurking underneath and an unhappy ending.

In startling similarities to the previous crime, Madison had been killed by blunt force trauma to the head. One of Jake's championship baseball bats was found nearby covered in blood. Chillingly, Jake had scratches on his arms and tissue had been found under Madison's too-long fake fingernails.

About a week after the arrest, Lauren was on her way to work when her cell phone rang. "Hey, Sugarless," Lauren teased when she picked up the phone, knowing Candace secretly loved the nickname she had been given for being tough rather than sweet.

Candace cut to the chase. "I've got news that some colleagues leaked to me, but you have to keep this top secret. Nobody's listening in on your conversation, are they?"

"Nope. I'm alone in my car. What's up?"

"Preliminary blood tests came back on the baseball bat in the Wakefield case."

Lauren's pulse quickened. "And?"

"The baseball bat was covered with Madison's blood."

"That's good, right? It helps the Prosecution make their case."

"But that's not the big news. They also discovered trace results for a second blood type on the bat."

Lauren's heart began to hammer in her chest. "Do they know who it belongs to?"

"The immediate assumption was that it might belong to Jake. Maybe he had been injured in the attack, but the DNA came back negative as a match for Jake."

What was Candace trying to tell her? "So they don't know who the second blood belongs to?"

"On a hunch, they decided to compare it to Liz's DNA."

"And?"

"It was a match."

Chapter Seventy-three

(Wednesday, February 12)

"Lauren, did you hear me? Are you still there?" Candace was saying on the other end of the phone.

"Yeah, I heard you. I just can't believe it. He used the same weapon for both murders?"

"Apparently so. God, I wish we had that bat for the first trial. I don't know how we missed it. Was it hanging on the wall of his trophy room back then?"

"No. I've been hearing on the news it was the bat he used during the World Series." She shook her head with disgust. "He continued to use that bat after he killed my sister with it."

"So, it would have been with his baseball equipment."

"Yeah, he probably left it with the team equipment when he returned early from D.C."

"And by the time he became a real suspect in the case, who knows where he stashed it," Candace sighed. "I think they're going to get him this time. The evidence is overwhelming and most people think he already got away with murder once."

"Will they introduce both blood samples in court?" Lauren asked, wondering how a judge would handle this. Jake could not be tried again for Liz's death. Double jeopardy.

"They're not supposed to. No information about the previous case will be admissible because he was found not guilty, but I'm willing to bet the prosecutors will fight tooth and nail to get that evidence before the jury. I know I would if I was trying this case. Anyway, I wanted to let you know. I imagine this information will get out soon. This case has more leaks than a rusty bathtub. Once the press gets ahold of this, they're going to come looking for you. You didn't hear this from me, but it wouldn't hurt if you tried to get the injustice of Liz's case back in front of the public. You can remind potential jurors that Jake killed your sister and got away with it."

"I don't know, Candace. I don't want a starring role in this new production in Jake's life. I'd rather watch from the sidelines like everybody else."

"If wishes were dollars, we'd all be rich. Mark my words, the media's going to come looking to you for comment. All I'm saying is it wouldn't hurt to give them a sound bite, reminding the future jurors out there that Jake already got away with murder once."

Lauren smiled at how Candace's mind worked. "All right, I'll do what I can."

"The camera loves you anyway," Candace said. "So work your magic. Maybe Jake will end up where he belongs after all."

Chapter Seventy-four

(February–October)

Fortunately, or unfortunately perhaps, the information about the second blood type on the baseball bat had not been leaked to the press. However, reporters Lauren had known well from the first trial did start calling her for comment. And, true to her word, Lauren utilized each opportunity to express outrage at the outcome of the first trial, stating that Jake's acquittal had set a murderer free to kill again.

On February seventeenth, the preliminary hearing started. The new Prosecution team carefully presented the evidence to a judge who concluded there was enough evidence to bind the case over for trial.

This case generated even more frenzied media coverage than the first one. Lauren found herself feeling sorry for Madison's family. The news followed them everywhere with media shots of Madison's father leaving work, her mother going to the bank, her older sister buying tampons, and her younger brother leaving wrestling practice still wearing his unitard. The Hart family was baffled by the sudden interest in their everyday activities. Lauren was very sympathetic about how their lives had been turned upside down by this craziness.

Of course, the media also followed Jake's every move. On television clips, he looked upbeat on his way to fancy restaurants or playing golf at exclusive country clubs. He never missed an opportunity to speak to the media, always saying essentially the same thing. "I am completely innocent of this crime. I'm confident the truth will prevail at trial and I'll be acquitted."

Lauren was heartened to see Jake had lost a lot of his supporters from the first trial. Nearly everybody now believed that Jake must not only be guilty of the murder of Madison, but also surmised he had indeed been guilty of the murder of his first wife, Elizabeth. He was suspended from the Diamondbacks pending the outcome of the trial and lost all of his lucrative endorsements.

The legal pundits all speculated Jake Wakefield would be found guilty this time. Many thought he would accept a plea bargain. Still, Lauren feared he would wriggle out of the charges once more. She refused to get her hopes up this time only to later see them dashed again by another acquittal.

After months of delays by the Defense team, the case finally went to trial in the fall. At night, Lauren and Ryan watched the trial coverage, evaluating the proceedings ad nauseum. These discussions reminded Lauren of the conversations she and Ryan once shared in the quiet interior of his government sedan, arousing feelings of nostalgia for those early days of falling in love along with painful reminders about the outcome of that first trial.

As they watched the Prosecution roll out their case, they were impressed by the totality of the evidence. The baseball bat had only Jake's fingerprints on it, the blows were inflicted by a left-handed person, Jake had scratches on his forearms, and his DNA was found under Madison's fingernails. The police had discovered Madison's battered body in the living room of the Wakefield home. There were no signs of forced entry and nothing was disturbed in the house.

Lauren and Ryan couldn't imagine how Jake would be able to defend himself especially given his early admissions that he had been home all night. One interesting tidbit was Madison's car was inexplicably missing along with her purse and car keys. The Defense team alluded to the missing car as often as they could, trying to convince the jury that the missing items were somehow evidence of Jake's innocence.

Ryan and Lauren debated whether Jake would testify. Lauren, who felt Jake was too arrogant to miss an opportunity to perform for an audience, predicted he would. Ryan didn't think Pratt would risk it this time. When Jake chose to testify, Ryan owed Lauren dinner at her favorite restaurant.

Jake testified that Madison had left the house at about 8:15 on the evening of February third. He denied they had an argument, but admitted she left the house without telling him where she was going. On the stand, he dismissed this, stating that Madison was a grown woman who could go wherever she liked. Jake speculated Madison had gone out drinking that night, suggesting she did this frequently. He testified he went to bed around midnight or so after watching some movies in his media room. He fell asleep quickly, slept soundly, and wasn't aware there was any sort of problem until he was awakened by a ringing doorbell at around five in the morning, which proved to be the police responding to reports of a disturbance. Jake testified he was flabbergasted when Madison's body was found lying on the living room floor, maintaining that he had no idea what had happened to her. He asserted Madison must have brought somebody home with her, who had then killed her in the house, and stolen her car and purse. He had no rational explanation for the scratches on his arm, insisting he had no recollection of those injuries.

Jake smiled convincingly on the stand, seemingly certain of his ability to charm the jury into believing his rendition of events.

The Defense underscored the missing car no less than seventy-two times in a closing argument that lasted only ninety-four minutes. "Find the missing car and you will find Madison Wakefield's real killer," Fisher offered in another polished closing argument.

It took the jury three hours and forty-one minutes to reach a verdict. Lauren wanted to be present for the reading of the verdict so Candace arranged for seats for both Lauren and Ryan. Lauren was reminded of old times when she exited the hospital to find Ryan waiting for her. She slid into the passenger seat and they smiled at one another, but said little on the way to court, each absorbed in their own thoughts.

Ryan used his police credentials to circumvent the traffic blockades that surrounded the courthouse for miles. Media coverage had reached full fury.

They walked into the courthouse hand in hand, no longer needing to hide their affection for one another.

They cleared the metal detectors and entered the courtroom reserved for high-profile cases, the same one they had spent so much time in three years earlier. There was a distinctive familiar smell of leather and lemon furniture polish. Ryan and Lauren slid into the row behind Madison's family. Madison's mother looked exhausted, but smiled at them as they took their seats.

Lauren felt somewhat nostalgic as they stood while the judge entered the courtroom and she watched the jury nervously return to their seats in the jury box. She tried to ascertain the verdict by the actions of the jury, but could be sure of nothing.

Lauren noticed Jake now, looking the same as always. Perfect hair, crystalline blue eyes, slim build. He didn't look like a hardened murderer. Had the jury been able to see the cruel person inside that good-looking shell?

They would soon find out.

Lauren felt detached from her body as she observed the familiar proceedings. The judge's usual admonitions that there should be no disruption upon the reading of the verdict sounded as if it were coming from underwater.

The verdict was passed to the judge to be read aloud. Time stood still momentarily. "We the jury in the above entitled action find the defendant, Jacob Charles Wakefield the Second, guilty of murder in the first degree."

The courtroom erupted into absolute pandemonium. Ryan squeezed Lauren's hand in a silent sign of victory. Jake was shaking his head in absolute disbelief, Pratt whispering consolingly into his ear. Fisher was nervously smoothing his hair as if preparing for his next big press conference. People were whispering throughout the courtroom, reporters typing frantically into mobile devices. Jake hugged his sobbing mother before being handcuffed and escorted out of the courtroom. Lauren let out an enormous sigh as if she had been holding her breath for over four years. It was over. It was finally all over.

Chapter Seventy-five

(Thursday, December 16, one year later)

Christmas songs were playing on the car radio, but the sun shone pleasantly through the windows of Ryan's car.

"Are you sure you don't want me to go in with you?" Ryan offered again, a worried look on his face.

"No, this is something I need to do on my own," Lauren said from the passenger seat beside him.

"Okay. Go do it. I'll be right here if you need me."

She gave him a kiss before slipping out of the car. She had paid extra attention to her appearance today, looking sharp in a fitted gray and black Calvin Klein dress made of soft wool and an expensive pair of black pumps. Her legs were toned from years of running and tanned thanks to an extra long Indian summer. Having always felt like an ugly duckling next to her glamorous older sister, she had blossomed into a beautiful swan over the past several years. Stronger, more confident, more outspoken as a result of her ordeal. More secure and happy as a result of her relationship with Ryan.

She crossed the short distance from the car and strode into the lobby of Arizona State Prison Complex-Lewis, located in the small town of Buckeye just west of Phoenix, site of the longest prison hostage situation on record.

She was greeted in the lobby by a plump woman with a friendly face and beautiful dark curly hair, wearing civilian clothes. "Dr. Boyd?"

Lauren stood and shook hands as the woman introduced herself as Correctional Officer III Patty Lopez. "I understand you have a special visit scheduled today with one of our high-profile inmates. You must have friends in high places. I'll be escorting you. There are no other visits scheduled today so you'll have the visitation room to yourselves. You're not allowed to give the inmate anything nor is he allowed to give you anything. You may have a brief three-second hug at the beginning and end of the visit. Your visit has been authorized for sixty minutes. When your allotted time is over, you must return with me. Do you have any questions?"

"Just one."

"Okay, shoot."

"Are we going to be separated by glass?"

Officer Lopez smiled. "You learned all you know about prison from television?"

Lauren laughed and Officer Lopez answered, "Inmate Wakefield is housed in protective custody because of his celebrity status, but he is entitled to face-to-face visits. There's no barrier. He's already waiting for you in the visitation area. Are you ready?"

Lauren's heart was racing and her palms were sweaty. It wasn't too late to call this whole thing off. Instead, she nodded.

Lauren was surprised to see inmates moving freely about the yard inside the Buckley unit. Some appeared to be engaged in productive activity, such as raking rocks, but many were milling about aimlessly. Most of them did not attempt to disguise their stares as they brazenly looked Lauren up and down. She was glad to be accompanied by Officer Lopez, who firmly admonished several inmates to "get back to work."

Officer Lopez checked a window before saying, "Inmate Wakefield has been searched already and will be again before he leaves so ensure you do not pass anything to him. The room is monitored by video, but not audio. I will be waiting right outside this door if you need anything. Otherwise, I'll let you know when your time is up. Your visit will be over at 5:13 p.m. Do you have any questions?"

"No, thank you." Lauren took a deep breath, determined to appear confident and composed. She pulled open the door forcefully. The room resembled a large fishbowl, with floor-to-ceiling windows. She could see Jake tipping back casually in a plastic chair next to a small round table with one other empty chair as she shut the door behind her.

Jake got to his feet. Whether this was remnants of the proper manners his parents had attempted to instill into him or his own effort to establish control of the situation, Lauren wasn't sure.

Lauren took in Jake's appearance, surprised at what she saw. Other than the unappealing outfit comprised of an orange jump-suit and cheap orange shoes resembling Vans, Jake still looked devilishly handsome. Same perfect haircut, suntan, and teeth. He looked like he had been working out, upbeat, not like a guy who'd been handed a life sentence without possibility of parole.

He met her eyes and shot her a crooked grin.

She took a seat in the uncomfortable chair on her side of the table and he resumed his own chair.

"The accommodations aren't much…" Jake joked, "…but it's all gratis."

"For you," she shot back. "Not for the taxpayers. They've paid plenty for your two expensive trials and lifelong imprisonment."

"You're so testy. I'm pretty sure I paid enough in state taxes to cover all of this grandeur." He swept his hand around the room grandiosely. "So, were you just in the neighborhood or did you want to reminisce?"

Lauren ignored his efforts to get a rise out of her. "I came to trade information."

"I doubt you have any information I want."

"Oh, I think I do."

"And how do you come by your knowledge?"

"Because I did it," she told him quietly.

Chapter Seventy-six

(Thursday, December 16)

Jake stared at her as if trying to size up what she had just told him. She held his gaze. Neither said anything for quite some time.

Finally, Jake broke the silence. "How do I know you aren't taping this?"

"I went through security," she held up her arms, exposing her empty hands. "Besides you've already been acquitted of murdering Liz. You can't be charged again."

He cocked his head at her and contemplated for a moment. "I don't have to tell you anything."

"No, you're right. You don't, but if you don't tell me, I don't tell you. It's a simple formula."

Lauren could see he was mulling this over, saying nothing.

Then, after several minutes of silence, "Okay, they say confession is good for the soul so, here goes. I killed your fucking sister, is that what you wanted to hear me say? Now you go."

"You're talking to me, remember? The one person that already knows with certainty that you killed her. What I want to know is why. I want to know what happened. And I want to know why you tried to blame it on me."

Jake vanished a bit in front of her as he recounted the night of Liz's murder. He began to speak in a monotone as if he were in a trance.

"I was packing for my trip to D.C. and Liz was acting weird. She had recently learned I'd been with other women and she'd been bitching and moaning about it. But that day, she was acting fake, like everything was fine. I could tell it wasn't. I started to wonder if she was stepping out on me. What if that bitch had been cheating on me the whole time she had been making a stink about my dalliances? Maybe she was even sleeping with somebody I knew. All my teammates always said how hot she was. What if she had taken up with one of them to get back at me? They're all a bunch of cheating liars."

Jake's teammates had protected him throughout both trials. None of them had ever betrayed Jake. Lauren was astounded he didn't recognize how loyal his teammates had been, but she said nothing to interrupt him.

Jake continued his trancelike narrative. "I decided to check the bank charges. I kept a tight eye on her expenditures anyways. Maybe I'd find evidence as to what she had been up to. So I get on the computer and I checked the banking account. And, holy shit, she had just written an enormous check to some lawyer. When I looked that guy up on the Internet, I find out he's a divorce attorney. That bitch was planning on leaving me and taking me to the cleaners."

"I confronted her and she says she's leaving me. After all I did for her? That girl would be nothing without me. She never even finished college. She said she was planning to move out of the house while I was gone for the weekend and we could sort out the rest of the details with the lawyers. So then I knew for sure. She had to be cheating. I start demanding the slut tell me who she's sleeping with, but she keeps denying it. I grab my favorite bat off the bed. I was getting ready to pack it for the trip and I hold it up. I tell her I'm going to bash her brains in if she doesn't tell me the truth, but she still won't confess. She just keeps denying she was cheating. So I swung that bat with a nice level swing and I landed a good one on the side of her head. She's bleeding and she tries to get the bat away from me, but she still won't tell me the truth. If she had, I would have stopped.

But she didn't so I hit her again and she crumpled to the floor. She was still making gurgling noises and I can't let her live now because she might go to the hospital or the police so I wind up and take one more big swing. Three strikes and she was out." He smiled at his own morbid joke. Lauren felt sick to her stomach.

"As far as trying to pin it on you, it was nothing personal. The fact that Liz had changed her life insurance pissed me off royally, but it made you a convenient fall guy for me when I needed one."

Jake smiled at Lauren. His attractive appearance in sharp contrast to the gray cinderblock walls, prison uniform, and the content of what he had confessed was eerie. "Anything else you want to know?"

"So Madison lied for you in court?"

"That dumb bitch. She would have done anything I asked. I thought for sure I was going to beat the rap but our mock juries kept coming back with convictions. Even after I testified. When that didn't work, I started to panic. And Pratt says to me, 'Too bad we don't have a better alibi, like somebody that saw you between the hours of six and seven that night. Of course, it would have to be someone that saw you close to home because your cell phone says you were in that area.' That got my wheels spinning.

"I drove through McDonald's that same night and the girl at the drive-through can barely speak she's so excited to see me. The funny thing is she didn't even follow baseball. She never would have recognized me if it weren't for the trial, but that doesn't seem to matter to her. She's still tripping over her words and asking for my autograph and the light bulb goes on. So I ask if she wants to go out with me after work. I start meeting up with her, making her believe I care about her. God, that's so easy to do with chicks."

Lauren felt the personal sting of his remark, but said nothing. She didn't want him to stop talking now.

"I buy her some stuff, make her feel special. She's not the best-looking girl, but at least she was a virgin so that was a bit of a bonus. Anyway, I've only been working on her for a short time before she starts boohooing about how much she's going to miss me if I get convicted. Of course I have her convinced that I'm innocent, that the police are trying to frame me for something I didn't do. I tell her what Pratt said, that I just need somebody to confirm my alibi and I'm scot-free. But I was alone in my car driving to the airport at that time, I tell her, so there's nobody to confirm my whereabouts. I set it up so good I made her think it was her idea. Then I feed her everything to say on the stand and, I must say, for a dumb bitch, she did a pretty decent job. She rehearsed it so much, she almost convinced herself it was true. It made her feel special for people to believe I would cheat on my wife with her. Agreeing to marry her was a small price to pay for her testimony. For my freedom. Plus, after we were married, I could keep an eye on her, make sure she didn't turn on me. The only one on the chopping block now was her, for perjury. I made sure to remind her of that frequently to make sure she never confessed to anyone.

"Of course, we weren't married in any real sense of the word. I still did my own thing, saw other girls, did what I wanted."

"So I guess you were never really married to Liz either," Lauren snapped.

Jake's eyes narrowed. He clenched his jaw. His hands balled into fists. Lauren wondered how closely the prison officers were watching the video feed, but then Jake relaxed his posture.

"Liz never got more than she deserved."

Lauren's blood ran cold. She knew she wasn't going to be able to make Jake see the distortions in his thinking nor did she feel compelled to try. For the rest of his life, he was confined to an environment where he could no longer manipulate, control, or victimize women. "And now you're finally getting what you deserve for killing Liz."

"But I wasn't convicted of killing Liz. I was convicted of killing Madison. Only I didn't kill Madison."

Chapter Seventy-seven

(Thursday, December 16)

Lauren smiled. "I know you didn't."

"I told you everything. Now tell me what I want to know."

Lauren got to her feet. "No, I got what I came for. I think I'll take my leave now."

"What?" The metal legs on Jake's chair screeched against the linoleum floor as he pushed back his chair and stood up, staring at Lauren now in an intimidating manner. "We made a deal. Now spill."

Lauren took a step back. "It sucks to be lied to, doesn't it?"

Jake lunged across the table and made a grab for Lauren's neck. She stepped back again, narrowly avoiding his fingertips as they whiffed past her neck.

A door opened loudly and several officers dressed in brown trousers, khaki shirts, and combat boots rushed into the room. One was on a radio requesting an IMS, another ordered Jake to calm down and back up, while a third reminded Jake that he would be subdued with pepper spray if he did not comply.

Ignoring them, Jake yelled at Lauren, "Tell me now, you fucking bitch."

The officers were cautiously approaching from several directions, one clearly brandishing a canister of pepper spray.

Lauren lowered her voice. "Too bad you only played one perfect game. And you wasted it on baseball."

"I'll fucking kill you myself when I get out of here."

"Without possibility of parole. That means you're never getting out of here." Lauren smiled and headed toward the exit as the officers muscled Jake to the ground.

As she exited the front entrance of the prison, she felt free. The air seemed sweeter, the sky more expansive, the sun setting in a glorious blaze of red, orange, and pink.

Ryan greeted her with a firm hug and gentle kiss. As he had so many times before, he gallantly opened the passenger door for her.

Chapter Seventy-eight

December 31, the same year

Unlike Phoenix, it was cold in the small town of Tehachapi, California, where Liz and Lauren had grown up. Lauren glanced around at the familiar rolling hills and majestic oak trees. Fortunately, there was no snow on the ground. She pulled her long winter coat tightly around her and sat on the frigid grass next to the granite marker topped with an angel. After more than a year of wrangling with the Wakefield family lawyers, Lauren had finally gotten legal permission to relocate Liz's cremains to this scenic location nestled in the foothills of the Sierra Nevadas.

"I wish you could have been here for your 'real' memorial service," Lauren said to the angel. "You really would have enjoyed it. I swear your entire graduating class showed up as well as half of mine. Even Lori Grimwood came. You would be impressed to know that she has six children now. She'll be able to supply our alma mater with an entire volleyball team in a few years." Lauren laughed briefly and then continued in a more serious tone. "I know you always felt confined by this little town, but they really turned up in droves to show their respects. There were lots of stories about how funny and creative and fiercely loyal you were. Say what you want about this crazy hometown of ours, but these people really knew you. And they really loved you.

"You should have seen Jake's face when I saw him at the prison a couple of weeks ago. Orange, by the way, is not his most flattering color. He was so furious that he was practically frothing at the mouth. But now I'll tell you what I refused to tell him."

"I've been working at a hospital in Scottsdale since I finished my residency. I was working late one night, about 12:30 in the morning. I was supposed to get off at midnight, but I had just finished up with another case. The ER was really busy that night, and we had just gotten a call from Scottsdale Fire about another incoming. They were bringing in a victim from a single vehicle accident. The victim wasn't responding to resuscitation efforts, but paramedics can't call death so they had to bring her in. I figured I'd go ahead and take it. I was already right there. Why bother another doctor just to call a time of death? I'd just call it real quick and then go home.

"The paramedics were still performing CPR when they arrived, but they were shaking their heads. DOA. It was a Jane Doe case. She had been pulled out of the car right before it caught on fire so they hadn't been able to recover any ID. We tried shocking her a couple of times, but it was no good. She'd been down for too long so I called time of death. After that, I finally looked her over. She had massive head trauma to the right side of her head. I was taken aback because her injuries looked so much like yours. That's why I decided to dismiss the nurses and clean up the body myself. As I was pulling the sheet up over her mangled head, I realized she looked familiar. She was pretty messed up, but her hair color was distinctive. When I looked closer, I realized who it was. The same girl that lied to get Jake acquitted in your trial. I was thinking about the irony of her coming into my ER on a night I was working. It was all too coincidental. And that's when I got the idea. I propped Madison up in a wheelchair and rolled her right out of a side exit, one of the ones without video cameras.

"It was actually pretty easy after that. But the plan was only going to work if Jake hadn't changed the home security code or locks. But of course, he hadn't. Why would he? In reality, he knew I wasn't any real threat. I snuck into your guys' house and put a cloth soaked in Sevoflurane in front of his nose as he slept. It's a nice little inhalation anesthetic. I needed to make sure he wouldn't wake up for a couple of hours while we set things up.

"The one thing I still needed was something that could serve as the murder weapon. Madison wasn't wearing her seatbelt and she had struck her head on the rounded frame of her sports car. I spotted Jake's championship baseball bat centered so lovingly on the trophy room wall and figured that would work nicely. Of course, I didn't yet know that was the same weapon he had used on you. I made a point to get a nice set of Jake's fingerprints on the bat. I was wearing gloves and scrubs from the hospital, a great little idea that Jake's defense team had provided. Oh, and I also made sure to use Madison's fingernails to scratch Jake a little bit while he was knocked out. Lucky for me, she had those ridiculous long fake nails, which made it pretty easy.

"I couldn't hit her head with the bat because forensics would reveal post-mortem wounding. So I drew a vial of her blood with a syringe from a discreet location on her body where it wouldn't be detected and put that on the bat. I swung the bat a few times in order to get the blood spatter right for the forensics experts. I guess it must've worked pretty well. Lucky for me, I swing a bat left-handed.

"Now that everything had been set up in the house, I let myself back out, making sure to set the alarm and lock the door behind me. All that was left to do was alert the police to loud screaming coming from Jake's house earlier that evening. I made a quick anonymous phone call from a nearby pay phone. I said I was a neighbor and I was worried about the blood-curdling screams I had heard coming from the Wakefield home. I mean, at first, I figured Jake and Madison were just having another domestic dispute, but the more I thought about it, the more I wondered why the screams had stopped so abruptly. I mean, after all, Jake had been accused of killing his first wife. I knew the cops would respond, even if just out of curiosity to meet *the* Jake Wakefield. The anesthetic should have been wearing off by then so Jake would be alert enough to answer the door when the cops arrived. I made sure to leave the body so as to be visible from the front door. I figured Jake would enter the front hall from the side so he wouldn't even notice the body before he opened the door. I must say, it worked like a charm.

"Of course, I couldn't pull that off all by myself. But, luckily, I married the most amazing man.

"Madison's car had been pretty well destroyed by the fire and it was hauled off to a junkyard where it was completely destroyed. Ryan made sure the license plate also disappeared. He's an expert on the city computer system so he made sure that all of the documentation on that Jane Doe case disappeared. Scottsdale Police and Fire share the same databank for incoming calls. Isn't that convenient? And, I was able to make sure that the treatment record got deleted from the hospital system, too. No loose ends."

There was some condensation on the grave marker, and Lauren used the sleeve of her coat to wipe it off.

Elizabeth Rose
Beloved Daughter, Granddaughter, and Sister
Never Forgotten

"I dropped the Wakefield from your name. You're back with Mom and Dad now." Lauren looked at the nearby marker that contained the names of her parents. "When I went in to emergency medicine, I wanted to try to save accident victims like Mom and Dad. And sometimes we do. Just the other day, I had an amazing save. The other doctor had given up, but I wanted to try one more thing and it worked. I saved the life of a forty-five-year-old car accident victim, mother of three teenagers. But you know what else I do a lot of at my job? Counsel victims of domestic violence. Did you know that women are treated in ERs for domestic assaults more often than car accidents, muggings, and rape combined? So I really try to empower them to get out of unsafe situations. It really seems to help when they recognize me as your sister. I feel like I'm making a really big difference in that area.

"We finally got justice, and Jake will never be able to hurt another woman again. I hope you are still proud of me.

"Rose-ma is doing really well. Still taking everybody's loose change in bridge games at Desert Pointe. She was here for the memorial service. Ryan took really good care of her while I exchanged memorable stories with friends. I really wish you could have met him. You promised me that I would meet the perfect man some day. And you were absolutely right."

Lauren paused to artfully arrange the bouquet of fragrant lilies she had brought with her. "I love you, Liz. Always remember that you're my favoritest sister."

To receive a free catalog of Poisoned Pen Press titles, please provide your name and address through one of the following ways:

Phone: 1-800-421-3976
Facsimile: 1-480-949-1707
Email: info@poisonedpenpress.com
Website: www.poisonedpenpress.com

Poisoned Pen Press
6962 E. First Ave. Ste 103
Scottsdale, AZ 85251